To: Anne

Thank you for w...

With All the Best Wishes.

The Azadi Trilogy

Book I

Doctor Margaret's Sea Chest

A Novel

By

Waheed Rabbani

What the Beta Readers of *Dr. Margaret's Sea Chest* have said ...

"Very impressive intriguing novel, filled with mysterious circumstances and suspense. The story unfolds combining interesting historic facts to the present with descriptive vivid imagination. The characters surrounding Doctor Margaret's Sea Chest are alive and introduced to us in a gripping way, colourfully taking us back in time. I commend this book to be a very enjoyable read ... my interest was captivated to the very end ... "
—**Micheline Beniusis**, English Teacher

"The story takes one on an adventurous trip with a compelling mission to discover a life lived through different continents, warfare, joys and sorrows. Portrays lives in 19th century, exposes the reader to understand our diverse societies and cultures considering history and changing times. The captivating story often kept me up way after the midnight hours till the end ..."
—**Al Beniusis, Accountant**

"I can see this story as a 'Masterpiece Theatre' movie—just thinking of the costumes and the dramas is exciting. You set each side of the border in such picturesque settings, in Grimsby, Niagara-on-the-Lake and New Jersey. We all see some of the Persian and Indian settings on a regular basis on the news today. Most of the costumes are available already..."
—**Diana Stevens-Guille,** School Principal

"The basic story I did enjoy. The plot was developed in such a way that I did want to find out more about Margaret and how her life is linked to the contemporary story..."
—**Dr. Janette MacDonald,** Mount Sinai Hospital, Toronto

"Story was very intriguing and enjoyable and kept me wanting to read and know more—it grabbed me right from the beginning ... enjoyed the jumping from past to present and the history/period descriptions it

provides ..." —**Dr. Josie Marciello,** Toronto

"*I like the idea of the dream at the beginning of the novel ... The plot is not only captivating, there is an aura of mystery—and the conflict between Margaret and her family fuels the fire as there is tension on all fronts. The setting that you have chosen is the beautiful 1960s, in stark contrast with the 1850s. You have described them beautifully ... the first person narration is very effective...*"
—**Sheila Abedin,** Human Resources Professional

"*The first person, first Doctor Wallidad, then the grandfather and Margaret, is an effective approach ... the story is good, weaving the past and present dramas. You have included so much detail on Margaret's life that is really interesting. It held my interest throughout ... I believe that the historical element of this story enhances its interest. The details of the underground railroad and the Crimean War are great. Adding Florence Nightingale also adds interest. The promised detail about the rebellion also sustained my interest. You have included much rich detail ...*"
—**Margaret Smith,** Senior Advisor, Socio-Economic Assessment

"*The frame story? Yes, it works ... Although I must admit I prefer Margaret's story. Partly because it's historical and partly because of her personality ... I like your descriptions of settings. They're evocative. Well done. I also like how Dr. Walli notices gardens wherever he goes. This is one memorable aspect of his personality ...*"
—**Guylaine Spencer,** Hamilton, Ontario

"*Two plot frames? I like it. Adds richness and depth to the story ... It was a very effective opening. It definitely gives incentive to wade into the introductory section of the story. Also really enjoyed how we kept coming back to that dream, the woman on horseback, hair streaming. It helped tie Walli's story together and tie him to Margaret as well. Was it an enjoyable read? It usually takes me a month to read a novella. I read your novel in 2½ weeks. You decide.*"
—**Stephanie Hill**, Dress Designer.

For my wife, Alexandra, without her love, help and continuing support this work may not have been possible.

Also

In fond memory of my beloved mother and father, who unfortunately did not live to see this book in print.

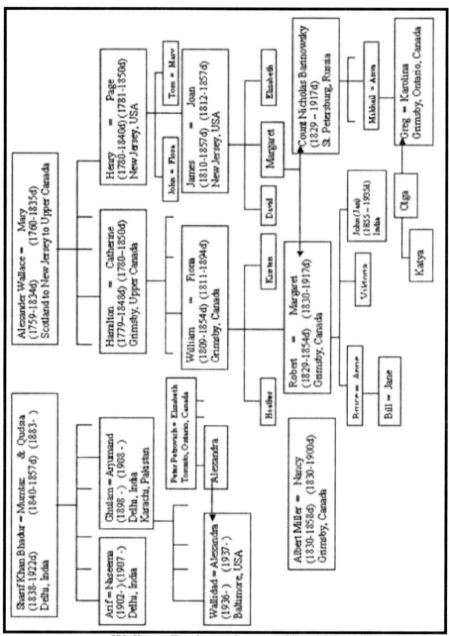

Wallace, Barinowsky and Sharif Families

Prologue

[Ah ko chahie ek umr asar hone tak]
A sigh needs a lifetime to assail,
[Kawn jeta hai teri zulf ke sur hone tak?]
Who lives long enough for your charms to prevail?

--Mirza Ghalib, Delhi, 1797 - 1869

THE FULL MOON hung in a cloudless sky, like a lantern held by an invisible force. We galloped over a treeless plateau that sloped down to the glittering waters of a wide river. The mighty Ganges, I thought, eyeing the numerous smouldering pyres visible along the *ghats**. The river flowed endlessly on, seeming to drain into the star-studded heavens to deposit the ashes of the departed. While I had gazed at the flickering stars countless times before, there seemed something strange about them that night, although I could not determine just what. Was it the weird pattern they had formed, or their unusual brightness? In the hot night-air, sweat poured down my face and body, drenching my light cotton tunic and riding breeches.

The rider charging ahead of me, clad simply in a white wrap, waved frantically at me to keep up. Were it not for the fact that the rider rode sidesaddle, and had long, blonde hair that shone in the moonlight, I would have taken her for a man. Her horsemanship was flawless; in the bright moon-glow, she jumped her mount over dry gullies and manoeuvred around large boulders without breaking stride.

Tall mountains loomed ahead, above the long shadows cast by clusters of leafy trees. Apart from the clatter of hooves, the unmistakable, albeit faint, sound of cannon fire reverberated like

---

* A glossary of non-English words is at the end of this book.

distant thunderclaps from the far side of the mountains. I leaned down to make sure my musket was still in its saddle holster, for I feared that the Godiva-like maiden, rushing headlong forward, was surely leading me into battle. While I knew a rebellion had broken out across the land, whether we would fight for the Indian revolutionaries or on the British side, I could not comprehend.

Suddenly, a silhouette, of another rider on a white charger, appeared along the crest of a small hill, moving briskly towards the heights. Something about the horse and rider looked odd, almost eerie. The rider sat slumped in the saddle, head on the horse's mane and arms wrapped around the creature's neck. The animal ran hard, as if driven instinctively to a specific destination.

"Hurry up. We have to save the Rani." the blonde figure up ahead shouted to me, pointing towards the injured rider.

A Rani? It was only when we drew closer that I noted the other rider's colourful garb, resplendent as an Indian queen. She appeared injured, almost lifeless. Her long, dark hair flowed down the pale horse's neck, which looked streaked with blood. I continued my efforts to keep up with the two women ahead as they galloped across the now steeply rising land, dotted with increasing amounts of vegetation.

"Why? Why do we have to assist her?" I hollered back.

"Look at the stars."

I stared up at the sky again, and it was then I perceived the strange formations of the planets and the stars. The outer planets, Uranus, Neptune, Pluto and others, had formed themselves around the moon into a Yod—a major configuration—also referred to as an Eye-of-the-God or the Finger-of-Fate. I had heard that this configuration of planets in the form of sextiles and quincunxes was extremely rare. The formations occurred only once a millennium or so, and thought to have major dynamic influences on the persons they shone on. These people then became the chosen ones, who would go on to perform miraculous deeds.

I wondered if we were being followed. I stood up in the stirrups and glanced back. Sure enough, some distance away in the valley, a contingent of riders was visible. From their glinting helmets and their rigid riding formation, they were definitely British cavalry.

We galloped on, following the Rani's horse. Finally, it seemed that our mysterious destination loomed up ahead. On the remote mountain slope in a small dell, virtually hidden by the surrounding ridges and trees, moonbeams shone on some sandstone pyramid-like structures, likely those of a temple. It looked to be a perfectly secluded spot to hide from the enemy.

The blonde woman was getting far ahead of me again. I heard her shout once more, "Come along, before it is too late. The Rani of Jhansi is India's last hope for freedom."

"How can we save her? There are only two of us. The whole British army is behind that mountain," I yelled back.

"Kali will assist us. Don't you see the goddess flying over the mountaintop?"

I peered intensely towards the peak. For a while, other than the treetops, I could not see much. Then suddenly, as if by magic, she appeared on the horizon. It was the four-armed lady, riding a tiger. She held a sword in one hand and in the others what looked to be a trident, a severed head, and a cup brimming with blood. She wore a skirt made of human arms and a garland of white human skulls that glowed white in the moonlight. She looked down at us with fiery red eyes that smouldered within her dark blue face. It was the mother-goddess. Kali.

My labouring steed's mouth foamed, yet in an attempt to get a last burst of energy out of him and to get closer to the two exotic women and Kali, I spurred hard. The creature neighed shrilly and stumbled to his knees. I was thrown from the saddle and tumbled onto the dusty ground, my ears ringing.

*****

The loud ringing in my ears, I realised at last, was from my bedside alarm clock. Once again, I had awakened in bed-sheets wet with perspiration. It was another of the recurring nightmares that had tormented me ever since I had arrived in Delhi from the United States. The mysterious blonde Godiva look-alike met me in my dreams, at different locales.

The clock read six a.m., which suggested it was time for me to roll out of bed, shave, shower and get ready for another busy day at the hospital. Or so I had thought.

Chapter One

A Fascinating Discovery

1965, May: Delhi, India

THE BUSY DAY ahead was on my mind as I switched off the Volkswagen Beetle's engine in the *Doctors Only* parking area of the Lady Dufferin Hospital. However, I had no idea that it would launch the most intriguing chapter of my life on the Indian subcontinent.

Despite having been back in India for nearly a year, as an American visiting doctor from Johns Hopkins University Hospital, I had not yet reacclimatized to the intense heat of that part of the world. As I stepped out of the car, the humid air greeted me, hinting at the start of the long, hot Delhi summer. Emerging from the concrete parking garage into the bright sunlight, I walked through the hospital's scenic garden, returning the *namestes* and *salaams* of the *chaukidars* and the *maalis*. Fountains spewed sparkling streams of water and sprinklers showered the plants, trying to make up for Nature's broken promises of rain. Eye-catching beds of oleander, hibiscus and roses, filled with colourful flowers in reds, yellows and purples, bordered the paths. They danced in the gentle breeze, as if in merriment, straining to drink drops of the passing sprinkled water.

The Lady Dufferin's red sandstone, two-story, imposing structure, created in the flamboyant Mughal style, looked more like a nawab's palace than a hospital. My wristwatch showed it was close to eight o'clock. Aware that the main lobby would be thronged with patients and visitors, I walked briskly on the paths among the manicured lawns and entered the hospital through the back door. I made my way through the labyrinth of antiseptic-smelling passages, towards my office.

In the central corridor, I spotted Premila, our Surgery Unit's nurse, rushing towards me, waving a slip of paper.

"Doctor Sharif."

I waited for her and she handed me a message slip, breathless from her scamper. Before leaving, she smiled and bid me a *nameste*—with the palms together and a slight nod of her head. I thanked her and returned the greeting.

The note was from my chief, Doctor Rao. It read, in his scribbled handwriting:

Wallidad, could you please see me, first thing in the morning.

In my office, I called the head nurse to hold my appointments for a while. I hung my beige suit jacket in the wardrobe and changed into a white doctor's coat. Stepping to the mirror to comb back my dark, wavy hair—which, in the humid conditions, had a tendency to slide over my forehead—I could not help but notice how the Indian sun had tanned my face to a copper tone. This transformation made me look once again like a native son of the land I had left as a teenager, nearly eighteen years ago. While striding to the other end of the surgery wing, my personal thoughts were on my impending return home to Baltimore.

Opening the polished mahogany door with *Doctor S. RAO - Chief of Surgery* engraved on a shiny brass plate, I wondered what could be so important that Doctor Rao wanted to see me immediately. Normally, I did not see him until after my morning duties.

Nurse Premila walked through the waiting room into his office to announce my arrival. Doctor Rao himself came to the door, dressed in a white shirt, dark trousers and a thin, red tie.

He greeted me in a loud voice. "Doctor Walli, how are you?"

Smiling, I nodded and asked about his health. He was a slim, tall person with the dark brown complexion of those from the central Indian provinces. Shaking my hand, he put his other hand on my shoulder and led me into his office. He gestured at me to sit in his visitor's alcove by the bay windows that presented a picturesque view of the garden, while he went to his desk and shuffled some papers, apparently looking for something.

"What's up, Doctor Rao?" I asked, sitting down on the tan leather sofa. I noted a book—the title, *Lara's Story*, printed in Cyrillic looking gold embossed letters along the spine—lying on the mahogany coffee table, among some magazines. The title intrigued me. A Russian novel? However, knowing his love for literature, I gave it no further thought. He sat down on the opposite sofa and must have noted my impatience when I gestured a "no thank you" in response to his offer of coffee. He came right to the purpose of calling me in.

"It's a matter of returning a sea chest to its owner."

I consider myself a person not easily fazed, at most times, but this apparent mention of someone's luggage baffled me. "A sea chest, you say?" I finally asked, not sure if I heard right.

"Yes, indeed, an old sea chest. A large trunk, belonging to a lady doctor," he said and, glancing at the slip in his hand, continued, "named Margaret Wallace. We understand she was one of the first lady medical workers at St. Stanley's. I heard they initially requested Florence Nightingale to join them, but she was busy in the Crimea then, and Doctor Margaret was sent in her stead. But she probably wasn't British, because the label on the trunk shows the address of the American Mission in Futtehgurh." He paused, likely wondering if I was getting impatient with this story. When I was noncommittal, he came to the point and asked, "Would it be possible for you to locate her family? I mean, when you return to America, and deliver her trunk to them?"

"Yes, I suppose so. But why am I being asked to take this chest back to her folks?" I inquired respectfully, suppressing my urge to ask more directly what any of this had to do with me.

"Well, you see, Doctor Sharif, this is not an ordinary trunk. It has been here in our hospital's storage for quite a while, and prior to that was at some other hospital, likely the one in Jhansi, for a long time."

"She worked at St. Stanley's! Wouldn't that be in the mid-1800s?" My raised voice betrayed my disbelief. All types of possibilities swam in my head concerning the owner and the personal possessions the trunk might contain. A female doctor? What could have possessed her to go into a profession so stubbornly guarded by men in those days, and then to come all the way to India? Furthermore, his mention of Jhansi rang a bell in my mind, but could not place it just then.

I heard Doctor Rao saying, "Yes, the Custodian believes it has been here at least since 1857. As no one claimed it, the coffer lay locked away, forgotten, in a storage room."

This additional information astonished me. I blurted, "1857! Then she must have been here at the time of the Great Muti … er … Rebellion." I swiftly checked myself from saying "Mutiny," for I knew most Indian patriots were rather sensitive about that word and preferred to call that historic event "India's First War of Independence", although in practice, most historians referred to it as a Rebellion. I implored, "Again, Doctor Rao, why is it *me* who has to take this trunk back to America?"

"Our Board of Directors, whose meeting I attended yesterday, considers that you are the most appropriate person to return the trunk to its owner's descendents. We feel, being originally from this part of the world, and having been, shall we say, 'naturalized' in America," he smiled, "you could be trusted with this important task. And, I dare say, a somewhat sensitive mission."

"Why, thank you. I am glad to hear the Directors have so much confidence in me. Nevertheless, I'm not promising anything. I'll have to think about it."

"Yes, certainly. Take your time. However, we need to know soon." Doctor Rao crossed his legs. "By the way, Walli, weren't some of your close family unfortunately caught up in the 1857 Rebellion?"

"Yes, according to some of the stories my grandmother has told me. My grandfather served under the last Mughal king in Delhi, and later in the Rani of Jhansi's cavalry. How about you, Doctor Rao? Wasn't your family also involved in the conflict?"

"Yes, regrettably so," he replied, and then asked quickly, as if wanting to change the subject, "How is your grandmother?"

"She's over eighty now, and keeping well. Thank you." I knew Doctor Rao's family was originally from Jhansi and, as my grandfather had been there during 1857–1858, I was hoping to learn a bit more about that kingdom. It then came to me. What a coincidence, I thought, to have seen the Rani in my dream just the night before. However, on earlier occasions whenever I asked him about his family background, he was elusive. I got the feeling Doctor Rao did not wish to speak much about them or Jhansi. Hence, I did not press for details.

"By the way, Walli, please keep this crucial information to yourself, at least until we have delivered the trunk to your or someone else's home in America, and the owner's descendants are located."

"Why the secrecy, Doctor? Is someone else after the sea chest?"

"No. But just a precaution." He smiled. I noted he put the tips of his fingers together in the typical manner he used when he did not wish to go into details. "To keep the inquisitive and the bounty hunter types away. I'm glad to hear you will consider assisting us. Let's discuss this further over lunch, shall we?"

Getting up from the sofa, I nodded and left for my office.

I spent the rest of the morning getting through my usual hectic schedule as the hospital's Gastroenterological Specialist for gall bladder and other internal organ problems. In addition, I was learning more about tropical diseases like cholera and malaria. Hence, I did not get a moment to reflect further upon the strange yet seemingly important task the chief surgeon had called upon me to undertake. The usual queue of patients filled the anteroom. Examining them took up the entire morning.

I met Doctor Rao again for lunch in the cafeteria. We sat at a corner table. A turbaned bearer came over and took our orders. Doctor Rao, a vegetarian, selected only meatless dishes: rice, vegetable curry a n d *masala-dosa*. I ordered a couple of pieces of my favourite *tandoori* chicken, lentil curry and naan bread. The waiter brought over our drink orders of *lassi*. We sipped the refreshing beverage from copper tumblers with intricate engravings around the edges. After a bit of small talk about our immediate families and general matters, we discussed the intriguing issue of the fascinating discovery—the sea chest. Doctor Rao enlightened me with more details. We spoke at some length, until our food order and, shortly thereafter, other colleagues arrived to join us at our table. We were drawn into chatting with them and got busy eating.

After lunch, I hurried off to perform a major gall bladder cholecystectomie, planned for the afternoon. At that time, we were improving the laparoscopic technique—first tried on humans by a Swedish doctor in the early 1900s. It involved minimizing the extent of the incisions in patients' abdomens. Compared to the standard major surgical procedure, the cases benefited considerably from this new process, as they typically went home the very same or the next day after the operation. The interns were keen to get as much experience in this practice as possible, during my scheduled, short one-year stay at the hospital. As a result, in those last days of my tenure, I was swamped with requests for guidance and training in this method.

That afternoon, with all the pressures of work, I nearly forgot about the sea chest. However, later, back in my office, the request from Doctor Rao returned to my thoughts. Goodness. What was I to do with the trunk I was being handed? I should at least see it before it was shipped to my home.

When the late afternoon sun stretched its lazy, golden fingers through my second-floor office windowpanes, signalling the end of the day, I sighed in relief and walked out onto the balcony for some fresh air. This higher vantage point revealed the real artistic symmetry of the garden below. The typical Mughal *charbagh,* with lawns bisected and quartered by watercourses and fountains, presented a soothing sight to weary eyes. The garden ended at a boundary wall with bougainvillea vines tumbling over the barrier, bearing their exquisite red, yellow and purple flowers. Beyond lay the vibrant city.

The sounds of the city traffic, like screams from the centuries-old civilization it had cradled, reverberated to me. In the distance the metropolis, bursting with people, vehicles, minarets and skyscrapers—an intermingling of old and modern buildings—shone in the evening sun's rays. On one side lay Old Delhi, the city built by previous rulers, the Mughals. On the other side stood the city Sir Edwin Lutyens had designed, New Delhi—the city constructed by the subsequent occupiers. I often wondered how a time traveller from the past empires that had flourished here for centuries would react upon witnessing the fascinating mixture of ancient and modern architecture the capital now comprised. I peered into the distance to locate the circular Connaught Place, where my uncle, Arif Sharif, still ran his jewellery boutique. He and my grandmother were among the last surviving Delhi residents from the old generations of Mughal families. They had endured through the numerous wars with the Afghans, Persians, Sikhs, Indian Rajahs, the British, and lastly the civilian riots during the days following the 1947 Independence and Partition of India.

It occurred to me that, as day must turn to evening and evening has to give way to darkness, all civilizations have to eventually transform themselves into distinct entities. The lengthening sundown shadows falling from high-rise buildings, domes of the mosques and tall trees presented a picture of Delhi at sunset, the same one which perhaps inspired historians to call the last days of the Mughal Empire, prior to 1857, the Twilight Era.

From the last of the Mughals, my thoughts turned to Doctor Margaret's sea chest. Good heavens, it had been lying here for over a hundred years. Why had she not returned to retrieve it? Where was she from? Where did she go?

*****

That evening, on the drive back to my apartment, the meeting with Doctor Rao popped into my mind again and replayed like a scratchy old homemade movie. Driving through the hectic rush hour required skills learned only on Delhi roads. One needed to manoeuvre through not just the traffic, but also the mass of pedestrians. They spilled over from the sidewalk, dodged vehicles and crossed the streets as if out for a walk in the Shalimar Gardens. Bicyclists weaved in and around the moving cars, buses, taxis and rickshaws. The beeping air horns sounded like trumpeting elephants in a stampede, each trying to overtake the other. The scene reminded me of an often-repeated saying, "In Delhi, the right of way belongs to the bigger vehicle."

While overtaking an overcrowded bus, with passengers hanging on for dear life from doors and even poised on the rear bumpers, I could not help thinking about the efforts humans beings have to make and our reliance on each other for a helping hand, to survive in this world. It was then Doctor Rao's voice came back to me, requesting me to help find the lady doctor's relatives and return her trunk to them. I had thought agreeing to the assignment would be a morally right thing to do, as a symbolic act of appreciation for my term at the historic hospital. The Lady Dufferin Hospital was established during the Raj and named after its patron, the wife of a British viceroy. However, there appeared to be another, possibly mystical, reason. This trunk, it seemed to me, was like one of the last remaining vestiges of the presence of the British in India. Chronologists usually ascribe the beginning of the British domination to have been in 1757. That year, Robert Clive, leading the East India Company's forces, had routed the French out of their settlement at the south Indian town, Chandernagore. Then, at Plassey, he defeated the army of Siraj-ud-daulah, the nawab of Bengal. Although those battles did not last long, the events that followed had everlasting consequences for both nations, and indeed the whole world.

These worldly thoughts made returning the sea chest seemed so important, something I believed Lady Dufferin herself asked me to do, through her regal gaze, from the portrait done in rich, red, blue and touches of yellow oils that hung in the hospital's lobby. The painting had confronted me again at noon, on my way to the cafeteria. Lady

Dufferin's eyes arrested me on the spot, as if reminding me of the hospital's benevolent history. "You owe it to this tenacious lady doctor, one of the first to come to India. Restore her sea chest to her family. Help her soul rest in peace," the portrait seemed to command.

Evading another taxi coming towards my car, I recalled some scraps of the conversation Doctor Rao and I had held in a low voice over lunch.

He said, "Walli, there's another reason I believe you are suited for this undertaking." He ignored my blank stare and carried on. "I think your lovely wife might be able to assist us in finding Doctor Margaret's family. I remember meeting Alexandra at the Christmas reception last year, when she was over for the holidays. If I recall correctly, she mentioned she was originally from Canada?"

"Yes. We met while I was studying at the University of Toronto. But why do you believe she could help?"

Doctor Rao smiled. "Although the trunk's label indicates that Margaret was from somewhere in the United States, I sense she was more likely from Canada."

That information puzzled me. "Why Canada?" I blurted.

Doctor Rao took a sip of his drink, smiled and said, "Let me show you something." He pulled out from his jacket's pocket an envelope. Inserting two fingers inside the packet, he slid out a small card with a cellophane paper covering and placed it on the table in front of me. "It's from one of my nephews' collection."

I stared at the card. It was the kind stamp collectors used to display their valuable sets. Through the transparent paper, three similar stamps were visible. They showed a faded image, on a blue background, of a young Queen Victoria, with pursed lips and large, expressive eyes, wearing a jewelled crown, a necklace and matching pendulum earrings. *Canada Postage Twelve Pence* was written on an oval frame around the picture. From photographs I had seen, the Queen's portrait seemed to be one of her earliest, probably done in 1837, the year of her accession to the Throne. I picked the card up and examined it closely. The stamps looked genuine, for their postmark, although smudged, read "1856". I gulped and looked at Doctor Rao in disbelief; he, by then, had put on a Sherlock Holmes type of gaze. "These seem to be the very first issued Canadian stamps. Where did your nephew get them?"

"Oh, they have been in our family possession for a while. My nephew says they were given to him by his grandfather, who believes they were found on an envelope in an old English novel."

"Does he have the envelope?" I asked.

"No, unfortunately not. Someone steamed the stamps off and discarded it."

"And this was in Jhansi?"

"Yes, in Jhansi. So you see, Walli, this information should make it easier for you and your wife to locate the inheritors of the trunk."

"How can you be so sure that these stamps came from a letter addressed to Margaret?"

"I am not positive, of course. But there are rumours in our family circle that a lady doctor had lent that book to one of our relatives," he said, and concluded with, "It's a good possibility she was from Canada."

I was impressed, for this was the first time he had confided at least this much about his family. Nevertheless, it was obvious he did not wish to divulge any further details. I simply said, "You know, Doctor, Canada is a vast country."

"Yes, but it has hardly the population we have here in India." I kept silent and he persisted, "And on the other hand, your own family connections here in Delhi could help you. Surely your grandfather must have known her."

I must admit I was intrigued by the extraordinary possibility that Grandfather had actually met this lady. Having married and settled in North America, I was not on good terms with my parents. In fact, I had not seen them for a long time. Hence, as no one had told me about him, Grandfather's life was a mystery to me. I had wished, for a long time, to learn more about his role in the Revolution.

Upon further coxing from Doctor Rao to accept the assignment, I finally said, as if moved by an invisible supernatural force. "Okay, I will see what I can do, Doctor. I will have to speak to my wife first, though. Returning the trunk to Doctor Margaret's family could be an impossible task. Don't be surprised if you receive a shipping slip that it's sent back here," I said.

He laughed. Just then, our colleagues joined us at the table and Doctor Rao quickly put the historical stamps back in his pocket. It did puzzle me, a bit, that he did not wish to show them to the others. I put that down to his usual enigmatic nature.

While turning the car into the driveway of the Delhi

Intercontinental Apartments, I made a mental note to call Alexandra the next morning at around six a.m. Considering the time difference, it would still be the previous evening in Baltimore, a convenient time for her. After her usual extended day, she should be home from her law office.

*****

"Hi, dear, how are you?" Alexandra's voice sounded cheery as soon as she spoke on the telephone. The long-distance operator would have mentioned the call was from Delhi.

"Pretty good, honey, and how about you?" I tried to be as lively as possible, to prepare her for the important news I wanted to share. After the usual pleasantries and asking about our families and jobs, I came to the point. "Listen, dear, a trunk will arrive in a few weeks, via an international shipper. Please accept it and have it stored away in the basement, unopened."

"My, is it full of all the gifts you're bringing for us?" she teased.

"There might be some presents in there, but not for us. The trunk doesn't belong to me."

"Oh! Whose is it, then?" she asked in a surprised tone, over the static on the telephone line.

"Hon, you won't believe this. It belongs to an American or, Doctor Rao thinks, a Canadian lady doctor." I gave her the particulars and told her what I was being asked to do.

"But why can't they return it themselves?" was her obvious question.

I could picture her twirling her blonde hair between her fingers, which she did whenever she was a bit confused.

"It's a long story. Looks like they lost track of her during the 1857 war. She simply disappeared."

Alexandra persisted, "But haven't they tried to locate her family?"

"I believe they have. Doctor Rao tells me they made several attempts through the normal government channels, the Missionary Societies which, they believe, originally sponsored her, and even the Red Cross, but to no avail. All those attempts led to dead ends with no record of Doctor Margaret or her family's whereabouts."

"Hmm … wonder what makes them think you'll succeed," Alexandra murmured, obviously bemused at this surprising piece of news. I imagined her—her lovely blue eyes shining, one hand around her chin, and her face wearing a quizzical look—in deep thought. After a bit of silence, she asked, "So, what's inside this trunk?"

It was an opening for me to give her the other part of the extraordinary news. "You won't believe this, darling, but we don't know. Actually, no one knows."

"What! Why's that? Haven't they opened the trunk yet?"

I tried to remain as composed as possible, before replying, "No. The trunk has not been opened, as far as I know, possibly ever since she packed it."

Alexandra's fervent question was, "But why on earth not?"

"Well, you see, dear, it has to do with some of the religious customs and traditions in this part of the world. You already know they don't like to touch strangers, preferring to greet one another from a distance. I'm not very knowledgeable on this subject, but several groups here believe in the sacredness of the spirit of the deceased person; they consider that a part of the person's soul remains in any possessions left behind. I don't know, but it seems they think it would be an extreme disrespect to Doctor Margaret's spirit to allow her trunk to be opened, and her items in there touched and fondled freely, by anyone other than her immediate family members or descendants. It would be as if they had violated the sanctity of the trunk."

I tried to further explain these spiritual sanctum concepts in the rather long-winded manner I often adopted when explaining the intricacies of Indian culture to North Americans. However, from a lack of response, I seemingly had little success.

"My, my, this is heavy spiritual stuff. So am I to understand that we aren't supposed to open this coffer, only to locate Doctor Margaret's family and deliver it to their doorstep?"

"Yes. Those are the directives."

"If you ask me, it sounds like some sort of cover-up," she said, talking like the lawyer she was.

I said, like a simpleton, "No, no. I don't think it's anything like that. It looks to me the hospital is merely trying to live up to its responsibility by delivering the possessions of a notable doctor, safely and properly to her relatives." I added with a chuckle, "Her being American, you know."

She laughed at that deduction. "So, whatever became of Doctor Margaret? Did she die there?" Alexandra asked.

I tried to respond to her question, based on what I'd learned from Doctor Rao so far. "Well, that's also a complete conundrum. I gather there are several theories on her whereabouts after she left St. Stanley's Hospital here in 1856, just before the war. They believe she received a request from the Rani of Jhansi to treat one of the princes, who apparently was seriously ill. The last time anyone saw the doctor in Delhi was a glimpse of her in a carriage, escorted by some of the Rani's *sowars*, heading towards Jhansi—you know, the city a few hundred miles south of here. Then the Rebellion erupted, and while everyone knows what happened to the rebels, no one knows what occurred to her."

"Aren't there any street legends on whatever happened to the Rani and the good doctor?" Alexandra asked, sounding fascinated.

"Doctor Rao told me of some bazaar rumours. Apparently, several Russian military men were attached to the Rani's forces, in an advisory capacity. Some believe their real motive for being there was to instigate the Rebellion—"

Alexandra interrupted excitedly, "Well, it sounds like they were saved by the Russians."

"It's possible, but we still don't know what became of her, and who or where her surviving family is—"

Alexandra again interjected. "Wait a minute. Didn't your grandfather also serve in the Rani's army? Wouldn't he have known something about Margaret?"

"Yes. Possibly. I'm going to see Grandmother soon. I'll ask her."

Alexandra paused for a moment. She seemed to have become interested in this story. "I suppose I could ask some of my cousins in Russia if they've ever heard of an Indian Rani being helped by an American doctor and Russian officers. You know, gossip travels like the wind, especially in St. Petersburg and Moscow circles."

I wondered aloud about Doctor Margaret's possible Russian connection. "But why would she have asked the Russians for assistance? Couldn't she merely have gone over to the British side? Why wouldn't they have supported her?"

"She could have. For all you know, she might have come back to North America," Alexandra said.

"It's a good possibility, and that's what the hospital believes. However, Doctor Rao's thinking is, based on those old stamps, that she returned to Canada. So, dear, can you also please ask the Toronto side of your family to see if they could discover any descendants of a Doctor Margaret Wallace in Ontario, or anywhere in Canada?"

"I'll see what I can do." Her voice took on the firm tone it did whenever she committed herself to a major undertaking.

*****

One morning, a few days later, while driving out from my apartment building's driveway onto the street, I noted a dark blue sedan parked on the curb. From its huge, distinctive chrome-plated front bumper and the miniature racing-hound motif on the hood, I recognised it to be a Russian Volga. The driver was reading a newspaper, but it looked as if he was using it more to veil his face. Driving by, I managed a side glimpse. He had a sunburned face, short, blond, crew-cut hair and unmistakable Slavic features. I had a gut feeling he was Russian.

I drove towards the hospital, taking care to avoid the usual slew of buses, taxis, rickshaws and other rush hour traffic, all striving to overtake each other and me. I noticed the blue Volga again in the rear-view mirror, through the twin oval back windows of my VW Beetle. It remained there every time I looked, all the way to work. The driver did not attempt to pass and kept a respectable distance. When I turned into the hospital's entrance, the sedan did not follow me.

After parking my Beetle, I waited in the garden and looked towards the road and both the hospital's entrances, to locate the car or the driver. I couldn't observe either. Thinking it was just an odd coincidence, I continued to my office.

That afternoon, over lunch with Doctor Rao, I mentioned this curious incident of the dark blue Volga following me right up to the hospital. I remarked in jest, "Looks like the Russians are after me, Doctor sahib."

While he seemed to look concerned, he just laughed it off. "Oh, Walli. You're reading too many of those Cold War espionage novels."

"But, sir, could it have to do with my acquiring that old trunk?" I asked. "You did say someone else might be interested in it?"

"No, no. That's not possible. The trunk is safe with us. We have security guards here all the time. Don't worry about that car. It was probably there just picking up some other Europeans, foreign embassy staff, perhaps, staying in your apartment building."

While this opinion was plausible, as there indeed were other

Europeans residing in my building, I was still curious about the sea chest. I asked, "So, Doctor Rao, when can I see this precious trunk?"

"Of course. I think you should have a look before we ship it. I'll ask Mila to arrange it."

We finished lunch and went our separate ways. However, that afternoon, while I was on the balcony for some fresh air and gazing towards the City, the morning's events came back to my mind. I recalled the earlier conversation with Alexandra, and telling her about the rumoured involvement of Russian secret agents in the 1857 Rebellion. Alarm bells rang in my head. Good heavens, was the KGB aware of this trunk's existence? Had they listened in on my overseas call to Alexandra? What could be in the trunk that was so significant to the Russians, after all this time?

That evening, having just returned from a good workout in the hotel's gym—on the machines and boxing and karate exercises routines—I was sitting in my small living room, reading a newspaper and enjoying some jazz music on the Voice of America broadcast, when the doorbell rang. I turned the radio down, then walked over and opened the door to find an attractive blonde woman, wearing a blue jacket and short skirt, standing in the hallway. She held a book in her hands, and some more volumes stuck out from a canvas bag at her feet.

She gave me a dazzling smile and said, "Hello, Doctor Sharif, my name is Katya."

We shook hands.

"You like to buy this book? Only five hundred rupees," she said in an unmistakable Russian accent, holding the book towards me.

While I was trying to recover from the surprise of seeing her, the sight of the book and its title, *Lara's Story*, staggered me. It was a copy of the book I had seen lying on Doctor Rao's office coffee table, a few days ago. I leaned on the door-knob for support and stared at the hardback for a moment, and then at her. Her deep blue eyes looked steadfastly at me.

Finally, having regained composure, I took the book and opened the door wider. "Okay, I might be interested. Would you like to come in?"

She looked back and nodded at a beige-suited, heavyset man, wearing a straw fedora with the brim bent over his eyes, who stood at the end of the corridor. He nodded in return, turned and proceeded down the staircase.

"Thank you," she said to me and, picking up her satchel, walked in.

As she passed me, I noticed her slim, athletic figure, but a few wrinkles in her face betrayed her age, which I put close to fifty. I motioned her towards the sofa. She sat down and attempted to smooth the skirt over her shapely knees.

"Can I get you some tea or coffee … a drink, perhaps?" I asked, sitting down on the chair opposite the sofa.

"No, thank you. Me okay."

"So, what's this book about? Did you write it?" I asked, leafing through the pages, while trying to remember where I had heard, or read in a novel, about a character named Lara.

"It's Russian story."

Then it suddenly came to me. "Oh, do you mean the lady in Boris Pasternak's novel?"

"No, no. He don't write the real account of our people. I write the true story here."

"Really! I enjoyed *Doctor Zhivago*. Is this book similar?"

"No. It tell story of my grandmother."

"So, this one is a biography. Hmm … might be interesting. Okay, I'll buy it. I see that you got it published here," I said, looking at the Delhi publisher's name at the bottom of the first page, below the title and author's name, Yekaterina Barinowska.

"Yes. They translate it for me."

"Interesting. So, do you live here? How long have you been in India?"

"For two years. I working at the Soviet Embassy."

The mention of the Soviet Embassy immediately rang warning bells in my head. I could not help but stare at her. Doing my best to remain calm, I said, "I believe you have been to see my boss, Doctor Rao. Haven't you?"

She did not look surprised at all. She nodded and her hair, which she had done up in a chignon, shook with her head.

"Has it something to do with Doctor Margaret's trunk?"

"Yes," she whispered.

"So, why don't you tell me the real reason for coming to see me?"

"Okay, I tell you. We hear that your hospital find that lady's box. My boss call Moscow and they say we must get it from the hospital."

"But why? Why does your government want this old trunk?"

"They not tell. But say they want it. So, I go see your Doctor Rao. He buy my book, but say hospital directors do not want to give us the suitcase. They say it must go to the family of Margarita. Now my boss say to me to see you. Ask if you can help us get it. We give you good money for your job. You interested?"

"So that's why you are having me followed?"

Katya nodded.

"How much is your boss willing to pay?"

"We make you rich. How about five hundred thousand dollars?"

"Half a million! Hmm ..." I mused. "Well, Katya, I'll have to think about it. I can't decide right now," I said, getting up.

"Okay, Doctor Sharif. Tell me soon, please." She fished in her handbag and pulled out a card. She got up and, after pushing her tight skirt down, handed me the card.

I took out my wallet and paid her for the book.

After she left, I sat for a long time, sipping a glass of red wine, and contemplated the amazing turn of events. Half a million dollars. I mulled over what I could do with it. It would fetch a nice-sized property and set me up in private practice in Florida. Alexandra and I had been wanting to move down to the warmer climate there.

My thoughts were diverted again towards that mysterious lady, Doctor Margaret. I wondered what could be so important in her sea chest. Was she the one I was seeing in those nightmares? In one dream, she had visited me in my office, at the hospital. While I had sat engrossed in a report, she glided in silently and placed on my desk three leather-bound volumes of what looked to be journals or diaries. A melodious voice had whispered to me, "Doctor Sharif, I'd like you to read these."

I looked up, but before I had a chance to speak, the barefooted, white-sari-clad figure, with long, blonde hair that flowed to her waist, sailed out of the room, just as quietly as she had come in. While her incense-like perfume lingered, I opened the first volume, titled *My Life in America*, and started to read what appeared to be a memoir.

Chapter Two

The Toy Medical Box

1856, May: Jhansi, India

THE EARLIEST I can remember expressing a desire to become a physician and travel the world was as a little creature barely able to tie her shoelaces. It was usually voiced during those stormy evenings when we sat in the parlour, and my parents' response invariably sounded like a bolt of lightning. Even now, as I write my memoir, here in India in the Rani of Jhansi's Palace, on some stormy nights, when the sounds of rain and thunder come crashing in, the visions of my childhood often loom before my eyes. However, I leap to the day of the twelfth year of my birth in Elizabethville, New Jersey.

*****

1841, May: Elizabethville, New Jersey

"Margaret, are you ready, Puppet?" Mamma called from downstairs. She must have been anxious to have me dressed in time for my special-day dinner, as we were having company.

"I'll be down shortly, Mamma," I called back from my bedroom. However, the truth was that I was nowhere near ready. The blue gown and the pinafore, my mother's choice, still lay folded on top of the bed, while I stood in my undergarments, gazing out the window, hoping my friendly robin would fly over. I wanted him to nibble on the piece of bread placed on the ledge. I loved the way he looked at me while pecking away at his treat, by turning his oval head from side to side.

Where was he? What could be keeping him? I hoped he was not sick. My thoughts were for the poor soul as I peered out of the second-floor window, searching the oak and maple trees lining the street.

We lived outside Elizabethville in New Jersey, on a quiet street not far from the Presbyterian Church, where Papa served as the pastor. That two-story frame house was my first home, for I was born in that dwelling. On many wintry evenings, as we sat by the fireplace, Papa used to recount my birth to me: "On a dark night, thunder, lightning and heavy raindrops beat down on the windows. It was close to midnight when it was time for me to fetch the midwife." He would dramatize, by waving his hands, how he had rushed out in his carriage. I usually stood beside Papa with my elbows on his wing chair's armrest, my face in the palms of my tiny hands, listening with wide eyes. Mamma habitually sat on the opposite chair, attending to her crocheting. Papa would show how he cracked the whip at the horse to make him gallop, and swing his arms and make noises to indicate the bolts of lightning that flashed around. It made me giggle. He would relate the near-mishaps, such as mending a broken wheel or fording a swollen stream—a new obstacle each time he told the tale—and, on his return, rushing up to the front door in the pouring rain, with the midwife in tow. Invariably, Papa stopped the story just at that point, ending with the same words, "And then you were born." Regardless of how much further I wanted to hear and urged him to continue, he would not divulge any more and returned to reading the newspaper.

Mamma would hush me up with stern words that always commanded, "Margaret, go and fetch your storybook and read like a good girl."

I loved to read, especially books about strange lands, like *Gulliver's Travels*, which increased my desire to voyage the world as a physician. Nevertheless, whenever I mentioned this yearning to my parents, their enduring reply—usually Papa's—was, "Margaret, the medical profession is undeniably not suitable for women."

Nonetheless, my interest in medicine flourished like a wild flowering bush that continues to blossom despite neglect, even in the most arduous surroundings. I was forever bandaging injured birds, cats and any other friend or relative who cared to play along.

I can recall that spring day in May 1841 quite vividly, when my longing for medical practice reached another peak. It was my eleventh birthday.

The door of my room flew open and Mamma rushed in, looking most annoyed. She still wore her workday garb and an apron. Her blonde hair was all dishevelled and face flushed from spending the better part of the afternoon in front of the wood-burning stove. Her displeasure was further exacerbated at seeing me not dressed; her blue eyes filled with anger.

"There you are. Not clad yet. Just as I thought." Grabbing me by the arm, she pulled me away from the window. "Pray, what are you doing at the window in your petticoat? Playing with the birds again?"

"Mamma, my robin hasn't come to take his lunch."

"Never mind that wretched bird. Have you washed your face yet?"

I shook my head. The blonde ringlets, curled by Mamma that morning, danced about my face. She dragged me to the washstand and gave my face a good scrubbing with a rough, wet washcloth. It very nearly made me cry.

"Now wipe your hands clean, up to your elbows and, mind, under the armpits too," Mamma said, handing me the towel.

"What about Robin? What has happened to him?" I asked, drying my hands.

"Nothing's happened to him. He probably nibbled elsewhere."

"How could he? He always eats here. I think he is sick."

"Don't be daft. Birds don't get sick. Now, then, let's have you put on your nice clothes." She unfolded the gown and pulled it over my head.

"Mamma, do I have to wear this blue one?" I asked, as she did up the buttons at the back.

"Why not? Don't you like it? You look so pretty in it. It matches your lovely blue eyes, and see this nice white bow in the back," she said, turning me towards the mirror that hung on one side of the wardrobe's door.

"I want my robin," I insisted, and recall looking rather miserable in the mirror.

On seeing me so unhappy, and possibly because it was my birthday, Mamma relented. It was most unusual of her.

"Look, if you want, I have a wee robin already made up in fabric. I can pin it up here for you. Would you like that?" she asked, tapping the right side of my chest.

I nodded, brightening up at the thought of the little bird fastened to my dress, like a flower. My mother went quickly to her room and fetched her sewing basket. She showed me the miniature bird made cleverly in grey, white and red materials. It was padded with a bit of wool and its eyes and beak made from the tiniest buttons. I jumped up and down with glee while she expertly stitched the little stuffed bird, all the time asking me to be still.

"There, now, doesn't it look so grand?" she asked, turning me towards the mirror again.

"Yes. But where's my real robin? Do you think he's sick?"

"No. He is not. Listen, why don't you leave the bread outside the window? He'll come, by and by, to eat it when he is hungry enough. In the meantime, put on your shoes and come right down."

I picked up the pinafore, but she said, "Leave it. No need for that now. All the work's done. Your aunt and uncle will be here shortly. Don't you want to play with your cousins?"

"Yes, Mamma." The thought of playing with my friends elated me.

"Don't be long now. I still have to get Elizabeth and David ready." With those final instructions, she rushed off.

I looked into the mirror to admire the miniature bird and ran my fingers over it a few times. My blue dress was made of a soft taffeta fabric with borders of white crocheted trim around the neck and sleeves. The hem, tucked up in places, was eye-catching. Nevertheless, I would have preferred to wear the red one. I pinched my cheeks the way Mamma did hers, until they appeared like red-spotted apples. I turned to take a last look at the window to see if Robin had arrived. Alas, he still was not there. With a deep sigh, I stepped down the oak staircase to the parlour. The aroma of Mamma's cooking wafted from the kitchen.

I heard voices from the parlour and, standing in the hallway, peeked round the door. Aunt Flora and Uncle John were seated talking to Papa. They looked fetching, neatly dressed in their going-out clothes.

"There you are, Margaret," cried Aunt Flora. "We were wondering if you would *ever* come down."

"Come in, dear, don't be shy—it's your birthday." added Uncle John, extending both his arms towards me.

I tottered over to Uncle and Aunt to give them hugs and kisses.

"Happy birthday, darling. My, what a beautiful blue frock we're wearing. Do you like it?" Aunt asked.

I replied, "Mamma made it."

My cousins, Agnes and Jonathan, trotted over and, after giving me hugs, handed me a greeting card signed by all of them.

"What's that?" Jonathan asked, pointing at the stuffed bird pinned to my dress.

"It's Robin's brother," I replied, petting the bird.

"Where's Robin?" Agnes asked.

"He's sick. He could not come for my dinner," I replied, and saw smiles on my aunt's and uncle's faces.

Papa stood with his back to the fireplace, looking dapper in his black trousers, chequered waistcoat, dark frock coat, and a white cravat held by a pin with a golden cross. His blond hair and moustache were trimmed, as he had likely been to the barber that afternoon. Glancing at me with his blue eyes, he said, "Look, Maggie, see what your aunt and uncle have brought you. Just what you need—"

"Pray, what does she need?" Mamma said, entering the room with Elizabeth and David in tow. She looked decent enough, with her hair brushed and done up in a chignon. She wore a blue cotton, pleated dress with long sleeves, over a white silk blouse. A brooch, with ornamental jewels in a flower pattern, was pinned to her chemise. I believe it was the only piece of real jewellery she owned. Aunt and Uncle complimented her on her attire.

"I was just saying Flora and John have brought the perfect gift for Margaret. One she can put to good use, to take care of her sick birds," Papa explained.

I looked at my father and then at my uncle. My lips formed an "o" of confusion.

"Here it is. Happy birthday, dear." Uncle John lifted a small box from behind the chair.

"What is it?" I asked, accepting what looked like a cigar box, made of polished oak, with a pink ribbon tied around it.

"Why don't you open it," Aunt Flora suggested.

I untied the ribbon and lifted the box's lid. "Yoo-hoo," I screamed with delight upon observing its contents. "Thank you, Aunt Flora and Uncle John." I ran and hugged them again.

It was an exquisite little box, likely made by Uncle himself, for he was a carpenter. It contained a number of toy medical instruments: a stethoscope, a magnifying glass, rolls of bandages and bottles of colourful powders made to look like medicines, among other playthings. My daughter, in Canada West, has that medical box now, and no doubt cherishes it just as much as I did.

The item I treasured most was the toy listening device, made of brass with the ends flared like a blow horn. I asked, "Uncle, what's it for?"

"It's a stethoscope, dear, used for listening to patients' heartbeats. Come here, let me show you."

I handed the cylindrical object to him. He applied the larger end to his chest and asked me to listen at the smaller side. I heard thumping sounds. That was the first time I had ever heard a person's heartbeat. I was thrilled. My cousins and younger siblings gathered around, also wanting to hear the thuds. They shrieked with delight. We rummaged through the box. David grabbed hold of one of the bottles with red powder in it, and began pulling on the cork. When I stopped him, he screamed.

Mamma came over and snatched the bottle out of his hands. "Children! That's enough. Margaret, place these things back in the box, just as you found them, and put it away in the cupboard," Mamma said, and turned towards the others. "No doubt you must be peckish. Dinner is ready. Why don't we all go into the dining room?"

While we seated ourselves at the dinner table, Mamma came over from the kitchen, carrying a cauldron of steaming soup. From the aroma, I knew it was clam chowder, my favourite. After she filled our bowls, I could barely stop myself from tasting it. But we had to wait until Papa said Grace. He was, happily, brief. Although, after thanking God for all the bounties we were about to receive, he did continue and said a few kind words and a prayer for the well-being of his eldest girl-child and may she have a long life. Amen.

"I dare say, Joan, you make the most delicious clam chowder," Aunt Flora remarked, sipping on a spoonful of hot soup.

"The best along the Atlantic coast is no match for yours." Uncle John chimed in.

Mamma thanked them. She followed up the soup with courses of stewed beef, vegetables and herb-roasted fowl—all done according to her special Celtic recipe. I helped, by serving Mamma's sourdough bread she had baked specially for the occasion.

"How are Cousin Will and family faring in Canada?" Uncle John asked, passing his plate to Mamma for a second helping of beef stew.

"Very well, as far as we can gather. I had a letter from Fiona the other day," she said and, turning to me, asked, "Margaret, what did you do with the picture-card your cousins sent you?"

"It's in my room, Mamma. I think," I replied in a low voice.

"After dinner, why don't you bring it down and show us. There is a lovely painting of their farmland on the front and it's signed inside by all of them."

I kept quiet. However, when we were nearly finished, she reminded me to go and fetch the card.

"No. I don't want to show it," I said, like a stubborn child.

"Oh, why not, dear?" Aunt asked, looking surprised.

"I think we know the reason." Papa said with a chuckle.

Mamma hastened to explain, "Oh, it's nothing, really. Her cousin, Robert, has marked three exes besides his name. He's just a child, hardly twelve, you know."

"Oh my goodness. Robert fancies you, my dear." Aunt Flora said, looking at me with wide eyes, and clasped her hands, as if to signify a match made in Heaven.

"Don't worry, Margaret, we won't tell anybody, even though he's a Loyalist." Uncle John teased, and the others laughed.

I must have blushed crimson in embarrassment. I sat back in the chair, bent my head down and covered my face with my hands. In fact, I really wanted to hide under the table or have the earth open up and swallow me.

Mamma saved me from further loss of composure. Getting up, she announced, "It's time for Margaret to blow out the candles. Children, please clear the table and place fresh platters, while I get the cake."

Taking the empty dishes to the kitchen, in my mind's eye I saw Robert's writing on the card. He was from the part of our family that had moved to Upper Canada. My great-grandparents, having migrated in the late 1700s from Scotland, had settled in the Mohawk Valley. However, at the start of the American Revolution, around 1775, the kinfolk had split up. While roughly half the relations decided to remain loyal to the British Crown and moved north to the safety of Upper Canada, the other half, my grandfather included, had supported the Patriots and remained resolutely in New England.

With dinner and the happy birthday wishing over, we retired back to the parlour. The grown-ups, glasses of wine in hand, seated themselves by the fireplace; the little ones played on one side of the room. Elizabeth and I fetched our new dolls to show Cousin Agnes. We three convened in a corner, making small talk with the dolls. David brought out his toy wooden train set. He and Jonathan took delight in rolling, the miniature engine and carriage sets on the floor. Some of my smaller dolls became passengers inside the wagons. However, I did not raise a fuss for, after all, it was my special day.

I overheard Papa ask Uncle, "Have you finished that new book you showed me the other day, John? What was it called, *A Thousand and One Nights?*"

"Aye. *Arabian* nights. Ach, no, not finished it yet. Ah, but you should read it too. What fine tales that Scheherazade tells the Caliph of Baghdad."

"Scheherazade. Wasn't she the princess?" Mamma asked.

"No. She was a concubine of the Caliph—"

Aunt Flora exclaimed, "Can you believe it? She narrated those yarns, each night, to save her life." Looking at Uncle, she added, "I've been peeking through that book too, you know, John."

All this talk of Scheherazade and the Caliph of Baghdad intrigued me. I dropped my doll in Agnes's lap and crawled over to sit on the rug beside Mamma's chair.

Papa asked, "Who wrote this book, and how in Heaven's name did he hear those Arabian fairy tales?"

"A French physician in the court of Baghdad's Caliph had transcribed them from Arabic into French. This book is an English translation of the French novel, by a Scot, of all people. "

I got up and stood beside Uncle's chair. "Are there really a thousand and one stories, Uncle John?"

"Aye. That's what the title of the book says."

"So many. And what are they about?"

"Well, there's the one about *Sinbad the Sailor*. He's somewhat like … er, do you know *Gulliver?*"

"Yes, I have a picture book called *Gulliver's Travels.*"

"Aye, that's the one. Then there's one about *Ali Baba and the Forty Thieves.* All told by the concubine to save herself from the gibbet."

I must have looked rather innocent when I asked, "Uncle John, who is a concubine and why does she have to die?"

"Well, let's see. She's a slave girl …" He didn't finish the sentence. Instead, he looked at Papa, as if to ask whether he should answer the second part of the question.

Papa cleared this throat and announced, "That will be all for now,

Margaret. This book is for grown-ups."

"Oooh … you always say that, Papa," I said, likely with a long face, and shuffled over to stand behind Mamma's chair.

Mamma was probably thinking of something else, because she abruptly asked, "Oh, that reminds me, Flora. Is that runaway slave girl still hiding in your …" She paused when Aunt Flora gestured at Mamma, with her eyes, towards me. Mamma turned around and, looking at me with an irate face, said, "Listen, children, why don't you all go and play some games upstairs. Puppet, show them the new chequers set Papa got you."

I pursed my lips and took the little ones up to my room. Setting up the chequers board on the bed, I asked them to start the game. I was curious to learn more about the runaway slave girl. I tiptoed downstairs.

I heard Aunt Flora say, "Yes, her parents will be joining her soon."

"The poor lass. How long can they all stay in your loft?" Mamma asked.

"As long as it takes, Joan. It's getting dreadfully difficult to find conductors to take these creatures across," Uncle John said. "That's why I was asking earlier about Cousin Will, to see if we could—"

There was a creaking sound. I had stepped on a loose floorboard. I froze.

Mamma called out, "Is that you, Margaret? I thought I told you to go upstairs."

"Yes, Mamma. Just getting a glass of water," I replied, trying to sound as innocent as possible. Walking back up the stairs with the glass of water, I thought about the other slave girl, Scheherazade. Wouldn't it be nice to work, just like that French physician, in the Caliph's court? I could treat the concubines and listen to their yarns. Would my parents let me go? Papa never. Mamma might. I must ask her to get Papa to agree. With a sigh, I trudged upstairs to play chequers with my cousins.

*****

I loved my toy medical box and carried it everywhere. I played ceaselessly with the stethoscope, and went around applying it to my parents' and other visiting family and friends' chests to listen to their heartbeats. I would only stop when told sternly by my mother to do so.

A few weeks after that day, another defining moment of my life awaited me. It was a Monday. I woke up early, possibly from the chiming of the grandfather clock in the hallway downstairs. I remember counting six chimes and being happy, for it was not yet time to get ready for school. I lay curled up in bed and daydreamed. The cool breeze blowing in from the partially open window felt good. My mind wandered and I remembered the events of the previous day.

It being Sunday, there was a special meeting in the church after the service. Mamma had me wear the same blue dress, for it "wasn't ready to be washed yet," she said. Except that since it was getting a bit soiled around the collar, she added a clean while tucker around it. On the way to church, while helping me into the carriage, Papa remarked how adorable I looked with my hair in ringlets.

After the service, we stayed on to listen to a talk given by one of our Presbyterian missionaries on furlough from an American mission station in northern India. Papa introduced him and the reverend came up to the lectern, amid polite applause.

"Pastor Wallace, sisters and brethren," the visitor began, "while it is a pleasure for me to be amongst you here in your fine town, I do not rejoice in what I am about to relate to you. May the Holy Spirit honour us with his gracious presence, in this meeting, as he has manifestly done in our gatherings at the missions in India. I thankfully acknowledge the good hand of our God upon me through the long journey of many thousands of miles, over numerous oceans and lands, in various climes. I had the privilege of meeting people of customs and manners much different from ours. I found their religions not only strange, but also akin to heathenism, and I dare say those that engage in many pagan rituals. However, just a few years ago, the northern provinces of that land, having experienced recurring crop failures from lack of rain, were visited with a severe famine whose effects are still being felt. The nauseating scenes of suffering by the starving masses are just too dreadful to describe. People lay by the roadside, dying in the hundreds. Those with enough energy crawled up to the travellers, begging for a morsel of bread. Looking at their gaunt faces and sunken eyes, one could not help but remember Shakespeare:

Famine is in thy cheeks.
Need and oppression starveth in thy eyes.
The world is not thy friend.

"Riding through the villages was fraught with danger. Haggard shapes, with skin shrunken to the bones, shuffled through the streets and the empty bazaars, ready to pounce on any lone wayfarer they believed might possess a loaf or even one *chapatti*. In front of their huts usually squatted a family that reminded one of Ugolino from Dante's *Inferno*. Most of all, my dear brethren, it is with a painful heart that I must relate to you what I have seen with my very own eyes. The shocking sight of women, with tears flowing down their sunken cheeks, running up to us with their babes in their outstretched arms, and offering them for a few shillings or a bag of flour."

"No!" gasped some women in the audience. "How could they?"

"Yes, ma'am. Those were desperate acts," the reverend replied. "Although one of our native priests, Reverend Gopinath Nundy, believed that the women likely felt happy, knowing their little ones would be cared for by us. There was also a grave danger of the famished babies being carried away by starving wolves or tigers."

While the reverend continued his speech, describing the calamitous situation, my mind wandered. I shuddered at the mental picture of human babies being taken away by wolves or tigers, held in their jaws.

I heard someone ask, "Did the government not provide any famine relief?"

"Indeed it did. The Governor General, Lord Auckland, and his sister, Lady Emily Eden, toured the area and distributed food and blankets. Large ovens were set up to supply bread to the masses. I am told Miss Eden could be seen feeding some of the urchins herself."

"How about our American Mission—did we not help?" another gentleman asked.

"We most certainly were there. It was through the special orderings of Providence. By the efforts of our brother, Reverend Wilson, and a British Captain, Wheeler, we were able to set up an orphan asylum. We also acquired the good services of Reverend Gopinath, his wife and others. Here we housed hundreds of those unfortunate children who had either been orphaned or given up by their parents. Sure enough, following normality, some of the children were claimed back, while others are happily left in our care."

"How are the waifs doing now?" a parishioner asked.

"The task of restoring these unfortunates was no ordinary one," the missionary replied with a sad look. "They had initially arrived in our care much incapacitated and diseased. Even with what medical treatment and attention we could provide, I am heartbroken to say many died within a short period. It seems that the famine-fever has long-lasting effects. It is hard to say if many of the remainder will reach their mature years, or if they do, whether they will be in good health. They need the kind blessings of our Saviour and the helping hands of our brethren. We are planning to add to the orphanage a Mission Station and a church—"

"Don't famines happen in cycles? Why can't they predict them and do something before they come about?" someone interjected.

"Well, sir, I have heard of a most curious method the good folks down there use to predict a famine. You see, they have those large forests of bamboo shrubs that seldom flower. However, their witch doctors, if I may be permitted to call them that, believe that the year a bamboo plant flowers will be a famine year …"

My mind again wandered with the vision of the sick children lying dying in their little cots without much medical aid. I wanted to do something for them, like take them in my arms, rock them and sing a lullaby.

I heard another question. I believe it was Mamma. "What about the education of the orphans?"

The reverend replied, "Indeed, ma'am. Both their mental and spiritual needs are being cared for, again within our limited resources. With the help of our Lord, our labours have not been without fruit. If I may be permitted to celebrate, for just a moment, as many of them have become members of Christ's kingdom. The blessed effects of Christianity are being exhibited in the lives of those who still survive. Let us pray for the salvation of the souls of these children of God …"

While we joined him in prayer, I looked around. His poignant message must have touched the hearts of the congregation. I spotted many ladies dabbing their eyes with kerchiefs.

After the lecture, there was a social get-together over tea and biscuits. Papa knew the minister personally, and brought him over to where we stood, teacup and saucer in hand.

"Brother Duncan, allow me to introduce my family." Papa told him our names.

"Reverend Duncan, where in India is this new American Mission?" Mamma asked.

"Ah, yes, madam. In addition to our establishment in Allahabad, we're now planning to build another church in the village of Futtehgurh. It's also situated on the Ganges River, but closer to the Mughal Empire's capital city, Delhi."

"Why, isn't that a bit distant from Calcutta? In event of any difficulties, how would they get help from the Company's forces?"

Papa interjected, "My wife's family has several members serving in the East India Company."

"Oh, how commendable of them. Indeed, ma'am, it's a bit out of the British area, but we aren't expecting any problems from the natives there, really. We're going there in peace and have plans to open a school as well."

Papa must have remembered something, possibly from the church newsletters, and asked, "Is it true, our church has managed to secure land over there?"

"Indeed, Brother James. The British have taken over that whole area and pensioned off the nawab. The government has been kind enough to grant us land, in total about sixty acres, at a most nominal rate. Our plans are to build adjacent to the asylum not only mission bungalows, but also a church, a school, a carpet-weaving enterprise and, I am proud to say, a Christian village to house the ever-increasing population of our native brethren."

"How many missionaries are you planning to have there?" Mamma asked.

"Up to a dozen staff members. So far we've recruited a couple of local native Christian priests and are expecting some volunteers from our American clergy or parishioners," he said, looking at Mamma and Papa, as if inquiring whether they might be interested.

Papa said in his priestly voice, "We will pray for your success in all your undertakings, Brother Duncan. May God grant you strength in your endeavours." He apparently was not interested in going to India.

"Amen," replied Reverend Duncan.

Mamma asked the missionary some more questions about the weather and general living conditions over there. From her inquisitiveness, I could not help thinking that despite Papa's lack of enthusiasm, being a schoolteacher, she might have been entertaining the idea of teaching in the new school Brother Duncan had mentioned. Was it the money, or her desire to raise her social status, I wondered?

Nevertheless, I was still intrigued by all the sicknesses the priest had talked about, and especially that the people there were still suffering from the famine-related diseases. I could not subdue my curiosity and tugged his jacket sleeve. When he looked down at me, I asked, "Brother, why are the Indy children not getting well?"

His good-natured reply was, "Because there are so few doctors out there, young lady."

To that I said, looking towards my mother, "I have a medical box, Mamma. Can I go to Indy to help the sick people?"

Mamma looked dourly at me and spoke in her strong tone of voice, "That's enough, Margaret, you be quiet now." There was much laughter from those standing around us.

I felt annoyed at my mother's harsh reply and covered my face in the folds of her kilt to hide the tears. Mamma hugged me and ran her hand over my head.

*****

As I lay in bed with those events of the previous day churning in my head, my attention was drawn to the birds chirping outside. Just then, as if by a supernatural force, an inner voice spoke to me. The voice sounded like it came from a long tunnel. *It is time for you to begin your journey to India. Go there and help the ailing children.* I jumped out of bed. I recall donning my bonnet, but still in my nightshirt and slippers, I picked up the toy medical box and tiptoed downstairs. I walked out of the front door, onto the porch and into the street.

We lived in a pleasant, semi-rural area. It being early, the sun was just beginning to come up and shone through the oak trees. I do not recollect seeing many people as I ambled down the street, swinging the toy medical box in my little hand. I strolled in the direction of the stagecoach stop, hoping to take the next carriage to India!

I might have awakened my parents, from either the creaking of the stairs or the opening and closing of the front door, or possibly they were already up. However, no doubt, they must have been horrified when they spied me from their bedroom window, wandering down the street.

I had sauntered just a few yards when I heard my father: "Maaggiee!"

I turned around and saw him running towards me. He came up to me and picked me up in his strong arms. With his face close to mine, he asked in a stern voice, "And where do you think you are going this morning?"

"To Indy, Papa."

"And, pray, what would you be doing there?"

My reply was, "To make the Indy children well, Papa."

Papa put me down and, with me holding his fingers, led me home without another word. I am sure he must have subdued his temper and the urge to box me about the ears. Nevertheless, some other punishment would follow on some other day.

Chapter Three

The Sea Chest

1965, May: Delhi, India

I WAS BUSY in my office, reviewing patients' files, when someone knocked on the open door. I looked up and saw nurse Premila, or "Mila", as we called her, hovering there shyly with a half smile on her face. I waved her in. She was a young woman, pretty, with striking dark eyes and shoulder-length, raven hair. Her light olive complexion and high cheekbones suggested she was from northern India. She looked charming in her uniform, a white sari with a blue border, draped across the front over a tight-fitting blouse. A white headscarf and matching shoes completed her outfit.

"Yes, Mila?" I asked, sitting back in my chair and gazing up at her.

"Doctor Rao is asking if you are free this afternoon, to see that sea chest?"

I hadn't forgotten about the visit Doctor Rao was going to arrange. The mysterious trunk was very much on my mind, among other issues. I was anxious to look at it, believing it would somehow reveal its secrets to me. "What time does he wish to go?"

"Would two o'clock be okay?"

I consulted my diary and replied, "Yes, that'll be fine. I'll come over to Doctor Rao's office." Then I noticed another appointment, written in my scribbled hand, in the five p.m. slot: *Mila jewellery shop.*

Before I could remind her, she asked, "Are you still able to take me to your uncle's jewellery store?"

"Yes. I have to go there anyway. I haven't seen him for a while."

"Thank you. Okay, see you then." She smiled again and gave me the customary *nameste*. I put my palms together in return and she departed.

I closed the diary and, while putting it away to one side of the desk, a business card fell out of it. It was Katya's, which she had given me the evening before. I held it in my hand and stared at her name, telephone number, other details, and the hammer and sickle emblem embossed on one corner.

I had agonised over the Russians' alluring offer for most of the night, but was unable to come to a decision, even by the time I arose with the sound of a *moazzen's* call to prayer from a nearby mosque. I believe I made up my mind on the drive to the office, when I observed the homeless sleeping on sidewalks and those living in their meagre huts on the side of the streets. People were waking up and preparing perhaps their only meal of the day on the makeshift stone cookers, using dried cow-dung cakes for fuel. It was a sight I had seen every day and yet hardly noticed. However, that morning, it bore a special nuance—a message I had been ignoring. While it had been less than two decades since Indians had gained their *azadi*, their freedom, I wondered how much longer it would take for the plight of these destitute people to improve. Were not all the sacrifices they had made during the ninety-year struggle—from 1857—enough? However, who would make the effort to improve the quandary of the impoverished? It dawned on me that it was incumbent on not just the politicians, but also on all the professionals like myself—engineers, lawyers, doctors and others—to put our hands to the *chakra*, the wheel, that is imprinted on India's flag.

I put Katya's business card down and, picking up the telephone receiver, dialled the number on the card. The Russian Embassy receptionist put me through to her immediately. I told her I had been reading her novel and, having found it very interesting, wished to buy another copy for a friend. "Can you deliver it to me this evening?" I asked.

She said, "Me very happy to hear you like book. I bring one more book to your flat, after dinner."

At two p.m., I arrived at Doctor Rao's office and found him waiting for me. After the usual greetings and handshakes, we headed down the hallway with the brisk steps doctors and other professionals take in urgency. We went down the stairs leading to the hospital's annex at the rear of the property, where the storage rooms were situated. My eyes blinked in the brilliant sunshine, and the hot, humid air welcomed us as we stepped out of the back door. While on the garden path towards the annex, I looked up to see if there was any prospect of rain, but the blue sky seemed as bare of clouds as a calm ocean without whitecaps.

"Another hot day, Doctor Rao?"

"Yes, too bad. A cloudy, rainy day here is a cause for celebration, Doctor Walli. Do you remember, we skipped school to go on picnics on such days?"

We both laughed.

"Is the trunk still in one piece?" I inquired.

"Yes. I was amazed when I saw it. It is in splendid condition."

"That's remarkable, considering it has been missing all these years."

"It might be a benefit of mislaid baggage kept in storage. It remains undisturbed by nature and humans."

I nodded, and wondered how its owner, after all these years, would react if she could see us probing her trunk.

We entered the annex and found the storerooms supervisor, along with a couple of his aides, waiting for us outside his office. He was an older man with a greying beard and a broad handlebar moustache, fashioned in the manner typical of a British army sergeant. They were dressed in the hospital maintenance staff's khaki uniforms, grey turbans, baggy trousers and loose shirts.

"*Nameste*, doctor *saa'bs*," they greeted us.

"*Nameste*, Narinder Singh. This is Doctor Sharif. You know, the grandson of Sharif Khan Bhadur? He will be taking the trunk back to America."

"*Nameste*," I said, and shook hands with Narinder. He clasped my hand in both of his. His eyes gleamed at the mention of my grandfather, whom he would have remembered as a renowned freedom fighter during the Rebellion.

"Yes, I hear you now working in this hospital. It is great honour for me to finally meet you, s*aa'b*. I know you grandfather a great *bhadur*. I am retired soldier too, you know."

"Retired, truly. You look so young. Were you in the Second World War?"

"Thank you, *saa'b*. Yes, 1944, me serve the British Indian Army. Going to Europe."

"Really, and which countries were you in?"

"Me fight in North Africa and Italy."

"Oh, so you were part of General Montgomery's forces, against Rommel?"

"Yes, s*aa'b*. We fight in the desert."

"Yes, I've heard a lot about those battles, Narinder *Bhadur*," I said, imagining those turbaned soldiers with bayoneted rifles in hand, storming the German tanks. I called him a *bhadur*, to return the compliment.

Doctor Rao interrupted, "Please tell us, where is the American lady's trunk?" He likely feared that Narinder would go into a long reminiscence of WWII events.

"I show you. Please follow me." Narinder led us into the building and down a hallway with storerooms on either side. We walked behind him solemnly, as if on our way to view a coffin. He stopped before a door, pulled out his chain of keys, unlocked the door, and pushed it in. It opened with an eerie screech. Beams of sunlight shone down on us from the few windows close to the ceiling, injecting some brightness into the gloom. The damp, humid air smelt like old, rotting paper and made me cover my nose with my palm. Wooden and cardboard boxes, medical equipment parts, files of decaying old medical records and such items were kept on lines of metallic racks. Narinder led us to the back of the room and pointed to a box on the last row of rusting shelves.

"Here it is, doctor *saa'bs*."

A layer of dust covered the chest. Narinder frowned and, using his old sergeant's commanding voice, barked at the assistants. "Look, *kamchors,* how dusty it is. Clean it, *jaldhysay*."

The two assistants scrambled to wipe the coffer with the dusting cloths they carried on their shoulders.

Although it was over a hundred years old, apart from a few bumps and scratches, it still looked like a fine piece of an old-fashioned sea traveller's chest. A typical storage box, made of oak hardwood, with a curved lid. Its length and depth were nearly three feet and almost two feet in width. It certainly appeared to have withstood the test of time, likely because it was evidently handcrafted from solid wood, with ornamentally carved wooden strengthening ribs around its girth.

Reinforcing strips of brass were riveted to the wood along the edges. The brass would have shone in its original days, but had become tarnished over the years. There were flowery patterns around the edges of the brass plates. A square, brass address-label holder was attached to one side. I looked closer—a label was still there. On yellowing whiteboard, in firm handwriting, likely using a quill ink pen, someone had written in an elegant script:

Dr. Margaret Wallace, American Mission, Futtehgurh, India

The box had a solid padlock, which looked preserved and strong as ever, like the expertly crafted locks made in those early days. I recalled flipping through similar ones in antique markets. I reached over and cradled the padlock in my palm. A strange energy and warmth emanated from it onto my wrist, as if I had touched the hands that had locked it over a century ago. In the gloom of the dimly lit storeroom, I thought I saw a dust cloud coalesce into an apparition in the shape of a woman. Blinking, I strained to see her face. The image looked similar to the one I had seen in my terrifying dreams: the same person with the Godiva likeness who had tried to lead me onto that mountaintop temple. Before I could get a clearer look, the form faded into one of the sunbeams. No one else seemed to have noticed anything, for they stood calmly looking at me.

"Where was this trunk found?" I asked, resting my hand on the top of the chest, trying to recover from my trance.

"*Saa'b*, we find it by chance, between the broken furniture, desks and cabinets, over there." Narinder pointed towards the back.

"How long has it been here?"

"Oh, it is there for long time, sir. Even before I start work in this hospital. Before twenty years ago, I am believing. First, we think it is empty. Then, one day we clean out that room, because we need more space. One *jamadaran* tell me that the box too heavy to move. She think something inside. I go take a look and find, yes, it heavy, something in there. I look at the name of the Aamrican madam and say, oh *Bhagwan*, and I call *bara saa'b* at once." Narinder looked clearly proud at having made the discovery, for he said these words standing erect, with his chest out.

"Where did this trunk come from?" I asked, looking at Doctor Rao.

"From one of the neighbouring hospitals, I think, when it was closed down. It was possibly from the one in Jhansi."

"But the address label says *American Mission, Futtehgurh.*"

"This is the mystery, and that's why the Directors believed the doctor to be American and not British," Doctor Rao replied. "Usually these trunks contain the personal possessions of deceased persons. Their relatives are notified and either they take the coffer away or, if they do not want it, it is emptied and just kept in the storage room. We have several similar old sea chests lying around here."

"And this one hasn't been opened yet?"

"Yes. You know, our hospital's policy is not to open a person's luggage without the presence of their surviving relatives, or at least their written permission."

"Yes, I believe this is the common procedure in most reputable hospitals," I agreed.

"That's why you see, Walli, the Directors want it returned unopened to the family of this lady."

Narinder was listening intently to the discussion. Grasping my arm for emphasis, implored, "Please, sir, take this trunk back to the doctor *sahiba's* children yourself. I do not sleep for nights to see this trunk here and not know what happen to *bechari.*" He shook his head, looking sorrowful.

"We have to locate them first." To comfort him, I added, "Narinderji, believe me, I will do the best I can."

"Thank you, *saa'b. Bhagwan ki madat say*, you will find her family."

We thanked the storage staff and, bidding farewell *namestes*, strode back through the garden towards the main building.

On the way, Doctor Rao asked, "Have you spoken to your grandmother yet?"

"No, not yet." I was again intrigued by his interest in determining any connection between my family and the owner of the sea chest and, especially, why he had not disclosed to me Katya's visit to his office. I spotted a park bench under the shade of a huge mango tree in an isolated corner of the garden. I pointed to it and asked, "Can we go and sit there for a minute? There is something I wish to discuss."

He agreed readily and we walked over to the bench. The shade of the mango tree was a wonderful reprieve from the heat of the blazing sun. We sat there for a while, enjoying the cool breeze, and mopped drops of perspiration from our foreheads. Crows squawked in the branches overhead and *maalis* hoed the flowerbeds in the distance. I informed him about Katya's visit to my apartment, but took care not to mention the offer of the large sum of money. He listened patiently and nodded when I finished by saying, "It looks to me the Russians really wish to obtain this trunk at any cost."

"Yes, that lady, Katya, came to see me as well. She used the pretence of selling her novel and then asked that we give the sea chest to them. I checked with the Director and his answer was a definitive no. Imagine the international incident it might create if we handed over to the Soviets this trunk that really belonged to an American."

"Yes, I would agree. Margaret's relatives would be most disappointed with Lady Dufferin's careless attitude. But why didn't you tell me about Katya's visit earlier?"

Doctor Rao did not meet my gaze. He looked into the distance and replied, "I didn't think it was that important. I felt it would have alarmed you unnecessarily. Besides, we were planning to ship the trunk soon and the subject would have been closed."

"But what if the Russians try to steal it?"

"Now this looks serious. I didn't think they were *that* interested to approach you and, as you say, they might even resort to theft. I think we should send it to your home in America as soon as possible."

"When will you be able to do that?"

"It might be in a month or two. You know the paperwork for these things takes time. But I am now worried that it might give the Russians an opportunity to try and steal it."

"In that case, I have a plan that might get them off our backs, so to speak," I said in a steady voice.

"Oh!" Doctor Rao looked at me, his eyes wide. He asked with raised eyebrows, "What do you have in mind, Walli?"

Looking around to be sure that no one else was within earshot, I leaned closer to him and whispered my proposed plan. I concluded by saying, "Of course, much depends on whether Narinder Singh can be trusted."

Doctor Rao looked amused and wore a smile. "Hmm … it might just work. Don't worry about Narinder. He is a very trustworthy fellow. One of the old guard. I have known him for a long time."

"So, how soon can you make the arrangements?" I asked, happy to see that my plan was acceptable.

"Oh, very soon, possibly in less than a week. Let me go and make some inquiries."

We got up from the garden bench and walked back to our respective offices.

Later that afternoon, Doctor Rao passed by my office and, coming closer to my chair, whispered, "Your plan will work. You can do it this Saturday night."

"Are you sure Narinder can be trusted?" I asked again.

"Absolutely. I have just spoken to him and he is willing to take care of all the details."

*****

The air-cooled engine of my Beetle resonated with its familiar rattle as I drove along the wide boulevards of New Delhi towards Connaught Place, one of the major shopping venues.

"You must stay for dinner," Uncle Arif had said when I called him earlier that afternoon.

"No, thank you. I won't be able to stay late," I explained. "I have an early surgery tomorrow." I also declined his dinner invitation knowing that dinnertime in Delhi was closer to nine o'clock, which was too late for me. I still had not become accustomed to those late dinners and preferred to eat at the North American suppertime.

Mila rolled down the window a touch on the passenger side, to get some fresh air into the car. She looked lovely, having changed into her traditional *shalwar-kameez* outfit, which comprised a silken, knee-length shirt in light blue with white flowery patterns and matching baggy, white silk pants. As I rounded a corner, the aroma of her heavy eastern perfume, a mixture of jasmine, night-queen, roses and other flowers, drifted towards me: a pleasant change from the nauseating smells in the operating rooms. Noting that she wore light sandals with blue and golden leather straps, I turned the airflow to the floor and asked, "Is it warm? Shall I open my window a bit more?"

"No. It's fine now."

"So, tell me, what type of jewellery are you looking for?"

"Oh, something elegant. It's a gift for my best girlfriend who is getting married."

"Jewellery is a very special wedding gift, isn't it?"

"Yes. She is a close friend of ours. I know your uncle is famous for his jewellery sets. So, I thought of asking you to take me there.

Perhaps I can get a discount. No?"

"No. I'll ask him to charge you extra, so I can get a commission."

She giggled. "Oh, Doctor Walli, you are picking up the bad habits of the Delhi-*wallahs*."

"Don't forget I was born here. Some habits are hard to break," I said with a smile.

She laughed, throwing her head back.

At the mention of my past, and possibly because of Mila's presence, my thoughts turned to my parents and my childhood sweetheart, Anjuli. My parents were descended from the Mughals, who arrived in India from Central Asia in the sixteenth century. My father and his brothers, in the tradition of Mughal craftsmen, were reputable jewellers of Delhi and carried on the craft, using the special knowledge of metallurgy and gemmology handed down from father to son for centuries.

In 1947, after a struggle lasting over ninety years, India finally won her freedom from the British. However, the final price paid was the partition of the country into India and Pakistan. When, because of the separation, the inevitable rioting broke out between the majority Hindu and the minority Muslim populations, most Muslims feared for their lives. Nevertheless, the Sharif family's Hindu neighbours had assured them that no harm would come to them; they were persuaded to remain in their homeland. This was likely because my family were reputed to be sincere and compassionate employers of persons of all faiths, including Hindu, Sikh, Christian and Muslim. My relations were treated with honour and respect in the community.

However, there was likely another, more important reason for the assurances of our safety. The credit for that has to go to my grandfather, Sharif Khan. He had earned the title of *bhadur*, having served valiantly in the armies of the last Mughal Emperor, Shah Zafar and the Rani of Jhansi, in their battles with the British in 1857—1858.

Although statues and images are considered inappropriate in the Muslim religion, a portrait of Grandfather in brilliant oil colours nevertheless existed; he sat gallantly on horseback with a *talwar* in hand. The painting still hung in my uncle's store. I remembered, as a young boy, looking up to that painting in admiration, as did many other visitors from the city and surrounding areas. They came to the store specifically to see that painting, as if it were in an art gallery. Sharif Khan *Bhadur*, having fought for his homeland in India's First

War of Independence, was a folk hero and much loved by all the citizens of Delhi.

My uncle, Arif, the youngest of my father's brothers, was among the last of our family members still living in Delhi. My father and other aunts and uncles had decided to leave Delhi for Karachi, in 1947. I hadn't seen Anjuli since that tearful parting of two eleven-year-olds. I often wondered: Where was she? How was she? Was she married? But that is another story.

"Look, there's the India Gate. Doesn't it look wonderful, reflecting the rays of the setting sun like that?" Mila's comment jolted me back to the present.

"Goodness. I've never seen it shine so brightly," I remarked. We drove on the roundabout road circling the monument, the famous landmark built by the British Raj to honour the fallen soldiers during past wars. The India Gate: some consider it the divide between Old and New Delhi, signifying the ushering in of the new era of Western influence. Tour operators usually referred to it, lovingly, as India's answer to the Arc de Triomphe, for it bears a striking resemblance to that other famous memorial.

I had not visited this site for a long time. With the Rebellion so much on my mind, I asked, "Does it have the names of the soldiers who died in 1857 as well?"

"No. There is another one, the Mutiny Memorial."

"Yes. I've heard about that one."

"It's much smaller. It's hidden away, nearly forgotten."

"I don't recall seeing it. But I was only eleven when we left in 1947."

"Really, so you are now, what, about thirty? But you look much younger," she said, looking at me with her entrancing, dark, almond-shaped eyes.

"Thank you, and you aren't older than sixteen or so?" I teased, for I knew she was about twenty.

"No. I am much younger than sixteen," she said, laughing, and tried to cover her face with her hands to hide the crimson blush on her cheeks.

"So, where is that memorial?" I asked, changing the subject to put her at ease.

"It's on the Ridge. I can take you there, if you like."

I knew the Ridge, a famous landmark of Delhi; a small hill near the

Red Fort and the River Jamuna. "Yes, please, take me there some time. I would very much like to see it."

Evading the heavy traffic of buses, cars and rickshaws, I took the turn for the road around Connaught Place. The circular layout of this district resembles those in London or Bath, having the same pattern of outer and inner ring roads dissected by radial arteries. I turned into a radial road to reach the central complex. It was still early evening and, thankfully, the shopping crowds had not arrived yet. I found a parking spot not too far from Uncle Arif's shop.

We walked along the concave walkway of the buildings towards the jewellery store. A large, neon-lit sign, with *Sharif Jewellers* emblazoned on it in golden letters, was visible from some distance. The store was typical of what one would find in any modern shopping plaza around the world. The glass front windows displayed attractive exhibits of the latest jewellery items.

The heat poured down on us from the sky like a waterfall of hot air. We rushed to get to the air-conditioned store. I wore a light blue summer suit, but even from the little walk up from the parking lot, the heat and humidity brought beads of sweat to my forehead. Dabbing my face with a handkerchief, I glanced at Mila. She looked relatively cool in her light silk dress, walking with a leather handbag slung over her shoulder and her long, dark hair flowing behind her.

Aunt Naseema must have spotted us through the windows, for she was already at the door, holding it open for us. She wore a green silk sari with a border of gold thread work. A charming jewelled necklace and several golden *karas* on each wrist complemented her attractive personality.

She greeted me, "Wallidad, my dear *Beta*, you are really a sight for sore eyes."

"*Salaam*, Aunty Naseema," I said, giving her a light hug, and introduced Mila. "Do you know Mila, from the hospital?"

"Yes, sure, I know Mila. You have been here before. Yes?"

"*Salaam*, Begum Sharif. Yes, I have been here many times, and my mother too," Mila said, making the *salaam* greeting in the Indian Muslim way—a slight bow of the head, and bringing the tips of the fingertips of the right hand to the chin.

The half-dozen or so employees in the shop were mostly women and, I believed, related to me in one way or another. To the bewilderment of the customers, they rushed out from behind the glass-cased service counters to greet me. Although I had a difficult time remembering each of their names, it was easy to respond by just calling them *bahen*. There was much hugging and *salaaming* and asking, "How are you?" and "How is Alexandra *Bhabi*?"

Uncle Arif, a short, balding man of about sixty, had the usual weight problem—mostly around the belly—common to those who have to spend long hours at their work desks. He must have heard the commotion in the store and came out of his office, from the back of the shop. He was dressed in the traditional Muslim Delhi style, in a white cotton shirt, a short, silk waistcoat, tight pyjama-type trousers and a white *topi*. He greeted me with extended arms and a loud, "There you are, *Beta*. We have been waiting all afternoon for you. How are you and how is Alexandra, that pretty wife of yours?"

We hugged each other in the traditional Muslim way, right side, left, and right side again. I introduced Mila and he bade a *salaam* to her, as it was considered improper in our culture to shake a lady's hand. I sometimes did forget this protocol, and on several earlier occasions when being introduced, had to restrain myself from extending my hand to Indian women.

"Alexandra's fine, thank you. Sorry, Uncle, for being late. We couldn't get away early enough from the hospital and the traffic was so heavy."

"It's all right to be late—as Mirza Ghalib would say, *der ayat durust ayat*." My uncle loved to quote his favourite Indian poet.

"Exactly, Uncle. In America we say 'better late than never'."

"We have suggested so many times to get yourself a chauffer, like all respectable people here. But you insist on driving in this maddening traffic."

"Uncle, my odd working hours just do not permit me to hire a driver."

My aunt interjected, seizing her chance to repeat her pet complaint to me. "And what about a cook and a bearer? I just don't understand it. How you alone can do all the housework and cooking too?" she said, putting a palm to her cheek and shaking her head.

"Aunty, I just have a small apartment. Cleaning is no problem, and I mostly eat out."

"Talking of eating, it's past five o'clock. Why don't we have *chai*?" Uncle suggested.

I realised he must be famished, as the evening tea there was usually a sumptuous affair, no doubt a leftover tradition from the Victorian days. We moved to the back of the store, where some rooms served as offices, storage areas and a kitchen-dining room. A teakettle was put on the electric range and a servant dispatched to fetch fresh *rasmalai*. My cousins started opening boxes of snack food and laid the appetizers out on the dining table. There were many different types of delightful cakes, pastries, *samosas*, *pakoras* and other Indian hors d'oeuvres. After sampling quite a few and declining the others as politely as I could, I was soon full and realised I would have to skip dinner that evening. Nevertheless, I could not refuse a second helping of *rasmalai*, my much-loved dessert.

My aunt took Mila around the display counters, showing her the latest jewellery sets in fashion. Uncle and I retired to his office, our cups of tea in hand, and seated ourselves on chairs beside his desk.

"How are *Naushabhai* and *Bhabijaan*?" he inquired about my parents in Karachi, Pakistan. "Have you talked to them recently?"

"No, not for a while. I called them several times to tell them I am here. But each time I overheard my father tell the maid to say they were not home. Have *you* heard from them?"

"Yes. *Naushabhai* called here a few days ago. I tried to talk some sense into him. Told him you are his eldest son. What's the use in keeping grudges? I believe Naseema also tried to talk to your mother. Our heart aches to see they are still very upset with you."

"Believe me, Uncle, if there is anything I can do to make amends, I will do it. But Father is his stubborn self. It is either his way or no way at all."

I thought about my dear mother and father. He was also a jeweller and although in his late sixties, would likely be hard at work, as always. My two elder brothers and sister were married and must be engaged in their separate lives in other parts of the country. However, I was the maverick of the family. I had chosen the medical profession, moved to America and, what was more, married a Canadian woman. However, that was not the only reason for my estrangement from my parents.

I felt Uncle Arif's hand on my shoulder, and his question brought my mind back to the present. "*Beta*, we pray that Allah may bring you all together. He will, *inshallah,* do what is best for you. Anyway, you mentioned on the phone something about a trunk, the hospital wishes you to take back to America? Whose is it?"

"We don't know. All I know is the name on the trunk says Doctor Margaret Wallace."

"And who is she?"

"That's what they want me to find out. Apparently she was a doctor employed by the Rani of Jhansi at the time of the 1857 Rebellion."

At the mention of the Rani, my uncle stared at me for a moment, as if he remembered something. He looked up at my grandfather's painting hanging on the wall, and said slowly, "So, the hospital thinks *Baba* may have known her?"

From my uncle's question, I could not help but wonder if he felt uncomfortable having his father involved in this matter. I replied, attempting to ease his mind, "It's just a thought, Uncle. It is possible, isn't it? After all, *Dada* was there at the same time. Do you remember him ever mentioning an American lady doctor?"

"I cannot say for sure. But come to think of it, he did once say there were several Europeans in the employment of the Rani. Russians, mostly."

"No, Uncle, she had to be either English or American. Margaret is a very British name."

He was again silent for a while, and I had the uneasy feeling he did not wish to discuss this matter.

"I was very young when your *Dada* died," he finally said with moist eyes, and suggested, "You should ask your *Dadi*. She may know something about this strange lady. A doctor, did you say?"

"Yes, that's what the hospital tells me. There certainly are a lot of mysteries surrounding the Rebellion, aren't there? How it started, how many died, and what happened to the missing …"

He nodded and added, "You know, *Beta,* as our poet Ghalib used to say, 'Only Allah knows what happened that day … He will make the tally, on Judgment Day'."

"Indeed, who knows how many perished in the War," I agreed, and asked, "So, do you suppose it is possible that Grandfather might have mentioned meeting Doctor Margaret to *Dadi*?"

"It's possible. But, *Beta*, you know she is now in her eighties, and her memory is failing. She was Baba's second wife and much younger than him; he may not have confided in her. And I never knew your elder *Dadi*, for she died during the Rebellion."

"Yes, I've only heard of my *Dadi-Amma*. However, I hope that at least *Dadi* can tell me which country this lady came from. Then we could concentrate our search in that part of the world."

"Yes, do ask her. She might tell you. It's up to her."

I was wondering what Uncle meant by "It's up to her", and if there were some things they did not wish me to know. I looked up at the painting of Grandfather, mounted on a white stallion, smiling down at us. He looked so real. I felt as if I was there inside the painting, standing beside him. Then a shiver ran down my spine when I noticed the background of the painting depicted a terrain very similar to that I had seen in my dreams, where I galloped behind that lady with her long, blonde hair flowing in the wind. The same foothills loomed in the back and, good heavens, the same domes of the distant temple peeked over the mountaintops.

I felt a gentle squeeze from my uncle's hand on my wrist. "*Beta*. Before I forget, I was going to ask you. Your *Dadi* wants you to have dinner with us next Saturday. You don't have to perform an operation or something that evening, do you?" he asked with a smile.

"No, no. Not on a Saturday night. Unless it's an emergency," I replied laughing. "Yes, I would very much like to. What time shall I come?"

"How about eight o'clock? Would that be too late for you?"

Just at that moment, my aunt came into the office with Mila behind her. She caught the tail end of Uncle's question and interjected, "*Beta*, you have to learn to eat late. I don't understand how you young people can have dinner at five o'clock." As she said this, she rotated the palm of her right hand in the inquiring gesture.

"Yes, Aunty, I suppose when in Delhi, I have to do as the *Dilli-wallahs* do." I raised my eyebrows to emphasize the joke. She tapped my shoulder in a friendly admonishment.

Mila showed me a slim, red-velvet-lined case that contained the jewellery set she had selected. There was an exquisite necklace with matching ear, nose and finger rings. The necklace was made out of heavy gold with elaborate patterns inlaid with bright red rubies and pearls hanging along the edges. The matching earrings were also set in gold with rubies and dangling pearls.

"My, this is an attractive piece," I said, taking the large pendant in the palm of my hand.

"Oh, I am so glad to have found this set for my best girlfriend. She loves rubies, and I am sure will be very happy to receive it," Mila said, beaming with excitement.

It was getting late. We said many thanks and bade farewell with hugs and *salaams* to my aunt, uncle and all their staff, my cousins.

"Don't forget. Dinner at Sharif Mahal this Saturday," Uncle reminded me, bending down to look at me through the car window.

"I'll be there," I replied, waving at them all standing outside the shop, as we drove off.

The evening sunlight had given way to a bright orange twilight. With the approaching darkness, the lights of the shops in Connaught Place's circular promenade were on. The brightly lit neon sign, *Sharif Jewellers,* reflected in my VW's rear-view mirror.

"So, your grandmother still lives in Sharif Mahal?" Mila asked.

"Yes. It's our family home. Uncle Arif and his family also live there. I was born there."

"Why don't you stay there now?"

"I would have liked to. But it's a bit out of the city and the drive in rush hour traffic would take too long to the Lady Dufferin. Besides, my erratic working hours would drive Aunty crazy." However, I didn't wish to reveal to her my real reason for not wanting to stay there. It would have brought back too many childhood memories, some pleasant and some not so. Especially those happy days Anjuli and I had spent playing together in the *gullies* there.

"Sharif Mahal is a fascinating *haveli*. I always admire it when I drive by there. I love the red sandstone architecture and those intricate archways," Mila said.

"But you should see the inside. It's hardly the grand mahal it once was. Over the years, time has taken its toll. During the wars there was much pilferage and damage."

"Washing all those marble floors and dusting the ornate pillars and mouldings must take a lot of staff."

"I believe one of my forefathers received it as a gift from a Mughal Emperor in appreciation for his heroic service in the wars. They used to have many servants in the past, but just a few now. It's difficult to get good help."

"Yes, my parents have the same problem. So, when did your family change from being the Emperor's soldiers to jewellers?"

"The jewellers are from my grandmother's side. Grandfather married her after his first wife died during the Rebellion."

"Oh, his first wife was killed. I'm sorry to hear that. So he became a jeweller?" Mila sounded very curious.

"Yes. I understand the events of the Rebellion disheartened him. He didn't wish things to have happened that way."

"The killing of the British civilians, women and children, you mean?"

"Yes, everything. The initial mistreatment of the Indian population by the British, the Sepoy Rebellion and murder of innocent Europeans, the War where even some Indians helped the British, the treachery of some kings and princes, the heavy-handed reprisals by the British, and in general the whole episode." I sighed. "He gave up his sword for good. He brought up his children to be peace-loving and kind to all human beings regardless of race."

"He sounds fascinating. I would have liked to meet him."

"Actually, I don't know much about him. Although I've heard he was probably among the first to have come up with the philosophy of non-violent revolution."

"Really, much before Gandhiji?"

"Yes. Although he had battled with the Rani of Jhansi's forces, he had apparently come to the same conclusion that war was not the answer to achieve our goals, even *azadi* from an oppressor."

We drove by Chandni Chowk, another famous bazaar in Delhi. I tried to imagine the time when my grandfather had started his shop there, and what it would have looked like, lighted with oil lamps, about a hundred years ago. The glitter of gold and silver from the shops there and mention of the Rani brought a thought to my mind. "Mila, do you know where the Rani is supposed to have died?"

"I don't remember ... yes, I do. It was at the Kotah-ki-Serai."

"Where is that?"

"The Serai is near Gowalior. I believe she was cremated in a small temple on one of the mountaintops. Why do you ask?"

"Oh, I don't know. It's probably nothing, really. It's just that I keep having this recurring dream," I said, feeling rather sheepish talking about a personal vision to her.

"A dream. About the Rani?"

"Yes, at least I think so. But there is another woman, a European, in the nightmare. She keeps wanting to take me to a temple in the mountains."

"How exciting. But we will have to finish this interesting discussion later. Look, there's my house. Would you like to come in for some tea or coffee?"

I wanted to stay and continue our discussion, but remembering the appointment with Katya, for later that evening, said, "You are most kind. However, it's getting late and I have some early appointments. Some other time, perhaps?"

I drove into the entrance of her parents' imposing house. I knew her father, who was also a doctor, but in private practice.

"Yes. My parents want to have you over for dinner soon. Thank you so much for taking me to your uncle's shop."

She alighted from the car; I leaned over and we shook hands through the passenger side door's window.

"Please, say *nameste* from me to your mother and father."

She nodded, looking happy enough. I figured my uncle hadn't charged her a lot for that elegant ruby necklace set.

Back at my apartment, I changed and, settling down on the comfortable leather sofa in the living room, read the newspaper. It was not long before I heard a knock. Opening the door, I saw Katya there, dressed again in a blue jacket and tight skirt. The same man in the straw fedora stood some distance away. I asked her to come in and offered a drink. This time she accepted, and asked for a glass of red wine. We settled down, wine glasses in hand, on the sofa. She came straight to the reason for her visit.

"You want to help us, yes?" she asked.

"Yes." I informed her that I was willing to help them, because I needed the money to set up a private practice in America. However, since it involved stealing the trunk from a secure warehouse, I could not do it alone. Fortunately, I had been able to entice a maintenance staff member to assist. But it would take an additional 50,000 rupees for his support. "He is a poor man with a large family," I added.

"Oh, extra 50,000 rupees is lot of money. I suppose you need money to keep him quiet, no?" she said.

I nodded.

"I speak to my boss. I think he say okay. If not I call you. So, what you tell Doctor Rao when he find out suitcase is missing?"

"Oh, I don't know. Nothing, I suppose. The security of the trunk is not my problem. My man says he can make it look like it was sent to some other hospital, a mix-up of paperwork or some such bureaucratic bungling. These things happen here a lot, you know," I said, looking at her with steady eyes.

She contemplated my information for a while. Took a sip of wine and said, "Okay, your *programa* looking good to me."

From her ready acceptance, I thought that perhaps I should have asked for some more money. I further suggested, as a precautionary measure, the transportation of the trunk be done during off hours, preferably after midnight. However, I would not bring it to the Soviet Embassy, but rather meet her at a secluded location. She proposed I take the trunk to the parking area of Humayun's Tomb. It was normally deserted at night and we could transfer the trunk from my car to her embassy vehicle, which would be waiting there. She asked when the plan could be executed. I mentioned it might be this Saturday night, but I would have to call her to confirm the time.

"Okay. I am waiting on Saturday night in my office for your call."

Having established the arrangements, she gulped the last of the wine and got up to leave.

I had to ask, "So, when would I get paid? And could I have it in cash?"

"When you bring the box," she replied, and waddled out of the apartment.

After she left, I kept sitting, stretched out, on the sofa for a long time. I was in no mood to catch the Voice of America News, as I normally did at that time. I poured myself another glass of red wine.

As I sipped the pleasant wine, I wondered about *azadi* and *daulat*. I reflected on how former invaders of India had used promises of freedom and money to bribe and entice some of the populace to turn against their own neighbours. The divide and rule technique had been put to good use. In addition, since my family was also on my mind, I could not help but wonder if my father's decision to leave Delhi had been the right one. By comparison, Uncle Arif appeared to be doing very well, even though he was part of a minority group in the huge masses of the Indian population. It was for our *azadi,* Father used to say when asked about his choice to come to Pakistan. So, what is *freedom-denied*? Is it confined by some narrow definition, where one would be caged like an animal, deprived of personal movement to do as one pleased? Or a bit broader, where limits or restrictions are placed on people's decisions, on choices in life, or even, in a much wider scope, on limits to advancement by invisible barriers, like a "glass ceiling"? Are we human beings really ever *free* in this world, and can we survive in a money-less environment?

I considered the lives of the common people under Communism around the world. In the USSR and Eastern Europe, in Africa, in China, in Cuba and South America, were they free? Probably not. They were confined to act within their rigid state-established systems. But then, how about the public in the so-called democratic countries, like Britain, France, Canada and the USA? Sure, they had certain privileges, but were they really free? To do as they pleased? How could they be free if they had to follow certain governances and set rules? How about the so-called *azad,* free persons, the deprived people of India?

I refilled my glass. In due course, the pleasant wine seemed to take over my mental faculties, and I came to the startling concept that no one was really free in this world. Ultimately, we all have to follow established behavioural patterns, in the end set by nature and mankind itself, especially those related to the exchange of services using the monetary standard.

As I stumbled towards my inviting bed, I questioned myself. What would it be like to be *really free* of all encumbrances? To live in a world without money? To do just as one pleased? However, then, on the other hand, was it worth giving one's life away for the sake of *azadi* as sacrificed by my forefathers, and millions of others? Eventually, was it all worthwhile for India to obtain her *azadi?* What part had the good lady doctor, Margaret, played in the Revolution? Were my grandfather's thoughts, and later Gandhiji's non-violence movement, the appropriate way? My mind did not respond to these questions, as by then, I was falling down a deep precipice into the calm ocean of sleep.

Chapter Four

The Dinner Party

1965, May: Delhi, India

IT WAS A BALMY EVENING. After the setting of the scorching sun, Delhi had begun to cool off. I walked beside my grandmother, through the dining room's French doors, onto the veranda overlooking the garden. We wanted to admire the brightly lit stars in the clear night sky. Just beyond the walled area lay our family burial grounds. I had visited there earlier that evening to pay my respects to the deceased. The marble domes of the mausoleums shone in the moonlight.

"There will be starlight forever on your grandfather's grave," my grandmother said.

I turned to face her. Although she was in her early eighties, she looked fit and walked without the aid of a cane. She wore a plain white silk *shalwar-kameez*, no make-up, and little in the way of elaborate jewellery. Her taste ran to a set of gold stringed buttons on her shirt, golden *karas* on her wrists and slippers woven with gold threads. Her long, silvery-grey hair complemented her dress. She was diminutive, but still was very much like the Mughal princess she had been, back in the glory days. Although after the fall of Delhi, in 1857, all those related to the King were purged from the city, her family had returned and managed to re-establish their jewellery business, no doubt with the help of my grandfather.

"Yes, *Dadi*, the moon and stars will always shine brightly on him, for he was such a noble man." I sighed and put my arm around her shoulder as we gazed at Grandfather's memorial, which resembled a miniature Taj Mahal—except for those four minarets. I assumed that it was built in the honour of his first wife, Mumtaz, named after the famed Empress. However, despite searching all around there, I was unable to find her crypt. I asked, "Is *Dadi-Amma* also buried there?"

She did not reply, instead dabbed her eyes with an embroidered handkerchief. I felt sorry that my question had likely saddened her, and memories of her beloved husband would have come floating back to her, like faded family photographs. "I wish Khan-*bhadur* could have been here today with us," she whispered.

Indeed, Grandfather would have enjoyed the evening. We had just dined on a splendid banquet of pullao rice, lamb, beef korma, curry chicken, and my favourite, barbecued partridges. For the Hindu guests, there were several vegetable curries, among other vegetarian delicacies. A procession of maids and bearers served the superbly cooked food, curried with a delicate blend of spices. Later, I was too full to even sample the wide selection of dessert dishes of different varieties of Indian sweets. My light eating habits dismayed my aunt and cousins, who constantly implored me to "please have some more".

"*Huzoor*, coffee is served in the *Diwan-e-Khas*," the head bearer announced, bringing my thoughts back to the present.

"Thank you. We'll be there," I said and, keeping my arm around Grandmother's shoulders, led her to the exclusive drawing room used only for special occasions.

Uncle Arif and the other guests were already there. All settled on comfortable *divans*, propping our arms over the long, round cushions covered in blue, green and red silken material, interwoven with gold thread work. Strong, extra sweet Turkish coffee was served, in fine copper cups etched with flowery patterns. The caffeine no doubt helped the guests—most of all me—to remain awake after the heavy meal.

Entertainment followed, to round out the evening. A group of musicians and a striking *naatch*-girl appeared. They bowed, *salaamed* and took their places on the Persian carpet at one end of the room. One played a *sarangi*, another a *harmonium*, while a third beat out rhythms on two *tablas*. The dancing girl, a young maiden, had long, raven hair tied in two braids that fell to her slim waist. Apart from her costume jewellery and heavy make-up, the mascara on the long eyelashes of her captivating brown eyes accentuated her looks. She was dressed in a long, pink silk shirt with gold and silver embroidery. Strings of bells tied around her ankles jingled when she walked. I was looking forward to the dancing, which was to be in the classic style with songs and *ghazals* of the Mughal period.

The *naatch*-girl came to the centre of the floor and looked in my direction. She startled me by first *salaaming* and then asking, "In honour of the American Doctor Sahib's visit, I wish to present Mirza Ghalib's medical-*ghazal*, *Dil-e-Nadan*. Would Doctor Sahib permit me?"

Slightly embarrassed, I looked around the room to see who had put her up to this. Just as I thought, it was my cousin sisters. I saw a group of them sitting on a divan across the room, and when I met their eyes, they immediately covered their mouths with their silk shawls. However, they were unable to hide their giggling. I nodded at them, acknowledging their mischief.

"It is permitted," I finally replied. The *naatch*-girl *salaamed* me again and took her place in the middle of the dance floor to begin her song and dance performance. Her starting position was similar to one that an ice skater might take at the start of a dance competition: arms up, torso bent sideways and one leg angled with feet curled and resting on the toes. She tapped her raised foot gently a few times to jingle the ankle bells, a signal to the musicians. When she swirled around in her dance, her skirt flared up like a fan in a breeze, revealing her tight, pink silk pyjamas. While she spun by twirling around her arms, there wasn't much hip swaying in the routine. The hand and foot movements were, however, curiously similar to ones I had seen in dances by the Hawaiian Islanders.

The *Dil-e-Nadan* ghazal, written in the early 1800s by the famous Indian poet, Mirza Ghalib, was about a lovesick individual longing for his sweetheart and seeking some medicine for his troubled heart. The *naatch*-girl sang in a melodious voice the *ghazal* that—translated into English—was as follows:

> My troubled heart, what is it?
> This pain I feel, is there medicine for it?
> I am amorous, but she is annoyed,
> Dear God, what is the reason for it?
> I have a tongue to speak,
> If only she would ask, what is it?
> It's been a while since we met,
> This confusion, God, what is it?

Her fabulous face comes from somewhere,
Those charms and flirtations are part of it.
Her amber locks, those gorgeous curls,
The eye shadow and the mascara are part of it.
The green grass and the roses, where do they come from?
What are clouds, and what is air, what is it?
I have hopes of faith from her,
But it seems she doesn't even know faith; what is it?
Be good to her, and she'll be good to you,
A beggar's prayer, this is it.
I'll give my life for her,
But a prayer, I don't know, what is it?
I agree that Ghalib is worth nothing,
But if he comes for free, how bad is it?

The girl ended her dance in virtually the same pose she had begun. Loud applause from the gathering followed, for this old love poem is much cherished by the Delhi-*wallahs*. She bowed to us, bending as deeply as she could. Some of the women left the room dabbing their teary eyes. I must admit I had watery eyes as well, for I had thought about my dear wife while listening to the words of the poem.

With a one-hundred-rupee note hidden in my palm, I extended my arm to the dancer. She came over with rapid steps, graciously accepted the gratuity and returned backwards, smiling and *salaaming* me a few times.

While the song and dance show continued, I moved to an empty spot on the settee beside Doctor and Mrs. Rao.

"Hello. Are you enjoying the show?" I asked.

"Yes, very much. This girl, Surrayia, is the best *naatch-walli* in Delhi. We simply adore her singing and dancing," Mrs. Rao remarked and Doctor Rao nodded.

"What part of India are you from, Mrs. Rao?"

"Oh, please, none of this Mr. and Mrs. business. You can call me Geeta. I am from Bithur and my husband, Subash, is from Jhansi—that you probably know."

I nodded and, remembering something from my history lessons, asked, "Bithur? Wasn't it in Raja Nana Sahib's kingdom?"

"Yes, until the poor fellow lost it in 1857. I hate to admit it, but I can trace my family roots back to him," Mrs. Rao replied.

I saw Doctor Rao was smiling. I asked Geeta another question. "Whatever happened to him? We haven't heard much about him after the Rebellion."

"Wallidad, that's one of my family's great tragedies. We are all so heartbroken, for a long time, not knowing what happened to our beloved Raja Nana Sahib. Our hearts will not be at peace until we know where he is buried." She dabbed her eyes and continued, "When Subash told me of his hospital finding that poor lady doctor's trunk, I thought that perhaps the American woman might have known something about him."

"Really. Why do you believe that?"

"We know that after the fall of Jhansi, the Rani, with a good number of her soldiers, and certainly her Europeans advisors as well, took shelter in the neighbouring Gwalior Fort. The final battles were fought there. It is very likely that Doctor Margaret was with them. And did you know, we heard that your grandfather, Sharif *Bhadur*, was also in the Rani's cavalry?"

While I nodded, Doctor Rao, who had been silent thus far, commented, "It's curious that the Rani, Nana Sahib and the Europeans all disappeared, as if they had ridden over the Himalayan mountains."

I smiled at the analogy and said, "Yes, it does sound bizarre. Although Grandfather returned to Delhi after the war, but I don't believe he told anyone very much of what happened during that summer of 1858."

Mrs. Rao said, "Wallidad, there is also the matter of the Taj of Jhansi, which has some of the largest and most precious jewels. It was also stolen and hasn't been recovered yet. The people of Jhansi are anxious for its return."

"Really, a crown like the one with the Koh-i-Noor. Wouldn't it also be with the British monarchs?" I asked, amazed at the possible existence of another set of crown jewels. I knew the Koh-i-Noor, allegedly the world's largest diamond, had been in British possession after the Sikh Wars in the 1840s.

"No. They are denying ever even having seen it. Perhaps this lady Margaret's family might know of its whereabouts? Also, we would like to know how the Rani and the Nana *actually* died."

"I'm not sure, Mrs. ... er... Geeta, if they'd know. What's more, the family has to be located first."

Just then, a bearer interrupted and offered us, on a silver tray, paans —vine leaves rolled with betel nuts, tobacco and other condiments. Doctor Rao and I declined, but Geeta took two, remarking, "Paan and betel nuts are something I can never live without."

A whiff of familiar perfume drifted by me. I turned to see Mila sitting on a chair nearby. She was dressed exquisitely in a purple shirt over a red *lehnga* and delicate jewellery, no doubt taken from her collection for this special occasion. She said, while chewing on a paan, "I know where the Rani died. It was at the Kotah-ki-Serai. Didn't I tell you, Doctor Sharif?"

"No, no. She didn't die there. It was her look-alike, Jalkari Bai." Mrs. Rao spoke in an authoritative voice. "Otherwise, why would they have cremated the body so quickly?" Not waiting for a reply, she answered herself, "It was because they wanted the attackers to believe the dead warrior was the Rani. The British may think they killed her. But we know otherwise."

"So what happened to Raniji, then?" Mila asked, looking perplexed.

Geeta replied, gesturing with one hand, "No doubt she was injured in the fighting. But her faithful horse ran away from the battlefield, with her on his back. That was the last time her soldiers recall seeing her."

I was stunned on hearing this account, for I had seen that very image, of the Rani and her horse, in my dream. Puzzled at this conflicting information, I asked, "Doctor Rao, since your family is from Jhansi, have they shed any light on this mystery?"

Before he could reply, Mrs. Rao said, "Subash, what about those Canadian stamps your nephew has? Couldn't some Canadian or Britisher have given them to your grandfather?"

"We don't know that for certain. The stamps have always been in our family's possession," Doctor Rao said and, turning to me, replied to my question. "Walli, I am not sure if they can reveal any more than is already known."

"So, what did your grandfather do in Jhansi?" I asked.

"He was a merchant there."

"Did he escape with the Rani following the British attack?"

"No, he remained in the city and, fortunately, survived the assault."

Mrs. Rao interjected, "And he helped to rebuild the city. For that the British awarded him some land—"

Doctor Rao interrupted, "Geeta, you know it's only hearsay. We don't know that for certain. We believe he purchased the land from his hard-earned savings."

That information intrigued me. I wondered how a simple merchant could save enough to procure a large tract of land, for I was told the Rao family had holdings that comprised several villages. I wanted to ask some more questions, but Mila's parents, whom I had not seen for a while, interrupted us and we got busy conversing with them. A bearer passed by with a tray of tea and coffee; we picked up cups. I asked Mila's father and Doctor Rao if they would like some brandy, for I knew my uncle kept some in a special cabinet in his library. They smiled at my offer of liquor and said they would love to have some.

I went into the library for the brandy, but first telephoned Katya. As planned, she was waiting for my call. Since Delhi streets do not empty till late into the night, we fixed our meeting at Humayun's Tomb for two o'clock.

"Do you have my money and the extra fifty?" I asked.

"Yes," she replied in a low voice.

I then rang the hospital's annex office. Narinder was also waiting for my buzz. I asked him to get the package ready for my pickup. I mentioned it would be after one and asked if he did not mind waiting that long. He answered with a smart, "Yes, *saa'b*. No problem about late night."

I was returning to the drawing room, holding the three brandy glasses in both hands, when I met Mila in the hallway. I noted her elegant outfit and remarked, "That's a nice *lehnga*, Mila. You look like a Mughal princess."

"Thank you. I wear one sometimes. But today it's in honour of your grandmother's dinner." She did a pirouette like the *naatch*-girl.

I laughed. "Seems that you are enjoying the party?"

"Yes, very much. But you know, despite what Mrs. Rao says, I still believe the Rani died in battle, fighting for her land."

"I am confused as well. I think I will have to go to Kotah-ki-Serai to find out for myself."

"I have never been there. Can I come too? I am getting very interested in this mystery."

Her request surprised me. "What will your parents say?"

"Nothing, if I go with my college friends. We are planning to go somewhere for a holiday. We could meet you there, if you like."

I felt relieved on hearing that we would not be travelling alone. I thought they would be good company and could help with translation, for I was not familiar with the dialect in that part of the country. I replied with a smile, "Sure. You and your friends are welcome to join me on the trip. I haven't set the date yet. I'll let you know."

"Oh, thank you. I would like that. But can you tell me where is the ladies' room?"

I pointed the direction to her and proceeded to the living room, with the brandy goblets in hand.

It was past midnight when the guests prepared to depart. From their jovial mood, they looked to have enjoyed the soirée of dinner, songs, dances and pleasant conversation. While waiting in the foyer for their chauffeurs to bring up their automobiles, they expressed their appreciation by thanking Grandmother, Aunt, and Uncle a number of times. They bid goodnight to me with *namestes* and handshakes, and each family said, "Don't forget to visit us before your return to America."

Uncle told the head bearer to turn off the bright lights and leave just the candelabras on. I look a short stroll down the darkened hallways. The crickets sang out in the centre courtyard garden. The flickering candles cast long, mysterious shadows around the Mahal, making it look like it would have in the 1800s.

I returned to the drawing room. A bearer poured me another coffee. Cup in hand, I took a place on the divan close to my grandmother and rested my elbow on the same bolster as hers.

Aunty Naseema came into the room; her rouge and gold-threaded sari shone in the candlelight. "Oh, I'm, how you Americans say, dog tired. My feet are simply killing me."

"Indeed, Aunty, you must be exhausted after throwing such a grand dinner party. You were busy all evening, making sure everything was in order."

"Oh, we have to look after the whole thing now. It's not like in the earlier days when the servants took care of it all. Now it's getting very difficult to find good help."

"Well, Aunty, at least you can get some maids and bearers here. In America, it's hard to even find any."

"Yes, I know. Poor Alexandra was telling me. I cannot imagine how she can manage having only one cleaning lady come over, just twice a week, is it?"

"No, it's only once a week, Aunty." I corrected her with a smile.

She raised her eyebrows and shook her head in amazement. "Well, I think I'll have to be biddy-byes now. *Beta*, why don't you stay over a bit and talk to your grandmother and uncle? They haven't seen you for quite a while." She then turned towards the kids, seated on a divan, and said firmly, "Come, children, the party's over. It's time to go to bed now."

On that instruction, the teenagers reluctantly rose from the settee and proceeded upstairs, bidding us goodnight. Even though they had sleepy eyes, I supposed they were eager to stay and listen to the grown-ups' conversation.

With all of them gone and the servants dispatched, there was silence in the Mahal. I looked pensively into my coffee cup.

"What is it, *Beta*? Are you thinking of your *Dada*?" Grandmother asked.

"Yes, *Dadi*." I informed her of the strange discovery of the sea chest in the hospital, and also recounted some of the nightmares I was having. I told her I felt there was some connection between the trunk's missing owner and *Dada*. "Did he ever mention meeting an American lady doctor while he served the Rani of Jhansi?"

"I'm not sure, *Beta*. I don't recall him telling me about an American. Now, wait a minute, he did once talk about having been treated by a woman doctor for a wound to his arm. He remembered it because of the medicine she'd given him to drink. It made him feel very strange and he'd seen all the colours of the rainbow before his eyes. He said he'd slept the whole day after that."

I smiled and conjectured, "Oh, it must have been laudanum. It had some opium in it, you know. But did he reveal her name, or where she was from?"

"I believe he said she was French, as she used to speak in that language with all the European officers. Let me think, yes, he said her name was 'Madame'."

"Oh, *Dadi*! You know, all French married women are called 'Madame'." I laughed. "But it *is* interesting to know there was a European lady doctor there. Tell me, how did *Dada* come to join the Rani's service? Was he not with the King in Delhi at the beginning of the Revolution?"

On this question, my granny remained silent and stared into the ceiling for a while. Regaining her composure, she replied, "My son, even though I was not born then, the incidents of those days are just too difficult for me to repeat." She was again quiet for a while. Her eyes looked moist. She dabbed them. "Khan-*bhadur* told me, because his family was in Delhi, he did not wish to go Jhansi."

"Then why did he go?" I asked, with raised eyebrows.

Dadi reclined back on the long cushion. "Let me start from the beginning. The Rebellion started in the month of May, in Meerut, not here in Delhi, as you know. *Dada* was then only a nineteen-year-old youth in the King's Palace Guards unit. When the revolutionaries arrived here in Delhi and begged the King to assist them while promising to make him the Emperor of India, your *Dada* warned Shah Zafar of their wild ways. He feared for the safety of the European civilians, particularly the women and children, and the looting of the city. However, no one listened to him. It happened exactly the way he'd dreaded. There was widespread killing of the few British soldiers here and nearly all the Europeans as well. A few families did escape, the fortunate souls."

"When did the British army arrive?"

"In just a few months—in July or August, I think—they came in full force, with large cannons, thousands of soldiers. And would you believe, merely for the sake of money and plunder, some of our own Hindustani northerners joined them. They camped on the Ridge above the Red Fort. *Dada* told me that the bombardment of the Fort went on for days. People said the ground trembled, as if from an earthquake."

"Yes, I've heard about the cannonade from the Ridge and the eventual assault on the Fort. They say *Dada* was the one who rescued the King? Can you tell me about it?" I asked, for although I had read about the fall of Delhi in history books, I wanted to hear a personal account, which my family had been reluctant to give me.

"He did it, for his King and Begum Zinat, but alas, he could not save the princes. That was the biggest disappointment of his whole life. He often used to speak about it." Her eyes filled with tears.

I put my arm around her shoulders. "*Dadi*, don't cry. What is the use of tormenting yourself now? It happened so long ago."

"Yes, *Beta*. However, those memories are still etched in my heart. Anyway, since you ask, I want to tell you what happened next. Numerous attempts by the rebels to attack the British failed miserably. They were shot before they could reach even halfway up the Ridge. Finally, the King appointed General Bakhtiar Khan as the commander. He led a daring raid, in the middle of the night, around the Ridge. As bad luck would have it, a thunderstorm arrived. That attack was also unsuccessful; they suffered many casualties. It seems the British were ready for them, as if they had gotten wind of the attack. How, I'll tell you shortly. The sepoys were disheartened and squabbled amongst each other. Finally, due to the siege, an acute shortage of food and armaments developed. Not many of the neighbouring kingdoms came to help—"

I interrupted and asked, "What about the citizens of Delhi? Did they not assist?"

Dadi smiled sarcastically. "The pillaging by the rebels had made matters worse. And the curse upon our nation, the Hindu-Muslim discord, raised its ugly head."

"Oh, how did that happen?" I was curious, as the history books had not mentioned that.

"Our *Bakra Eid* arrived during the middle of the crisis. Although the King had forbidden sacrificing of cows, some of our Muslim brothers disobeyed and slaughtered cows in the middle of a bazaar. Naturally, what would you expect? The Hindus were incensed. It led to riots. The people of Delhi started fighting among themselves.

"Anyhow, let me continue *Dada*'s story. Soon enough, the situation became hopeless. From the fierce cannon fire, it became clear that the British were going to breach the wall and storm the Fort. *Dada* knew of a secret passage out of the Fort that led to Metcalfe House, by the river. The Metcalfes had fled Delhi, and the officers of the rebel army occupied the building. He believed he would find our General Bakht Khan there, who might have assisted the King to escape. He urged the King to leave by that passage. After much soul searching, Zafar eventually agreed to the suggestion."

"Where was Begum Zinat?" I asked.

"Oh, *Beta*, she proved to be a treacherous woman. As soon as the fighting started, she left the Fort, with her beloved son, for a *haveli* in the west end of the city. From there she was in touch, through some spies, with the British."

"Really! Why did she do that?"

"Oh, she wanted her son, Jawan, to be appointed the King's successor. But Zafar was not agreeable to it, since Jawan was a much junior prince." She wiped her eyes and continued her narrative. "Anyhow, *Dada* led the King and some members of the royal family through that tunnel out of the Fort. When they reached Metcalfe House, they found it empty and General Bakht was not around. There weren't any boats at the waterfront, either. Fortunately, *Dada* found some horses still locked in the stables. They travelled south along the river to the old fort area, where the British assault hadn't reached yet. Thus, they managed to escape unnoticed and took shelter in Humayun's Tomb. Zafar sent for his favourite wife, Zinat, and Jawan to join him there."

"Didn't General Bakhtiar go there to help them?"

"Yes, Bakht did visit them and implored Zafar to flee with him to Lucknow, which was still in the rebels' control. Although *Dada* begged the monarch to take this opportunity, I believe Zinat persuaded the King to refuse the offer. She managed to convince him he was safe there, for the British would not harm him, the last Mughal Emperor. In reality, I think, she had made a secret deal with a British officer that, if the King surrendered, it was likely that her only son, Mirza Jawan, could be put on the Delhi throne. So, with her pleading and his unwise thinking, Zafar refused to leave."

I thought that even I, had I been there, could have told the King that Begum Zinat was too naïve in her thinking. Eager to learn more of the details, I asked, "So how long did they stay in Humayun's Tomb?"

"Only for a day or so, until a small British unit led by that officer arrived there, likely on Zinat's correspondence with him through those spies. It is said that a large civilian crowd of thousands of men, women and children had collected there. They were willing to protect their King with just their bare hands."

I said, "Yes, I'd heard about the throng of Delhi citizens present to support Shah Zafar. But what's really amazing is that a small group of British soldiers were able to capture him."

"No, they didn't exactly *capture* him," Grandmother corrected me. "It is believed that the British officer, on his own accord, offered the King and his kin a safe passage out of Delhi."

"What did *Dada* think of the offer? Did he advise the King to agree to it?"

"No. He suspected a trap. He didn't believe that after the killings of the Europeans, the British would let him go so easily, and advised the King against accepting the deal. He told me he was ready with his musket, several revolvers and *talwar*. If Zafar would have listened to him, he was prepared to fight off the few British soldiers himself and, putting the King on a fast horse, make another escape. Although they would have had to leave the Begum and the princes behind. Alas, it didn't happen that way."

"Why did the King consent to the British offer? Surely he would have known that the Revolution would fail if he surrendered."

"I think it was due to his love for Zinat. Despite her deceitfulness, he could not bear to part with her. Although, *Beta*, what else could he do? The situation looked hopeless, the Red Fort had almost fallen and —"

Uncle Arif, who so far had kept silent, interrupted. "Shah Zafar was a noble king. I believe he didn't wish to use those innocent civilians like a shield from the British bullets and bayonets. He must have known that more British soldiers and cavalry regiments were on their way. If he hadn't agreed, the Hussars would have had a field day, slicing the heads of the people gathered there."

"Goodness! It would seem that he prevented a Jallianwala Bagh type of massacre." I remarked.

Grandmother said, "He decided against continuation of the bloodshed. He walked out of the mausoleum and surrendered to the British officer—what was his name, Arif?"

"Captain Hodson," Uncle Arif answered.

"Did Hodson take the King and family all together? In one coach?" I asked.

Grandmother said, "No. There were two carriages. One took the King, the Begum and Prince Jawan out first. The second one, with the other three princes, followed sometime later. It might have been the next day. I'm not sure. My memory is failing."

"And the princes were shot as they were riding in the carriage?" I wanted to know the facts, for I'd heard conflicting accounts.

It seemed the memory of the killing of the Mughal princes was too much for Grandmother. She could not speak anymore and, putting her handkerchief to her eyes, she started to sob.

My uncle, who until then had sat calmly through the recounting of the historical events, finally lost his temper. He jumped up from his chair and paced the room. Slamming one fist into the palm of his other hand, he said, "That damn Englishman. We Mughals should never forget that cold-blooded murder of our princes. Terminated a three hundred-year-old dynasty. Their names shall be engraved in our memory forever." Raising the palms of his hands in a prayer, he loudly iterated their names, "Mirza Mughal, Mirza Kizr Sultan, Mirza Abu Bakr. May Allah grant you a peaceful life in Paradise. *Ameen.*"

I became concerned about my uncle's excited state, for I knew he had high blood pressure. I was worried he might suffer a heart attack or a stroke. I jumped up from the divan and put my arms around his shoulders. "Now, now, Uncle. What's the benefit in exciting ourselves? It happened over a hundred years ago. You know, atrocities took place on both sides. It's common in wartime. People do all kinds of fanatical things. Act like animals."

I was happy to see that he calmed down a bit. I led him back to his sofa, where he sat with his head resting, inclined, on the back cushion.

I looked at my wristwatch and noted it was getting close to one o'clock and I would have to leave soon. Nevertheless, still curious about the whereabouts of Grandfather, and aiming to change the sensitive subject, I asked Grandmother, "So, where was *Dada*? Did he remain in the Tomb?"

My grandmother, recomposed by then, continued the fascinating story. "*Dada* felt very uneasy when the second carriage with the princes left from the Tomb, under the British guard led by Hodson. *Dada* feared for their lives. He lost some time looking for a horse. Finally, having found one, he galloped after the carriage. However, he hadn't ridden long when he heard the three shots. He told me that although he had heard many a rifle shot, those were the loudest ones he ever heard. He kicked the horse to make it race towards the cart, but arrived there too late. The British soldiers saw him charging. They blocked the road and levelled their rifles at him. Fortunately, he reined in the horse, making it rear up on its hind legs, to stop just in time for the soldiers to hold their fire. He spied the dead princes, undressed down to their underwear, lying by Delhi's outer perimeter wall gate, the Khooni Darwaza. He told me it was a horror scene he would never forget."

I knew that was why that gate was named the Gate of Blood. But I was curious about the state in which the bodies were found. I asked, "Why were the princes undressed?"

"That's why we are convinced their killing was premeditated by Hodson. Not because they were trying to escape or some such reason, as he would have us believe."

"What did *Dada* do next?"

My uncle picked up the narrative, as Grandmother, with tears in her eyes, had fallen silent once again. "He turned his horse around and came here to see if his wife and child were unharmed. You must have heard that the streets of Delhi were so littered with dead bodies he had difficulty riding his mount through all the carnage."

"Yes, I heard about the rivers of blood that flowed through the streets."

"*Baba* said the stench and the sight of corpses even made the horse sick and reluctant to enter the *gully* leading up to Sharif Mahal. He jumped from the horse and ran up the lane, sword in hand, to this house. He must have realised something was wrong when he saw the front door was smashed. He ran into the empty house, along the hallways, shouting the name of your elder *Dadi*, 'Mumtaz … Mumtaz,' and the name of his daughter, 'Jahanara … Jahanara …' Sadly, there was no answer. The whole house had been ransacked. Every chandelier and crystal piece was shattered, and any jewels in them pried out. The silk drapes and divan cushions were slashed. All the ivory carvings, ornamental items and jewellery pieces were missing. Anything of value which could be carried away was gone."

I could not bring myself to imagine this house after its pillage. I did not press about the fate of my elder grandmother and other members of the household, as Uncle went silent. I realised that recounting those details was too much for him, especially with my younger grandmother listening. Previously, I had heard that all the occupants were killed. Someone had told me it was with sabres and bayonets. I consoled myself with the hope that they had not suffered and would be living a peaceful life in Paradise.

To save my uncle from describing the gory details, I asked, "Grandfather then went to Jhansi?"

"Yes. There was nothing left for him to do in Delhi," he replied, dabbing his eyes.

Still puzzled, I had to ask, "But why Jhansi? Why did he go there? Why not to Cawnpore or Lucknow? Didn't most of the rebels regroup there?"

Uncle looked inquiringly at Grandmother. She stared at him for a while and finally nodded, as if to grant him her permission to say something.

"*Beta*, since you are so curious, we should tell you a family secret. Your grandfather had asked us to keep it in the strictest confidence. So far, only your *Dadi* and a handful of others know it. We were sworn not to reveal it, except only under very exceptional circumstances. Now with the recent discovery of that lady doctor's trunk, it looks like the time has come for you to learn of this enigma."

These words perked me up. I gulped the dregs in my coffee cup and awaited the next piece of information. Uncle motioned with his hand for me to stay as he walked down the hall into his library. He returned with a large envelope, from which he pulled out an old, yellowing paper and another item that looked like a diary. He unrolled the parchment and extended it to me. It read:

IN THE NAME OF ALLAH THE BENEVOLENT AND THE MERCIFUL
P R O C L A M A T I O N
MARCH 1857
THIS PROCLAMATION IS ISSUED BY THE KING OF PERSIA.
THE PEOPLE OF INDIA ARE NOTIFIED THAT A PERSIAN ARMY IS
COMING FOR THE RELEASE OF INDIA FROM THE GRASP OF THE BRITISH
IT BEHOVES ALL TRUE MOHAMMADENS TO GIRD THEIR LOINS
RESOLUTELY
THE UNBELIEVERS MUST BE FOUGHT AND DRIVEN OUT OF INDIA

SIGNED
Mohammed Saleem

The sight of that document astonished me. I had heard about it, of course, and even seen it reproduced in history books. My hands shook as I realised that I held what appeared to be the original parchment of the poster: the one that had initiated India's First War of Independence.

"Was this the one that appeared mysteriously, pasted on the walls of the Jami Masjid?" I asked, my voice quivering with excitement.

"Yes, this was one of them."

"But no one knew who Mohammed Saleem was. I don't believe he was ever found. Was he?" I asked Uncle. He just stared at me, and then smiled as if to convey a message. It then dawned on me. I gently slapped my forehead and asked, "*Dada?*"

Uncle just nodded and handed me Grandfather's diary.

It was now getting past one a.m. and, remembering my rendezvous, I stood up to take my leave. I embraced Grandmother, who still had tears in her eyes. "*Dadi,* I'm extremely happy to have known you, and am sorry that I did not meet my elder grandmother."

Grandmother arose from the divan. She looked at me with her grey, moist eyes and said, "*Beta*, you have asked many times how she died, and we have not told you. Do you honestly want to know?"

My elder grandmother's mysterious death, with all the rumours attached to it, had bothered me from childhood. It seemed that the moment had arrived for me to find out the truth. Gathering up my courage, I replied, "Yes, *Dadi*, I want to know. Please tell me."

"Come, *Beta*, follow me." She led us to the courtyard in the middle of the Mahal. The quadrangle's air was full of the aroma of jasmine, night-queen and the other fragrant flowers of the small garden planted there. Starlight and moonbeams dropped down from the clear sky. She reached the centre of the area and stopped beside what I knew had formerly been a well, which had long been covered up. There was a knee-high, circular, marble wall around it, and a fountain stood at its hub. We reached the well and looked at the fountain. Grandmother's subsequent words stunned me.

"When the farangis broke into this house, rather than face their torment, your elder grandmother picked up her child and jumped into this well."

The news staggered me. I knelt down and put my head on the marble wall. I looked at the base of the fountain, and the images of the bodies of my elder grandmother, Mumtaz, and her tiny daughter, Jahanara, lying deep in the well came before my eyes. I remained prostrate for some time and wept bitterly. Grandmother put her hand on my head and gently ran her fingers through my hair. Finally, I arose, and with tears streaming from my eyes, I raised my palms and joined Grandmother and Uncle in a prayer for my elder grandmother and her daughter. May their souls rest in peace and Allah grant them *Janat. Ameen.*

*****

I drove through the Lady Dufferin's entrance gate and parked in front of the Annex, beside Narinder's Harley Davidson. Except for in the Emergency area, few persons were about.

Narinder must have spotted my VW and came out of the office. He had put on what looked to be his old military uniform's khaki jacket, complete with the cross-belt and revolver holster. Goodness, was he expecting trouble? He greeted me with his customary *nameste*. I nodded, and he understood it to mean to bring out the sea chest. He went back inside and returned, holding it by the side handles with both his hands. In the darkness, it looked like the one he had shown me earlier. I popped the latch of the front hood and held it open. But the chest was too large for the small boot of the Beetle.

"I think dickey too small. It go on the back seat, *saa'b*," Narinder said.

"Yes." I opened the side door and moved the passenger seat's back down.

"It okay here," he said, sliding it onto the rear seat. "I come with you. Yes?"

"No, Narinderji. It's not necessary."

"No, *saa'b*. You don't know those *Russki-log*. I help you," he said, patting his holster.

"No, no, Narinder *Bhadur*. I absolutely insist. I am not expecting any problem," I said with a wave of my hand. "Thank you very much for all your help. You will get your reward on Monday," I said, getting into the driver's seat.

"Okay, *saa'b*. But tell me where you go?"

I thought that it was a good idea to at least tell him that. "Humayun's Tomb," I replied.

"Good luck, *saa'b*," he said and saluted in perfect British-Indian military style, including a stamping of the right foot.

I gave him an American Army-type salute and drove out. Motoring speedily on the nearly deserted streets, I felt relieved that Narinder had not insisted on coming with me, for I did not wish the Russians to see him. Furthermore, I feared he might pull out his revolver and it could lead to unnecessary complications.

It was nearing two o'clock when I turned from the main road into the access way leading into Humayun's Park. Driving though the empty playgrounds and picnic spots, I reached the deserted lot of the Tomb's entrance and parked in one corner. The streetlights and a few lamps around the park cast ghostly shadows of the tall trees. A concrete wall with a steel fence encircled the Tomb's garden. At the centre of long, straight walkways dotted with flowerbeds and fountains, the monument's onion-shaped dome shone in the floodlights. The entrance gates were closed and there was no light in the ticket office. I was happy to see that the authorities had not placed a *chaukidar* there. Or if they had, he had probably gone home. I rolled down the window and some fresh air, although warm and humid, blew in. I breathed deeply and felt relaxed. I waited, listening to the sounds of crickets and an occasional bus or biker that roared by on the main road, in the distance.

Grandmother's account of Grandfather's involvement at the start of the Rebellion came back to me. I had seen a painting in a London museum that depicted the King of Delhi's surrender to Captain Hodson. I felt as if I were on that very spot where the historic event had taken place. I wondered how the Rebellion might have turned out if Shah Zafar had heeded Grandfather's advice and accompanied the rebels out of Delhi. Could their final stand at Lucknow have transpired any differently?

The clunky sounds of a badly tuned engine broke my reverie. The familiar dark blue Volga drove in and parked at some distance from me. There were three persons in the car. I recognised Katya in the front passenger's seat, and the driver as the same one I had seen earlier. I could not place the third person, sitting on the back seat. He got out and walked towards my car. He was a blond-haired, burly chap; his dark trousers and white tee shirt accentuated his muscular build. I stepped out to meet him.

"You have box?" the beefy guy asked.

I opened the passenger side door and pointed at the sea chest. "Help yourself. Do you have my money?"

"You get later," he said and, reaching into the VW, pulled out the trunk. Holding it with both his hands, he proceeded towards the Volga. The chauffeur got out; he still wore a straw fedora and beige suit. Opening the boot, he helped place the chest in there. I expected Katya to step out and hand me a package or something. When she did not move, I started to walk towards her.

The chauffeur quickly stepped in front of me, blocking my way to their car.

When I got closer, I said, "I want to talk to Katya."

"Niets," he said in a rough voice.

"I want my money."

"She say you get money later," he growled again.

"No. I want to talk to Katya," I said, and started to step towards her. The second man, by this time, had closed the Volga's boot and advanced towards me. I heard the faint sputter of a motorbike starting somewhere in the park, but paid no attention to it.

As I tried to walk past the man in the straw fedora, he put his hand on my chest and shoved me backwards. The other guy had come behind me and held me with his arms around mine. When I saw the chauffeur raise his right arm with the fist clenched, I realised it was the classic situation of two goons beating up a loner. Balancing myself on my left foot, I swiftly gave him a flying kick, with my right foot to his chest. His fedora went flying and he fell to the ground. From the twisting motion, I had managed to free myself, partially, from the guy holding me. In the same action, I rotated on my left foot and gave the man behind me a karate chop. I hit him with my left hand on his neck. Although the cut was not strong, he must have felt it. He released me and staggered back, holding his neck with his left hand. He glared at me. From the corner of my eye, I noted the chauffeur was on one knee, pressing the side of his chest with one hand, trying to get up. The burly guy started towards me with his fists balled, arms extended, like a clumsy heavyweight boxer. I took the karate defensive stand: with my feet apart and bent at the knees, arms extended and palms ready for chops. The chauffeur had managed to get up and was also stumbling towards me. Although my heart pounded, I was ready to have another round with them.

Suddenly, a motorcycle roared into the parking lot. Although the biker had a helmet on, I recognised Narinder's black Harley. The Russians and I looked towards him. He came speedily towards us and, raising his right arm, fired a shot in the air.

Katya screamed something in Russian. She had gotten into the driver's seat and started the engine. The two guys ran and, opening the doors, jumped into the car. With tires screeching, the Volga sped away.

Narinder stopped his motorbike beside me. "*Saa'b*, you okay?" he asked, holstering his revolver.

"I'm fine. But we had better get out. Your shot may have attracted attention."

"Yes, *saa'b*. I follow you."

I picked up the Russian's fedora and ran to my VW. I started the Beetle and revved its engine up and down a bit, to get the rpm up. Putting it in first gear, I raced it out of the park. I noted, in the rear-view mirror, Narinder following close behind.

Reaching the centre of the city, I drove into the parking area of an all-night café. Narinder parked his bike beside my VW. I invited him for some chai and he readily accepted. He took the helmet off and quickly put on his turban, which he kept in the side pocket of the motorbike. We went into the restaurant. He looked a bit shaken up; I felt the same myself.

We sipped the hot, extra sweet masala-tea and bit into some spicy *samosas*, in silence. Soon our nerves calmed down.

"That was a very brave thing you did. How did you know I would get into trouble?" I whispered to him, for I saw some customers giving us strange looks.

"*Saa'b*, I tell you before. Those *Russki-log* not to be trusted," he said in a low voice, shaking his turbaned head.

"Narinderji, I must say, you are like a magician," I said. He gave me a puzzled look. "First you produced a near duplicate of the sea chest and then you suddenly appeared at the Tomb."

"No problem, *saa'b*. I find one more same old trunk in the hospital."

"What did you put inside it?"

"I go to *purana* market and buy old British women's clothes they leave behind. Big, long dresses and wide petticoats, like I see in the films." He held his palms wide, indicating the size of the hips. "Also, Doctor Rao *saa'b* give me old books to put inside."

"I suppose that should keep the Russians happy. For a while, anyway."

"You think they find out the trunk is not same?"

"I imagine, sooner or later, they will. This duplicate will give us time to have the real one shipped out."

"Okay. I now understand, *saa'b*. You very clever," he said with a smile.

I took out from my pocket an envelope with five thousand rupees in it and placed it on the table. "Without your help, this wouldn't have been possible. Thank you. Here's your reward." I slid the envelope towards him.

"No problem, *saa'b*. Also, no money for me. I do this for *bechari* Aamrican doctor. I receive payment from my god."

"No, Narinderji. Doctor Rao said he would compensate you for your service. It's from both of us. It is for your family." I had added another two thousand to the three thousand rupees Doctor Rao had given me.

Having finished our tea, we got up to leave. I thanked Narinder again for all his help. He wanted to escort me right up to my apartment. I managed to dissuade him, pointing out that it was getting late and he lived some distance out of the city. He reluctantly agreed and we parted with a handshake.

On the way home, I was relieved the Russians had not paid me. But if they had, I wondered what excuse I would have made to return it to them.

*****

Riiiing...ring, ring...riiiing. The shrill ringing of the telephone on the night table woke me. The repeated one long and two short rings were the jingles of a long-distance call. I looked at the clock on the end table. It read six fifteen. I had overslept and my wife, tired of waiting for my usual six a.m. call, was calling me. I reached over and lifted the receiver.

"Hi, dear," I said, trying to sound as normal as possible.

"My, that must have been some Saturday night party." She spoke with a bit of a laugh in her speech. Obviously, my voice betrayed the grogginess.

"Sorry, darling, I slept in. Yes, it was a grand affair. Would you believe it lasted till two a.m.? Too bad you weren't here."

"Two a.m.. That good, huh? Sorry to wake you up, hon."

"It's okay—I was going to get up soon."

"Was there a *naatch*-girl show as well?"

"Of course there was a *naatch* show. A Saturday night party in Delhi is never complete without one," I replied, stifling a yawn.

"Well, in that case, I can still come over—it's only Saturday evening here in Baltimore," she joked, although her voice lacked cheerfulness. I suspected that this extended period of long solitude was affecting her.

"Sure, just hop on the plane. I would love to have you in my arms now," I said, trying to comfort her, thinking about her wonderful warm embrace, when she would hold her arms tightly around my chest and rest her head on my shoulder.

"Don't I wish," she said, almost with a sob.

I pictured her lovely blue eyes filling with tears and her fingers twirling her soft, shoulder-length, blonde hair. "Aw, I am sorry, darling. Are you feeling lonely?"

"Does it show? I'm okay, dear. But spending Saturday nights alone is not my favourite pastime, you know. Anyway, sorry for being emotional. How are you keeping?"

"I'm okay, sweetie. Busy as usual, not enough hours in a day. Missing you a lot, though. But look at the bright side—I'll be home next month."

"Wow. I just can't wait. Did you talk to Doctor Rao about not accepting their offer of an extension?"

"Yes, I did. I told him I definitely wished to return home. Besides, Johns Hopkins is anxious to have me come back, and very likely wouldn't agree to the extension, anyway. He was sorry I couldn't stay another year, but still asked me to reconsider."

"Well, one year is enough. Time you were home, love. You can always go back after a few years, if you wish."

"Yes, it has been an interesting year. The teaching aspect was most satisfying. Doing my share, extending a helping hand, assisting the hospital develop towards providing better medical aid to the millions of needy here. It was spiritually very rewarding."

"I am sure they appreciated your help very much. Besides, you will be helping them in another mission even from here: finding the family of that trunk's owner."

"Yes, that's pretty much on my mind too. Looks like it will arrive home before me."

"Sorry that I can't come to Goa, as you were suggesting. The caseload in the office is very heavy; too many court dates are coming up. I just can't get away."

"Too bad. Lawyers are always so busy. It would have been nice to meet you there. We could have taken a small holiday. "

"Oh, I need a *big* holiday. So, how is Grandmother? Did she have any information about the mysterious Doctor Margaret?"

"She couldn't recall much specifically about an American. Except she did mention that Grandfather said he was once treated, in Jhansi, by a French lady doctor whom he named, guess what, *Madame*."

"Hmm. Well, that makes sense. I would think she was Canadian, then."

This quick assertion, coming from her legal mind, surprised me. It was still too early in the morning for me and I was about to ask how the name *Madame* made her a Canadian. Then it suddenly dawned on me. I slapped my forehead with my free hand and exclaimed, "Ah! A *French*-Canadian, you mean?"

"Possibly. You know, there were quite a few French-Canadian women serving with the British."

"Yes, but the label on her trunk said Doctor Margaret Wallace, which is a Scottish name, and gave the address of the American Presbyterian Mission in Futtehgurh. By the way, did you call the

Mission Offices?"

"Yes, I called their head office in Boston. None of the priests was around, so I left a message. A most pleasant Reverend Paten called back. We spoke at some length. He told me all about the American Mission, school and church in Futtehgurh. It opened in the 1840s to help the children orphaned by the famine."

"Did he know of the Wallaces?"

"He looked into their records, but found only scanty lists from that period. Their names were not on those. However, he said this did not mean the Wallaces could not have been part of that Mission."

"How could that be? Don't they have names and other information recorded in registers, books or ledgers?"

"Yes, they do. The pastor said that records were maintained quite dutifully, but bookkeeping being what it was in those days, there's always a chance of misplacement of papers due to fires, renovations, moving and so on. It could well be that the Wallaces and their daughter, Margaret, were at the Futtehgurh Mission in 1857. But unfortunately, the rebels burned down the whole place and all the records were lost. He was most sorrowful in recounting the details of the martyred missionaries. Most of them were Americans, some British, and a few native converts as well, he said."

"I'm sorry to hear of the burning of their church. That may well explain the loss of records," I said with a sigh.

"Yes, unfortunate, isn't it. But did Uncle Arif know anything?"

"No, not much either. He was very young when Grandfather died. Except that he *did* give me Grandfather's diary." I said this as casually as possible, taking care not to mention the original parchment of the 1857 Proclamation from the Shah of Persia, nor about that night's events at Humayun's Tomb. I feared that an inquisitive long-distance telephone operator—or the KGB—might be listening.

"My, that diary should make interesting reading." Alexandra said, her voice rising with excitement.

"Yes, I am going to spend the remainder of the day reading it. How are you going to pass your weekend, darling?"

"Guess what? I picked up some books from the library on the history of India and its First War of Independence. So, I'll be cramming on Indian History 101."

"That should keep you busy. You can educate me on all the extraordinary events when I return home."

"And you can tell me all about Grandfather's life and times you read in his diary."

Finishing the telephone conversation, tired as I was, I stumbled downstairs to the apartment building's exercise room for a good workout. I took Grandfather's diary with me. It was a bit larger than normal book size and was a hefty, brown-leather-bound tome, with a few dog-eared pages, which I separated carefully. Except for some smudged sheets and insect-bitten holes, it was still in very good condition. I read the diary while on the treadmill and the stationary bicycle.

Following a hot shower, I felt refreshed and hungry. I walked across the road to the Intercontinental Hotel's restaurant to partake in their sumptuous lunch. I had the diary propped up on the table while I ate. Needless to say, I was totally captivated by its contents.

After dining, my head buzzing with the information I had ingested with my food, I felt like a walk to clear my head and mull it all over. I strolled through some of the nearby bazaars and flea markets. The marketplaces were vibrant with activity. Multitudes of people ambled about, buying items from rugs, slippers to saris and *paans*. I tactfully dodged all the aggressive vendors and begging children, an art I had mastered by then, and arrived back at my apartment.

Settling comfortably on the couch with my feet up, and assisted by a glass of red wine, I continued reading the thrilling diary. It was written in old Urdu, using a lovely poetic style, and embellished with liberal uses of Persian phrases, very much like English scholarly works use Latin expressions when emphasising a point.

Reading the diary was like taking a step back into the historical events of over a hundred years. It opened for me a new window on India's First War of Independence, as it was filled with Grandfather's firsthand account of the events of that time. In my excitement, I could not help but race forward, skipping over some of the detailed passages, for I craved to find any mention of the lady doctor, or any clues related to her disappearance. Indeed, there were several references to the enigmatic "Madame", and *even* a "Margaret", but alas, there weren't many details. The chronicle also finished rather abruptly, as if the writer had lost interest in recording the episodes of the day. This seemed to corroborate what I had been told by others, of his change of heart. But the reasons for these second thoughts were not clear.

By 1856, India's Great Mughal Empire was practically broken up.

The last surviving "Emperor", *Bhadur* Shah Zafar, having lost most of his empire, was virtually a detainee in his own palace in Delhi's Red Fort. Although he was left alone to go about his business and he retained the title of "King", his authority extended no further than the metropolis of Delhi. Some British soldiers jokingly called him "the Sheriff of Delhi".

While historians differ on the motives of Shah Zafar, I do believe that he must have longed to be a real king once again, like his fabled ancestors, Babur, Humayun, Akbar and others, just like in the glory days of the Mughal Empire, which had stretched across the entire Indian subcontinent. Who would not have such dreams?

Skimming through the diary, I learned that Grandfather, even at the young age of nineteen, was a strong, muscular, heavy-set warrior type. He had become proficient in wrestling, fencing, riding, shooting, and all forms of battle tactics. King Zafar took a particular liking to him. Also, since Grandfather was from a Mughal family, one that had served the line of kings, he was dependable, and his trust in the King was absolute. Before long, he was promoted to the trustworthy special Palace Guards unit. Grandfather served his King admirably and acquired the title of *Bhadur*, among other honours.

However, after many courageous battles, he threw down his sword and returned home a crestfallen hero. He chose to change his profession, from a warrior to a jeweller. The reasons for his *volte-face*, like that of a person converting to another religion, I tried hard to find in the diary. Nevertheless, I was experiencing uneasy feelings. Ever since I had touched the padlock of Doctor Margaret's trunk and seen what appeared to be her apparition, not to mention the nightmares, I felt that some perplexing secret was going to be unveiled to me. But by whom, how or when, I knew not. Could it be that there was some bond between Margaret and Grandfather?

Following are some excerpts, which I noted while searching for answers to my questions, by reading through, that Sunday afternoon, the diary of my grandfather, Sharif Khan *Bhadur*

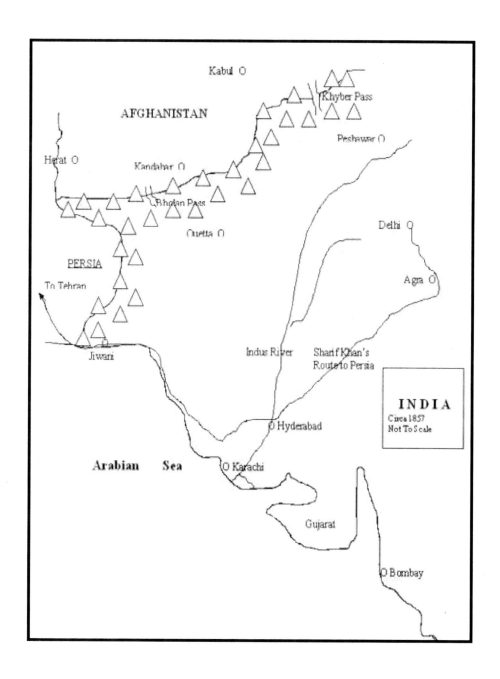

Sharif Khan's Secret Route to Persia

Chapter Five

Sharif Khan Bhadur's Diary – Part 1
(As translated by Wallidad Sharif)

1856, July: Delhi, India

THAT AFTERNOON, having barely passed my nineteenth spring, I was in the blacksmith's workshop sharpening my *talwars*. Due to the summer heat, further intensified by the ovens and the sparks from the grinding wheel, I had stripped down to the waist. Sweat dripped off my chest and biceps as I hammered the hot blades on the anvil, when I heard *Subedar* Farid-uddin come to the door and call out, "Sharif Khan, the King summons you. Go immediately to the Palace." He pointed at my bare chest and added, "And put some clothes on. I don't want a complaint from the *Harimzadi* that her girls swooned again over your muscular body."

I hurried to my room, washed up in haste, put on a clean blue uniform robe, tied on my sword by its gold belt and rushed to the *Diwan-e-Khas,* the King's private chamber. I was led in without delay.

The sentry, entering the chamber, tapped his lance on the marble floor and announced, "Sharif Khan, the bravest of the braves, Sepoy of his Majesty's Guards, presents himself."

I walked across the red Persian carpet, bowed and *salaamed* his Majesty, *Bhadur* Shah Zafar, who sat on colourful cushions over the granite throne. Two maidens dressed in silk shirts and baggy pants stood on either side of the chair, fanning the king with peacock-feather fans. The silver and gold linings on the walls, with jewels embedded in them, dazzled the room, as if it were lit by a thousand stars. Sunlight and fresh air filtered through marble lattices that covered the windows. The Persian inscription, painted in gold, glittered above the throne. It read: *If there is Paradise on Earth, this is it, this is it, this is it.*

Bhadur Shah, being in his eighties, looked frail from a distance, but in the few times I was near him, he mesmerized me with his grandiose personality. He sat cross-legged on the Mughal throne, wearing the crown embedded with numerous sparking jewels, dressed in a gold braided jacket, and several garlands made from beads of pearls and precious stones adorned his neck. His hands showed the strength and steadiness that once could shoot down a partridge while riding on horseback. His well-trimmed, greying beard and handlebar moustache covered a dark and, even then, handsome face with the long, hooked nose typical of the northerners.

"Sharif Khan, I have chosen you to be part of a very important undertaking," King Zafar advised, looking solemnly at me with his piercing dark eyes. "May Allah be with you and grant you the strength to accomplish this mission successfully."

Alhamdulillah, it was bewildering to learn that I was chosen for a journey to Persia, which was to commence the very next day. I was to be part of a small contingent of special guards who were to escort a group of emissaries from our King to the Shah of Persia.

[…]

Our contingent comprised a dozen guards, six servants, and three elderly emissaries. Although I had seen those noblemen before and knew their leader, Mirza Ahmadullah Khan, a friend of our family, they remained aloof and hardly conversed with us. We were to go on a most secret mission of the utmost importance to the future of India, and especially the Mughal Empire, was all we were told.

[…]

I was curious about the route we were instructed to take to Persia. As India is ringed in the north and east by a range of high mountains, and on the other sides by the Indian Ocean, there are only two land passages leading out of the country: the north opening, through the Khyber Pass to Afghanistan, and the eastern one, via the Bolan Pass, also to Afghanistan. I knew both these border crossings were heavily guarded, which would have made it very difficult, if not impossible, for a party representing the King of Delhi to go unnoticed. But I was informed that instead of through the Passes, we would journey on the ancient route taken by Alexander the Great on his retreat from India in 327 B.C.

We were to follow this relatively little known course: east along the Indus River and then up the Baluchistan coast to the village of Jiwani, close to the border with Persia. Although Alexander, who called this region Gedrosia, had sailed away on Macedonian ships lying in wait at a port close to what is now the town of Gwadar, we would continue on foot up the coast. We were informed there was a small bay there, like the point of a curved sword, at the foot of the mountains that rise from the Arabian Sea to join the Himalayas. At low tide, *inshallah,* we were assured that it would be possible to cross over unnoticed into Persia. I was apprehensive, on receiving this information, for if there wasn't a passage through the beach, climbing the steep, rocky cliffs with horses would be next to impossible.

[…]

1856, July: Agra, at the Taj Mahal

We travelled secretly, dressed as merchants on a trading mission. Several of the mounts were laden with goods to justify our disguise. We had no difficulty passing through the Delhi Fort's gate without generating any suspicion in the minds of the few lethargic British sentries. From Central India, we travelled south through the little known trails towards the Rajasthan desert. We crossed the Jamuna River at Agra. From the riverboats, Allah be praised, the Taj Mahal was a remarkable sight. The marble dome of the tomb and the four minarets around it reflected in the moonlight on the waters of the gentle river.

[…]

We travelled mostly at night and prayed to evade discovery by the British military patrols. Our prayers were answered. Although this area was recently captured from the Sikh Maharaja, Ranjit Singh, there were few British army units around. Possibly, they did not relish the heat, sand storms and lack of water in the desert. We passed through the towns of the Sindh province to reach Hyderabad, on the banks of the majestic River Indus.

[…]

1856, August: Hyderabad

The River Indus is so wide that I could not see the bank on the other side. I wondered how we would cross over. I inquired aloud, "How did Alexander, with his massive army of thousands, navigate this river?"

"He built his own boats here," one of the elders informed me. "But we will have to silver the palms of a farmer to take us across the mighty river."

After the Indus crossing, we turned north-westward through the deserts of Sindh. We avoided the big city of Karachi, which was in British hands since 1840, for we knew large contingents of British troops were stationed there.

[…]

The arid mountains of the Hindu Kush loomed in the distance, separating the lands and marking the three borders between India, Afghanistan and Persia. The peaks then disappeared into the Arabian Sea, like a giant diving into an ocean.

[…]

We turned westward, and when we approached the ocean, we felt the refreshing, cool, moist breezes of the Arabian Sea on our faces. It was especially exciting for me, for it was the first time I had ever seen an ocean. We dismounted and walked across the sandy beach to the water's edge. Facing westwards, towards Mecca, we got down on our knees and raised our hands in a prayer. With the surf running around our waists, we prayed to Allah to grant us the energy to reach the tall mountains in the distance, and to help us locate the small beach with the passage through to cross over into Persia. *Ameen.*

[…]

1856, mid-August: Along the Mekran Road to Persia

The first day along the seashore was very fatiguing. We were short of drinking water and food. We trudged along the sandy coastal paths with our cobs in tow.

One of the elders told us, "Alexander lost many a man from starvation and heat stroke on this stage of his journey."

I spied something shiny in the sand and picked it up. It was a silver coin. Although the inscriptions on the coin had faded, what looked to be the head of an emperor was visible, along with writing in a Greek script around the circumference. I showed it to an elder.

He exclaimed, "*Wah*! Allah be praised. You are His chosen one. He has bestowed upon you a gift of an ancient coin from Alexander the Great. Cherish it. Wear it around your neck. It will provide you his strength."

The presence of the Macedonians was still evident there. We saw many ruins of brick and stone buildings. I was told those were temples. Some had only the foundations still standing, as if defiantly mocking the winds of time.

[...]

1856, late August: Jiwani Village

This morning we arrived at a tiny fishing village by the sea. A crowd of the native Baluchis gathered around and stared at us curiously with their fierce dark eyes. Although they appeared intimidating in their long beards, *shalwar-kameezes* and turbans, *Alhamdulillah*, we were fortunate to find that the fishermen were friendly. They welcomed us and were especially cordial when Mirza Sahib opened his money belt and passed rupee notes all around. In return, he received their word, in the name of Allah, to keep our journey a secret. We were able to buy fresh fish, food, water and accommodation in their huts. Sleeping on *charpoys* in the hut—which I shared with three other sepoys—with the soothing sound of the Arabian Ocean waves pounding on the beach was the most relaxing night I had in over a month of travel.

In the morning, as I lay alone on my bed, I overheard an interesting conversation. It was between Mirza Sahib and the village chief, while they sat on a cot by a cooking fire, smoking *hookahs*.

The chieftain said, "Mirzaji, be particularly careful when travelling in Persia. Do not get mistaken for Afghanis. You may not have heard, but there is a strong rumour that the Persians have assaulted the Afghani City of Herat. Persia is now at war with Afghanistan."

I looked out of the hut's window and noted that Mirza Sahib merely nodded. He did not look at all surprised on hearing this significant news. It was as if he was expecting it.

He said calmly to the chief, "It was bound to happen soon. The last Persian attempt to capture Herat, eighteen years ago, failed."

The chief then asked him, "Will the Persians succeed this time?"

"Oh yes, *Inshallah*. Certainly, as they have much better Russian support this time."

I noted the quizzical look on the old chieftain's face. I am sure he was wondering how Mirza Sahib knew of the Russian help to the Persians. However, he kept quiet and continued pulling on the *hookah*, which made a bubbling sound as the smoke was drawn through its water bottle.

I remembered a history lesson at school, where the teacher had told us that in the 1838 Persian-Afghan war, a lone British officer had helped the Heratis. He was called the "Hero of Herat". Lieutenant Potter, was it? I could not remember his exact name just then. In addition, I think the Russian officer who helped the Persians at that time was a Count Victor, or some name like that. So, who was this other Russian officer helping the Persians now? Surely not the same Count Victor? It was rumoured that British secret agents had assassinated him in 1840, in St. Petersburg, and his death made to look like a suicide. I made a mental note to ask Mirza Sahib for some details later. I didn't wish to disturb him in his conversation with the village chief, just then.

(Margin notes: Lieutenant Pottinger, Count Vitkevich)

[...]
1856, September: India-Persia Border
Mashallah, we arrived at the critical part of the route into Persia. The majestic mountains on the Indian border with Persia were before us. Nevertheless, to our apprehension, barren, steep, hundreds-of-feet-high cliffs that sloped down into the ocean confronted us. The angry sea waves pounded their rocky feet, churning the water into thick foam. Was it possible for the tide to recede sufficiently to enable us to slip across? When would that happen? Could it be that our scouts had led us astray?

We made camp on the sand in the shadow of the mountain ledges. At nightfall, Mirza Sahib instructed us to sleep in the tents in our travelling clothes and be ready to depart at a moment's notice. The village chieftain had told him there was only a small, perhaps half-hour time period, sometime in the middle of the night, with the moon at a certain point on the horizon, when the tide would be low enough for us to get across. When that time came, we would have to make haste.

In the middle of the night, *Subedar* Farid-uddin awakened me, with a three-times shaking of my shoulder, the specific signal that it was time to leave, immediately. It was arranged that the emissaries and the Guards would start first, to be followed by the servants. They would need some time to break and clean up the camp, so as not to leave any trace of our presence there.

I ran towards my faithful Punjabi stallion, Shahbash, and, grabbing his reins, led him swiftly towards the foot of the heights. There was an eerie silence all around. The partial moon shone with a hazy, yellowish light that was hardly enough for us to get our bearings and detect the path ahead. The Arabian Sea was indeed at low tide. The waves had receded, but only just.

Alas, *Shaitan* was at work. The rough, pebbled beach between the rocks and the ocean was not wide enough for us to ride through. This was a setback, for we had to walk in single file, leading our horses. The emissaries and other Guards were ahead of me.

"It is getting late. Make a run for it," was the message whispered down the line. The shore was hardly a foot wide, and littered with sharp rocks that made us stumble. The surf lapped at the edges, wetting our feet and ankles, and inching higher all the while. How long before the tide rose to wash us into the furious ocean?

I pulled hard on Shahbash's reins to make him trot along behind me. He shied a bit. Looking back, I saw he had his ears perked up, his eyes shone with nervous fright, and he blew air through his nostrils. I feared that our Central Indian horses, having never experienced salt-water conditions, would resist walking through this narrow passage. I looked ahead and saw the other Guards were having similar trouble pulling their mounts along. When Shahbash reared up on his hind legs and neighed, I scrambled over to him and, rubbing his neck and mane, whispered in his ear, "Easy boy, Shahbash, easy, good boy." I continued to stroke his neck and rub his nose gently, which seemed to calm him down.

Suddenly, a large wave came crashing down on a piece of rock jutting out into the ocean. The water spray drenched Shahbash and me and those behind us. I held firmly onto his reins, as the cool water shower made the horse want to rear up again. It seemed the noise of the waves pounding on the rocks and the sounds reverberating from the cliffs were making the horses jumpy.

There was a loud snort from a horse behind me. It belonged to one of the sepoys, Shafi-uddin. The charger had broken loose. Neighing and snorting streams of moisture, he dove into the water, desperately trying to escape the cacophony. Shafi ran after him into the water, trying to catch the poor animal. The strong undertow immediately carried the horse away. I knew Shafi did not know how to swim and was taking a big risk trying to bring the horse back. I wanted to help. But Shahbash was jumping wildly by my side and I was having a difficult time just trying to keep him restrained.

On hearing the commotion, Farid-uddin came running back. I handed Shahbash's reins to him and prepared to run into the water. The *Subedar* grabbed my arm when he realised what was on my mind, forcibly holding me back. The ocean was getting rougher now, and just then, a large wave lifted Shafi up and smashed him down onto a rock protruding out of the water. The *Subedar* gasped and covered his mouth with one hand. I thus managed to wrench my arm free and plunged into the water. Shafi's motionless body lay on the rock. By then, his horse was carried away quite a distance, looking like a small boat bobbing up and down in the sea. I swam up to Shafi, fighting the waves trying to roll me over. Grasping his body in the crook of my right arm, I began the swim back, using just my left hand and kicking furiously. Definitely, the Angels were helping me, because it seemed that just for a few moments, they held back the large waves and I was able to make my way to the shore. Others scurried over and took Shafi from my arms.

While I sat exhausted on a rock, panting to regain my breath, the sepoys examined him. He bled from his left shoulder and arms, which had taken the brunt of the crash on the rock. Fortunately, he had not hit his head. Although breathing irregularly, possibly from a state of shock, he did not look fatally injured. They carried him to a makeshift canvas stretcher. We peered into the dark ocean for any sign of the poor animal. Alas, the horse was nowhere to be seen. The unfortunate beast of burden had helped us in the long journey from Delhi, only to drown in the Arabian Sea.

Mirza Sahib scampered down the line to us. "Move along quickly," he urged. "Ahead, water is already up to the knees."

We resumed our frantic, seemingly unending scurry along the narrow beach. The tide was returning and the water was up to our waists by the time, *Alhamdulillah*, we reached the other side of the mountains. All knelt down on Persian soil, in obeisance to Allah, completely exhausted.

[...]
1856, September: Persia
The next night, we resumed our travel up the Persian mainland towards the Caspian Sea and the capital city, Tehran.

One day, emerging from a hilly area onto a flat plain, we spotted a group of about two-dozen tribesmen riding in our direction. From their attire and ferocious faces, we recognised them to be Turkmen, who were known for their involvement in slave trading. They stopped and sat on horseback, blocking our path. On getting nearer, we made the usual *salaams* and "God is Great ... peace be onto you" salutations. However, from the way they eyed our possessions, it was clear they did not come in peace. Upon receiving a wink from Farid-uddin, the prearranged signal to attack, we pulled out our swords and heeling our horses, charged towards the slavers. The element of surprise was on our side. They were not able to pull out their rifles or revolvers. After a brief fencing skirmish, we struck five of them down. The rest escaped, galloping away into the desert with their loud curses ringing in the air. Some of us pulled out our muskets, but Farid ordered us not to fire. He likely feared attracting the attention of other marauders. From the way Sepoy Shafi parried on a spare horse, I was relieved to see he was none the worse from his earlier near-drowning incident.

We hastily buried the dead and mounted our horses. Holding the palms of our hands together, we said the *namaz-e-janaza* prayer for them. Farid gave us the order to gallop, knowing that those who had escaped would return with reinforcements.

Although this was a much more arduous route to Persia, we purposely did not take the easier, better known northern passages via the Khyber or the Bolan Passes, for they were known to be heavily guarded by the British on one side and the Afghans on the other. On the other hand, our King was likely well aware that the Afghan ruler, Dost Mohammad, was not particularly friendly towards India. Although he was deposed in 1839, following the First Anglo-Afghan War, and replaced by Shuja ul-Mulk, Dost had regained the throne, having massacred the retreating British Indian and European soldiers, together with their families and camp followers; Shuja was also assassinated. Although we knew that Dost was hostile towards the British, it was a complete surprise when we heard that last year he had signed an alliance pact with the British government. This overture to the British we assumed was probably with an aim of gaining a portion of Northern India—the region around Peshawar—which the Afghans believed belonged to Kabul. Furthermore, it was known that the British needed his support to hold the Russians' advance into Central Asia towards India at bay. It was interesting to learn from the Jiwani village chief that the battle to take Herat by the Persians, likely with Russian help, had begun. How long would it be before the Russians marched into India?

[...]

1856, late September: Tehran, Persia

We reached Tehran, the ancient capital of an ancient empire. At the city gate, the Tehrani guards looked as if they were expecting us. We were escorted directly to the royal palace. I spotted the Shah standing on the central balcony, in regal attire. He waved us in. We were treated royally, like long-lost cousins, and quite rightly so, as we Mughals are indeed related to the Persians. We dined on superb Persian cuisine of barbecued meats, pullao and delicate leavened bread. Although I found the food a bit bland for our Indian tastes, for it lacked the exotic spices and chillies common in our dishes. There was the usual nightly entertainment, dancing girls and so on, but none of us took any part in it. We kept to our strict regimen of going early to bed and waking up before sunrise. After morning prayers, we spent the day in the usual routine of exercise, wrestling, gymnastics, riding and other training. We kept ourselves in shape and were ready for any eventuality.

[...]

1856, October: Tehran, Persia

On an early autumn day, I awakened to much excitement in the city. News came that the Afghan city, Herat, had fallen to the Persians. There were many prayers of gratitude and a fireworks display at night.

A few days later, while I was exercising in the yard, our leader, Mirza Sahib, came to see me. He drew me aside.

"*Salaam* Sharif *mian*. How are you and your eminent Delhi family?" This was the first time he had spoken to me in private, all through the long journey from Delhi.

"*Walaikum salaam*, Mirza Sahib. By the grace of Allah, we are all well."

After more pleasantries, he asked, "Would you be willing to take on another, even more important mission for the Persian Shah and our King?"

"You know, sir, I have never shied away from dangerous undertakings."

"But, Sharif *mian*, I must warn you that it will be perilous. If captured by the British, you would surely be hanged as a spy."

"Mirza Sahib, I am willing to lay my life down for our King."

"*Subhan-Allah!* I knew I could count on you. I should also tell you the assignment is to be treated with the utmost secrecy. Can you be trusted to hold this information in complete confidence? The slightest leakage of this operation to anyone would certainly result in your beheading."

Without hesitation, I affirmed, "Mirza Sahib, I am a member of the long Mughal dynasty, and I can be trusted to the last droplet of blood in my body. It will be an honour for me to be given this assignment."

He looked pleased and said, "This is exactly the kind of reply I was expecting from a son of the great Sharif family." He also reminded me that the Emperor Shah Alam had awarded my family the mini-palace in Delhi—the place we called Sharif Mahal—after similar earlier sacrifices by my ancestors. He then departed, advising me that later that evening, while the others were partaking in the Herat victory celebrations—which would involve much drinking, feasting and performances by dancing girls and such entertainers—I was to follow him. We were to meet with the Shah himself, in his private chamber.

At the end of the sumptuous banquet, the after-effects of which I was savouring as I relaxed on a settee, I saw Mirza Sahib pass beside me. He nodded, the signal for me to follow him. He led me to where the Shah was seated. He rose from his reclining position on the divan and walked towards his private chamber. His entourage of courtesans accompanied him, with Mirza Sahib and I following discreetly. On reaching the doorway of his private quarters, the Shah turned and waved at the courtesans to leave. They departed, their eyes down, looking somewhat disappointed. He then gazed towards me and stared straight into my eyes, as if gauging whether a nineteen-year-old, one of his Mughal cousins from way back, could be trustworthy and capable of accomplishing the secret mission. I met his gaze steadfastly. The meeting of our eyes lasted a moment, and the Emperor of the Persian Kingdom seemed to see something in the depths of mine sufficient to satisfy him. Finally, without saying a word, he turned towards Mirza Sahib and, after nodding at him, passed through the doorway of his private chambers. We followed silently. Two guards closed the solid wooden doors behind us.

Expecting to see a few women in the Shah's private chambers, I was surprised to observe only two European men there. They stood up from the colourfully cushioned couch, wine goblets in hand, to face us. At nearly six feet, I considered myself tall, but one of those gentlemen literally towered over me. The other older man was a bit shorter.

The King introduced the shorter person as General Duhamel, the Russian Representative in Persia. The tall one was presented as Count Nicholai Barinowsky, a special envoy of the Tsar. While I had met many British men, these were the first Russians I had regarded. We know that when introduced, the British prefer to remain aloof and may nod their heads, or a few might even shake your hand feebly. These Russian gentlemen surprised me by coming forward and embracing me in bear-like hugs and kissing me on the cheeks, three times. I was later informed that this was the normal Russian greeting.

There was much discussion between the General, the Count, the Shah and Mirza Sahib, while I stood quietly to one side. They pored over a map of Central Asia that showed the Russia-to-India regions. They drew pencil lines across from Russia to Persia, and then to Afghanistan and India. There was considerable debate on the lines, which were frequently pencilled in, erased and redrawn. Finally, they came to some settlement and agreed upon two sets of lines. Being a military man, I knew what a line on a map meant. But why two lines? That decision puzzled me.

The Shah, having ignored me all this while, finally turned around and beckoned me to his side, with a slight wave of his right hand. I marched over and stood before his Majesty stiffly, with my head bowed. The Shah picked up a rolled parchment, tied with a red silk ribbon.

"I desire you to take this proclamation and present it to your King, *personally*. Do you understand?" he said, handing the impressive-looking scroll to me.

I received the parchment in both my hands and, after touching it to my forehead, told his Majesty, "It shall be done just as his Excellency wishes."

Mirza Sahib then approached me and with a stern look in his eyes said, "Guard it with your life."

I bowed my head in reply. The Count looked at me with a steady gaze, and then turned away, it seemed with a satisfied expression.

Servants were beckoned. They appeared with wine and sherbet glasses. Mirza Sahib and I, being abstainers, selected only the non-alcoholic beverages. It was only after we raised our glasses and toasted to "The Tsar" and "Victory over the British" that the real significance of my secret mission dawned on me.

I was finally told that my operation was to escort Count Barinowsky to Delhi for a personal meeting with our King. Thereafter, I was to take him on to Jhansi, where he was to remain secretly in the remote fortress, as a special councillor to the Rani. For the sake of speed and secrecy, only the two of us were to travel together. The parchment, maps and other secret papers were hidden, rolled up in the barrels of two muskets. These muskets were marked and loaded, ready to be fired, thereby instantly destroying the maps, if capture by the enemy appeared imminent.

[…]

1856, October to November: Tehran to Delhi
We travelled in disguise. The Count was now outfitted as a European-French *hakim*, since it was accepted for European physicians to wander in India, administering medical assistance to the needy populace. My screen was that of the *hakim's* servant. Mirza Sahib had papers, complete with the forged signatures of the relevant British District Commissioners and their seals affixed, already prepared for us.

[…]

The Count and I retraced the route I had used earlier with the King's emissaries to get to Tehran. We met the same rough sea and the harrowing night passage through that small beach at the Persia-India border. *Alhamdulillah,* we crossed without problems and made camp on Indian soil the night we traversed the beach.

The next morning delivered a bright and hot sun, beaming down on our tent from over the mountains. Since the last few days had been tiring, we elected to rest a bit and breakfast before continuing the journey. Sitting on a rocky ledge awarded us a beautiful view of the Arabian Sea, while we enjoyed our salted beef and biscuits, washed down with hot tea. I declined the Count's offer to spike my tea with vodka, from a bottle he carried in his pocket. Suddenly he sprang to his feet, pointed at something out in the ocean and, running up to his horse, pulled out a spyglass from the saddlebag. He opened the telescope to its full extension, placed it at one eye and peered out into the sea. Shading my eyes with my palm, I tried to make out what the Count was looking at so excitedly. I then saw, among a few dhows bobbing in the ocean, what seemed to be the billowing sails of a substantial fleet of ships with reddish-looking flags on their masts.

I asked, "Is that a British fleet, sir?"

"Yes, it is," he exclaimed. "Here, take a look for yourself." He handed me the telescope, saying, "Let me write down their particulars."

I rotated the lens to focus it for my eyesight and pointed it at the flag of the main vessel. A chill went down my spine when I saw the red blur turn into a red flag with the Union Jack at its corner. Other ships flew several different standards, indicating their status in the convoy.

Count Barinowsky hurriedly took notes. He said he recognised two of the large ships as the *HMS Himalaya* and *HMS Malabar,* troop ships he had seen in the Crimea. Several other smaller schooners and frigates escorted the larger warships. *Allah!* British troops were being transferred from the Crimea to India, but why? Were they already aware of our plans?

Count wanted the telescope back. While I was handing it to him, I noted a name etched on the barrel. It read *Lieutenant Wallace.* That being a British name, it puzzled me. After he had finished making more notes, I asked, "Is this telescope yours, sir?"

"Ah! No. Not mine. It belonged to—it's a long story. I'll tell you some day. Right now, we had better get out of here before the ships' lookouts spot us. If they haven't already."

[…]

We purchased more provisions from the friendly fishermen at the Jiwani village and continued on our travel, eastward. This time, riding back through the desert, we met several sandstorms. These required us to shelter in the small tent, with a meagre stock of food and limited water supply, for days. Nevertheless, we managed to brave the adverse conditions. I was much impressed with the Count's courage. For even though he was of noble birth and obviously used to the comforts of servants and the like that a privileged life provides, he bore the hardships with hardly a murmur of discomfort or pain.

One day, as a sandstorm buffeted our tent, we whiled away the long hours, the Count regaling me with his exploits in the recent siege and capture of Heart, and the earlier wars in which he had participated. He was particularly proud of his previous service in the Cossack Regiment with the forces of Prince Menshikov in Crimea. I had heard about the infamous charge of the British Light Brigade against the large Russian battery of cannons at the end of the valley. I asked him about it. He expressed his surprise at the British resoluteness in that action. He told me that contrary to popular belief by Russian soldiers that the British were drunk, intelligence reports stated the charge was due to a mix-up of messages from the command post, up on the height, down to the horse brigade in the valley.

"Count Nicholai, sir, did you take part in the cavalry skirmish that followed the charge?" I asked, as I'd heard that the Cossacks, who were hidden behind the Russian battery, had used their swords on the men of the Light Brigade who had managed to reach the cannons.

"No, fortunately not. I did not take part in that battle. I was assigned intelligence duties instead, and was held up in the interrogation of a most beautiful American lady. And what's most interesting is that she claimed to be a doctor."

"Really, sir? Where did you find her?"

"It wasn't me. It was my scouting force. They had caught her spying, or so they believed, for the British, on our Russian troops' movements."

"An American lady doctor, spying for the British." I exclaimed in disbelief.

"Yes, honestly, that's what she *said* she was," the Count stressed, and added, "It was her spyglass you saw the other day. I had confiscated it."

"So, she was a British officer?"

"No. She said the telescope belonged to her husband and she had borrowed it that day."

"Really. So, what did you do, sir? Did you imprison her?"

"No. From the cross-examination, I believed her story of being a doctor. I noted she was anxious to get to the battlefield and take care of the wounded. So I released her—without her spyglass, of course."

Little did I know at that time that our three stars—that lady doctor's, the Count's and mine—were shortly to meet over the turbulent red skies of an India in the flames of war for freedom.

[…]

When we approached the city of Hyderabad, we made camp on the north shore of the River Indus. That night, I found the same friendly farmer to take us across. So far, luckily, we had evaded detection, due to travelling light and mostly at night with our four horses.

Nevertheless, our tranquillity was short lived. Winter months were approaching and, wishing to reach Delhi before the cold winds started to blow down from the Himalayas, we started travelling during the afternoons. I had mentioned to the Count the British preference of resting during the afternoons, and he agreed to start each day at noon. One day, late in the evening, as we approached a shady oasis that comprised a knoll of palm trees around a pond, suddenly a group of British troopers emerged from the shade of the palm trees and rode up to us. They asked us to halt and dismount. We complied. Their leader, a sergeant, came over to us.

"'Ello, where you folks headin'?"

"Good afternoon, Sergeant. I am Doctor Pierre Dubois from Karachi. This man here's my servant, Saleem. We are going into Hyderabad, to treat a Nabob's young wife who's very sick." The Count spoke with an odd accent, which I took to be French-English.

"Oh, you're French, then, I take it. Got any pypers?"

"Yes, sir. Here they are," the Count said, handing him the forged documents.

The sergeant looked at the papers, and then, looking at me, asked, "You speaky Englishy?"

I did my best to look puzzled, and shook my head.

"Cor blimey. What am I to do?" Then he asked one of the soldiers, "'Ere, where's Captain Walker?"

"'E's down yonder, sir. Waterin' his 'orse."

"Wait 'ere. I'll go talk to 'im." The sergeant cantered off towards the pond.

Our horses were thirsty and I motioned at the soldiers, pointing to the horses' frothy mouths and to the pond. They nodded their heads. I led our four horses to the pond, deliberately choosing a spot close to where the captain and the sergeant stood talking. As I was in between the horses, I believe they either did not see me, or if they did, they likely supposed I could not speak English, and they continued their conversation.

I heard the sergeant saying, "If you ask me, sir, 'e's no more a doctor than I am a mullah. An' 'is illiterate servant, bein' too fair an all, don' look like from these parts, either."

"Right. His papers say his name is Pierre Dubois. Hmmm … Genuine-looking documents, I dare say. Wonder what he's up to?"

"Beats me, sir. Shall I arrest 'im?"

"No. Not yet. Let's let them go and see where they're headed. Sergeant, can you go straight to the post and telegraph a message through to HQ?"

"Yes, sir. An' what would the message be, sir?" The sergeant took out his notepad.

"The Count has arrived. Stop. Travelling under the guise of a French physician named Pierre Dubois with a servant called Saleem. Stop. Being kept under surveillance. Stop. Awaiting further orders. End of message. "

While the sergeant galloped off towards their station, the captain ambled over to where Count Barinowsky was standing, under guard. He took off his white pith helmet and mopped his brow. Even in that intense heat, he wore his full red-jacketed uniform. I finished watering our horses and brought them over to the party, making sure I arrived from the direction opposite to the captain's. By that time, a group of curious native Indian onlookers had gathered around and stared intently at the proceedings.

I heard the captain say, "Well, Monsieur, if you say there is a very sick lady you have to attend to, you had better be getting along, then."

"*Merci, mon Capitaine,*" the Count replied, and bowed in the perfect French style, with one foot extended and a swing of his right arm.

We did not need to be told a second time to leave. The Count and I quietly mounted the steeds and continued on our way.

I sighed with relief and could not believe our good fortune. Earlier, I had visions of being lashed, tied to some prison bars and having to endure insults from leering British soldiers. Hence, I asked, "Do you believe, sir, we managed to foil the troopers? With our cover story, I mean?"

"Not likely. I am certain we will be watched."

"Yes, I heard the captain order the sergeant to telegram their HQ a welcome message about your arrival. He did say 'the Count'."

"Indeed. As I thought, when I saw the sergeant gallop away. He rode just too fast in this heat. I imagine they already have some information about us."

"We should try to lose their trailing party," I suggested.

"You're the expert in these matters, Sharif Khan. I am in your hands."

"Well, sir, in such instances, we immediately change our disguise."

"What do you propose?"

"How about we change into North Indian frontier Pathan tribesmen? You'll make a terrific Pathan. Being descendants of Alexander's army, they are just as fair as you are."

"Pathans? Hmm ... All right, let's change into Pathans."

"I'll see if can buy suitable clothing in the next village. Let's see, we'll need long robes, baggy pants, and turbans. And yes, multicoloured waistcoats. That should do it."

"Don't forget the curved daggers." The Count was smiling now.

In the next village, I left the Count at a friendly *serai* and managed to procure what we needed. We quickly changed into our new disguise. In addition, as another diversionary tactic, we altered our direction and joined a caravan travelling northwards, the least expected course our trackers would have anticipated we would take. It worked. Soon enough the red-coated party we had been spotting in our telescope was nowhere to be seen. No doubt they were feverishly enquiring about a French doctor and his helper from every caravan and in every *serai* they could find.

[…]

1856, December: Delhi

Varying our travel direction several times, the Count and I reached Delhi safely. We stole silently into the Red Fort, via an underground secret passage I knew of, thus managing to avoid the British sentries. We went straight to King Zafar's Palace.

It was still before dawn. Our arrival was announced to Shah Zafar, who was up, likely for his morning prayer. He asked to see us immediately. The King's usual fierce eyes mellowed. He looked at us with happiness as we stood before him with our heads bowed. Holding it in both hands, I proudly presented the rolled parchment from the

Persian Shah to the King. He took it and, pulling on the red silk
ribbon, unrolled it. It had the following message with the Persian
Shah's emblem, a lion holding a sword in one paw, embossed in red, at
the top of the page:

P R O C L A M A T I O N
THIS PROCLAMATION IS ISSUED BY THE KING OF PERSIA
THE PEOPLE OF INDIA ARE NOTIFIED THAT A PERSIAN ARMY IS
COMING FOR THE RELEASE OF INDIA FROM THE GRASP OF THE BRITISH
IT BEHOVES ALL TRUE MOHAMMADENS TO GIRD UP THEIR LOINS
RESOLUTELY
THE UNBELIEVERS MUST BE FOUGHT AND DRIVEN OUT OF INDIA

King Zafar had tears in his eyes. He raised both his hands in a
silent prayer to Allah. I believe he must have asked for the fruition of
the Shah's wishes. The Count and I did the same.

Count Barinowsky looked delighted to meet the King, a survivor
of the long line of Mughal Emperors. The Count had brought word
personally from Tsar Alexander II. There was an offer of help to the
Indian rebel forces who, we later learned, were being secretly put
together. They would comprise the patriotic sepoys, willing to mutiny
against their British officers, and any other native partisan. There was
to be both monetary and military assistance in our struggle for
freedom.

While I stood guard outside the *Diwan-e-Khas*, I heard the Count
speak in perfect Persian, as did King Zafar. Although I did not listen to
all the details, I picked up some basic information. There seemed to be
plans for an invasion of India by a combined Persian-Russian force.
From my post in the outer gallery, I saw through the marbled lattice
windows the King and the Count poring over the maps we brought
from Persia. Those two lines drawn across from Tehran to Delhi were
clearly visible. I still did not understand the meaning of the two lines.
Could those be routes of a dual offensive army? But that would need a
much larger force, wouldn't it? Did the Russians have that many
resources? That many men? That many guns?

[...]
1856, December: Delhi-Jhansi
Count Nicholai was provided comfortable accommodation in a secret
room in the Red Fort, where he remained virtually unseen. After a few

days of rest in the luxurious facilities of the Red Fort, he had recovered wholly from the ordeal of the trek through the mountains and deserts and looked again like a vigorous nobleman. I again admired his resilience, because such a journey would have drained many a tough soldier.

For my valiant service, the King awarded me the title of *Bhadur*, which I could add to my name. To have received this honour at such a young age was most gratifying, as soldiers typically earned it when they were more than twice my age and after many wars and years of service. Henceforth, I was to be addressed as Sharif Khan *Bhadur*.

There were several events, gatherings, meetings and such in the Red Fort, to which I was not always invited. I was happy to be home in the loving arms of my beloved wife, Mumtaz, who was expecting our first child.

One day, a great banquet was held on the birthday or engagement of a prince—or some such occasion; the exact reason escapes my mind. Heads and other dignitaries from neighbouring kingdoms were invited. As I was on duty on the ramparts, I did not observe the arrival of all the guests. But I did see the entrance of some notable persons, among them the Rani of Jhansi; Nana Sahib, the acting Peshwa; his assistant, Azimullah Khan from Bithur; and another person who—I was advised later—was the representative of Begum Hazrat Mahal from Lucknow. The local British Resident and other officers also partook in the feast. However, I noted that after the festivities and the departure of the British and other guests, the special dignitaries I had noted retired to another secluded area of the Fort. From my vantage point, I distinctly saw Count Nicholai, dressed in flowing robes and turban, in the guise of a Pathan, being escorted to that location. It occurred to me that an important meeting was very likely taking place that night.

The next day, I was summoned before the King. He advised me that arrangements had been made for the Count to serve as an advisor to the Rani of Jhansi. I was instructed to escort the Count to her palace, and cautioned, again, to take all the necessary precautions to avoid the Count's detection by the British officials. In accordance with the agreement with the Rani, Count Nicholai and I rode out for her kingdom, on a cold and rainy December night.

Chapter Six

Seeking Margaret's Relatives

1965, July: En route, Delhi to New York
I BUCKLED THE SEAT BELT of the first class cabin's window seat. The four giant jet engines of the Pan American Airways Boeing 707 roared like crouched lions, straining for a dash. Noticing an empty seat beside me, I put my reading material on it and stretched out in a comfortable position as the plane started to roll down the runway. Outside the window, Delhi's Palam Airport buildings passed by, slowly at first and then sped up, as if on a movie screen. It was another hot day and speaking with some of the crew, earlier in the lounge, I was informed the aircraft would need to speed up to 250 kilometres per hour for the takeoff. The enormous plane bounced a bit from its tires bumping along the uneven runway, as it raced along with its engines screaming in a high-pitched wail. Finally, just when it seemed there was not going to be any runway left, with a shudder, the big bird lifted off the ground.

As the airliner soared and banked to enter an unmarked skyway westwards, Delhi's skyline came into view. The steaming metropolis, a juxtaposition of Old and New Delhi buildings, extended almost endlessly. The sunlight gleamed off the domed minarets and the waters of what looked like a silver necklace, the Jamuna River. The river snaked around the city and flowed by the red sandstone boundary walls of the Red Fort, as if still trying to protect it from the marauding armies that had attacked its ramparts for centuries. The plane inclined a touch more and the low, mountainous Delhi Ridge at the north end of the Fort appeared, looking like a grey, sleeping whale. The ingenuity of the British assault from that Ridge, in September 1857, suddenly dawned on me. From my vantage point, it looked to be the perfect strategic spot from which to blast the Fort with cannon fire. My thoughts drifted to my last visit there.

*****

"There it is," Mila said, panting a little from the uphill walk, pointing towards the Mutiny Memorial. We had parked the car on the Rani Jhansi Road and walked up the Ridge towards the Memorial, which she had promised to show me.

The Memorial appeared over the crest. It was in the shape of a tall, spiral sandstone Gothic structure, decorated with ornamental mouldings in trefoils and clover leafs. It reminded me of Prince Albert's Memorial in London, minus his seated statue. Overgrown weeds and shrubbery covered the base and made it look like an ancient tomb from prehistoric times. Creepers had reached the top of the spiral, which was decorated with a Presbyterian or lantern cross with a circular halo around the top. Dismayed to see this historic monument in need of much cleanup, I subdued the urge to roll up my sleeves and start pulling out the weeds.

"There's a plaque here somewhere," Mila said, parting the weeds at the base. She found it and, spreading the wild plants with her hands, bent and read out the fading inscription. "It says, '*In memory of those officers and soldiers, British and Native, of the Delhi Field Force who were killed in action against the enemy, or died of wounds or disease between 30th May and 20th September 1857*', and there is a long list of names of persons who died fighting the *enemy*. Interesting, don't you think? They called the people who owned the land the *enemy*."

"Ah, but look at this," I said, noticing another plaque on the other side, which looked to be of newer construction. "This one says, '*The 'enemy' mentioned in the original inscription on this monument were those who rose against Colonial rule and fought bravely for National Liberation in 1857...*'"

"Oh yes, I remember. This one was installed later by the Indian Government to set the record straight about the real *enemy*," she said with a smile.

We turned and looked down the hill towards the panoramic vista of

Old Delhi, foregrounded by the Red Fort immediately below the Ridge. The Fort's walls, bastions, domes and minarets of the palaces and mosques shone in the bright midday sun. I peered at the Emperor's Palace and located the *Diwan-e-Khas*. Its magnificent walls of marble, with its flowery inlays of a few remaining silver linings, gold and jewels, still glinted.

I pointed to it and said, "That's where Grandfather brought the Russian Count Nicholai, and presented King Zafar with the Russian invasion plans. Most likely Doctor Margaret would have met him there as well."

"The Russian forces never came to help in the Rebellion? Why not?"

"They didn't. What really happened is a mystery. But it seems the Tsar changed his mind, for some unknown reason."

"*Bhagwan*, what a betrayal, and what a tragic end to the great Mughal Dynasty. India would have been a different country had the Revolution succeeded." As she said this, she turned towards me and I saw tears streaming down her olive-complexioned cheeks.

I put my arms around her and drew her gently towards me. She rested her head on my chest and sobbed. I had tears in my eyes as well. For a brief moment, I imagined my spirit soaring into the sky, and from above I peered down upon the two children, representing the Hindu and Muslim cultures of Mother India, embracing each other in memory of all the fallen, brave souls who gave their lives for the freedom of their homeland.

*****

"Would you like a drink before lunch, sir?" I was jolted from my thoughts, and back to my seat, by the gentle hand of the Pan Am stewardess on my shoulder.

I looked up to see a tall, blue-uniformed blonde woman with a radiant smile playing on her face. "Yes, please, I'll have a scotch on the rocks," I replied in a hoarse voice, suppressing a sniffle.

"Is anything the matter, sir?" Her smile changed into a concerned look.

"No. It's nothing. I'm just glad to be going home. Thank you for asking, Diane," I answered, noticing her name on the gold-plated nametag.

Our eyes met. She returned a puzzled look. Her deep blue eyes gave the impression of searching for something in my teary ones. Being in an emotional state, I could not speak. However, she appeared to read my thoughts. She smiled again, as if she understood my feelings, preferring not say anything. Instead, with a gentle squeeze of my shoulder, she turned around and walked down the aisle with the quick, short steps airline people use, to fetch me the drink I needed.

*****

1967, May: Baltimore, USA

A couple of years had passed since that "Walli, could you please see me first thing in the morning" note and conversation with Doctor Rao. I had returned to the States and settled into my normal medical practice, teaching, research and other routines at Johns Hopkins. Doctor Margaret's trunk did arrive at our home in Baltimore, and we carefully stored it away, locked in a spare bedroom down in the basement. Alexandra could not get over the fact that although it was over a hundred years old, apart from a few bumps and scratches, it looked very sturdy.

The box's solid padlock was still there, well preserved and, although tarnished, looking strong as ever. No, we had not dared to pick the lock. Honouring the strict instructions from the Indian hospital Directors, and not gambling to chance a venture into the mystical world by breaking the spiritual proscription against opening a deceased person's personal effects, we did not even think about peeking in the trunk. Hence, it just sat there, hidden away in our cellar.

There was the occasional question from a relative or guest who happened to notice it, having wandered by there, but we usually replied, yes, this was an interesting piece of luggage, which I had picked up in an antique shop in India. In return we usually got an understanding nod with a suggestion like, "It's such a fine piece of furniture. You should bring it up to the living room."

We continued our quest to discover the whereabouts of any surviving family members of Doctor Margaret. We placed notices in some of the major North American newspapers, only to have our hopes wane from a lack of response. I personally made numerous telephone inquiries, sent letters to medical institutions and missionary societies throughout the United States. Alexandra did the same in Canada. She also wrote to some of her relatives still living in Eastern Europe, asking if they knew anything of the infamous Count Nicholai Barinowsky. While we did get some encouraging replies, the message was mostly negative. None could recall such a person. Nevertheless, we followed up on any promising leads that our respondents forwarded. Through these contacts, we managed to make a list of a number of American and Canadian missionary women doctors who were among the first to go to India. Some of the notable names given to us were Doctors Clara Swain, Ida Scudder, Margaret Mackellar, Belle Oliver, Marion Oliver, and others. While we found documented accounts of their stay in India, they had been there in the late 1800s or early 1900s. This was many years after Doctor Margaret was there.

We contacted the surviving family members of some of these ladies. Most expressed their disbelief on hearing of a young doctor having gone there as early as 1854. Their general opinion was that travel to oriental lands by western women—and young, unmarried ones at that—was highly discouraged in those days. With light humour, someone told us, "The male heads of the missions preferred to send more 'mature women', for they were likely too old to arouse any interest in the amorous minds of the maharajahs out there."

Our friend, Doctor Rao, telephoned us regularly from Delhi. However, after a while I found his calls somewhat annoying, and wondered what his real motives were for inquiring frequently if we had any luck in our search. Nevertheless, I kept him appraised. Upon hearing the negative reports, he always advised us to be patient. "Do keep on trying, and one day you will find them," were his usual encouraging remarks.

One day, when I returned home after work and was hanging up my jacket in the front closet, Alexandra rushed out of the kitchen into the hallway. After a kiss, she showed me a letter. "Darling, look at this—it came from Cousin Agnes in Toronto. She has sent some newspaper clippings of reports on 19th Century Canadian soldiers and doctors."

"Really." I took the papers from her and read the report with anticipation, hoping there might be some mention of Doctor Margaret. The Toronto newspaper article was only a recapitulation of the early Canadian Victoria Cross recipients. The first four awards were noted as follows:

1st: Colonel Alexander Dunn, born Toronto, for valiant service in the Charge of the Light Brigade, 1854.

2ⁿᵈ: Assistant-Surgeon Herbert Taylor Reade, born Perth, Ontario, for service beyond the call of duty during the assault on Delhi, September 1857.

3ʳᵈ: Able Seaman William Hall, born Summerville, or Horton Bluff, Nova Scotia, for gallant service during the relief of Lucknow, November 1857. The first black person to win a VC.

4ᵗʰ: Doctor Campbell Douglas, born in Quebec City, awarded the VC for bravery in the Andaman Islands, Bay of Bengal, 1867.

However, even after going through the article from top to bottom a couple of times, regrettably, I could find no reference to our good doctor.

"Too bad," I said, "no one seems to have heard of her. Nevertheless, dear, why don't you write back to Cousin Agnes, thank her for this interesting information and ask her to keep inquiring?"

"I'll do that," was her cheery reply.

*****

Well, miracles do happen, and such an astounding day did arrive. Lady Luck indeed smiled on us. One afternoon in the summer of 1967, I was busy in my office, going through my patients' case history files, when the telephone rang. It was Alexandra on the line.

"She was from Grimsby," she shrieked with excitement.

Of course I knew right away whom she was talking about, and felt a rush of exhilaration. However, I must have sounded a bit apprehensive when I said, "So that means we will have to take a trip with the trunk to England—"

Alexandra interjected, "No, darling. I mean Grimsby, Ontario. Not Lancashire."

"Oh, that's not too far from us, is it?" I recall saying with some relief.

"Yes, rather close. Just on the other side of Niagara Falls."

"Have you contacted her relatives?"

Alexandra replied that she had. Actually, it was the other way around. They had called her. It seemed that while our newspaper ads were not successful, all the personal inquiries in Toronto, Boston, Moscow, St. Petersburg and elsewhere had likely paid off. Through a stroke of good luck, some kind angel possibly carried word of our pursuit to the family of Doctor Margaret Wallace and advised them of our wish to get in touch with them.

"Amazing. How did they get our telephone number?"

"William Wallace called me and told me, 'the exact details of how I came to learn of your inquiries are not important. What is more momentous is that we have made contact, at long last'."

"And who is this gentleman?"

"He's the grandson of Doctor Margaret."

"Really. And how old would he be?"

"Well, I asked if he was still working the farm and he replied that he'd just retired. So, I suppose that would make him a bit over sixty-five?"

While I was happy we had found him, I could not help getting an uneasy feeling that Mr. Wallace was being a bit coy about how he came to hear of his grandmother's trunk and us. Why would he want to keep that information from us?

We learned the Wallaces had migrated from Scotland in the mid-1700s, originally to the Mohawk Valley, what is now New York State. During the American Revolution, the Loyalist side of the family had taken refuge in the Niagara Peninsula. They eventually made their home in the village of *The Settlement at the Forty,* now named Grimsby, established by the United Empire Loyalists around 1787. In compensation for having lost lands in the Mohawk Valley and in return for "Loyalist Service" in the armies of the British Crown, they had been granted a large tract of fertile land along the Niagara escarpment, where the present town has flourished since.

We arranged to visit the Wallaces in Grimsby, and Alexandra's parents in Toronto on the upcoming Fourth of July long weekend.

*****

1967, July: Grimsby, Canada
Driving up from Baltimore, we crossed the US/Canada border at Niagara Falls. Doctor Margaret's trunk was stowed in the back of our Buick station wagon, where it was visible through the rear windows. The Canadian Customs officer, at the border crossing, inquired about the purpose of our visit. I advised him it was to see our family, and saw him glancing at the trunk. I felt my pulse quicken.

The officer remarked, "That's a fine antique piece. We don't see many of them these days."

"Oh, it's an old family junk box—I wish it was a historical item. Then we could sell and make some money from it," I replied with a smile.

"Let me know whenever you wish to get rid of it," the officer said with a laugh, and waved us on. Alexandra and I let out sighs of relief after I pulled out of the booth. We could not have opened it, had he asked, not having even the key for the lock.

We spent that night in the picturesque town of Niagara-on-the-Lake. On the way to the Inn, by the Niagara River, we drove past historic Fort George's wooden spiked fence barricade, which looked just like in the paintings from the War of 1812.

The next morning, after a late breakfast, we continued towards Grimsby. Following the signs on the highway led us onto a winding road at the foot of the Niagara Escarpment. Passing by several fruit farms and Victorian-style homes with gingerbread trim, we reached the quaint town, and stopped at a gasoline station. I asked the young service attendant for directions to the Wallace Estates.

"That will be the Grimsby Castle, just a few miles further. Go up on Mountain Road and make a left on Ridge Road, you won't miss it," was his quick reply.

Our arrival at the sprawling Wallace Estates, surrounded by fruit orchards and vineyards, that unseasonably warm Sunday afternoon, felt like entering a small piece of heaven on earth. *Wallace Hall* read the chiselling on a slat in the stone boundary wall, at the entrance to the property. The wrought-iron gates were open and we drove up a long, winding farm road to the mansion. An eye-catching lily pond, with weeping willows on its banks, lay on one side of the road. The main building was a red brick, rambling Victorian-type manor house, perched atop the brow of the Niagara Escarpment. The two turrets at either ends of the two-storey structure indeed gave it the appearance of a castle. Beyond the edge of the escarpment, the drop provided a glorious view of the complete southern part of the Lake Ontario basin. One could see clearly the neighbouring towns and cities all the way up to the Toronto skyline, and even beyond.

William and Jane Wallace must have spied our car from the mansion's bay windows and walked out onto the driveway from the front stone portico.

"How are you, Mr. Wallace?" I asked, shaking his hand.

"Good, thank you. Please call me Bill. We're not formal here."

Their lean, tall, sturdy figures and Jane's kilt underlined their Scottish heritage. Both looked very youthful, far younger than their nearly sixty-five years of age or so would suggest—some of it spent, no doubt, in the hard working conditions typical of those in a farming way of life. Behind them there gathered an army of family members, of all ages from infants in arms to toddlers to teenagers, and a number of middle-aged and older persons, likely Wallace brothers, sisters, cousins and their spouses. Alexandra and I were thrilled to note that it looked like the whole Wallace clan of Grimsby had come out that afternoon to greet us. There was much hugging and hand-shaking, which made us feel like their friends, visiting from the far-off lands their kith and kin had visited.

"They brought Great-Grandma's suitcase all the way from India 'cause she forgot it there," I overheard one of the kids whisper to another.

Walking up to the ivy-covered walls of the mansion, I glanced about to admire the fine landscaping around the home. Sizeable lawns in all directions suggested a small golf course. The garden circling the house had colourful flowering shrubs and bushes with borders of boxwood. On one side lay an inviting rose garden, and I saw some farm buildings in the distance. Several tractors were driving up to the barns, pulling flatbed wagons loaded with fruit baskets. Workers unloaded the baskets and carried them into the storage barn. Most of them were dark skinned, dressed in farming coveralls, typical of the offshore help brought in from one of the Caribbean countries. However, I noticed several other blond-haired workers, dressed a bit differently, in jeans and chequered shirts.

I asked Bill, pointing in the direction of the fair-haired persons, "Are they also family?"

He replied, "Aye, from our Russian side. They are a bit busy picking apricots that have ripened early on account of the hot spell we've been having. They aren't ignoring you, mind. They will join us later."

That sounded like a good enough reason to me, for I had heard that farmers do not quit until the "job is done".

Bill guided us into the house, saying, "Don't worry about the trunk, the boys will carry it in. We'll open it after we've had some lunch."

Alexandra and I entered the mansion's large foyer, and the first item to catch our eye was a large painting hanging on the wall along the curved staircase leading to the upper floor. It depicted an attractive lady with blonde, flowing hair, deep blue eyes, and the same high cheek-boned features as Bill had. She was in a cheerful pose, sitting sidesaddle on horseback. The painting looked very much like those of queens and princesses we had seen in museums in Europe. Several other paintings hung on the wall going up the staircase, which disappeared from my view. The next picture was that of a cavalry officer, also sitting elegantly on horseback. But my attention was drawn back to the first painting. I had the familiar feeling of having seen that person somewhere before. It then dawned on me. It was the same face from my nightmares and in the vision in the Delhi hospital's storage room. It was her.

I looked inquiringly at Bill, who nodded and, pointing to the painting, said, "Yes, that is Grandmother Margaret."

At that moment, I was tempted to ask all the questions about her that were stored away in my head all these years, but checked myself, for I realised this was not the time or place. There would be other opportunities later. I did, however, want to ask who the cavalry officer in the next painting was, but Alexandra spoke first.

"What a lovely painting. Where was it made?" She obviously couldn't restrain herself.

Jane replied simply, "In St. Petersburg."

I was astonished at the reply. Good heavens, the rumours in India were true. She had survived the Rebellion and managed to escape to Russia. There were several other details I was longing to learn. I followed them into the living room. Since it was getting late, we were asked to come to the dining table presently as lunch was ready.

We all sat at a long table in the dining room with the sun shining through the large bay windows, which also provided a breathtaking view of the lake beyond the gardens. Maids and a butler served us a most sumptuous feast of delicious pumpkin soup, various types of salads, breads, game, fish and poultry. Most of the fine food and wines, I was informed, were from their own Estate, which added to the pleasure of dining while gazing out onto the picturesque surroundings.

Overwhelmed by the grand welcome reception and the pleasant conversation, Alexandra whispered to me, "Don't you get the feeling they want us to consider ourselves a part of their family?"

To that I nodded and replied, "Very much so." However, I couldn't help noticing the absence of the "Russian side of the family" at the dinner table. I again reconciled it as being due to the urgency of bringing in the apricot harvest.

I was jolted from my thoughts when Bill, seated across from me, asked, "So, Doctor Sharif, which part of India are you from originally?"

"Call me Walli, please. I'm not too formal either," I replied and explained, "My parents are from the North of India, around the Delhi area. But we have family in nearly all the neighbouring cities there, such as Agra, Lucknow, Cawnpore. Have you been there, Bill?"

He nodded, but the mention of these towns must have stirred some of his deeper memories and he asked further, "Then you must be a descendant of the Mughals?"

While I was impressed with the question, I laughed and replied, "Oh, perhaps the last of the Mughal 'mohicans'." There was much laughter from those around us at this allusion. I added, "Except for my uncle in Delhi, we are scattered all over now. God only knows how many of us are left in India."

Jane said, "Well, you folks did put up a heroic fight for Independence. Which year was that? And whatever happened to the last Indian Emperor?"

I replied, "1857. Yes, it surely was the last stand by the Mughals. Apparently, they were not as organised as the Americans in their Revolution. The last Emperor, *Bhadur* Shah Zafar, was captured by the British and exiled to Rangoon. He died a few years later."

Bill remarked, "Those were tragic times."

I could not help noticing a faraway look in his eyes, which seemed to indicate some personal sorrow of which he was unable to speak. I again suppressed my desire to blurt out the questions I had for him about his grandmother's life during those years and thereafter, perhaps because I felt he might not be able to speak about those events just yet. I waited. All in good time, I thought.

Nevertheless, Alexandra, being the curious person she was, did ask, "So, when did Margaret return to Canada?"

There was a long silence from those at the table around us. It seemed this was a question they had been expecting, but one for which they did not have an answer. Jane had tears in her eyes, which she dabbed at with a kerchief. Bill finally said with moist eyes, "She never came home. The last time Father heard from her was a letter written in

1901. I was about one then."

Both Alexandra and I became a bit emotional as well. I asked, with a lump in my throat, "Is she buried in St. Petersburg?"

"Somewhere in Russia," was Bill's barely audible reply. We grew silent, each enveloped deep in our own thoughts about the great lady.

A question from one of the children reeled us back into the real world. "Grandma, when are we going to open Granny's suitcase?"

Jane responded, running her fingers through the little girl's hair, "Soon, sweetheart, soon."

As the *raison d'être* for our visit to their home was to deliver the trunk, we assumed they would prefer the trunk's unlocking and the revelation of its contents to be a private family matter. Hence, we proposed returning to the Inn. However, both Jane and Bill would hear none of this, and insisted we stay for the opening. "After all, you have brought it all the way from that enchanting country," Jane said.

Bill and his family were indeed very impressed that we had not opened the sea chest, even though it was in our possession for a couple of years. More so, they marvelled at the resolve of the pious people in India who, having found it, had respected its sanctity and kept it locked. It had remained undisturbed through all those tumultuous years: there had been the two World Wars, endless conflicts in the struggle for independence and with the departure of the British, major upheavals and ethnic violence stemming from the partitioning of the country into India and Pakistan.

All gathered around in the spacious living room, decorated in quaint, Victorian-style furnishings, with eye-catching tapestries and paintings. On the side tables and the fireplace mantel rested memorabilia from the wars of American Independence and the 1812 days. Other items looked to be from their travels abroad, and I spotted a few objects, like a tiger and elephant figurines, apparently from India. However, the object that most caught my eye was a finely polished silver samovar that stood on a side table. Definitely Russian.

A couple of muscular farm-boys carried in their great-grandmother's trunk and set it in the middle of the living room. We sat around it in a circle, wherever we could find seats, on sofas, chairs, cushions and on the carpet.

I glanced around to see if any of the "Russian relatives" had joined us. Not seeing any new faces, I asked Bill if we should wait for "the others", not wanting to call them "Russian". He simply indicated there was no need as, having toiled very hard, they might be tired from the daylong ordeal. I was again taken aback by their absence, for I had thought that Doctor Margaret, having lived in Russia, must have had close ties to those "relatives", and hence they should be an integral part of the main event of that afternoon. Their exclusion from the festivities seemed to be premeditated, and that perplexed me.

Bill motioned to one of his sons. "Go ahead, Jim."

Jim was a locksmith and had come prepared with his tools for the occasion. He inserted a couple of thin plier-like lock-picking tools into the padlock's keyhole, and after just a few twists, the lock sprung open.

Children cheered and clapped with excitement. They appeared to be more anxious than the adults to see what was inside the mysterious trunk. Jim took the lock out from the bolt clamp and slid the bolt back, but did not open the lid. Instead, he motioned to Bill to come forward. The honour of opening the sea chest was rightfully reserved for the eldest surviving grandson of the great lady.

Bill swung open the top to reveal a fine lining of cedar wood on the back of the cover and in the interior of the trunk. The cedar must have been of the finest aromatic quality, as it still looked fresh and had maintained its rosy tinge even after all these years. It appeared that the aromatic cedar had managed to preserve the contents of the trunk in good condition. All stood up, peering anxiously into the trunk to observe its contents, which had been packed over a century ago.

It looked as if the contents of the trunk had been folded neatly, in a manner that suggested its owner was leaving on a journey and would be away for some time. The top layers contained neatly folded Victorian dresses. Some were fine silk with skilfully embroidered collars and gold-threaded corners. Jane held up these to the sounds of admiring "ah"s from the women. Most of the other garments looked to be of Indian origin. There were exquisite, colourful silk saris and shawls with rich patterns.

I found it curious there were none of the khakis or riding breeches worn for travelling by European women in India those days. This indicated to me that Doctor Margaret would have packed those in another case for a journey. There were some ornamental items and decorative pieces, intricate wooden carvings, small statues and figurines in ivory, brass, silver and gold made by skilful Indian artisans. Everyone, and most of all the children, admired these. They picked up each artefact and turned it repeatedly in their hands to look at it from all sides. What interested me most were the old medical instruments, aged stethoscopes, bullet-pulling forceps and other tools used by early pioneer medical practitioners. These I had seen only in old medical textbooks or in museums. Indeed, there were a couple of those medical textbooks in there as well. Bill handed these on to me and I was busy thumbing through one, when there was a gasp from Jane.

"Oh, my God! Would you look at this?" She drew out from the bottom of the box a large regal crown wrapped in a pink silk cloth. The coronet was made of fine, shining gold, with rings around it studded with colourful jewels, noticeably rubies, emeralds, pearls and others I did not even recognise. The most striking object was the centrepiece, which appeared to be made of a brilliant array of diamonds. Everyone in the room, young and old, was mesmerized by the sight of the tiara and stood speechless, watching it held up in Jane's both hands. The evening sun's rays passing through the bay windows reflected from the jewels in the crown and cast brilliant specks on the walls.

"Do you know what this is, Walli?" Jane asked finally, breaking us out of the reverie.

"Er …" I hesitated a bit, but I suddenly recalled what Mrs. Rao had told me at the party in Delhi. "I believe that would be the missing crown of the Kingdom of Jhansi."

There were loud exclamations of "Really! The crown jewels of a kingdom."

I mentioned I had heard that the State of Jhansi was anxious to find that crown, and there likely was a big reward for its return. I speculated, "It would seem the Rani possibly gave the crown to Doctor Margaret for safekeeping."

"But why?" Jane asked.

"I suppose it was when the Rani escaped from the British siege of her fort. Possibly she thought it was safer with Margaret," I said.

Then it was Bill's turn to exclaim. He drew out some more items from the bottom of the trunk. "Now, what do we have here?"

I saw him holding three ledger-type books, which seemed to be journals or diaries. He handed them to me. The ledgers were labelled, on the cover, *Margaret Wallace's Journal* and itemized as *Volume I*, *Volume II* and *Volume III*.

"Ah, at last," I remarked. "These journals will definitely contain the information surrounding the mysterious events of those turbulent days. We may now finally know what happened."

Jane, with the crown still in her hands, asked, "But what are we going to do with this gorgeous crown?"

"I will take that crown," said a gruff voice in a heavy Eastern European accent.

All turned towards the door of the living room, where stood a muscular, heavyset man with cropped blond hair. I took him to be one of the family members from the "Russian side", as Bill had put it.

"It belonged to my grandfather. Give it to me." The man walked towards Jane, who held the crown in her hands.

"Now look, Gregorze, we talked about it earlier and you agreed that you will stay out of this matter. It is Margaret's trunk," Bill told him in a raised voice.

"No. I want that crown," the man said and pulled out a revolver from his jacket pocket.

Everyone gasped at the sight of the pistol. Some kids screamed "Mommy!" and clung to their parents. Bill tried to lunge forward. I restrained him by holding onto his arm.

Gregorze did not listen to any of our pleas. He calmly strode over to Jane and, pointing the revolver at her, snatched the crown from her hands. Just as calmly as he had come in, he backed out of the room, his pistol held in his right hand and the crown firmly grasped in his left. He ran out of the house, slamming the front door closed with a loud bang.

It appeared that while we were all engrossed in watching the contents coming out of the trunk, Gregorze had come in and observed the proceedings unnoticed from the hallway outside the living room.

Bill was most apologetic. "Please excuse the intrusion, Walli. Gregorze is my stepbrother. He's been quite disturbed ever since we heard the news of the discovery of our grandmother's belongings. This is a family matter and we will have to deal with it. You know we don't get to choose our family members." He tried to smile after his last remark.

Although I was relieved to see Bill unfazed, I was concerned that he, at his age, might suffer a heart attack from all the excitement. I comforted him by saying, "That's for sure, Bill, family is family. It's okay. Don't act too hastily. Gregorze looks distressed at the moment, and might repent his action later, after cooling off." I asked Jane and

Bill and the others if they were all right, and whether there was anything I could do. I asked a few times if they were feeling okay after what had just transpired.

There were nods all around and, thankfully, everyone said they were well. I hugged Alexandra and asked how she was. She nodded, indicating she was all right. I thought about advising them to call the police, but I didn't wish to bring any more stress on the older family members than they had already gone through that evening. Bill again emphasized that it was a family matter and they would prefer to deal with it privately.

Bill asked the butler and the maids to pour us some more wine and drinks, obviously attempting to retrieve the situation. We retired to our seats and tried to put the incident out of our minds. We admired some of the other items from the trunk, and engaged in small talk. The children resumed passing around the various objects that had intrigued them.

Bill asked me to tell him all about my medical practice, and Jane quizzed Alexandra about her life in the United States and whether she was happier there, having left Toronto.

Nevertheless, I was struck by Jane and Bill's calmness after the strange turn of events.

I was glancing through a journal when I felt a tug at my sleeve. I looked up to see a little girl, barely ten, standing by my chair. From her blonde hair and features, she could have been a reincarnated Margaret.

"Are you really a doctor?"

"Now, Christina, don't bother Doctor Walli," a lady seated nearby said, likely her mother.

"It's okay," I said to the mother, and holding the little girl by the shoulders, replied, "Yes, I am. And what do you want to be when you grow up, Christina?"

"A doctor, 'cause I already have a medical box."

"A medical box. I'd like to see it. Can you show it to me?"

While Christina ran upstairs to get the box, Bill explained, "It's only a toy medical box. It belonged to Grandmother. She got it as a gift when she was about Christina's age."

"Really! And it has been in the family since then?"

Bill nodded and while we engaged in other talk, Christina returned, carrying a small wooden box in both her tiny hands. Although it did look worn out and had a few scratches, it was still in one piece and appeared to be made from the same strong oak wood as the sea chest. She opened it and showed me the toy medical instruments.

I was still examining the contents of the toy box when the telephone rang. Jane answered it. She listened to the caller for a minute, then hurriedly put the receiver down.

She turned towards Bill and said in a hysterical voice, "It was Karolina. Gregorze has some more mischief in mind, and is on his way back here. He now also wants to get Margaret's journals. He believes he can sell them and make a lot of money."

Bill said in a gruff voice, "That will be over my dead body. I will not have my grandmother's good name splashed in those tabloids all over North America, Europe and God knows where else."

But Jane was perplexed and, wringing her hands, said, "Well, what are we to do, unless—"

Bill asked, "Unless what?"

Jane said, "Unless we can ask Walli and Alexandra to take them away." She then turned to me and asked, "Look, Walli, you have kept Margaret's things safe and sound all this while, could you please keep these journals a bit longer, till we have decided what to do with them?" Her voice had a pleading quality.

There was not much time to think, for we knew Gregorze was on his way, with that revolver. I looked inquiringly at Alexandra and she nodded her quick agreement. I replied, "Of course we will take them back to the States. It's unlikely Gregorze will be able to get in there, or track us down. But if he does, we'll have the FBI after him."

Jane sounded relieved. "Oh, thank you, so much. I don't want to rush you, but look, Gregorze lives only about fifteen minutes away and is already on his way over here."

I said hastily, "Well, that gives us just enough time to get out of town and make a dash for the US border." I gulped down my drink and snatched up the three volumes of Doctor Margaret's journal. We bid a hasty farewell to the Wallaces scattered about the room. Bill shook my hand and, in a touching gesture, gave me a tight hug. We promised to be in touch, to discuss our future course of action.

Alexandra and I rushed to our car and drove off quickly down the Wallace Estate's driveway. In my haste, I might have stepped on the gas a bit too hard. The wheels spun and kicked up a cloud of dust as we rounded a curve. We reached the main road and turned in a southerly direction, towards Niagara Falls and the border. As we sped along, I saw a large, grey American car parked by the side of the road. Its hood was up and two tall, muscular men, one black and the other white, dressed in blue suits and hats, stood with their arms folded, leaning against the side of the car. They looked the other way when we passed them by. They don't look like farmers at all, more like gangsters we had seen in movies, I thought.

I had just rounded a bend in the road when, looking into the rear-view mirror, I noticed a dark blue Chevrolet pick-up truck coming up behind us at high speed. Even in the mirror, I could recognise the driver. It was a blond, crew-cut-haired, heavyset man. It was Gregorze.

Chapter Seven

Escape from Niagara

1967, June: Niagara Escarpment, Ontario, Canada
AT THE CROSSROADS, the sign read *Niagara Falls – 38 Miles*, and below it an arrow pointed to the road to the left. Without slowing the car, I rounded the left corner. The movement shoved us momentarily to our right side while the tyres screeched, as if warning of an impending calamity. Glancing into the rear-view mirror, I noticed the blue pick-up truck also turning and coming speedily towards us. Pressing the accelerator pedal down did not help. Our older model station wagon's big, eight-cylinder engine couldn't respond fast enough.

"Looks like he's definitely after us," I muttered to Alexandra, trying to keep the car on the winding road and expecting a bullet to come smashing through the back window at any moment.

"Walli, watch out. The madman's going to ram us!" Alexandra shouted, as she twisted in her seat and looked back.

The truck caught up to us. Slowing down to match our speed, its front bumper lightly thumped the back chrome-plated buffer of our Buick. The pick-up then speeded up and shoved our car forward. It felt like someone pushing with their hands on our hips. Our car lurched forward, jolting us back. This gentle nudging of our car, instead of the gunshots, puzzled me. It seemed the driver was trying to get our attention, rather than ram us. The bastard is clever—he wants us alive, I thought.

"I think he wants us to stop," Alexandra remarked, still look backward.

Gregorze blew his vehicle's horn. I glanced up in the rear-view mirror and saw him repeatedly pointing with one finger, motioning to the side of the road. The signal a trooper might make when ordering a car to stop.

"Not on your life," I mumbled, and slammed my foot hard on the accelerator pedal, pushing it all the way to the footboard. With a loud roar, as if by magic, the Buick's power of some 400 horses finally came alive. With tyres squealing like a crescendo, the car shot forward. We sped away. The truck slowly diminished to a small blue blob in the rear-view mirror.

"Let's take the side roads to Niagara Falls," Alexandra suggested, looking relieved to see the pick-up had disappeared from our view.

"Do you still remember the way?"

"Of course. Papa used to take us hiking here."

"Okay. Do warn me of the turns early, though. I don't want the car sliding into the farmers' fields."

Alexandra gave me the directions to the Falls while I drove, imagining myself a rally car driver. The car screamed at every swerve in the small roads that crisscrossed the Niagara Escarpment. Those deserted country lanes wove through picturesque orchards, vineyards and cornfields. As the rows of grapevines and fruit trees whizzed by, the wheels of the car barely missed falling into the drainage ditches. Making several right and left turns, zigzagging across the Niagara Peninsula, we managed to shake off the blue pick-up. Just to be sure, I kept checking down the side-roads and in the rear-view mirror, to reassure myself Gregorze had not somehow caught up with us to reappear at the next intersection, like a monster out of the woods in a bad movie.

I allowed myself a sigh of relief when I did not see a blue dot for some time. We sped along those eighteenth-century paths, which the Loyalists and the underground slave-railway runaways likely used in the bygone days, in their escape to Canada. Having foiled our pursuer, I imagined those fugitives might have experienced a similar sense of relief. However, the difference was that we were travelling in the opposite direction.

Suddenly, the memory of another blue car I had spotted in a different rear-view mirror, some years ago in Delhi, jolted my mind from the calm.

"Goodness, I just remembered something," I said.

"Oh, what's that?" Alexandra, who was also trying to relax, gave me a perplexed look.

I slowed down and parked the station wagon at the side of the road. She listened patiently while I told her about the sunburned blond man in the blue Volga, who had followed me around in Delhi, and Katya's visit to my apartment with the offer of money in return for my assistance. I informed her that I discussed it with Doctor Rao, and both of us believed the Russians were after the trunk. Hence, we had contrived to foil their efforts. However, I took care not to mention the incident of my skirmish with the two Russians in the parking lot of Humayun's Tomb. I did acknowledge that the promised prize money was never paid to me.

I finished the long narrative by saying, "It would appear the Soviets have either realised, or were informed, that the sea chest I gave them wasn't the real one. I suspect this Greg fellow is in league with them."

Alexandra sat silently for a moment and then broke into near hysterics. She asked questions in quick succession, wanting to know: why had I not mentioned it earlier, how and when it had happened, who was this Katya, and how did she come to know about the sea chest and me? Why did I choose to help her, and was I so naive to believe the Russians would actually pay me?

I tried to calm her down and made up reasons for not informing her, such as: I had not wanted to upset her unnecessarily, or that since the trailing occurred sporadically, it had not bothered me, or since we made that deal with Katya, and having given them a duplicate sea chest, they seemed to be satisfied, as neither Doctor Rao nor I heard back from Katya. I was not worried about the compensation. Just getting them off our backs was good enough for me. We believed it was the end of that incident. "Come to think of it, I'd forgotten all about it until just now," I concluded, attempting to placate her.

After some deep thoughts, Alexandra regained her composure, a little, and asked, "All right, at first you were not sure about the Soviet's surveillance. But did you at least report it to the police?"

"No. As there wasn't much evidence, I didn't wish to sound paranoid. Look, I did mention it to Doctor Rao."

"Yes. At first, he said it was nothing and he thought you were probably imagining it from reading too many Cold War spy novels. Right?"

"Exactly."

"But then, later, when you told him of Katya's visit, he informed you that she'd called on him as well. Did he agree readily to your plan to hand them a bogus trunk?"

"Yes. Doctor Rao thought it was a brilliant scheme to thwart them."

"Hmm … But why didn't he tell you about the Soviets requesting the trunk earlier?"

"I don't know. He didn't want to alarm me, I suppose. He did say to keep it a secret, for there might be some what he called 'bounty hunters' after the sea chest." I replied to her questions in the best way I could.

"Do you think he's been frank with you?"

"Ye … yes," I mumbled, although Alexandra's questioning did raise some alarm bells in my mind. I remembered that at Grandmother's party, Mrs. Rao told me she was related to Nana Sahib —a rebel leader during the 1857 Uprising—and she knew about the Rani's missing crown. It seemed strange that Doctor Rao had not mentioned this to me. Also, something else about his family I had discovered on the trip to Jhansi with Mila. Not wanting to complicate the discussion with Alexandra, I did not bring up my fears, or Mila, just then.

Alexandra still did not look satisfied with my answers. "I'd say Doctor Rao is keeping something from you," she said. After another silent moment, she asked, "Anyhow, tell me, are you sure the Russian beauty, Katya, didn't follow you around?"

"Am I on the witness-stand, madam lawyer?" I turned to see her face.

She was smiling and looked her cheery self once more. We both burst out laughing. She appeared so lovely, especially when she threw her head back and chortled. I reached across and kissed her soft lips.

Having recovered her composure, she asked, "No, no. I mean that car-trailing, did it continue after the Soviets picked up the fake trunk?"

"No, not that I'm aware of. Of course, I saw Katya a few times in the Intercontinental Hotel lobby. We just exchanged pleasantries, and that was all. The real trunk had been shipped and I left Delhi shortly thereafter."

"Did she say anything about the sea chest you had given her?"

"No. Not a word, except for a knowing smile and a nod. Actually,

I'm puzzled. I had been expecting much more of a reaction after our sting on them."

"One thing puzzles me, darling. If you didn't want the money, why did you go though the pretence of appearing to help the Soviets?"

I thought for a moment and wondered how best to answer her important question. "I'm not certain, dear. Although, I hadn't made that decision lightly, and agonised over it for some time, I still cannot resolve why I did it. I'm aware of the rumours that the Russians let the Indian people down in 1857. Hence, their wanting this trunk from that period sounded very suspicious to me. It seems that a strange force compelled me to act and outwit their effort. Although I'm glad we managed to get Margaret's trunk to her relatives, I'm sorry I failed in my endeavour to thwart the Soviets. But you know what, it doesn't make sense to me. They wanted the trunk for the Rani's crown, which they now have. So why are they following us?"

Alexandra squeezed my arm. "You have nothing to be sorry about, dear. You did your best. But their chasing us now makes sense to me."

"Really. Like how?" I marvelled at her legal mind for having figured out this riddle in a moment.

"We're getting their reaction to your Delhi troubles now. I'm certain they made sure the real coffer was delivered safely to the Wallaces, and now want something from inside it that we have."

"You mean these old journals?" My thumb jerked, almost involuntarily, towards the worn-out ledgers lying on the back seat. "What could be so important in there they want so badly?"

"Beats me. But I'd say the KGB agents will be waiting for us at the foot of the Niagara Rainbow Bridge to USA."

"You're probably right, darling, as always. Perhaps we'd better turn around. Shall we go to Toronto to see your parents, as we'd planned?" I suggested.

"Yes, why don't we? That should throw those hounds off our trail."

I made a quick three-point turn and headed the car back towards Grimsby and Toronto.

Speeding along on the farm lanes, I noticed a small blue-and-white painted road sign nearly hidden among the branches of some cherry trees. Its arrow pointed rightwards, reading *QEW Toronto*. Braking hard, I made a sharp turn, the tyres just missing the curb, to swing the station wagon onto a bridge and down the curved ramp leading to the Queen Elizabeth Highway. The traffic was light and we sped over to the fast lane. I was glad to have found the entrance to this highway, which would take us straight into the bustling metropolis of Toronto. There, among the narrow streets, which always reminded me of my university days there, we could evade the prying eyes of whoever was trying to follow us and inhibit their attempt to steal whatever treasure they believed we carried.

"I'm glad we're on the Queenie, dear," Alexandra remarked, as our Buick now hummed along smoothly. She looked relieved. No doubt the tormenting experience of being rear-ended by that maniac, followed by our nerve-racking drive on the country roads to lose him, was stressful for both of us. Not to mention my revealing to her the incidents in which I foiled the Soviets in Delhi.

"Yes, dear, so am I. Thank God we've lost that madman and we can drive in peace," I replied.

"I'm still wondering, though. What *is* so important in those journals that he's willing to kill for?" Alexandra asked.

"God knows."

"Let me see what I can find." Alexandra reached over to the back seat and retrieved the journals. She inclined her seat to a comfortable position and, placing the ledgers in her lap, opened one of them.

"Oh my. What could this be?"

As we were driving along a straight stretch of the highway, I glanced over for a moment. A sheet of folded paper had dropped out of the ledger. Alexandra opened it and, holding it with both hands, turned it towards me. At first glance, it looked to be an old map of Central Asia from about Turkey to India. Nevertheless, it seemed peculiar; precisely why it looked odd did not seem obvious to me. I returned my eyes to the road.

"That's strange." Alexandra remarked.

"What?"

"The map is in Russian." she said.

"Really!" Then it dawned on me why the drawing looked unusual. I took a fleeting look. The writing on the sketch illustrated the names of the countries and other landmarks in the Russian script.

"Do you still remember your Russian?" I asked.

"*Nyet!* Well, just a bit. I can make out the names of these countries, like Afghanistanski for you-know-where. There are some notations in small print—I'm at a loss to figure out those."

"Goodness, could this be the map that Grandfather wrote about in his diary?"

"It might be. But how did it get in this ledger?"

"I can't imagine Margaret would have stolen it. Unless she spied for the British?" I speculated, remembering the incident, mentioned in my grandfather's diary, when the Russians captured her in Crimea on that accusation.

"If she was a spy, why didn't she give the map to the British?"

"Someone might have stopped her from passing it on," was my feeble guess.

"But why is that guy in the pick-up, presumably a Soviet agent, after these maps, and what is of such strategic significance in them after all these years?"

"There might be something in them of vital importance to their national security."

"I'll get Papa to read the map. I'm certain he'll be able to solve this riddle."

"Good idea. Looks like we have a lot of surprises for your Mamma and Papa when we get there." I pressed on the gas pedal a bit more, to speed the car towards Toronto.

The QEW highway runs along the shores of the expansive Lake Ontario, from Niagara Falls to Toronto, much like a welcoming mat for visitors from Canada's southerly neighbour. As it approaches the downtown area, the highway changes into a lofty overpass that sweeps across the city. Drivers, soaring along on the bridges, get a bird's-eye view of the many boats and pleasure craft plying the lake to the south. On the northerly verges of the highway stand tall skyscrapers, representing the business hub of the metropolis.

It was getting late and the setting sun's rays shimmered on the waters of the ocean-like lake. We exited from the elevated highway down to York Street, which led us into the heart of the city. Driving along the majestic oak and maple-tree-lined boulevards, past a charming mixture of Victorian and Edwardian brick homes with eye-catching front gardens, we reached Rosedale, the city's affluent residential district.

I turned into the driveway of the two-storey Victorian-style home of my in-laws. We parked on the driveway beside a bed of roses. The colourful flower garden and green front lawn, with the commanding oak trees scattered around the property, gave the residence a tranquil atmosphere. Getting out of the car, the first thing I did was rush to the back of the vehicle to examine the wreckage I was expecting from the earlier thumping. However, since the blue pickup had nudged us lightly, there was very little damage from the impact. Just a couple of dents and some scratches on the chrome bumper were visible. It looked as if an expert, such as a trained policeman had done the jolting. Who was that madman?

"It doesn't look too bad, does it?" Alexandra remarked, having walked to the back of the car as well.

"It could have been much worse," I whispered as we walked up to the front door, our suitcases in hand.

"Hello, Mamma." Alexandra hugged her mother, standing on the porch.

"Olenka, dear. My, this is a pleasant surprise. We weren't expecting you till tomorrow." Mrs. Elizabeth Petrovich said. Then, smiling at me, she extended her right arm. "Hello, Wallidad. How good to see you." She embraced both Alexandra and me together.

"Hi, Mamma." I hugged and kissed her in the customary European way, three times on the cheeks. Alexandra's mother looked her usual elegant self, attired in a casual, printed summer dress and a beige cardigan. Her blonde hair, deep blue eyes and radiant features made her look much younger than her mid-fifties.

"Well, look who's here already." Alexandra's father, Pieter Petrovich, came into the hallway, newspaper in hand. His six-foot-tall, lean frame towered above the three of us. Although dressed informally in a blue shirt and slacks, his flowing blond hair and handlebar moustache made him seem more like a Russian cavalry officer than the University of Toronto history professor he was.

We had not seen them for a while, so there was much hugging, kissing and inquiring after each other's health. I explained the reason for our early arrival simply as having concluded our visit to Grimsby sooner than expected, and inquired, "I trust we're not inconveniencing you in any way? It's Saturday evening and you might have other plans?"

"No, no. Good heavens, you're welcome here any time. We don't have any other engagement. Your bedroom is ready. Why don't you take your suitcases right up there," Mamma said, motioning towards the stairs.

"I'll help you with the luggage." Pieter took hold of one of the suitcases and led the way up the curved staircase.

"Would you like tea or coffee?" Alexandra's mother inquired after us.

"I think we'll need some coffee, Mamma, to fortify our nerves," Alexandra responded, looking questioningly at me.

I nodded.

"Yes, I'm sure it must have been an unsettling visit to those folks in Grimsby. You will have to tell us all about it," Mamma said as we walked up the stairs.

"We'll probably have something stronger." Pieter winked at me as he opened the door to the bedroom.

"Of course, Pieter. We'll be down shortly," I replied, winking back.

I threw the suitcases onto the bed. We unpacked, changed and freshened up in the attached washroom.

Down in the living room, Pieter had the vodka already poured and waiting in crystal glasses. On a silver platter, he presented the drinks to us.

"To your health," I said, raising the glass.

"And to your safe arrival," Pieter rejoined and knocked back the drink in one swig. The rest of us took a small sip of the strong vodka.

"How did your meeting with the Wallaces go?" Pieter asked, smoothing out his moustache, as we settled into the comfortable sofa and chairs.

"Not too badly," I began casually. I briefed them on the family gathering at the Wallaces, about their farming estate, and mentioned as much information as we were given, so far, about their family connection to Doctor Margaret. They listened with interest to my narrative.

"Did you stay for the opening of the trunk?" Mamma asked, looking at Alexandra while she poured coffee from a silver coffee pot.

"Yes. Although we offered to leave, they wouldn't hear of it. Mamma, you won't believe what lovely silk clothing, ivory carvings and other beautiful ornaments came out of the chest."

"Working for that Rani, shouldn't she have been well rewarded?"

"Yes, it looks like she was," Alexandra agreed. "And you should have seen the most gorgeous crown, full of gold and jewels, they found in the trunk."

"Really, a crown. Was it a gift to the doctor by the Rani?" Mamma asked, leaning forward on the sofa.

I explained quickly what had transpired. We were not sure to whom the crown was given, but a grandson took it away at gunpoint. However, the Wallaces did not wish to call the police as they thought it was a family matter and wanted to resolve it between themselves.

"Except that we were almost knocked off the road by that same Russian madman!" Alexandra said in a raised voice.

"What!" Mamma exclaimed, putting a hand on her open mouth.

Pieter's jaw also dropped as he stared at us.

Alexandra was not shy in narrating the nerve-racking experience, in detail, to her parents. She also mentioned my encounter with the Soviet agents in Delhi.

"I'm so glad you two aren't hurt," Mamma said, appearing worried, and looked up and down at us. Seeing that we were all right, she turned towards Pieter and remarked, "Aren't the Russians all like that?"

Pieter smiled and cleared his throat. He also looked relieved on observing that we weren't harmed. "It does seem strange the Wallaces did not call the police. Hmm ... it would almost seem that Gregorze fellow is in league with the Soviets." he said, his brow furrowed, deep in thought.

"Oh, Pieter! You are too engrossed in the Cold War bit. Those poor souls had just received their long-lost grandmother's trunk and didn't wish to make it a newspaper headline. I think they were quite right in trying to settle this matter first, amicably, within the family," Mamma said, patting Pieter on the shoulder.

"But Walli, how about you? Would you like to report this Gregorze chap, to the police? Did you say he acted almost like a highway patrolman?" Pieter asked.

I looked at Alexandra, as if seeking a legal opinion.

"No, Papa. I don't think we need to involve the police," she said calmly. "No harm was done to us, and not much to our car either, strangely enough. On the other hand, we could end up with no end of legal hassles for bringing Margaret's trunk across the border. Not to mention that possible Soviet connection." She then turned to me and asked, "By the way, Walli, who do you think those two guys were? You know, the ones dressed in blue suits, standing beside that big grey sedan parked on the side of the road."

"I can't say. They didn't look like Soviet agents to me," I said.

Pieter asked, "Could they have been American, possibly the CIA? You know, blue suits and all."

"Yes. You may be right, Pieter. But why were they there? Unless —"

"All this talk of the KGB and CIA agents is beyond me," Mamma interjected, and defended our actions by saying, "I can't see what wrong you might have done, dears. After all, those were Margaret's possessions you brought back to her home."

I felt relieved on hearing their opinions and said, "Yes, I agree with Mamma and Olenka. Let's not get the police involved. It might also affect the Wallaces' family relationships. Why don't we leave it to them to sort it out among themselves?" I was happy to put this matter to rest, as I was in no mood for filling out lengthy forms and answering endless questions at the police station.

Pieter nodded. He refilled our glasses and asked, "Was there any more information about Margaret and the Count? Any papers found in the trunk?"

"No, not directly. If anything, it would be in Margaret's diaries. By the way, Pieter, we need your help in deciphering a map we found in one of them," I said, pointing to the ledger, which I had placed on the coffee table.

"Now, why don't I go and get dinner ready, while the two of you look through that notebook," Mamma said, getting up from her sofa. "Walli, dear, I was going to make some spaghetti with seafood, is that all right?"

"Yes, thank you, Mamma. You know that pasta marinara is my favourite dish," I replied with a broad smile.

"I'll give you a hand, Mamma." Alexandra followed her mother into the kitchen.

"This is the map we found." I spread out the drawing on the coffee table. Pieter put on his reading glasses and moved forward in his chair to examine it. I kept silent and sipped my coffee as he looked at it for some time. Finally, he removed his glasses, took another gulp of vodka, and looked at me with his blue eyes shining with amazement.

"This is unbelievable. Walli, this must be the original map of the Russian-planned invasion of India in 1857! I have heard and read much about it, but never saw this original document."

I took a sip of the vodka. "But, Pieter, is it genuine?"

"I believe so. Look, there's the unique seal of Tsar Alexander II. I have seen it before in other documents. Feel the texture of the map, it appears very authentic," he concluded, standing straight up and taking on his history professorial stand, as if lecturing to a class. "And if you want further proof, just look at this." He pointed to a red dot in one corner of the map, which had a handwritten scribble below it. "There it is, the signature of the Tsar."

The same two lines that my grandfather had written about in his diary were on the map, running from Persia to India. "What do you make of these two lines?"

"These are obviously the courses the military columns were to take. Ah! Here's the explanation. This line says," he pointed to one of the lines and peered down to read the Russian written in fine print, "'route of the main contingent', and this one says 'route of the diversionary force'."

We looked at each other silently for a while, in astonishment. I finally asked, "Pieter, do you believe they were really serious about invading India?"

"Judging by the details on this map, it seems much of the planning had been done, at the very least. This would indicate they were keen on capturing India and the warm water ports to the south seas."

"Yes, we know that was the dream of the Romanovs for quite some time. But did you hear specifically about this 1857 planned incursion?"

"Walli, as you know, I was born here in Canada, but my dear father, God bless his soul, spent a good part of his life in Russia. He definitely knew something, and used to discuss the plans with his friends."

"Did they talk about this map?"

"No, not a map specifically. However, what I recall, having overhead some of their conversations, is there were invasion plans. Except at that time, not many of his friends believed him. But I am happy to say this map now vindicates him."

"Why didn't his colleagues believe him?"

"You see, in 1856, after the defeat in Crimea, Tsar Alexander negotiated a peace treaty with Britain and France. That treaty imposed restrictions on Russian troop movements and naval activity through the Bosporus to the Mediterranean. Hence, we don't see any armada sailings indicated on this map."

"So these plans were made contrary to that peace treaty and would have been heavily safeguarded, much like, say, the Soviet space program?"

"Indeed they were, and looks like they still are."

"You mean the person who was chasing us this morning was actually after this map, not just Doctor Margaret's diaries or the crown."

"Exactly. I would think Premier Brezhnev would very much like to have this map destroyed, because if it were made public, it might add fuel to the rumours in some underground intellectual circles."

"What philosophical ramblings are those?"

"Walli, keep this to yourself. There are some murmurs from pretty reliable sources about a Soviet invasion of Afghanistan, and from what I have heard—"

"Have you discovered the whereabouts of that mysterious Count yet?" asked Mamma, entering the living room with a platter of *hors d'oeuvres*, followed by Alexandra, carrying serving plates and paper napkins. I made a mental note to ask Pieter later about the details of the alleged invasion of Afghanistan.

"No, Liz, not yet. So far we have just confirmed the authenticity of this map." He filled them in on what he had already told me, but said nothing about Afghanistan.

"Papa, did you hear anything from Uncle Stefan?" Alexandra asked, offering us the snacks.

"Ah yes," Pieter replied, biting into a pierogi, "Cousin Stefanovich did some research in the historical archives at the Leningrad library. In his last letter to me, he observed that Count Barinowsky's name did come up in a few documents—"

"And what about Doctor Margaret? Were there any references to her?" Alexandra asked, looking anxious.

"Sorry, Olenka. There was no mention of the good doctor. But I wonder, were there any women doctors in the 1850s?"

I knew the answer to that question. "Yes, Pieter, there were. The first woman doctor to graduate from a medical school in North America was Elizabeth Blackwell. That was in 1847."

"Hmm … how interesting. And which school did she qualify from?"

"I believe it was the Geneva Medical College in New York State"

"Ah. Jane Wallace mentioned it was a school close by to that one. The Philadelphia Women's College, which Margaret attended," Alexandra interjected.

"Oh, was she an American, then?" Mamma asked.

"Yes, she was born in New England, but married her Canadian cousin," Alexandra said.

"A Rebel who turned Loyalist." Pieter said with a chuckle.

"Yes, just like me," I joked, and there was a burst of laughter all around.

"So, *her* parents' home would still be in New Jersey, then?" Mamma asked.

"No. We understand she went to India with her parents. Her father was a Presbyterian Missionary," I replied, remembering what Bill had told me.

"And she met this Count Bari ... somebody there, remarried and moved on to Russia?" Mamma wanted to know.

"Yes, it would seem so. One of her Russian-born grandsons also lives in Grimsby," I said.

"That madman you mentioned?"

I nodded.

"Papa, what did Uncle Stefan say about Count Barinowsky?" Alexandra was still curious.

"According to Stefanovich, Barinowsky's name appears on some documents relating to General Ignatief. It seems that Count Barinowsky was on Ignatief's staff," Pieter informed us.

I had heard of a Count Ignatief, but couldn't remember in what connection. I asked, "Who was this Count?"

"Ignatief was the Tsar's agent who negotiated the famous treaty between the Russians and the Chinese, around 1850," Pieter said, "And you know, Walli, the picture is now getting a bit clearer."

"How so?"

"Cousin Stefan wrote that there is no official record of Count Ignatief having been to India," Pieter said, and added with a smile, "That's the official position. But we all know that India lies on the way from Russia to China."

Mamma, who was listening attentively, opined, "You never know, Ignatief could have secretly sent Count Bari-whatsit to India."

I remembered what Grandfather had written in his diary and exclaimed, "Yes, that's it. It was my grandfather who smuggled him from Persia into India."

While everyone looked at me in astonishment, I hastened to explain the connection between Grandfather and the Count.

Pieter still looked confused, though. Pressing the fingers of one hand with the other and counting out the items, he remarked, "Look, in the fall of 1856, the Persians attacked Afghanistan, most likely with Russian assistance, and took the city of Herat. In addition, by the spring of 1857, the Mutiny—or the Revolution, if you like—started in India. The British had their hands full quelling the rebellion. So why did the Russians not follow through with the invasion of India? This is still a great mystery, at least in my mind."

"Had they done so, it might have changed the map of the world. I could be speaking in Russian with you now." I joked, and they all laughed.

"This is all so confusing," Mamma said, rising from the sofa. "Dinner's ready, let's eat." She led us to the dining room. We followed with our heads down, each deep in thought.

Dinner was most delicious. Despite having feasted at the Wallaces earlier, I over-ate and drank more than I should have. It was the end of a long, unforgettable day. Both Alexandra and I were tired out, like two marathon runners. Drowsiness took hold of us by the ears, pulling down our heads and bodies. We took our leave from Mamma and Pieter and trudged upstairs to the comfortable feather bed. I do remember kissing Alexandra and saying, "Goodnight, dear," but not much else.

*****

I heard a swishing sound, like a petticoat dragging on the floor. I opened my eyes and turned my head towards the foot of the bed, where the sound seemed to have come from. I felt my skin prickle. I saw her standing, looking at me with her deep blue eyes.

It was the same image of Doctor Margaret I had seen in my dreams, in the hospital's storage room in India and in the portrait hanging in the foyer of Wallace Hall. However, this time she materialised more vividly. She wore a beige dress with frills on the low neckline. Her golden, wavy hair flowed alongside her gorgeous, beaming face, past her ample bosom and almost down to her waist. Catching my eye, she smiled. I must have had a bewildered look.

Her melodious voice sang in my head. "Thank you so much, Walli, for bringing my belongings home from India."

I tried to speak, but an invisible force held my tongue down. Although not saying a single word, it seemed we could communicate telepathically. I replied to her, in my thoughts, "You are very welcome, Madame. Was it you who arranged for me to bring your sea chest here?"

"Yes. How perceptive of you," she said with a smile.

"But why me?"

"I knew your grandfather. He was a very kind man. I owe him a *favour*. I want you to have his Greek pendant. Pray tell our story to the rest of the world."

"But I don't know the story. How can I narrate it?"

"My chronicle. It is all in my journals. Please read them."

"Yes, but I need your help." I threw the bed covers off my side of the bed and got out. She looked so real. I wanted to hold her hand. I took a step towards her. "Shall we go down to the library, where we can talk some more?" I asked.

"I have to go. Goodbye for now." She turned around and glided out of the room, flying through the open window.

"Please wait ... Tell me about my grandfather's *favour*," I cried silently after her. However, she was gone.

*****

The rustling of the window drapes in the wind woke me up. I threw the sheets off and, sitting up on the edge of the bed, ran my fingers through my hair. She had returned to me again, in another of those dreams. What's more, this time I was able to communicate with her. Cold shivers ran through my body. My limbs shook with fright.

"What's the matter, dear?" Alexandra said in a sleepy voice.

"Nothing. Go back to sleep, honey. I'm going down to get a drink."

I crept downstairs. With shaking hands, I poured myself a glass of red wine from the bottle at the bar and walked over to the living room. Slumping onto a sofa, I took a gulp. After a couple more sips, the wine had a calming effect and warmed me. The shivers gradually left my body, one by one.

I looked around, hoping the spirit of Doctor Margaret would reappear. I wanted to ask her if she knew the crown was now in the hands of her grandson. As for the Alexander's coin pendant, it had not been in the chest, although Grandfather had mentioned it in his diary and I remembered reading that he found the coin on the shores of the Arabian Sea while going to Persia to escort Count Barinowsky to

India. How did it come into her possession? Moreover, what was that *favour* he had done for her? Unfortunately, she did not return. There were far too many questions unanswered. The first volume of her journal still lay on the coffee table. I picked it up and opened it to the first page. An exquisite, neatly handwritten script in the Victorian style glimmered at me. The title page read:

My Life in America
by
Margaret Wallace

The writing looked familiar, as if I had read it before. I realised it was the same chronicle she had asked me to read in Delhi. It seemed the dream had come alive. I skimmed through the pages I had already seen and proceeded to the next chapter.

Chapter Eight

On the Underground Railroad to Canada

1841, July: Elizabethville, New Jersey

IT WAS A SUN DRENCHED SUMMER'S DAY. School was out and I sat in the parlour, in my favourite spot on the window-ledge seat, cross-legged like an Arab, reading *Gulliver's Travels*. The sun's bright rays streamed down at me through the windowpanes, bathing me in Heaven-sent energy. I was truly lost in a dream world of Lilliputians and suchlike when I heard a horse whinny. Looking out of the window, I spotted the postman, dressed in his blue uniform with a cape and cap, dismounting and tethering his horse to our gatepost. Since Mamma was busy in the kitchen, I ran out of the front door, across the porch, down the front steps, and along the path to the front gate, where the postman stood.

I asked, out of breath, "Any letter for me, sir?"

"Hallo, young lady. Now, let's see." He thumbed through the stack of envelopes and replied, "No. Don't see any for you, missy. Were you expecting any?"

"No, not really," I replied, trying to hide my disappointment.

"Ah, but there's one here from Canada, most likely from your uncle. Your cousins might have put a letter in there for you," he said in a consolatory tone, handing me a stack of letters.

"Thank you, sir."

I ran back into the house, shouting, "Mamma, Mamma, the mail has arrived. There is a letter from Aunt Fiona."

"Hush, child. You don't have to let the whole neighbourhood

know. Put the letters on the table. Now, then, weren't you going to cut the vegetables for the soup?" Mamma asked, wiping her hands on the apron, looking at me with eyes that appeared perpetually tired.

"Yes, Mamma."

"Well, you better get on with it, then. Your papa will be home shortly from church, for his midday meal."

"Elizabeth, David … where are you?" She hurried off, looking for my sister and brother, likely to make sure they were not up to any mischief.

I brought out the vegetables from the larder and placed them alongside the cutting board on the kitchen table, across from where I had put the mail. As I cut the vegetables, I kept glancing at the envelope from Canada, for it had a large, bright red stamp with the newly crowned Queen Victoria's portrait on it. I wondered if there was a letter from Robert in there for me.

As I cut the carrots into neat little circles, my mind drifted to thoughts of Robert and the last time I had seen him. It was the previous Christmas, when they had all visited for the holidays, "to escape the Canadian cold," Uncle Will had joked.

*****

"Too bad you don't have as much snow here. We got lots," Cousin Robert said to me as we sat, bundled up, on the swing-couch on our porch that cold December morning. Although he was only about a year older than me, he was much taller, and I had to look up to speak to him. How handsome he had looked, in his red-and-white-checked woollen jacket and a knitted cap snuggled over his blond hair.

"Why's that? What can you do with snow?" I couldn't imagine why anyone would want snow, of all things.

"Not *do*, silly—*play* in it."

"Play in the snow? You mean, like make a snowman?" I had made only a few of them, for we did not get much snow in our town.

"No. Not making a snowman. That's for girls to do. I prefer to ski."

"Ski? What's that?" I must admit he had me stumped. Although I had heard of skiing, I did not have a clue what that activity was all about.

"Well, it's like this, you see. You buckle two long wooden skis, which look like sleigh runners to your feet, hold poles in your hands, and you slide down the mountain." He got up to show me the ski position. He bent his torso, dipped his knees at an angle, and stuck out his bottom. His arms were extended forward, as if holding two imaginary poles.

He looked so ridiculous, like someone going to the toilet in the bush. I giggled.

"What's so funny?"

"You look so silly, crouching like that."

"No, I do not. You are so *stupid*," he retorted loudly and strutted to the house, like a soldier, stomping his feet on the porch's wooden boards. Entering the house, he slammed the front door.

My, what a temper. I simply returned to reading my picture book. Tucking one leg up on the swing-couch, I pushed at the floor with the other, gently rocking myself as I read. Come to think of it, I believe that was our very first quarrel.

*****

"There, that's a good job." Mamma's voice brought me back to the task at hand. She squeezed my shoulder, delighted at the sight of the neatly cut pile of vegetables all in perfect circles, squares and triangles; done just the way she preferred.

"This was a most delicious soup," Papa said, spooning the last of the soup from the bowl.

"Aye. Margaret helped to cut the veggies. She has a steady hand, our girl." Mamma smiled, looking at me. "Did you like the soup?" she asked Elizabeth and David, seated across the dining table from me. They simply nodded.

"It is good of you to help your mother, Margaret. Soon enough you'll be cooking the whole meal."

"Thank you, Papa, but I want to do more than cook. I want to be a doctor and go to foreign lands."

"We shall see," he said quietly, perhaps not wanting to start a discussion on that subject yet again. He wiped his lips with a napkin and, turning to Mamma, asked, "The children said there's a letter from Canada?"

"Indeed, Husband, there's one from Fiona. Margaret, would you be so kind as to fetch it from the kitchen table, dear?"

"Yes, Mamma." I jumped out of the chair and, running over, brought the two letters out of the Canadian-stamped envelope. I gave one to Papa and kept the other in my hand.

Papa quickly read through the letter and smiled.

"So, we are invited for a visit?" he said, looking inquiringly at Mamma, as if asking a hidden question that I did not comprehend.

Mamma nodded in agreement. "It's wee Robbie's birthday," Mamma said, looking at us.

"Well, let's see. Children, you would *not* like to take the long trip to Canada, would you?" Papa asked in his teasing voice.

Did we ever. It was like asking a fish living in an aquarium if she wanted to swim in the river. The three of us jumped off the chairs and, shouting, "Nooo ... we want to go. Yaaaay...", ran over and hugged Papa.

We were intoxicated with excitement at the thought of journeying to the Niagara region of Canada West where Papa's cousins, from his grandfather's side, lived on a large farming estate. It was situated on the brow of an escarpment overlooking a lake, in the town of Grimsby. We had heard so much about the beauty of the location and their lush orchards. Mamma said it was not too far from Niagara Falls, which we had been dreaming of seeing for the longest time.

I put my arms around Papa's neck from behind and inadvertently looked over his shoulder at the letter he held in his hand. I read something I did not quite comprehend.

"Papa, what does this mean—'do not forget to bring the packages'?" I asked, pointing to a line in the letter.

Papa quickly moved the letter aside to hide it from my view. He glanced curiously at Mamma, as if to ask whether I should be told about the *packages*. She pursed her lips.

"Oh, it's nothing, Puppet. Your aunt wants me to bring a few things over in a package. That's all," Mamma replied casually.

However, I felt there had to be more to it.

"Ah, I see there is one more letter that is being kept secret from us." Papa exclaimed in mock enthusiasm, looking at the other one in my hand. But more, I felt, to change the topic.

"She got a letter from Cousin Robert," Elizabeth said, in her solemn nine-year-old's voice, no doubt taking delight, as always, in telling on me.

"Why don't you read your letter to us, dear? We know you love to read, don't you?" Mamma asked.

I did not want to read it, but upon further coaxing from Papa, I obliged and recited the following letter:

Dear Cousin Margaret,
My birthday is on August sixteenth and I would like you very much to come to the party. Sorry I could not come for your birthday, as I was in school. When you come, can you bring your medical box? My pony's leg got hurt and I want to make it better. Do you have any medicine for it and have you got any bandages?
Please give my best regards to Aunty Joan and Uncle Jim and Cousins Elizabeth and David too.
Your loving cousin,
Robert
PS : Too bad there is no snow now 'cause it is summer and we cannot go skiing.
I am sorry for calling you stupid.

"Why, isn't it grand of him to apologize—don't you think so, Margaret? Will you write to him to tell him he's forgiven?" Mamma asked.

Although it looked to me as if someone had made him write that last sentence, I nodded.

Elizabeth said in her squeaky voice, "That's not all. She's hiding something from us. There are a couple of crosses at the bottom."

"No. That's all," I replied, while Papa playfully tried to grab me and snatch the letter away from my hand. I wriggled out of his reach and ran upstairs to my room, giggling. David and Elizabeth followed. I stood in a corner of the room and, hiding the letter from them, counted the "x"s again. There were three kisses marked by Robert, right beside his name.

"Goodbye, children." That was Papa calling out as he prepared to return to work. I rushed from my room to say goodbye to him. However, I stopped at the top of the stairs when I heard him speaking to Mamma. I thought he might be saying something about Robert's letter.

"After the Abolitionists' Committee meeting, I'll go over to John's workshop and give him the good news from Canada," Papa said.

"Yes, indeed. We do need to get Harriet away. I'm afraid she might get sick, cooped up like that. The poor creature," Mamma said, quietly.

"Quite so, especially now that her parents are also here."

"Oh, is that so? And where are they hiding?"

"They are at Tom's farm, most likely in the barn. Brother McHowat is visiting from Wilmington, and brought me the personal message from Tom."

"Oh, good. I am sure they will be safe there in his barn's underground cellar."

I did not get a chance to go down the stairs, for Papa put on his black coat and top hat and left the house. I returned to my room, where David and Elizabeth were playing with some toys. Standing by the window and gazing out at the birds flying around merrily without a care in the world, it seemed to me how wonderful it must feel to be free and do as one pleases.

Papa and Mamma's conversation came back to my mind. The mention of my favourite uncle, Tom, the youngest of Papa's brothers, intrigued me. The pieces of the puzzle that had juggled in my head for the past few days began to fit together. What I had figured out, so far, was that the runaway slave girl's name was Harriet, and her parents had also arrived here, most likely from a plantation in one of the southern states, and were hiding in Uncle Tom's farm near Wilmington. What was to become of them? What my then feeble eleven-year-old brain could not foresee were the events that would unfold during our journey to Canada.

*****

"It's all settled," Papa announced after dinner that night. "I spoke with John this afternoon. We leave for Canada in a fortnight."

"That's good. It will give me some time to prepare for the journey," Mamma said, likely going over in her head the many things she would have to do. "I'll send a reply right away to Fiona and Will, accepting their kind invitation."

"Would Uncle Tom and Aunt Mary be coming with us?" I asked with excitement.

"Yes, I have already sent a verbal message back with Reverend McHowat. He will deliver it personally to Tom. They must have finished planting their fields by now, and will be able to join us."

"That's wonderful. How are we going to travel, Jim?" Mamma asked.

"I have asked Tom to bring his farm wagon. John and his family will travel in their carriage, and we shall have ours."

"Can I go in Uncle John's carriage, Mamma? It is so much nicer than ours," Elizabeth asked. Her request did not surprise me, as I knew she loved her comforts, no matter where she ventured.

"I wanna go in Uncle John's carriage too, and play with Jonathan," David shouted.

"Hush, children. We know your uncle's carriage is newer and bigger than ours, but you can't all pile in there like chickens in a coop. What will your aunt think?" Mamma gave us a stern look.

"Our carriage might be old and the seats worn and loose, but we all have to make do with what the good Lord has given us," Papa said in his solemn voice.

Everyone looked delighted as we rushed around getting ready for the journey, making sure to do those little things one usually forgets when in a hurry. Just the thought of a holiday in Canada sent shivers of delight through my veins, not to mention the idea of soon meeting Cousin Robert again. I packed the toy medical box, the very first item to go into the travel chest that Mamma said I was to share with Elizabeth and David. But I deliberately had not replied to Robert to accept his apology. Let him stew a while.

*****

It was the day before we were to leave for Canada. I glimpsed, from the parlour window, Uncle Tom and Aunt Mary driving their wagon up the road towards our house. "Uncle Tom's here," I shouted and ran out of the house to meet them. Elizabeth and David followed close behind.

No sooner had their covered wagon reach our front gate than the three of us raised such a cacophony of delighted screams that it brought some of our neighbours out onto their porches, wondering what on earth was the matter. I noticed a couple of them starting to walk towards our house to greet our visitors.

Papa rushed out of the house and, after a quick handshake with Uncle Tom, advised him to take the wagon to our back yard. Our carriage also stood there, next to a small barn we used for stabling our horses. I wondered why he hurried them away without even giving them a chance to get down from the wagon. We walked behind the wagon as Uncle Tom drove it down the side lane to the back of the house. Its bed was packed full of all kinds of bags of grain and other farming things, all covered up with a tarpaulin. I wondered if there was going to be room in there for our bags, chests and other items for the journey, as there wasn't nearly enough room in our own small carriage.

"Hallo, Margaret." Uncle Tom hugged me. He was a young man, just turned twenty-five and recently married. Aunt Mary, an attractive young woman, came from a Quaker farming family in Delaware. They had settled in Wilmington on a parcel of land that was a wedding present from her parents. She hugged me and was about to talk to me when Papa came over hurriedly and interrupted us.

"Tom, Mary, you had better go to the front of the house. The neighbours wish to meet you. We don't want them coming over here, now, do we? You go on, I'll unhitch the horses."

"Aye, thanks, Jim. I'll go and stave them off," Uncle Tom said, nodding. Picking up both David and Elizabeth in his arms, being a tall, strong man, he walked to the front of the house along with Aunt Mary.

I was about to follow them when I heard what I thought was a suppressed cough. It came from inside the wagon. I hung onto the wagon's tailgate and, on tiptoes, tried to peer inside. Although my head reached over the boards, barely, I could not see anyone there.

Papa, removing the horses' harnesses, saw me and said in a stern voice, "Margaret, don't loiter there. If you wish to make yourself useful, go and fetch water for the horses."

"Yes, Papa," I said meekly and, picking up the pail, walked towards the well.

We finished our dinner and sat in the parlour. Aunt Mary came to me and handed me a large package, wrapped in brown paper and tied with string and a pink bow. "Margaret, we're so sorry we couldn't be here for your birthday. However, here's a belated present for you. Happy birthday, dear."

I thanked her with a hug and a kiss. She asked me to open the parcel, which I had already started to do with excitement. I undid the string and unwrapped the covering paper, making sure not to tear it, for I knew Mamma would want to use it again. Something soft and woolly was inside. At first I thought it might be a dress or a cardigan but, to my astonishment, it was a lovely quilt. Unfolding it, I could not hold all of it up. About half of it fell onto the floor. But it seemed just the right size for a child's bed.

"My, would you look at these lovely patterns," Mamma remarked, holding up the quilt to examine the square designs stitched skilfully all over the comforter.

"Margaret will love those birds on it." Papa was the first to spot the bird patterns, each the same, made out of a silky fabric, but every row a different colour, giving the covering a delightful dramatic effect.

"Mary, we'd heard about your quilting skills, but this is simply wonderful. What would you call this pattern?" Mamma asked.

"There are several names for this one, but the one I like best is 'Birds in a Cage'."

"Aye. An appropriate name. Indeed, it looks as if there is a menagerie of birds in there. Must have taken you quite a while to make it," Mamma remarked.

"She's been saving those scraps of material for over a year." Uncle Tom joked.

"No, it didn't take too long. Mütter helped as well. She's a much better quilter than I will ever be."

"Thank you so much, Mary. Margaret will cherish it. Won't you, Puppet?" Mamma looked at me in anticipation. From the movement of her eyes, I knew she wanted me to show some more appreciation for the gift.

"Oh, I love it, Aunt Mary. I will always cherish it. Thank you, so much. Let me see how it looks on my bed." I ran with it in my arms, upstairs to my bedroom.

When I came down, I heard Papa and Uncle Tom discussing the travel arrangements for the journey to Canada, which we were to embark on the next day.

I did not see Mamma and Aunt Mary in the parlour, nor were they in the kitchen. Where could they have gone? Just then, the back door opened and they came into the house, Mamma carrying an empty basket. When I looked inquisitively at them, Mamma simply said, "We went out to the barn to pick up a few things." Yet there were no "things" in the basket she carried. All I saw in there were some empty soup bowls and platters with leftover chicken bones and bread. I had a pretty good idea whom Mamma had taken the food out to in the barn, but I dared not say anything.

"I've heard there's a new toll road along the Albany to Buffalo

Canal. It goes through Rochester, where we have a reliable station," Uncle Tom said.

"That sounds good. However, we'll have to take care, won't we? I'm sure the others know about that station."

"Indeed, but the road's good and it looks like a risk worth taking."

"Yes, the roads from here up to Albany are not bad either," Papa remarked, looking at a old map of northern states.

I was dying to ask Uncle Tom what he meant by the *station* in Rochester and the *risk*, but he continued conversing with Papa, and I did not wish to interrupt.

"Where shall we cross the Niagara River?" Uncle Tom asked.

"In his letter, Will suggested we take the ferry crossing at Fort Niagara. It's located right across the river from the Canadian Fort George. Being quite a bit downstream from Niagara Falls, it isn't so rough at that point," Papa said.

"Let's try that one. The last time I took the barge at the Detroit crossing, the river was so choppy, it pretty near drowned us."

"How long will the journey be, Husband?" Mamma asked.

"We should be able to make it in four to five days, don't you think, Tom?"

"Aye, perhaps five. Last time I did it in three days, but I was travelling on horseback, mind."

"I am looking forward to staying overnight at some of those lovely inns in New York State we've heard so much about," Aunt Mary remarked.

"John and family will be arriving early in the morning. Let's leave as soon as they get here," Mamma suggested.

"Is Harriet coming with them, Papa?" I blurted out.

There was a long silence in the room. Everyone stared at me. Finally, my sister Elizabeth asked, "Who's Harriet?"

Papa gave Mamma a questioning look, and she nodded. Papa explained. "Harriet is a Negro girl about Margaret's age, whom your Aunt and Uncle will be taking to Canada. But, as she has just arrived from Virginia, pray do not say a word about her to any of the neighbours. Is that understood, children?" He fixed us all with his most solemn look.

We all nodded. However, I was still curious about her and asked, "Uncle Tom, will her parents come with us to Canada?"

Uncle Tom's eyes widened in amazement, likely wondering how I knew about the other fugitives. "Yes, they will get to Canada, by and by. But again, Margaret, would you keep this information to yourself, dear?"

"Yes, Uncle Tom."

"Well!" Mamma exclaimed with a sigh of relief. "Now all this is settled, I dare say it's getting late. Children, pray get ready for bed. We have an early start tomorrow morning."

At Mamma's instruction, we trotted upstairs. Nevertheless, I was far too excited at the thought of going on holiday—and, what was more, having Harriet come with us—to even consider sleeping. Why was Uncle John helping her and her parents get to Canada? Sleep would take a long time to come and close my eyes.

The stars still shone brightly and the roosters crowed in the early morning darkness as our convoy of two carriages and a wagon left on a journey towards the Northern Star. Our carriage's oil lamps cast a glow onto the driver's bench seat, at the top, where Papa sat. He had promised I could join him alongside by and by. I heard him gently slap the reins on the horses' flanks to nudge them along. Our travel chests were secured behind him on the roof, there not being enough room in Uncle Tom's covered wagon for our coffers.

Although it was summer, a cool wind blew in. We rolled the leather flaps of the carriage's windows down and secured them into the metal hooks. Mamma sat on one seat with David beside her, sleeping with his head on her lap. Elizabeth and I sat on the opposite seat with a stack of books between us. I looked at Elizabeth and saw she was still sulking from having been awakened too early. I had my new birthday present quilt snugly around me, and put my head on the panel of the carriage to try and make sleep return.

I thought about the last time Papa had taken us on a trip. I believe it had been about a year before, to Jersey City. He had to go there for a meeting, no doubt related to the abolitionists' movement he was involved in. I had heard him many a times preach in his sermons, "No man has the right to enslave another human being …" On other occasions, I heard him announce to the congregation, "Jesus himself had a skin much darker than ours. Would the Lord have asked us to keep people in bondage, simply because of the colour of their skin?"

After the meeting, he had taken us across to Manhattan on the ferry. It was great fun, peeking into all the fancy window dressings of the grand shops on Bloomingdale Road. We just stood in the street and only looked, through the windows, at the lovely merchandise, not daring to go into the stores. Mamma, no sooner than she had spied the price tags, would pull us away by the arm, muttering, "Too dear. Too dear." We would then move on to the next shop, where the entire process would be repeated.

The steady clatter of the horses' hooves woke me from my slumber. The carriage was finally moving at a faster pace and it went around bends with ease, for we were likely on a stagecoach road. However, my mind was still fixed on the windows of those elegant Manhattan stores. Why could we not buy those exquisite things? Why were we so poor? But the rocking of the carriage lulled me back to sleep, before another part of my brain could send me answers to my questions.

*****

At a rest stop, I was pleased to meet Harriet when Uncle John cautiously brought her down from his carriage and introduced her to me. She was a pretty Negro girl with curly dark hair, done in two braids. She was very shy and hardly said anything. Poor thing, she looked so frightened. When we stopped for refreshments at taverns and spent the nights in inns, Aunt Flora simply said she was her servant girl, and folks gave her nary a second look. But where were her parents, I wondered? When would they join us, as Uncle Tom had mentioned?

On the fourth day of our journey, Papa announced we would be in Canada by late evening or the next day. Except for the usual aches and pains from travelling in a swaying carriage, we were enjoying the trip, marvelling at the passing countryside dotted with pine forests and streams. Even Elizabeth looked happy, staring out of the window. David, as usual, complained to Mamma that he was hungry.

"Are we going to stop for lunch, Husband?" Mamma asked with her head out of the carriage window, looking up at Papa.

Papa shouted his answer back: "Yes. We are getting close to Rochester. We'll stop at a tavern soon."

In a short while, the carriage slowed. I looked out of the window and saw what appeared to be a group of farmhouses and a main building up closer to the road, with a sign over it that read:

New Holland Tavern — Come Rest Ye Weary Travelers.

"Look, Sister," Elizabeth said, "there is a quilt just like yours hanging on the clothesline there." She pointed to a washing line outside one of the farm homes.

Both Mamma and I peered out of the window and, indeed, there was a quilt with a pattern of birds on it, although not exactly the same as mine. The birds in this one had their wings extended, as if flying away.

"Ah!" Mamma gasped, putting her hand to her mouth. Her eyes shone with excitement, almost in fear.

"What is it, Mamma?" I asked, puzzled at the expression on her face.

"Nothing, child," she replied, putting a hand on my shoulder. When the carriage came to a stop, she said, looking grimly at us, "Children, I have to go and talk to your papa first. I want you to stay in the carriage. In no way are you to come out until I ask you to. Is that clear?" Her voice had never been sterner.

We nodded, too confused to speak. She stepped down the carriage steps and walked quickly towards Papa, who was at the front, holding the horses by their bridle. Uncles John and Tom strolled over, looking calm and carefree, and joined them. I saw the group speaking in quiet whispers. There was nodding all round. I leaned out of the carriage window, and tried to listen to their conversation, but could not hear what they said.

Ultimately, I heard Uncle Tom say in a calm voice to Papa, "Jim, why don't you take the family into the Tavern? John, Mary and I will tend to the horses and join you all shortly."

The children and I followed Mamma and Papa to the Tavern's door. Before entering, I turned back and saw our carriages and the wagon being led towards a barn with a Dutch-style hip roof, where other horses were being watered and fed. Harriet had not come with us. This was not unusual, as she normally did not go into restaurants and preferred to sleep in the carriage. Aunt Flora usually took out something for her to eat.

Papa found an empty long table in a corner of the Tavern and we all slid onto the oak bench seats. A plump waitress wearing a white-and-blue-checked dress, a white apron and a bonnet came cheerfully over to serve us. I must have stared at her wooden shoes, a type I had not seen before, for she saw me looking at them and smiled. Papa, with some prompting from Mamma, ordered the food and only water to drink. Aunt Mary and my uncles joined us at the table shortly.

"Everything all right?" Papa asked.

"Aye, all's been taken care of, not to worry," Uncle Tom replied airily as he reached for a glass of water.

While we ate our lunch and the waitress came by to refill our water glasses, Aunt Mary said something to her in Dutch. The waitress simply nodded and pointed with her eyes at a table across the room from us. A group of rather rough-looking men sat there.

After a while, those men gulped down the last of their tankards of ale and stood up, wiping their lips with the backs of their hands. As they passed by our table, I noted they carried revolvers in holsters around their waists. They touched their hats and bowed a bit, as if to appear friendly and respectful for the ladies. One of them did stop by Papa, while the others continued and waited at the door.

"Howd'y, Reverend. Y'all out for a ride in the country?" he asked. Papa was wearing his white collar.

"Good day to you, sir. No, we're going up to Canada for a family get-together. Are you gentlemen from these parts?"

"Naw. We all come up from Virginia. Lookin' for our escaped property. Say, you wouldn't have seen any Negroes running in these woods here, by any chance?"

"Nay, sir. I didn't see any in the woods. Did you, John, Tom?" he asked, looking at my uncles.

They simply shook their heads, trying to muster up expressions of helpful regret.

The southerner appeared satisfied with these replies. He touched his hat once more and walked away to rejoin his group. Through the open door, I saw them mount their horses and ride away, no doubt in the direction they believed their runaway slaves might be scurrying.

"They're a rough-looking bunch, if you ask me," Aunt Flora remarked. The grown-ups all seemed to visibly relax.

"Just as I thought when I saw that quilt with the 'Flying Birds' pattern, hanging outside," Mamma said, looking at Aunt Mary as if asking for confirmation. She simply nodded her head.

We finished our meal and prepared to be on our way. While walking back to our vehicles, to our delight, Papa told us children to sit in Uncle John's carriage. We had been clamouring to do this all along the journey. Not only was that carriage new and more comfortable, but we also wanted to play with our cousins, Agnes and Jonathan. I got into that carriage, expecting to see Harriet there. When I did not see her, I asked Aunt Flora about her. She informed me that Harriet was now riding in the carriage with Mamma. That surprised me, but I could not talk to Aunt anymore as she climbed up on the driver's bench to sit with Uncle John.

Our journey continued along the picturesque Mohawk Valley, which was covered in deep woods of maple, oak, and evergreen trees on both sides of the road. I grew tired of playing chequers and leaned out of the window to look at our carriage, rolling on in front of us. It looked like we were approaching a fork in the road. Papa slowed down and I saw a signboard that read *Fort Niagara Ferry to Canada*, with an arrow pointing to the right fork.

But there they were: the four mean-looking southerners sat on horseback, blocking the road to Canada. Another rider stood ahead of them, but he did not appear to belong to that group, for he was dressed neatly in a dark coat and trousers. Papa stopped the carriage and that man rode up to us.

"Good day, Reverend," the well-dressed person said, lifting his bowler hat.

"Good day to you, sir. Whom do I have the pleasure of speaking with?" Papa asked.

The gentleman unbuttoned his coat and moved the lapel sideways to reveal a shining sheriff's badge pinned to his waistcoat. "I am, sir, the Deputy Sheriff of this county. These gentlemen here claim you might be transporting some of their slaves across to Canada."

Before Papa could reply, the man who had spoken with him in the Tavern also rode up. "Howd'y again, Reverend."

"Good to see you again, sir. Have you found your runaway slaves?"

"Naw. Not yet. But you aren't taking any to Canada, are you, by any chance?" Without waiting for a reply, he continued, "Would you mind if we looked through the carriages? The sheriff here says we have the right to check for our missing property." He said this with one hand on the butt of his revolver.

Papa looked at the Deputy Sheriff, who said, "It is only fair, sir, that these men be allowed to search for their property. There hasn't been time to get a search warrant, but one can be obtained, if you were to accompany us to the county jail."

Papa said, in a loud voice, "This is most improper, sir. Waiting for the warrant is only going to delay us. Search the vehicles if you must. But you will only find our women and children there."

The sheriff nodded to the ruffian, who waved to his partners. "Check out that wagon, especially under the tarp." They spurred their horses and cantered over to the wagon.

My heart skipped a beat. I thought Papa was hoping they would believe him and not look through our carriages. I gritted my teeth and could almost not bear to look. I was certain they would find Harriet. I also expected to see her parents dragged out from under the grain bags in the wagon.

While the sheriff looked on, the leader peered through the windows of Papa's carriage and, tipping his hat to Mamma, asked, "Any Negroes in there, ma'am?"

"Why, sir. Would you expect me to ride in the same carriage with their kind?" Mamma replied, sounding most indignant, very ladylike.

The oaf simply nodded. He then rode over to the next carriage, the one we were in, and stuck his face—which clearly hadn't seen a razor for at least a week—into the window. The other children and I shrank back in the seat, terrified at the sight of his unkempt face. Not to mention that he smelled most foul. David started to cry.

"Pray, sir, you are frightening the children." Aunt Flora exclaimed from the driver's bench above.

"Sorry, ma'am." Satisfied with his examination, he touched the brim of his hat and rode over to the wagon. His partners had taken off the tarpaulin. It lay on the side of the road, fluttering in the breeze. While Aunt Mary and Uncle Tom stood by, watching, they put the tailgate down and unloaded a pile of sacks of grain. Two of them climbed into the wagon and, moving the farming items about, peered into the corners of the flatbed. Finally, they scratched and shook their heads, as if in disbelief on not seeing anyone hidden there.

"Find anyone?" the leader asked.

"Ain't nobody in there," one of the searchers said.

The leader removed his hat and hit it on his thigh. "Dang! I was sure they had them hidden in the wagon."

"If you ask me, Bubba, I reckon these here clever folks left the Negroes back at the Tavern," one of the ruffians said.

"Darn it, Rhett. You do come up with some fancy ideas. Let's go get them there."

The slave-catchers galloped off in a cloud of dust towards the Tavern. The Deputy Sheriff thanked Papa for his cooperation and, with some quick words of apology, rode off behind the brutes.

Papa and Uncle John helped Uncle Tom reload the wagon with the items the searchers had strewn about the road. I did not hear them say a word between themselves, but I noted the broad smiles on their faces and figured they must have hidden the Negroes somewhere. In another house, perhaps? I felt relieved and presumed we would be turning back to pick them up. However, since we rolled along on the road towards Fort Niagara and the ferry, I assumed we were not taking the slaves to Canada

It was late afternoon when the northern shore of Niagara River loomed before us. We stood beside our carriages on the ferry barge, which inched its way towards the Canadian Fort George. Just as Uncle Will had written, the water was calm and the ferry swayed gently. The boat touched the dock. The captain advised us to remain onboard until we were cleared by the Canadian officials.

Three red-faced Canadian military men, sweating in the heat—no doubt from being dressed in the full, red-coated uniforms of the British army—jumped aboard the barge. Our two carriages and the wagon were the first in the queue. The officer approached Papa while the other two, a sergeant and a private, inspected the vehicles.

As this was the first time I had seen British uniformed soldiers, I put my hands over my mouth to hide my smile. So these were the lobster-backs I'd heard so much about.

"Good afternoon, Reverend. Your papers, please," the officer asked.

Papa handed him our baptismal certificates, which he had collected earlier.

The officer glanced at them. "Hmm ... all American citizens, eh? And the purpose of your visit to Canada, sir?"

"Aye, all Americans. Family visit, sir, to our cousins in the Town of Grimsby."

He looked at the sergeant, who nodded, indicating the "all clear" from their cursory inspection. The officer said, "Right. Please proceed. Welcome to Canada. Next." He waved us forward.

When we got ashore, Papa said to us, "All right, children, you can sit in your own carriage now. Let's drive off."

We clattered off on the road towards Fort George, which loomed in the distance. Uncles John and Tom followed behind us. I hung out of the window, admiring the countryside. It was a thrill to be in a different country, Canada, but things did not look all that different. It was as if I had expected the soil to be the British red in colour, but it was just the same greyish brown as on our side of the border. They are the same people as us, I thought. Our cousins. Then why did we fight a war with them?

My thoughts were jolted back to reality when I heard the same low cough as earlier, but this time from inside one of the boxes whose covers formed the seats we sat on. I looked inquiringly at Mamma, and then my eyes widened in understanding.

She leaned her head outside the window and shouted at Papa. "I think you'd better stop, Husband, lest the poor creatures suffocate."

"Aye, it should be safe to stop now."

I saw him pulling up on the reins, getting the horses to slow down and stop on the side of the road.

"Children, pray get down from the carriage," Mamma said, and we obeyed.

As we stood outside the carriage, Mamma lifted up the loose seat boards, and to my amazement, out came Harriet and what looked to be her mother from one box, and most likely her father from the other one.

As I write these memories, sitting in the Rani's palace overlooking the lovely Indian landscape—and it has been many years since I made that memorable journey—the sight of those slaves breathing their first breaths of freedom is etched in my mind, like a timeless picture carved on the walls of an ancient temple. The three Negroes literally threw themselves on the ground, kissing it, taking the soil in their mouths and clutching it in their hands. My uncles and their family came over, running. We stood in a tight circle, embracing each other, tears of happiness flowing down our cheeks. Finally, Papa went over and, holding Harriet and her parents by the hand, made them stand. He took out his Bible. Standing before us with the opened Bible in one hand and the other arm raised to the sky, he said, "Let us pray."

His prayer was brief, but one of the most poignant of my life. He thanked God for having delivered us in safety from the clutches of evil, in good health and spirits. He offered special thanks to the good Lord for having set free the three caged souls from the powers of tyranny, bigotry and persecution. He prayed for our well-being, and especially for those beginning a new life in a new land. He asked God for forgiveness for our sins and instructed us to repeat some verses after him from the Bible. While the others repeated the verses, I could not do so. Overcome with much emotion, I put my arms around Mamma's waist and sobbed my heart out, while she gently caressed my head.

We dried our tears and got back into the carriages. Harriet and her parents climbed on top of the grain sacks on Uncle Tom's wagon bed. There was no need for them to hide under the tarpaulin any longer. Uncle Tom took the lead, as he knew the way to an inn in a nearby village where we were to spend the night. Papa followed him with Uncle John not far behind us. I leaned out of the window and saw the happy faces of Harriet and her parents cuddling together in the back of the wagon. Then I heard their gentle voices rejoicing in what I knew to be the Negroes' favourite song, "Let My People Go":

Ohhh... gooo... down Moooses,
Way down into Egypt's land
Tell old Pharaohooo ...
Let my people gooo ...

I knew that song and picked up its lines. Soon Mamma and my siblings joined in. Uncle John and his family, in the carriage behind, must have heard us, for they started singing as well. Soon all in our convoy were reciting, as if in a church choir, *Go down Moses ... let my people go*, as we jangled along on the road towards a little village called Niagara-on-the-Lake and the inn where we were to spend the night.

Chapter Nine

The Engagement at the Forty Mile Creek
(Re-enactment)

1841, July: Grimsby, Canada West

IT WAS NEARLY NOON when we left the Niagara Inn, having slept in and enjoyed a late breakfast. The sunbeams sparkled on the waters of Lake Ontario, while our convoy, of the covered wagon and the two carriages, reached the road that snaked along the ridge of the Niagara Escarpment. It was thrilling to observe the whole region like a bird would. From the mountain brow, except for some areas of sharp, rocky drops, as if carved by a chisel, the land sloped gracefully down a valley to the lake. Sailing ships, paddle-wheel schooners and fishing boats bobbed in the mere, going about their businesses or taking goods and people to far-off shores. These and the surrounding forested hills made the scene look like something out of a painting. I would like to sketch it one day, or so I wished, for at that time I had no idea what was written in my life history scrolls up in Heaven.

We passed a sign painted on a blue board that read *TOWNSHIP of GRIMSBY (formerly The Forty)*. A few yards further along, we drove under a banner strung across the road. It said *Welcome to the Festival at the Forty.* Dates were written underneath in small letters, which I could not decipher.

"Look, Mamma, there's going to a festival here." I shook her shoulder and pointed to the hanging.

"Yes, Puppet. Don't you remember? Your Aunt Fiona mentioned it in her letter. They have one here every summer."

"What happens at the festival?" Elizabeth asked.

"From what I recall, there is going to be a circus, a funfair with up-and-down wheels, merry-go-rounds and other rides. Also, I believe there will be a re-enactment of a battle."

"I want to go on rides. Can I, Mamma?" Elizabeth begged.

"Aye, you may, dear," Mamma replied, running her hand over Elizabeth's blonde locks.

I asked, "What's a re-enactment, Mamma?"

"That's when grown-up men chase each other with toy guns in mock battle, behaving just like wee children." Mamma broke into a broad smile and we all giggled.

"I heard Uncle Tom say that in 1813, the American army captured Grimsby. Is that true, Mamma?" I asked, still curious about the *battle*.

"Yes, I believe they had most of this Niagara Peninsula in their hands."

"So, why did the American army leave?" I asked.

"I know there was a peace treaty signed to end the war, but I'm not certain on the details. Ask your Uncle Will, he—"

"How far to go, Mamma? I'm hungry," David interrupted, looking agitated.

Mamma leaned her head out of the window and, looking up at Papa, asked, "How much further to go, Husband? The children are getting peckish."

"Oh, not too far, Joan. Another couple o' miles, perhaps. Ah, there's Wallace Hall, yonder. See the chimneys peeking over the trees?"

We poked our heads out of the carriage windows, anxious to catch the first glimpse of the mansion we had heard so much about. Finally, through a break in the trees, the manor house appeared, looking grand in the distance. It was a two-storey red-brick structure, and I counted five windows on the second floor and several on the ground floor.

Passing some cultivated fields tended by farm workers, the carriages slowed down. Uncle Tom waved to a person on horseback who looked to be the foreman, directing the workforce. He seemed to recognise Uncle Tom and hollered back that he would go up to the house and announce our arrival to Major Wallace. As he galloped off, we proceeded along the road leading to the entrance into the estate.

"The house looks huge, Mamma. How many rooms do they have?" I asked.

"Fiona said they have ten bedrooms, child."

"Ten bedrooms. For just," I counted on my fingers, "Robert and his two sisters, that's three, his mother and father, that's five, and there are also his grandparents. That makes only seven people for ten bedrooms."

We tittered and Mamma smiled.

"Who cleans all those rooms?" Elizabeth asked, for I knew she hated doing housework.

"Your aunt has servants, dear."

"Servants. How many?"

"Oh, quite a number, I should think. There's the butler, the two footmen and the two maids, that's five, and the cook makes six, plus some more, I reckon."

"Why can't we have servants, Mamma?" Elizabeth asked in her squeaky voice.

"We don't need any. Our manse has only four bedrooms, and with our small family, I can manage quite well, thank you."

I noticed that as she spoke, she had a faraway look in her eyes, as if remembering the childhood home she had left behind in Scotland. I knew she was from an affluent family, and had a brother or two serving in the East India Company.

We reached the entrance and saw *Wallace Hall* inscribed on a board outside a low stone wall marking the property. Our carriage swung through the open gate, following Uncle Tom's wagon onto the long driveway. A kidney-shaped pond with white water lilies floating on it lay on one side. Red, yellow, blue and other colourful flowering shrubs stood along the paths leading up to the manor house. To one side stood a number of barns, stables and other log-cabin-type buildings.

"Windmill," David said, pointing to the circular brick structure attached to one side of the house. He had probably seen a similar construction in one of his picture books.

"It's not a windmill, silly—it's called a turret. There are rooms inside. People live there," I corrected him.

"But why do they have three chimneys?" Elizabeth asked.

"Because they have a number of fireplaces," Mamma informed her, "in the parlour, the dining room and some in the bedrooms. One chimney is for the kitchen, I suppose."

I looked out of the carriage window, enjoying the surroundings, with my elbows resting on the ledge and my face in my palms. This looks like a fun place to spend one's summer holidays, I dreamt.

All the clatter from the horses' hooves and our vehicles, and the foreman we had met in the fields earlier, would have announced our arrival. Uncle Will and Aunt Fiona came out of the house onto the stone terrace. Behind them were Robert and his sisters, Heather and Kirsten. Their servants followed and stood in a line on one side.

"Ah! There you are, Cousin Jim. We're so glad you all arrived safely," Uncle Will said, shaking Papa's hand as soon as he alighted from the driver's seat. "Trust the journey was not too unpleasant?"

"Thank you, Cousin Will. The trip was agreeable enough, except for one incident. We needn't go into that just now. We're all here safe and sound, and that's all that matters."

"All's well. I'm most relieved. I see they came through all right?" Uncle Will asked, nodding towards Harriet and her parents, who alighted from the wagon and walked towards us, behind Aunt Mary and Uncle Tom.

"Indeed. The good Lord looked after us all along the journey," Papa replied with a glance up towards Heaven.

The sun was starting to disappear behind the trees surrounding the estate and dusk was creeping in from the forest. Birds circled, looking for a nesting spot for the night. However, in the twilight there was a festive scene in front of that manor that July evening, as members of the four families greeted each other like the long-lost relations they were. There was much hand shaking, embracing and kissing.

Aunt Fiona came to me and, hugging me, exclaimed, "Oh, there's the pretty one." She held me with her hands on my shoulders and said, "Let me look at you. My, you look just as fresh as a daisy, not tired at all. Did you have a good trip, dear?"

I simply nodded, too embarrassed to speak.

Robert came to me and we hugged and kissed on the cheeks. He whispered in my ear, "Sorry for calling you stupid."

"It's all right, I didn't mind," I whispered back, enjoying his cuddle.

Aunt Fiona ushered Mamma and Aunts Flora and Mary into the house. Uncle Tom and Uncle John started to unload our travel chests from the carriages. I picked up a few things, like books, water bottles and such, to bring them inside. I looked for Elizabeth to ask her to help. However, she had already rushed inside the house.

"Oh, no. Pray leave the luggage. The footmen will take it up to your rooms." Uncle Will came towards us, waving his hand. "But I would like you to meet my overseer, Mr. Broadbent. He spotted your carriages earlier and has been waiting so patiently here while we reacquainted ourselves." Uncle Will motioned at Mr. Broadbent to come forward.

A short, stocky gentleman, wearing a tweed jacket and a farmer's straw hat, stepped forward and shook Papa's and Uncle John's hand. "A pleasure to meet you, sirs." Then, looking at Uncle Tom and shaking his hand, said, "Good to see you again, sir. How long has it been since you were last here? A couple of years, I'd say?"

"Aye, it's been a while. How've you been keeping, Mr. Broadbent?"

"Can't complain. Thank you, sir." He then looked at Harriet and her parents. "I see you've brought another family willin' to work for us?"

"Can you use them, Mr. Broadbent?" Uncle Will asked.

"For sure, sir. With the fruit-picking season upon us, we need all the help we can get."

Uncle Will addressed the Negro family. "Are you good folks willing to work for us? We will provide accommodation and the same fair wages paid the other workers."

"Yes, massa, we be more than happy to work fo' you. Thank you, massa. Thank you." Harriet's father, holding his cap in hand, dropped to his knees and sobbed loudly, just the way he had done when we crossed the border. Harriet stood clinging to her mother's tattered dress, and tears ran down their cheeks.

Uncle Will walked over to Harriet's father and, holding him by the elbow, made him stand up. "Now, now, there is no need for that. What is your name?"

"Jenkins, massa."

"Mr. Jenkins, you are now in a country where people are free to do as they please, within the law. No one can force you to do anything against your will. Do you understand?"

Jenkins wiped his tears with the sleeves of his shirt and nodded.

"Well, that's settled, then. Mr. Broadbent, could you please show the Jenkins family to their cabin?"

As Mr. Broadbent led Harriet and her parents away, Uncle Will said, "Oh, and one more thing, Mr. Jenkins."

They turned around to look at him.

"Please don't call me massa. A simple 'sir' will do."

"Yes, *sir*," Harriet's father replied loudly and his face lit up in a wide smile. It was the first time I had seen a Negro man smile. I waved at Harriet and she waved back.

Aunt Fiona took us on a grand tour of the house. She was evidently very proud of it, and rightly so. It looked as if the manor had been transported brick by brick from a British countryside hamlet, complete with the dark wood furnishings, Victorian furniture, colourful paintings, red velvet drapery and, not the least, the floral wallpaper. On the ground floor, the entrance led via double doors to a grand foyer, from where a staircase curved up to the second floor. On one side of the foyer lay the dining room and the parlour. The library and the drawing room were on the other side. The kitchen, pantry and a baking oven were in an annex that could be reached from the centre of the building. Upstairs there indeed were ten bedrooms, five each on either side of the central hallway.

I simply adored the large bedroom we were given; I had never experienced anything like its sheer spaciousness. It was in the semicircular turret. One had a panoramic view of the estate through the lead-paned windows on three sides. I enjoyed running my hands over the glossy finish of the furniture and rubbed the red and golden drapes between my fingers to enjoy the exquisite feel of the soft-textured material.

"Now, don't be dreaming here too long, Margaret. Fiona wants us down shortly. It is almost supper time." It was Mamma, instructing us to hurry up and get washed and changed for dinner.

Dinner was a grand affair. I sat down next to Robert at the dining table, which glittered with the silver and crystal settings. Was this how the kings and queens I had read about in my storybooks lived, I wondered?

"Are you hungry?" Robert asked.

"I'm starving. Only had a small sandwich for lunch, on the way."

"Didn't you have any chocolates?"

I shook my head.

"I always carry some," he said. He took some out of his pocket and offered me one. I took it but kept it in my pocket for later, as Mamma did not like us eating candies.

There was still no food on the table. Thomas, the butler, served drinks to the grown-ups and then simply stood on one side of the room, as if in a military parade. I looked around and saw the elders conversing amiably. I was about to ask Aunt Fiona if I could help and bring the food out from the kitchen, but I did not wish to interrupt her. Finally, Thomas, on seeing some movement through the oval glass porthole in the door leading to the kitchen, opened the door. In came Frank, the footman, with a large cauldron of soup, followed by the maids. They placed the soup on the sideboard and Thomas doled out measured amounts into china bowls, which the footman and the maids served. This was my first formal dinner in a manor home. I felt like a princess. The soup, the meat pies, and a whole lot of other good things I cannot remember, tasted simply out of this world. I felt like I was in a castle.

After dinner, the women and children retired to the drawing room, while the men went into the library to smoke. I peered around the door into the library. They were discussing politics. There was some talk about the annexation of Texas and possibility of war with Mexico. The cigar smoke bothered my eyes and I retreated to join the others in the drawing room. Aunt Fiona and her daughters entertained us on the piano. Finally, the gentlemen came over, glasses of brandy in hand.

I was sitting on a settee, enjoying the piano music, when there was a tap on my shoulder. It was Robert, holding a parcel.

"Happy birthday, Cousin Margaret. Sorry it's late."

I accepted it, giving him a kiss on the cheek, and proceeded to open it, doing my best to contain my excitement and not tear the wrapping paper. It was a lovely white teddy bear, dressed in a red suit. I thanked him again. Then I remembered Mamma had packed something for him. I looked at her inquiringly. She picked up the gift-wrapped packet from behind her chair and motioned to me to give it to him.

"Happy birthday, Cousin Robert. From all of us." I handed it to him.

He opened it. It was a new book, bound in hardcover with the title in gold lettering: *The Last of the Mohicans by J. F. Cooper.*

"Thank you. How did you know I wanted this book?" Robert asked, his eyes wide with amazement.

"A little birdie told us, Robbie." Mamma replied.

Uncle John also gave Robert a present. It was a skittle board made out of shiny pinewood, which he no doubt had constructed in his furniture shop. Aunt Mary also gave him a parcel, which turned out to contain another quilt.

"Margaret's got one just like that! Now they can share each other's," Elizabeth exclaimed.

Everyone laughed. I was so embarrassed I could literally have wrung her neck. However, I maintained my composure.

Uncle Will announced, "You've arrived in good time. Tomorrow is the start of the festival, and the first event, in the afternoon, will be the re-enactment of the 1813 Battle of the Forty Mile Creek. Would you like to see the battle played out?"

"Yes, yes." the children cried out in unison, clapping their hands.

"Good. Fiona will take you, as Robert," he said, putting his arm around Robert, "and I will be part of the re-enactment."

"Oh, how nice, Robbie—what part are you playing?" Mamma asked.

Robert blushed and would not tell.

Uncle Tom interjected, "How about you, Cousin Will—are you part of the Canadian or the American troops?"

"You'll see tomorrow," he replied with a teasing smile.

"Uncle Will, who will win the Battle?" I asked, just as Mamma had suggested.

"You'll find out tomorrow, Margaret. All in good time." he replied with a wink.

*****

The sun's rays shone through the windows into my eyes. I woke up with a start, feeling guilty that it was late and I hadn't done my morning chores. I worried Mamma would be most cross with me. However, the lovely wallpaper and the drapes reminded me where I was, and then it suddenly dawned on me that there weren't any tasks for me to do. The servants would take care of them. I felt like a lady and slumped my head back onto the pillow. I noticed Mamma and Papa, who had slept in the big double bed, were gone, as was David. Elizabeth and I shared the smaller bed, but she was still sound asleep.

"Wake up, Lizzie, it's late. We have to go see the battle." I shook her. She murmured to leave her alone and that she wanted to sleep some more. "Suit yourself," I said and jumped out of the bed.

Mamma had already laid out my favourite red dress and

underclothing on the chaise longue. After a run down to the privy and a quick wash at the basin, I got dressed, brushed my hair and, most boldly, put on some perfume from a bottle that lay on the dresser. The bottle, no doubt, was Aunt Fiona's. Looking into the mirror, I pinched my cheeks, wondering if Robert would notice their rosiness. A full-length dressing mirror stood on a pedestal to one side. Looking into it, I turned on both sides to make sure my dress was on properly. Observing everything was fine, I did a small curtsey to myself in the mirror and proceeded towards the staircase to go down for breakfast. I felt happy and looked forward to the rest of the day.

An appetizing aroma of baked bread and coffee wafted from the dining room. Only Robert's grandfather was at the table, reading a newspaper. Through the bay window, I spotted Mamma, Papa and others out in the yard, where Aunt Fiona was showing them her rose garden.

"Good morning, Grandpa," I said.

"Good morning. Ah! Margaret. Do sit down. Pray, have some breakfast." He lowered the newspaper and, looking at me over his reading glasses, asked, "And how's the princess this morning?"

"Very well, thank you, Grandpa," I said, blushing and sitting down on a chair where the plates and cutlery were still set on the table. Thomas was standing at his usual post by the kitchen door. I looked at him and he simply smiled with a nod, as if to say good morning. About a minute passed. I was still sitting there, and no one had served me any breakfast. Grandfather continued to read his paper. Finally, Thomas came to me.

"Would you be having any breakfast, miss, or are you waiting for someone to join you?"

"No, I'm not waiting. Yes, I'd like some breakfast, please."

"Well, in that case, please help yourself, miss. We do not serve breakfast. It is all laid out on the sideboards. Here, let me help you." He moved towards the sideboards.

"Oh. Thank you, Thomas." I must have turned red. Picking up a plate, I walked over to the buffet table, which was set up with inviting croissants, French breads, jams, scrambled eggs, ham and other mouth-watering delicacies. Looks like I'll need a handbook of instructions to do anything in Wallace Hall, I thought as I filled my plate.

It was just past one o' clock, and the afternoon sun was trying its best to shoot hot rays at us through any gaps it could find in the clouded sky. The carriages dropped us off at the lakeside park's gates, where the re-enactment of the 1813 Battle of the Forty Mile Creek was to be staged. Aunt Fiona led the way into the park. A small group of hostesses and hosts, dressed in that period's costumes, greeted us at the entrance. A booth was set up to one side, which had a sign that read *Entrance Fee. Adults 2 pence. Children under 10 years: free.*

A tall gentleman approached us and said, "Good afternoon, Mrs. Wallace. I see you have quite an entourage here today." He removed his hat and bowed to Aunt Fiona. It seemed he was one of the officials of the show.

"Good afternoon, Mr. Stretch. Pray, meet our cousins, visiting from New Jersey." Then, turning to Papa and my uncles, "This is Mr. Stretch, the President of our Historical Association."

"Welcome. Good of you to have come all the way from New Jersey to our humble Town," the tall gentleman said.

"We are very pleased to be here, sir," Papa said, shaking Mr. Stretch's hand, and the others did the same.

Aunt Fiona opened her reticule and moved towards the ticket booth. Papa followed her; taking a silver-dollar coin from his pocket, he tried to get to the booth first. However, Mr. Stretch stopped them both with an extended arm.

"Nay, Mrs. Wallace. You don't have to pay. You and Major William do so much for our Association."

"Are you sure now, Mr. Stretch?"

"Absolutely, madam."

"Why, thank you kindly, sir. But where are William and Robert? They left hours ahead of us."

"I believe they are down yonder with the re-enactors, likely rehearsing their parts," he said, smiling, and pointed with his cane to a wooded area in the distance. "Why don't all of you go on to that left embankment of the creek? The best view would be had from there."

Groups of visitors began arriving at the park, all dressed in their Sunday best, no doubt in anticipation of a gay afternoon. We thanked the kind gentleman again and continued towards the spot he had suggested. It was a short embankment, which rolled down to the sandy beach at the mouth of a creek and slid into the gentle waters of Lake Ontario. The beach stretched for miles on either side, broken only by some docks and the occasional rocks that protruded into the ocean-like lake. Thomas and Frank, along with the two maidservants, caught up to us. They carried rolls of blankets and a folding table under their arms, and held baskets of food and refreshments for the picnic.

"Shall I find a place to spread the blankets, ma'am?" Thomas asked Aunt Fiona.

"Yes, please, Thomas. Do find us a shady spot, under that maple tree, perhaps. Goodness, it's getting hot already." She fanned herself with a folding fan she carried in her reticule.

"Ready for a spot of cricket, chums?" Uncle Tom bantered, doing his best to fake a British accent, as he settled down on the blanket.

"Aye. But it looks like the American team are on a bit of a sticky wicket," Uncle John said, pointing to the half-dozen or so tents at the cove of the creek with a US flag flying on a pole. He then pointed to a schooner anchored offshore, flying the British flag. A canvas covered its original name and a new name, *Beresford*, was written across it, on a banner. "That ship's cannons can blast this camp right off the beach!"

I stood at the edge of the ridge and looked at what was portrayed to be the American military camp. A group of soldiers walked about, setting up muskets on tripods, dressed in their regular army grey uniforms and black shako hats. Some looked to be militia units, as they wore leather jackets, white trousers and farmers' hats. From the intense preparations, it looked as if they were getting ready for a real battle! Two cannons were rolled up to the beach, while logs and tree branches were laid to form a small barricade in front of the tents. A wagon and horses stood to one side of the camp, and a row of boats were propped up on the lakeshore. It seemed those could be used for a speedy getaway, if needed.

A couple of campfires burned, where women cooked. That puzzled me. I turned towards Papa and asked, "Papa, were there women soldiers in the army those days?"

"Nay, Puppet. There aren't any women soldiers, not then and not now," he replied with a small laugh and, putting his arm around my waist, added, "Those ladies are likely wives of the re-enactors. They'll disappear into the tents once the battle starts. You'll see." Then Papa asked, "Tom, do you know how large the American force was?"

"'Round four thousand, I believe."

Papa raised his eyebrows and nodded in amazement.

Good thing we arrived early, for soon the park was teeming with people. All the available spots on the first row of the grassy embankments overlooking the lake were taken. We had found a good spot. Other families had to settle for positions in the second or third rows, just like at a cricket match. A military band played marching tunes from the gazebo in the centre of the commons. Children ran around, chasing each other. The ice cream, cotton candy, caramel-apple and other knick-knack vendors did a brisk business. My siblings and I walked around the park and on the beach with our cousins for a while. We were soon recalled by Mamma with instructions to stay quietly on the blankets, for the show was about to begin. I wanted a cotton candy, but did not dare ask Mamma, as she would never allow us to eat those treats. "Not good for your teeth, you know," she would tell us sternly.

I was getting thirsty and was delighted to hear Thomas ask, "Would the ladies and gentlemen be needing any refreshments?"

Yes, get me an ice cream and a cotton candy, I wanted to shout, but kept quiet. Thomas took the drink orders, first from the ladies and then the gentlemen. Drinks were mixed on the picnic table set up behind us. The two maids scurried about, serving the refreshments. Finally, it was my turn.

"And, what will you have, miss?"

"A cold drink, please," I replied in a barely audible voice.

I almost swooned when I heard him say to the maid, "Betty, an orange julep for Mistress Margaret," for no one had ever called me *Mistress Margaret* before!

Finally, just past the appointed hour of two o'clock, the re-enactment started. Another tall gentleman, dressed in a dark tailcoat and trousers with a matching bowler hat, arrived on the beach, carrying a bullhorn in one hand.

"Ladies and gentlemen, girls and boys, welcome to our re-enactment of the historic battle of the Forty Mile Creek, which we believe turned the tide of the war in favour of Canada. But first, a very special warm welcome to our American friends, who have travelled from far-off states to be with us today ..." The gentleman listed, one by one, the names of the states the visitors were from. We clapped, loudest, when New Jersey was mentioned. He also read off names of dignitaries and other notable personalities attending the show that day.

"Before we begin, a brief history lesson, and I promise it will be brief." There was a murmur of laughter from the crowd. "The United States declared war on Great Britain on June eighteen, 1812. The

Canadian General Brock got the news in Fort George during dinner, while entertaining some American officers from Fort Niagara across the river. It is rumoured that the American officers took time to finish their glasses of port and shook hands with General Brock and his staff before departing. Thus began the war of 1812 in the Niagara Peninsula."

There was much laughter from the crowd.

"So here we are, ladies and gentleman. It is the eighth of June 1813, about a year into the War. Picture a US army in the thousands, camped here on these very grounds at the mouth of the Forty Mile Creek. They are under the command of General Lewis and are awaiting reinforcements, for they had been defeated a day earlier in the battle at Stoney Creek, just to the west of us. And then, after regrouping, what would they want to do?" He raised his hand, pointing the foghorn towards the crowd, wanting them to answer his question.

The audience shouted, "Recapture Stoney Creek!"

"Ah! But we will not let them regroup. We will not let them go on to our neighbouring town, Hamilton. Help is at hand. It is in the form of the Royal Navy. On that very morning, Commodore Yoe arrived with a squadron of ships." He pointed towards the ship on the lake. "The waters were too shallow for sailing in. Nevertheless, they had the Canadian schooners *Beresford* and *Sydney Smith* towed in. The captain sends out a party to meet with General Lewis. Ladies and gentlemen, let the battle begin!"

We saw a small boat lowered from the ship. Four uniformed sailors picked up the oars and started rowing in unison towards the shore. As the boat drew nearer, I saw a red-jacketed Canadian officer at the helm, holding a white flag.

The American camp was located a bit inland from the beach, on the bay formed by the creek. The re-enactor playing General Lewis was dressed convincingly in the flamboyant uniform of that period. He stood with one hand on his sword, looking majestic in a general's large, plumed bicorn hat. The rest of the troops lined up behind him. He turned sideways and ordered in a loud, clear voice, "Sergeant major, escort the landing party in."

"Yessir!" The sergeant major wheeled and asked two of the men to fall out, and they marched smartly towards the point where the Canadian boat was about to land.

The boat hit the bottom of rocky shore with a crunching sound of wood sliding over pebbles. The Canadian officer jumped out, put on his cocked hat and straightened out his red jacket. His sword was missing from its scabbard. While the two American soldiers stood guard by the boat, the Canadian officer marched behind the sergeant major towards the camp.

"General Lewis, I have the honour of presenting to you a message from the captain of *HMS Beresford*." The Canadian officer held out a piece of paper to the general.

"Could you read it, please?"

The officer obliged. "General Lewis, Commodore Yoe considers it his duty to advise you that a squadron of ships is in front of you, and a group of Mohawk warriors are behind you, lying in wait in the woods, hungry for your scalps. The powerful Canadian army is closing in quickly on your left flank. In short, sir, in His Majesty's name, we demand your surrender."

"Surrender! I have not heard anything so absurd in all my life."

"Do you have a reply, sir?"

"Sergeant major, hand me your musket."

"Yessir." As the sergeant major handed General Lewis his musket, many in the audience, including myself, gasped. I was sure he was going to shoot the Canadian officer. Instead, the general put the butt of the musket to his shoulder and fired into the air. The loud bang and the smoke from the musket hung in the still afternoon. The noise scared some gulls from the trees, and they fluttered away, squawking.

"Sir, you can tell your commodore that this message is too ridiculous to warrant a reply."

The Canadian officer turned and, grim faced, marched back towards his boat. This was a poignant moment. The gathering fell silent. As the smoke from the musket fire slowly drifted towards us, I heard one person next to me start to clap. I looked up and saw it was Uncle Tom, standing up, applauding. Papa, Uncle John and the rest of us all jumped to our feet and joined him in the clapping. The other American visitors in the crowd also joined in. Shortly, like an ocean wave sweeping up to embrace a beach, the rest of the audience united in the standing ovation. As tears rolled down my cheeks, I clapped hard, until my hands ached.

However, the battle was not over. In fact, it was just beginning. The gun ports of the schooner *Beresford* lifted open and its cannons commenced a bombardment of the American camp. From the noise of the cannons, it sounded as if they were firing real cannon balls. Thankfully for us, the cannons did not have any shots.

General Lewis shouted his orders, "Field gunners to your posts. Engineers prepare to heat the shots …"

The US army engineers quickly heated up the cannon balls in one of the camp's cooking fires. Indeed, there were now no women to be seen, just as Papa had predicted. The engineers ran the heated shots in shovels over to the cannons. Shortly, the American cannons began firing back, with loud booms, at the Canadian ship. I was comforted to see that the re-enacting soldiers were not actually loading the cannons with the hot shots, but discreetly dropping the balls in front of the cannons' muzzles.

The Canadian ship stopped firing and was towed back by two boats. I looked inquiringly at Uncle Tom and asked, "Uncle Tom, why is the Canadian ship going back?"

He explained, "The captain of the *Beresford* fears the ship will catch fire from the hot shots, and is moving it out of range of the American batteries."

On seeing the ship cease firing and pull back, the American soldiers took off their shakos and, pumping them in the air, yelled, "Huzzah … huzzah … huzzah." However, their victory cries were premature.

We heard bloodcurdling Indian war cries and musket fire from the rear of the American camp. Indian warriors, dressed in leather and with painted faces, come in canoes down the Forty Mile Creek. The American soldiers quickly took cover behind the temporary barricade erected earlier. A fierce gunfight erupted. The sound of the musket fire was deafening.

"Those things make more noise shooting powder alone than with real balls in them," Uncle Tom said with a chuckle.

It appeared the Mohawks were fewer in number and hence had difficulty in returning fire quickly enough. The American soldiers slowly gained ground, advancing on the Indians, but not without casualties. Some fell to the ground, writhing in mock pain; many Indians were hit as well. One fell dramatically off a tree branch into the river. All playacted like children, just as Mamma had said. The Mohawks then suddenly fled, just as quickly as they had arrived.

General Lewis ordered, "Sergeant major, have the injured loaded into the wagons and get them on their way to Fort George." He then turned towards his commanding officers and said, "Please have the boats loaded with as many men as possible and make haste, along the lake shore, for Fort George."

"But, sir, the *Beresford?*" one captain protested.

"There isn't much wind. I don't think she'll be fast enough to catch us. But if she puts out her men on bateaux, be prepared to fight." He turned to the rest of the soldiers. "Men, you have put up a brave struggle. I am proud of you. Nevertheless, we are in a desperate situation. A large Canadian army, along with their native friends, is about to descend on us. We are not only outnumbered, but we have many sick and wounded. Our only option is to make haste for the safety of Fort George. I have General Dearborn's instructions to that effect. Those of you who cannot get into the boats, double-quick march to the Fort. God be with you."

"A wise decision under the circumstances, don't you think?" Uncle Tom whispered to Uncle John and Papa, who nodded.

Where were Robert and Uncle Will? What parts were they playing? I looked anxiously about to catch a glimpse of Robert.

General Lewis had scarcely uttered his orders when there was the unmistakable wail of bagpipes and military drums playing "Scotland the Brave", coming from the road that led into the park. The Canadian army had arrived. With great fanfare, they marched into the park. I saw Uncle Will, in the full regalia of a red-coated uniform, atop a horse, riding with a group of officers ahead of the marching troops. Where was Robert? Finally, I spotted him, walking with another boy next to the pipers. The two of them had drums hanging to their sides and beat them rhythmically with drumsticks.

"Look, Margaret, there's Robert, the drummer boy." Aunt Fiona, bending down, pointed him out to me. "Doesn't he look so bonny?"

I nodded, not knowing what to say. Indeed, he did look handsome in his red jacket with its brass buttons, and white trousers and a shako hat.

The Canadian troops rushed in and fired from the embankment on the retreating American troops, but they managed to get away. Some sped away on their boats, while the rest took to the road, with the Canadian troops in pursuit. The camp was now deserted, except for the presumed wounded and dead.

A couple of boats from the ship came ashore with their officers. The sailors lifted up on their shoulders the actor playing Commodore

Yoe. In the traditional manner of a British naval victory merriment, he was hip-hip-hoorayed, and the ditty "For he's a jolly good fellow … and so say all of us" sung for him.

The military band started to play again, which was likely the signal for the end of the re-enactment. The playing-dead soldiers and the Indians got up and dusted off their backsides. The crowd clapped and cheered loudly. The "escaped" American soldiers also returned, and all the re-enactors gathered on the beach in a line, just like at the ending of a theatrical performance. The gentleman with the megaphone appeared again. He asked if we had enjoyed the show and received a resounding *YES*. I was a tad disappointed that the Americans had been defeated, however. He asked for a round of applause for the re-enactors. The thunderous clapping went on for quite a while and the re-enactors bowed at least half a dozen times.

I ran down the embankment and over the sand dunes to Robert, who stood with his regiment on the beach. On seeing me approach, he beat a welcoming rhythm on the drum, which sounded like, "trrrrrrrruuuuumph".

"My, you can play those really well," I said.

"It takes a lot of practice."

"Can I try, please?"

"Aw… All right, here," he said, handing me the drumsticks.

I had only beaten the drum a couple of times when the other drummer boy, standing beside us, turned towards me.

"Girls aren't allowed to play the drums," he said.

I looked at him, puzzled. "Who are you?" I asked.

"He's the other drummer boy, Albert," Robert said.

"Pleased to meet you, Albert," I said and continued to beat the drum.

"Like I said, you are not allowed to play the drums." His voice had taken on a quarrelsome edge.

"Who says so?" Robert said, looking Albert in the eyes.

"I say so. Don't you know girls aren't permitted in the regiment?" Albert said and, snatching the drumsticks from my hand, started to run away.

Robert took off the belt holding his drum, placed it on the sand and ran after Albert. He soon caught up to him, as Albert, being rather pudgy, was a slow jogger and had his drum still in his belt. Robert knocked him to the ground and the drum went rolling away. Robert sat on his chest and snatched the drumsticks out of his hand. By then a crowd of onlookers had gathered. Robert made a threatening gesture with his fist, while Albert squirmed angrily under him.

"Robert! What's the meaning of this?" Uncle Will approached them, striding crossly.

"Albert started it. He grabbed these from Margaret's hands," Robert said, showing his father the drumsticks.

"That's enough. Now get up, the two of you," he said. When Robert and Albert stood up, he asked, "Albert, why did you take these away from Margaret?"

"I only took them to show her the correct finger positions, and all of a sudden Robert attacked me," Albert said with a devilish look.

"Now that's a lie!" Robert shouted.

Another person, dressed like a country gentleman, approached us. "Albert, you come with me. Sorry, Major Wallace. I will have a word with him," said the gentleman. He was obviously Albert's father.

"Thank you, Mr. Miller. No need to be hard on the lad. I'm sure it was all in good humour," Uncle Will said.

"Good day to you all," Mr. Miller said, as he led Albert away by the ear.

Uncle Will, Robert and I trudged up the embankment, back to our picnic spot.

"I'm hungry, let's eat," Uncle Will said, as Thomas handed him a glass of whisky.

A cold lunch was served. While I enjoyed the baked chicken, I did not care too much for the cucumber sandwiches.

"You did a terrific job, Will. Scared away the whole US regiment," Papa said.

"Aye. It was those highlander bagpipes, Jim. They work all the time." Uncle Will took another sip of whisky and everyone laughed.

After we had finished eating, Robert asked, "Would you like to see our docks, Cousin Margaret?"

"Yes, I would love to."

"Now, Robbie, don't go too far. We shall be departing soon," Aunt Fiona said as she saw us going towards the water.

"Yes, Mother."

Robert and I walked along the sandy beach. He pointed out various landmarks. There was the large Canadian city of York, right across the lake on the opposite shore. To the left of us were the towns of

Hamilton and Burlington.

"There's the Wallace Dock," he said, pointing to a pier where a sailing ship was anchored. Several men rolled large barrels along the pier, up the gangplank and onto the deck.

"What are they loading on the ship?" I asked.

"Fruits, mostly—they are in season now. Later they'll take corn and grains."

"Where do they take them?"

"To all the cities around the lake and down to Lower Canada, Montreal and Quebec."

"Do they go to England, too?"

"Aye. Some ships go there."

"Have you been to England?"

"No. But I will one day, soon. Would you like to come with me?"

"No."

"Why not?"

"I don't want to leave Mamma, and besides, I have to study to become a doctor."

"A doctor. Really?"

"Yes, really."

"Good. Then you can take care of my horses, as they get sick all the time."

"Yes, I like horses."

We walked a bit further and passed by a house situated a little way up from the beach. It had a small patio with some chairs and tables. A stone wall encircled it. The sign at the entrance to the patio read:

The Lake House Tavern.

As we approached the tavern, someone who had been hiding in a wooded area close by came running towards us. It was that same fat boy, Albert. He approached Robert and, before he could react, whacked him on the chest. The blow sent Robert flying into the sand. The very next moment, Albert turned towards me and pulled me by my ringleted hair. It really hurt.

"Ouch, let me go," I shouted at him and tried to hit him with my fists.

He let go. Before Robert could get up, Albert ran off into the forest. Robert tried to chase after him, but gave up. Obviously, the punch was hurting him.

"Are you all right?" Robert asked.

"Yes, I'm fine. How about you?" I replied, taking my bonnet off and smoothing out my hair.

"I'm well," Robert said, rubbing his chest where Albert's blow had struck. "I'll get even with the devil as soon as we get back to the park. I'll teach him a lesson he will not forget for hurting you."

"No, no. Please don't fight anymore. It's all right, I'm fine." Pointing towards the tavern, I asked, "What's that?"

"A restaurant."

"Let's go in there and see if you're injured. I want to nurse your wound."

"No, I'm okay. There's no blood. It doesn't hurt anymore. Honest," he replied, still massaging his chest.

"Can we go in there for an ice cream, at least?" I also wanted Robert to forget about this incident, for I was afraid it might lead to further quarrel between them.

He replied simply, "Not today."

"Why not?"

"I don't have any money."

"It's all right. We'll have it some other day. Let's go back to the park. Aunt Fiona will be looking for us."

Many years later, I was to learn of the terrible incident that took a part of my heart away. For what? I have often agonised over the reasons for that and still wonder if this little event on Grimsby Beach, over me trying to play the drums, was the cause of it?

Chapter Ten

Six Years Later

1847, July: Grimsby, Canada West
FROM FAR AWAY out on the lake, a flock of gulls spotted us, for they flew over the beach squawking and flapping their white wings. It was a sunny, breezy Sunday morning and Robert and I had gone out riding. We ended up at the Forty Mile Creek and, tethering our horses to a tree, strolled on the sandy shore.

"It appears they're welcoming you back, Cousin Margaret," Robert said as he pointed at the birds, his golden hair blowing in the wind gusting from the lake.

"You are such a romantic, Cousin Robert. The birds don't know me from Eve. It's likely my red dress they're after." I looked up at the birds, needing to hold onto my bonnet with one hand. Indeed, I was happy, just like the gulls, to be back—it had been six long years since I last visited Grimsby. This time, only Elizabeth and I had come over, although not without a chaperone. Mamma had made sure that one of her distant cousins, Aunt Clara, accompanied us.

"Romantic! Who, me? From what I've heard, you're the romantic one." Robert said, sounding much more mature than the young twelve-year-old I had walked with on that same beach the last time.

"Oh! And, pray, what have you heard?"

"That more than half the birds in New Jersey are in love with you."

"Well, I can't help it if they keep coming to my window ledge, can I?"

"Why don't you catch some one day and make a good meal out of them? I love bird stew."

"Never! Oh, you're so cruel, Cousin Robert." I grabbed his arm and tried to twist it playfully behind his back. He shook himself free and ran ahead. I followed in pursuit. He looked back and, seeing me falling behind, slowed down, I believe purposely, for even at eighteen, he had strong, long, muscular legs that could have outrun the best sprinter, let alone poor me. I reached him, grabbed his jacket collar, and pulled his face closer to mine. He had mischief written all over his countenance.

"I demand you take back what you said about killing and eating those poor creatures," I said, breathless and in mock anger.

"All right, all right. I'm sorry for even saying so, let alone doing it. Now will you release me or are you going to strangle me right here on the beach?"

"There, that's better," I said, letting go his collar and hitting him lightly on the shoulder.

"Thank you, your highness," he said, making a bow to me in the noble way, and a wave of the arm.

"You are forgiven, sire."

We had run quite a distance along the beach, and I was feeling hot in the high-collar, buttoned-up dress. Although I was then only seventeen, I had filled out. Mamma thought I had developed a bit too much and wouldn't permit me to wear a low-cut dress. I felt thirsty and, looking up at the embankment, spotted the Lake House Tavern in the distance.

"Look, Cousin Robert," I said, pointing to the tavern.

"Yes?" he asked with a quizzical look.

"Goot any money, gov'ner?" I asked, doing my best to mimic a poor cockney.

"Yes, I do. But why?" Robert still looked puzzled.

"Last time we were 'ere, m'lord, you didn't 'ave any."

At last the penny dropped. He burst out laughing.

He recovered, to say in his best English accent, "Well, m'lady, I have found a buried treasure chest. You only have to command me to escort you to that establishment."

"I command thee."

"It shall be done." He extended his right elbow to me and we walked on the path towards the tavern.

I stumbled, having stepped on a loose rock or something. Robert, turning swiftly, put his arm around me to support me. My breasts pressed against his muscular chest. At that contact and from his closeness, a pleasant sensation flowed through me. I felt faint and could not withdraw, which I should have done. Neither did Robert step back. We simply stood there in a trance, in the cuddle, looking into each other's eyes, savouring the moment.

Finally, I regained my composure. "Let's go, there are people watching us," I whispered.

The maitre d' seated us on the patio at a table for two, under an umbrella. The view of the lake, with waves beating on the shore, was a painter's delight. It was almost noon and we ordered ales and steak-and-kidney pies, the Lake House specialty. In addition, having missed it earlier, I fully intended to have that ice cream.

"Tell me, Cousin Margaret, how was the trip from New Jersey this time?"

"Much better, thank you. We came all the way to Niagara Falls by railway, and then by stagecoach to Grimsby. Too bad you still don't have trains in Canada."

"Aye. They're working on it. I hear there will be soon a suspension bridge over the Falls. Then I will be able to walk over to New York State."

"Don't stop there, though. Keep walking on to New Jersey. Do you think you'll be able to make it to Elizabethville?"

"At my speed, I'll be an old man by the time I get to your town. You may not recognise me."

"I'd identify you even after you returned from a voyage with Sinbad."

"I might have a black patch over an eye and a parrot on one shoulder."

"That'd make you look lovely."

"All right, and would you prefer a beard and a wooden leg as well?" Robert asked, trying hard to hold a grin.

"Sure, if you'll hop over any quicker to me."

Our eyes met. I tried to keep a straight face, but could not quite manage it. We burst out laughing, almost simultaneously. Robert reached over and held my palms. I felt his warm hands squeeze, and I squeezed back. We heard a voice behind us.

"Having fun, Master Wallace?"

Robert jumped up from his seat. "Oh! Yes, Colonel Mitchell, sir. I mean, no, sir," he said, blushing, and bowed to the rather distinguished-looking gentleman towering over us. Three ladies, obviously his wife and daughters, stood beside him. The family were dressed in their Sunday best and looked as if they had just come from church.

"Pray let me introduce my cousin, Margaret, from New Jersey." Robert told me their names and made a special mention of the elder daughter as, "Nancy, who is in my class."

Colonel Mitchell remarked, "Pleased to meet you, Miss Wallace. We're originally from New Jersey as well. I believe I know your family."

"Really, Mr. Mitchell," I stammered, trying to recall if I had heard their name before.

"How long will you be in Grimsby, Miss Wallace?" Nancy asked.

"For the summer, most likely. I'm helping my aunt prepare jams and jellies."

"Ah! So you're the niece working in the preserves line of business Fiona's just opened," Mrs. Mitchell exclaimed.

"I'm afraid I don't know much about making them. Aunt has been showing me what to do," I remarked, rather meekly.

"You're too modest, child. Why just yesterday, I met Fiona at her store in town and she told me you're doing a remarkable job."

"Thank you, Mrs. Mitchell," I murmured.

"Well, let us not keep you. It being such a nice day, we thought after church we should get some fresh air." Mr. Mitchell turned towards the lake and drew in a deep breath of the air, as if it were an elixir.

"Will we see you at our bonfire this evening?" Robert asked.

"Yes, certainly, we always love your annual event. I'm sure the girls will enjoy it. Won't you, girls?" Mrs. Mitchell said, looking at her daughters.

"Oh, yes. We won't miss the bonfire for anything," both the girls replied in their squeaky voices, almost in unison, nodding and wiggling in excitement.

As soon as they were out of earshot, I asked, "Who are they?"

"That's Colonel Mitchell, the commander of the British Regiment stationed here. A very influential person."

"How does he know my family?"

"Well, apparently there was, or possibly still is, a log cabin used as a gaol somewhere in New Jersey. Quite a few of our town's founders, being Loyalists, were jailed there in the 1770s. What's hilarious is that one of them had given a part of his land and even helped to build the very prison they got thrown into." Robert laughed and held up his arms.

"Now I remember. I heard that only one of them, your great-grandpa, managed to escape?"

"Yes, and do you know how he did it?"

I shook my head.

"He disguised himself as a Mohawk warrior, and with help from some natives, got safely to Canada."

"And this Colonel Mitchell's grandfather was with them in that same gaol. So he must be a good friend of Uncle Will?"

"Aye. But the important thing is that I want him to recommend me for a commission in the cavalry."

"Oh! And when will you be joining up?" I asked, rather surprised at his aspiration.

"Possibly next year, as soon as I finish school."

"What about your parents? Will they let you?" Having no love for warfare myself, I felt apprehensive at his desire and hoped they might dissuade him.

"They have no objections. In fact, Mother's father was a Hussar in a British Regiment in India. She's quite thrilled at the prospect of seeing me in a cavalry officer's uniform."

"Will they send you to fight in Europe?"

"No, not likely. The wars with the French and in India are all over. Also, we are now on friendly terms with the Americans. I don't think there's going to be another conflict."

The waitress came by. She picked up the empty dishes and asked, "Will there be anything else?"

"Would you like another ale?" Robert asked, looking at me.

I usually did not drink much, but the look in Robert's eyes suggested he wanted us to stay and talk some more. Although the appearance of Nancy was beginning to bother me, I thought "why not", and said, "Yes, I'll have another one."

"Tell me, wasn't Uncle Will also in the Army?" I asked Robert, continuing our conversation, as I wanted to learn more about his family.

"Yes, but he's only in the Militia now. He served in India too, you know."

"I heard. Didn't he meet Aunt Fiona there?"

"Aye. They were married there. She was the commandant's daughter—"

The waitress put down our fresh mugs of cold ale.

Mamma had mentioned that Robert and his sisters were born in India, but I was curious and asked, "Why did you all return to Canada?"

"We came back in 1834. I was about five, Heather and Kirsten a bit younger. Mother was getting worried about our education. We would have been sent to boarding school in either England or here. However, other events transpired. Great-Grandpa Alex died and Grandpa Hamilton was left to run the farm on his own. Then, unfortunately, he suffered a heart attack. So, Father had to sell his commission and we all came back."

"So that's why your grandpa is so sick. He hardly ever goes out. But couldn't your uncles have helped on the farm?"

"Ha! Are you serious? Uncle Alasdair is a lawyer in Toronto and Uncle Victor a doctor in Montreal. They hardly ever come by, except during hunting season. They don't like getting dirt on their hands," Robert said with a smirk, taking a large gulp of the ale.

I sipped a little of the beverage and asked, "What about your aunt?"

"Aunt Nora? Well, she's another story. She eloped with an American. They live somewhere in Charleston. I've seen her only a couple of times. Father doesn't wish to talk about them."

"Why's that?"

"They are southern plantation owners. They keep slaves."

"That reminds me. How are Harriet and her parents?"

"Doing well. Mr. Jenkins is a hard worker. Father has already elevated him to a lead-hand position. Harriet and her mother help in the kitchen. You know what? Good that you inquired about Mr. Jenkins. Father had asked him to arrange the bonfire, and I was to help him. Look, it's getting late. We'd better be going. We'll talk later. Let me go in and pay."

While he went to settle the bill, I straightened out my hair and adjusted the bonnet. When he returned, we walked towards the tavern's back gate, from where a stone walk led out to the creek. The Mitchells sat at a table near the exit. There was no way of avoiding them.

"Goodbye, Mrs. and Colonel Mitchell, Nancy, Judy. See you all this evening," Robert said in a cheerful voice as we passed by them.

"Ah, yes. Goodbye. Trust that you had a pleasant afternoon?" Colonel Mitchell said, while the women nodded. Just as we reached the gate, Colonel Mitchell called after us. "Ah, say, Miss Wallace."

"Yes, Colonel?"

"Has Fiona made her famous apricot chutney yet, by any chance?"

"Yes, sir. Apricots are in season. We poured a batch just yesterday."

"Ah! Good, good. Can we get some jars tonight? It tastes so delicious. Isn't it prepared from the secret recipe she brought from India?"

"Indeed, sir, it is. I'll put some jars aside for you to take home tonight."

"Ah! Good, good. So very kind of you," Colonel Mitchell said.

"I must admit Fiona has found a very able assistant." Mrs. Mitchell said, looking at her daughters.

Robert whispered to me, "We'd better go, otherwise we'll have to hear all the Colonel's war exploits."

Thanking them again, we scampered out of the tavern's back entrance. Outside, Robert stopped to pluck a rose from one of the abundance of rose bushes planted along the wall. I stood by, waiting for him. It was then I overheard Mrs. Mitchell say something intriguing: "Don't fret, Nancy, she's *only* Robbie's cousin."

I do not believe Robert heard her, or if he had, he didn't pay any attention to that remark. He came over with an exquisite red rose on a long stem. I must have turned crimson when he unbuttoned two of my dress's top buttons and threaded the stem of the rose through them.

"A token of my appreciation, Margaret, for spending such a lovely afternoon with me."

I was speechless for a while. I smelled the rose and murmured, "Thank you, Robert. It was delightful," and kissed him lightly on the cheek. I cannot say if it was the ale or the rose, but I felt like the gulls. I wanted to fly.

We walked back to the park to our mare, Taj, and pony, Babur. As they were on the creek's bank, they had all the water they could drink. They seemed happy and neighed, bobbing their heads in welcome. It was getting late in the afternoon and the park was nearly deserted. Down in the ravine, we were hidden from the view of the few remaining groups sitting under the shady trees. I was riding sidesaddle and needed Robert's help to mount Taj. He came to the side of the mare and cupped his right palm to enable me to get a foothold. I put a hand on his shoulder and tried to place a foot on his palm. It seemed that by that time, the second pint of ale had started to have its effect. My foot missed Robert's hand and I stumbled upon his sturdy frame. I giggled. He held me in his arms to keep me from falling.

"Whoa! Are you all right?"

I nodded. While he held me in an embrace, I felt dizzy and put my head on his shoulder. He tightened his hold and pulled me to him, crushing my breasts against his strapping chest. I felt his heavy breathing and his heart pounded against mine, as if we had just run up from the beach. We simply stood there, holding each other.

Just then, Nancy's face came before my eyes. I sobered a bit and asked Robert, as I traced his jacket collar with one hand, "Can you tell me one more thing, Robert?"

"Yes, what is it, dear Margaret?"

"Does your cavalry commission include Nancy?"

He laughed. "No. Never. She doesn't mean much to me."

"Are you sure?"

"Absolutely. You are the one I'm in love with, Puppet."

Those words were like music to my ears. A thrill passed through my body. I whispered, "I believe I'm falling in love with you too, Robert." I put my arms around his neck and looked into his radiant blue eyes as our bodies squeezed together, trying to become one.

He slowly bent his head down and kissed me. At first, it was a gentle brush of his lips against mine. Then he took my upper lip between his. It was a delightful feeling.

I felt faint and my knees gave way. I had to hang on to his neck. We succumbed to the passions that rose inside us like a volcano. We kissed passionately. He inserted his tongue inside my mouth and rubbed it over mine. That was something new for me. I enjoyed the delightful sensations just the same.

The screeching of the gulls broke our trance. We reluctantly parted our lips. The gulls flew over us again. It seemed as if they approved of our kissing.

I smoothed out my dress to recompose myself. "We'd better be going, Robbie. It's getting late," I whispered.

"I wish we didn't have to leave." Robert sighed as he helped me mount Taj, this time with success.

"Neither do I. This is now my favourite creek," I said. We then galloped up the Mountain Road in the direction of Wallace Hall.

I entered the foyer alone. Robert had gone to the fields to help organise the bonfire. Elizabeth, it seemed, was searching for me. She ran down the stairs, shouting, "Where were *you?*"

"Just out riding. Didn't you know? And you don't have to shout, Lizzie."

"Riding! Surely not for the whole day. Aunt Fiona is most upset."

Aunt Fiona hurried into the foyer. "Elizabeth, why don't you go upstairs and get ready for the bonfire? That's a good girl." Then, turning to me, she said sternly, "Let's go in the parlour, Margaret. You can tell me all about your day."

I followed her into the parlour. A tea setting with sandwiches was on a side table.

"Would you like some tea?" she asked.

"Yes, please. Let me pour it for you." I poured her tea in the exquisite china cups they used all the time, not just in company's presence, as at our house. My hands shook ever so slightly.

"So tell me, where did you and Robbie go?" she asked casually, sipping her tea.

I told her how Robert and I had spent that afternoon—except, of course, for the last bit at the creek. I mentioned we'd ridden over to the beach and at first had simply intended to have a brief walk but, being hungry, ended up having lunch at the Tavern. "And, oh yes, we met the Mitchells there. By the way, Mr. Mitchell wants a few jars of your apricot chutney."

"Well! That makes good sense, to have lunch there. I know my Robbie. He's such an impulsive child. When he gets engrossed in anything, he loses all track of time. I'll have to have a word with him again about that. Ah! So you had lunch with the Mitchells?"

"Well, not exactly *with* them. They arrived at the Tavern when we'd almost finished. We just exchanged a few greetings, and their request for the chutney, before we left."

"Ah, yes, the chutney. But, tell me, was Nancy with them?

"Yes, she was."

"Oh, good, then you met her? What do you think of her? Isn't she lovely?"

"Indeed, Aunt, she's beautiful. Has gorgeous auburn hair and hazel eyes—"

"Oh, I'm so glad you approve of her. Did she say she was coming this evening?"

"Yes, she did. But—"

"Oh, we'd better get ready, then. Goodness, where's Robbie? Is he still out chopping wood?" She rushed around excitedly, peering through the windows to see if she could spot Robert.

"Shall I go and fetch him?"

"Oh, no, no. You go and get ready, dear. I'll send Frank." She went to the door and called out, "Frank."

As I passed by her at the doorway, she looked up and down at me and said, "By the way, do you have any other, er … better dress?" Before I could answer, she added, "Do go and see if you can borrow one from Heather. She's the same size as you." As Frank did not appear, she herself hastened out to find Robert, for I heard her call out his name.

While I walked up the stairs towards Heather's room, my mind was puzzled by Aunt Fiona's remark about my approving of Nancy. I stood a while at the top of the stairs. What was there to *approve?*

"Come in," Heather responded to my knock on her door.

She was lying on a chaise lounge reading a book. It looked like she had already bathed and her blonde hair was in ringlets, ready for the party. We exchanged pleasantries and, upon her inquiry, I recited again the outing at the park—omitting the kissing part. Although she raised her eyebrows when I mentioned running into Nancy and her parents there, she did not comment.

I finally asked, "Can I borrow a dress, please, for the bonfire? Your mother wants me to look my best. I cannot imagine whatever for."

"Oh, I know why."

"Why?"

"Doona ya know, child? There be a whole lot of important people comin' to the party." she said, trying to mimic her mother's Irish accent.

"Aye, boot wot's it gotta do wi'v me, loove?" I asked, trying my awful cockney accent on her.

"You, my dear, are the most desirable woman in the whole town." she said with a wave of her hand.

"Really?"

"Yes, and Mother wants you to find the first moneyed beau and run away with him."

"Does she now? Has my mamma any hand in this?"

Heather nodded. "I believe she wrote something about finding a good match for you, in her last letter, which I just happened to read."

"Good God! Mamma's always meddling in my life."

"Now, now, calm down, missy. Let me find you a perfect dress that'll make you outshine the best of them, even Nancy." Heather said, rummaging through her closet.

I was wondering why she mentioned Nancy again. Did she know about Robert and me? However, my thoughts were diverted when she dragged out a gorgeous dress from the closet and, pulling it off its hanger, held it up to me.

"*Voila!* Here's a perfect dress for you, daahling."

I must admit it was a lovely gown, a green silk taffeta with a shocking décolletage. Mother would most definitely not have approved of it. There was hand-pointed lace and real gilt embroidery along the plunging V-neck, and it had short puffed sleeves that slid down the shoulders a bit. The dress was in the latest fashion of low waistlines and crinolines that were the rage in those days. Due to the stiffness from the mohair, the skirt filled out naturally and one did not need a whole lot of petticoats underneath to look rounded.

"Oh, I can't wear that. It's too low cut," I said, holding it over me. "I'm afraid my breasts will pop out of it."

"Nonsense. It's the very fashion these days."

I put it over me and looked in the mirror. It looked dazzling, and was exactly the right size for me. I was tempted to wear it, but on also seeing a low-cut waistline at the front, which seemingly went down to the navel, I tried to dissuade her, "Oh, Heather, would you look at this V-parting at the waist? Very suggestive, don't you think?"

"No. Not at all. You'll look like a princess, my dear," she replied impishly, giving me a peck on the cheek.

Again, to reassure myself, I asked, "What are you going to wear?"

"A similar one. Here, look." She pulled out another elegant dress, also with a revealing neckline, from the wardrobe. It was in a striking silvery brocade. "I bought both these on our last trip to Manhattan. Don't you remember? Mother and I passed through Elizabeth and spent the night at your place?"

I nodded and relented. "All right, if you're going to be so daring, so can I."

"Good, it's settled, then. You'll be the belle of the ball!"

"No. You'll look much better. Thank you, Heather. You're an angel." I hugged and kissed her.

I took a quick wash and put on the dress. I was sitting before the dresser, twisting my hair into a daring style, with a knot on the top and only my long back ringlets left free, when Elizabeth came in. The poor girl was wearing one of Mamma's handmade dresses. It was white cotton with red crocheted flower patterns on the buttoned-up collar and full sleeve cuffs. It just didn't go with her pale complexion. The dress was also worn out, having been hand washed too many times. She looked more like a sick ten-year-old child than her mature fifteen years.

"Where did you get that dress?" she asked in a raised voice, with more than a hint of shock, mixed with envy.

"Heather lent it to me."

"You're not going to wear *that* to the party, are you?"

"What do you think I'm dressing for? To wash dishes in the kitchen?" I regretted saying that. It was not fair, for Elizabeth grudgingly had to help in the kitchen whenever one of the maids was away. Nevertheless, she had annoyed me with her remark.

"Mamma would never let you wear a dress like that."

"Why not?"

"Look at you, your big boobies are just about to pop out. And didn't Mamma forbid us to wear short sleeves?"

"My dear, my breasts are perfectly well covered. Besides, it's too hot to wear a full-neck-and-sleeves dress. So why don't you run along like a good little girl and play outside. Hmm?"

"I'll tell Mamma. I'll tell her everything you've been up to." And with that she stomped out of the room.

Good heavens, what a nasty girl. Where did she picked up her spitefulness, I wondered as I continued dressing.

*****

It was a warm evening. The stiff breeze that had blown all afternoon had finally dissipated. Not a leaf of the large oak and maple trees surrounding the estate stirred. I walked out of the house, down the stone portico steps and onto the front lawn, the hem of my dress trailing with just the right amount of elegance. The dinner and dance were going to be held in the garden. The actual bonfire was safely lit much further away, on open land.

I had learnt earlier that it was a tradition of the Wallaces to hold the first bonfire of the season at their property. Similar festive events followed at the neighbouring farms. In fact, the farmers used the bonfires not only to burn away the brush and diseased logs from the spring pruning and replaced trees, but also as an opportunity for the folks to socialise and take a breather upon completing their heavy spring work.

Mr. Jenkins had organised the party very well, for everything was nearly ready and arranged in an orderly manner. I saw him, dressed in a blue frock coat and white breeches—no doubt hand-me-downs from Uncle Will—supervising the setting up of the dinner tables and chairs. Servants scurried about carrying things. A dancing area was set up to one side. The Regimental Band hired for the evening, probably courtesy of Colonel Mitchell, was tuning their musical instruments. Colourful Chinese lanterns hung on strings attached to poles. Although every face wore a happy smile, I had a strange, uneasy feeling, as if something was going to happen that night. However, I could not visualise it clearly and tried to put it out of my mind.

"Is that you, Missy Margaret?" Jenkins approached me, looking amazed.

"Yes, it's indeed that little girl you came here with, Mr. Jenkins."

"If you don't mind me saying so, missy, you are looking very beautiful in that new dress."

"Thank you, Mr. Jenkins. You are looking rather smart yourself. And goodness, have you been taking English lessons?"

"Yes, missy. Mr. Wallace is sending me and Harriet to school."

"That's good of him. But where are Harriet and her mother?"

"Jemima and Harriet are helping in the kitchen. We have roasted whole piglets, beef quarters, chickens, and cooked a lot of other dishes."

"You're making me hungry already. Is there anything I can do?"

"No, thank you, missy. Everything's taken care of. Look, there's Master Robert. If you'll excuse me, I have to go and see if the appetizers are ready." Jenkins hurried off towards the kitchen.

Robert strode over, looking very elegant in a dark frock coat and trousers. His white waistcoat sported a watch on a golden chain. I thought the silken cravat made him seem like an English aristocrat.

"Margaret, you are looking absolutely stunning tonight." He came up to me, all smiles, and gave me a kiss on the cheek. I caught him admiring my exposed bosom.

I blushed at his compliment and appreciative looks. "Robert, I believe Aunt is very upset at our having stayed away the whole afternoon."

"Oh, Mother gets overly concerned at the slightest unexpected event. Not to worry, I'll talk to her."

"She said something about Nan—" But before I could finish the sentence, his attention was diverted to the sound of carriage wheels coming up on the gravel driveway.

"Ah, there they are. Excuse me, Margaret."

Robert marched off to greet the first guests. It was the Mitchells. He helped them alight from the carriage and kissed Mrs. Mitchell and Judy lightly on the cheek. He probably wanted to give Nancy a brief hug and a kiss on the cheek, but it lasted a while, for she held him by the shoulders and only reluctantly disengaged from him. He then ushered them into the house. I was left standing on the lawn, wondering whether to accompany them. I chose not to.

By and by, other guests arrived, and the party got underway. Tables for groups of four to eight persons had been set up all around the garden. A long head table had been arranged for the Wallace family and important guests. Aunt Clara, Elizabeth and I were invited to sit there with Grandpa and Grandma, and other relatives. The Mitchells sat there as well. I noted Nancy rush up and grab a seat next to Robert. I was too late, for someone was already sitting to the other side of him. However, it did not bother me to sit some distance from him, for his words to me, when he had held me and kissed me that afternoon at the creek, still echoed in my mind. *You are the one I'm in love with, Puppet.*

Drinks were served and the band started to play. The festive atmosphere deepened. People walked about and mingled in groups, drinks in hand, exchanging recent happenings and old tales.

We stood in a small circle with Robert, Heather and some of their school friends. I recognised Albert, the fat drummer boy who had snatched the drumsticks out of my hands, struck Robert and pulled my ringlets that day on the beach, six years ago. I caught him staring at me quite a few times. Out of politeness, I smiled at him, and he nodded and winked at me.

"So, Miss Wallace, how was your ride this afternoon? Did you manage to get home safely, after all those pints of ale?" Nancy asked.

"Very well, thank you. A few pints of ale never bothered my riding. What about you, Miss Mitchell? How many pints did you have? Or are you too young to have any?"

Nancy turned red and, not wanting to admit her parents did not permit her to drink, simply said, "Oh, I don't care for alcohol."

"Nancy's just a bonny lass," Robert said. There was much laughter from the group. However, Nancy wouldn't give up. It seemed she was in a feisty mood, likely from having seen Robert and me together that afternoon. She went on the offensive again.

"What a lovely dress, Miss Wallace. Do you and Heather have the same dressmaker, by any chance?"

"Thank you. Indeed we do." The rest of the group looked puzzled by my statement.

"Oh! And where would that be?" Nancy asked, a bit triumphantly, as if I had walked straight into her trap.

"On Madison Avenue. Manhattan, of course. Have you ever been there, Miss Mitchell?"

"No, I haven't. But I could swear I've seen Heather wearing that same dress. Is it not so, Heather?"

Heather replied in her sweet, matter-of-fact voice, "Er, nooo. That one is Margaret's. I have a similar one. Margaret and I went shopping in Manhattan together, the last time I was in New Jersey. Don't you remember, I told you about our trip to New York?"

I could've kissed Heather then and there.

Robert came to Nancy's rescue and said, "This is all too confusing for me. I feel like dancing. Nancy, would you permit me the honour of a dance?"

As he led Nancy to the dance floor, she turned her head and glared back at me triumphantly. Heather and I just stood there, smiling back at her. I was glad that, quite perceptively, Robert had broken up Nancy's altercation with me. Nevertheless, somehow I had the feeling it was not the end of the event. Rather, just the beginning.

Albert sauntered over with a tankard of ale in his hand. He had grown up quite a bit and seemed to have turned his tubbiness into muscle, but was shorter and far less handsome than Robert.

"Hallo, Margaret. Do you remember me—Albert?"

"How can I forget?"

"How are you? And, I dare say, looking very lovely tonight," he said, brushing his dark, wavy hair back with his palm.

"Very well. Thank you, Albert," I replied and added quickly, to hide my embarrassment at his boldness, "How have you been keeping?"

"Not too badly. Just finished school."

"So, what are you going to do now?"

"My father wants me to work in his water mills, but I have other plans."

"Such as?"

"I want to be a soldier. I've already applied to join the cavalry regiment."

"Aren't you afraid of being sent to war?"

"Not at all. I would love to fight in a war. Especially with those heathens in foreign lands."

I was about to ask him what he meant by that, when Robert came back with Nancy.

"Oh, I see you two remember each other," he said.

"Yes. Albert is telling me he wishes to join the cavalry. Just like you, Robert," I said.

Nancy remarked casually, "Papa tells me there aren't many openings in the regiment."

I was about to say *who asked you*, but kept quiet.

"Colonel Mitchell will select only the very best," Robert said.

"I'm sure he can be persuaded," Albert said, looking at Nancy.

She smiled back coyly, fluttering her eyelashes a little.

"It's abilities that count, my friend," Robert said and, taking my arm, asked, "May I have this dance, Margaret?"

"You shall have a chance to prove your skills next week at the horse races," Albert remarked.

"I am ready," Robert said as he led me to the dance floor.

As we danced, I saw Albert talking intently with Nancy. What could they be up to?

Dinner was finally served, thankfully. I was so starved by that time I could have eaten the whole plate of appetizers served by Thomas, even though they were mostly those tasteless cucumber sandwiches.

For starters, there was a delicious Scotch broth, together with plentiful salads and vegetables that came from the Wallaces' own fields. Then whole piglets on skewers, sides of beef, mutton and chickens, all roasted on the bonfire, were brought to a buffet table set up in one corner of the garden. For dessert, there were numerous cakes of different types, trifles and a variety of fresh strawberries, apricots and other fruits in season.

I glanced up and saw Nancy sitting quietly next to Robert, hardly touching her food. She looked to be sulking. It seemed she and Robert had had a row or something. Let her vex, why should I worry, I thought, and decided to have a good time at the event.

It was much too formal at the head table. Hence, Heather and I and some of her friends, including Albert, moved over to a smaller table. We had a merry time there. We ate and drank heartily, and went to the buffet table numerous times to gorge ourselves. I must admit that Albert, however crude, was good company. He told many jokes, some of them ribald, which made us laugh.

After dinner, the dancing recommenced. Aunt Fiona brought over a steady stream of young gentlemen to meet me. Invariably she introduced them as so-and-so, the son of the owners of a large foundry, or a mill, or a large farm, or a high-ranking officer in the regiment, so on and so forth. The lads did ask me to dance and I accepted. Nevertheless, it seemed most were interested only in sneaking sly glances at my bosom instead of engaging me in any intelligent conversation. Each one complimented me on my looks and on how good a dancer I was. I was glad the money Mamma had scraped together to send me to dancing lessons was paying off. Usually they left with a polite "May I call on you sometime, Miss Wallace?" To which I, equally politely, replied, "Yes, of course."

The band struck up a waltz. Robert knew I loved to waltz and hurried over to ask me to dance. It was a wonderful feeling to be in his arms again. "What is the matter with Nancy?" I asked as we twirled around with a number of admiring eyes upon us.

"Oh, she's tired, not feeling well, I guess." His voice had a conciliatory, diplomatic tone.

"I have just the right medicine for her."

"What would that be, Doctor?"

"A few good clouts on her broad behind."

"Well, you'd better hurry up and administer the medicine, lest you miss your opportunity."

"Why?" I asked.

"They'll be leaving shortly."

I laughed. He smiled and drew me close to him, and our lower parts touched, sending waves of delighted shock through me. But I quickly stepped back, for I knew Aunt Fiona was watching us like a hawk.

The gay evening went on and on. Albert kept refilling my wine glass, and I was having a great deal of fun. I did not wish the festivities to end. I did dance with Albert, but had a difficult time not letting him draw me closer to him. At one point in the evening, Albert asked me to go for a stroll in the garden. Fortunately, I was sober enough to say a firm "no" to his suggestion.

Finally, it was past midnight. One by one, the guests departed. The Mitchells were the first to leave. I had asked Frank to put a couple of jars of apricot chutney in their carriage. I ambled over to bid them goodbye. Colonel and Mrs. Mitchell thanked me for the chutney, and wished me "a lovely stay". Nancy was already in the carriage and sat on the other side to where I stood. She looked away, talking to Robert, so I did not get a chance to say goodnight to her. It did not bother me at all.

The visitors having departed, everyone else moved into the house, except for some servants who picked up the last odds and ends from the tables. I lingered in the garden, savouring the warm night. I still had the ominous feeling that had swirled in my head all evening. It was as if something bizarre was about to happen to me.

Robert hurried over, looking disturbed.

"What's the matter, Robbie?" I asked, holding both his hands.

"My pony, Babur, is very agitated. He's kicking up a rumpus in his stall. I hope he's not going to hurt himself."

"No, he's not going to injure himself. He's probably just having muscle spasms. Did you work him hard today?"

"I might have. I'm training him for the steeplechase next week. I took him for a fast gallop after we came back from the park. The groom's gone home and I hate to call the veterinarian at this time of night. Do you know what I can do to calm him down?"

"It's probably only quivers. I believe they apply an essential oil to treat such cases. Do you have any?"

"Yes, there's a shelf full of bottles of different kinds in the stable. I don't know which one to use, though. Do you?"

"Can you show me the bottles? I'll see what I can do. But, first, let me go and change. I'll meet you in the stables," I whispered in his ear.

I ran inside, up to my room and took off my gown and petticoat quickly. I put on an older dress. It had a high waistline that needed to be tied just below the breasts. It was loose and flowed like a robe, and hence could be worn over just an underskirt. I hurried out to the stables.

The lanterns cast a dim glow inside the stable. No one else was there except Robert and the horses. Most of the horses were quiet, apart from Babur, who certainly was making a commotion in his stall.

"Here they are." Robert led me to the shelf with rows of bottles of different coloured essential oils.

I read their labels: *Basil, Chamomile, Eucalyptus, Frankincense, Geranium, Lavender*, and some others. I racked my brain for what I had read and heard about the uses of each of those. Robert stood by, looking quizzically at me.

"Do you know which one to use?" he asked.

"Let me think. I know eucalyptus is for warding off mosquitoes and bugs. That wouldn't be any good. Frankincense is a wound healer, so that's not going to help, either. Now, I'm not sure about basil or chamomile. Ah, here's lavender. I know it soothes hot and inflamed muscles. Is Babur hot?"

"Yes, he feels quite hot to the touch."

"Right. Lavender it is. Let's try it. Do you know how to apply it?"

"I'm not sure."

"Here, let me show you. Take some in the palm of one hand and rub your hands together. Then apply the lotion gently over his muscles. Stroke the muscle evenly, up and down and in circular motions." I moved my palms, with the imaginary oil, over his biceps—they felt strong and muscular. "Like this. Do you understand?"

"Ah, that feels good. Pray continue over to my back," he said, turning his back to me.

"Robert! Be serious."

"All right, I got it. It's simple enough."

"Also, here, put on this apron—try not to get the lotion onto your good clothes. It's difficult to wash off." I handed him an apron and put one on myself.

We went into Babur's stall. He recognised us and neighed a welcome, but shook his head and hopped a bit, obviously in pain. I patted him and gently rubbed his neck and nostrils. When I touched his leg muscles, he jumped. This was a definite indication that he had muscle cramps. I applied the lotion to the muscles of his front legs, while Robert worked on his hind ones. Initially, Babur was tense to our touch and breathed heavily, blowing air through his nostrils. However, slowly the lavender's pleasant aroma, and eventually the lotion itself, started to take effect. He calmed down and even began to enjoy our massaging his muscles, neighing his pleasure.

"That should do it, don't you think, Margaret?" Robert asked, after we had vigorously massaged the muscles for about a quarter of an hour.

"Perhaps. Let's wait a bit to be sure the lotion was fully effective. It could simply evaporate, and the poor creature would be back to the state he was in. In that case you would have to run over and fetch the veterinarian."

It had been a hectic day. I was tired, first from all the dancing and now the strenuous massaging. We took our aprons off, wiped our hands on clean rags and walked over to the back of the stable where the hay was kept. Robert spread a blanket over the bales and we plopped down on it. The soft hay felt good and comfortable through the blanket. My feet ached, so I curled them up, and laid my head on Robert's shoulder.

Robert took my hand in his and said, "Margaret, I am truly sorry for Nancy's disgraceful conduct this evening. I hope you weren't offended?"

"Offended? No, I got even. I gave the creature back exactly what she deserved. If you hadn't taken her away for that dance, I'd have done what I've heard they do in Jersey taverns to lasses who behave like her."

"Oh, and what do they do there?"

"Dump a glass of ale down their boobies!"

"Ah! That certainly would have cooled her off." Robert roared with laughter. "I'm glad it didn't come to that." He put his arms around me. "That's what I love about you, my dear Margaret. You are so feisty."

"And I love you because you are so gentle, kind and unselfish." These words had flowed sincerely from my lips.

Robert bent down and kissed me. At first it was in the same tender way he had kissed me by the lake. But then slowly, like a smouldering fire that has suddenly had fresh logs added, it did not take long for our passions to get inflamed. The touch of his tongue over mine sent shivers down my spine. I put my arms around his neck to hold him tighter. He touched my cheeks gently and then let his fingers slide over my breasts, cupping them. I massaged the back of his neck and the thick tuft of hair. He kissed me on the neck and moved his trembling lips down. He undid the ties of the dress to expose my bosom. I gasped when he rubbed the erect nipples between his fingers. It was so arousing, for no one had ever touched or kissed me there before.

"Oh, Robbie, Robbie," I moaned as novel, sensuous vibrations flowed from head to toe.

"Puppet, my love, my love," he said in a quivering voice.   He laid me down on the soft hay and gently moved on top of me. His body wrapped me like a cloak. He was breathing heavily, and just like me, he seemed intoxicated with excitement. I felt his hardened member through the thin dress. Needless to say, no one had ever lain over me like that before. It was a strange feeling. It seemed we were floating on air. We had lost all our inhibitions and self-control. He rolled to one side and, with one hand, pulled my dress up. He ran his fingers up and down, caressing my thighs. I had never known such sensations existed. When his fingers rubbed me there, it was like a bolt of lightning shooting through my body.

I felt as if Robert and I were floating on a cloud. In my mind's eye, on a cloud beside ours, his mother's stern face appeared, like an apparition. Her floating face looked at me over Robert's head as he kissed my nipples. She spoke some words, the same ones she had said to me that afternoon. They rang in my ears. "I'm so glad you approve of Nancy." Those words threw me back down to earth.

It was due to either the fear of the wrath of my aunt or my prudishness that I grabbed his hand and pushed it out of my dress. "No, Robert, no. Please don't."

"Why, Puppet? I love you. I want to marry you. Will you marry me?" he whispered hoarsely.

"No, Robert. It will never happen." I pushed him aside and sat up. I straightened my dress, did the ties up and brushed bits of straw out of my hair.

"Why not, Puppet? Will you not marry me?" he asked with an alarmed expression.

I kissed him on his cheek. "Robbie, don't you know? Your mother will never let you marry me. Nancy is the one she wants as her daughter-in-law."

"No. No. I don't want her. It is you I want to marry." He held my hands and tried to look me in the eyes.

I looked away. "No. It will never happen. I had better go. It is getting late." I attempted to get up, but he held me down, his hands clutching mine. "Please let me go, Robert. I really must go. Your mother will be looking for us."

He stared at me with a heartbroken expression that caused a sharp stab of pain deep within me. His eyes had lost their shine. It was as if he were far away, in another world. I wriggled my hands free from his hold and ran towards the stable door, feeling as though I would come apart from my grief.

"I'll talk to Mother. I'll make her change her mind," he shouted after me.

Chapter Eleven

Return to New Jersey

1847, August: Grimsby, Canada West

ROBERT'S AND MY relationship became strained, to say the least, after the incident in the stables. He tried to engage me numerous times in conversation, but I either replied brusquely or not at all, or quickly got out of his way. He continued to offer to take me riding, for he knew I loved to ride. Nevertheless, with a heavy heart, I refused steadfastly.

Uncle Will even asked me one day, "Margaret, why hasn't Robert taken you out riding lately?"

"Oh, Uncle, he's asked me a number of times. But I just didn't feel like it."

"You're not unwell, are you?"

"No, no, nothing like that. Nothing serious, I mean. Perhaps I'll go riding in a few days."

"I understand. When you're feeling better, you should get out and get some exercise, child."

"Yes, Uncle Will."

As it happened, some of the young men I had befriended at the bonfire did call, to take me out riding or whatever else I might fancy. However, after standing the whole day, lifting heavy pots in the hot cabin, making the fruit preserves, I was usually too exhausted to go out. I invariably begged off their invitations. On the other hand, it seemed my heart was still only for Robert.

One Sunday, Albert dropped by and offered to take me out riding. I was tempted, as I had not been out for weeks. At first I said no, but he persisted and I finally agreed. I had my mare, Taj, saddled up, and we set out. As we rode, he made small talk and told me jokes, some rather racy ones that made me laugh and likely turn red. I was beginning to enjoy his company. He took me to a lovely wooded area situated at the base of the Escarpment, where there was a waterfall called Ball's Falls. At the edge of the ravine, he reined in his horse, alighted, came towards me and extended his hand to help me down.

"Would you like to see the waterfall, Margaret?"

I hesitated a bit but, enticed by the prospect, relented and said, "All right, why not."

We walked up to the edge to see the waterfall. It did not look as magnificent as Niagara Falls, of course, being much smaller, but breathtaking nonetheless in the picturesque surroundings, with the trees all round and the water thundering down.

"Do you like it?" Albert asked, trying to make conversation.

"Yes. Thank you for showing me this. Robert never brought me here."

He took my hand in his and said, "I'd like to show you many more wonderful places than Robert ever will."

I thought he was humouring me again. I laughed and said, "I live far away, you know."

It was then that he put his other hand around my waist and drew me to him. I felt his thighs touch mine, which startled me. He looked at me with his dark brown eyes and said, "I want you to be near me, always."

"Oh, Albert. Be serious. Please let me go. Someone might see us."

"I am serious," he said and, pulling me hard against his strong chest, he bent down, trying to kiss me.

His breath and body smelled foul. I turned my face from side to side while he attempted to kiss me on the lips. "Stop, Albert. Please stop. Someone might come along," I implored him.

"Aww … come on, Margaret. There is no one here." He proceeded to run his hands over my back and down to my bottom, which he caressed and pinched. "Let's go over into that thicket, yonder, and sit on the grass," he whispered in a suggestive voice.

"No. I don't want to. Let me go. Let me go," I screamed and beat his chest with my fists.

I believe my crying out and the fear of being heard might have scared him.

He released his hold. "Why not? I've heard Elizabeth telling my sisters you and Robert like to roll in the hay," he jeered.

Hearing him say that filled me with rage. I slapped him hard on the face. "That's a lie."

He rubbed his cheek with one hand and said in a menacing voice, "I'll remember this."

"Don't you ever come near me again!" I shouted and, turning around, ran to my mare. Fortunately, there was a large boulder nearby that I could use as a step to mount her. I rode off, leaving Albert glowering by that waterfall.

*****

I busied myself with a single-minded attention to my work in Aunt Fiona's preserves-making business. After all, that was the main reason I was invited there, and she expected me to carry out my duties. She had set everything up in one of the log cabins. From morning to night I toiled there, washing jars, peeling and chopping fruit, putting the cuttings in a large pot and heating them to a pulp over a fire, constantly stirring lest the combination burn, and then adding the herbs and spices to the exact amount my aunt had written down in the recipe book. Finally, I spooned the mixture into jars and set it aside to cool. Afterwards, I poured a layer of hot wax over the preserve in the neck of the jar and, lastly, put a lid with a metal clamp on the jar to seal it.

Elizabeth was supposed to help me. However, she was more of a bother than help. All the time, she needed me to tell her exactly what to do and, on top of it, she was such a careless child. She dropped the jars and utensils all the time. I had to clean up hurriedly, before Aunt Fiona or anyone else saw the wastage. Although I never uttered one word of complaint about her, there was nary a word of sorry or thanks to me from her. So, whenever Elizabeth said she was getting tired and wished to go out and play with Kirsten, I gladly let her go. I was fearful that if I did not make the required amount of preserve, we would surely be sent back, and I needed the money to put away for going to college.

Aunt Fiona used to come to the cabin in the mornings, but only for a short while. After giving me my instructions for the day, she had Frank drive her to her shop in town. *Fiona's Preserves*, she called it, and it was there she spent the better part of the day, making a few sales but mostly gossiping with the other idle women, Mrs. Mitchell and the like. Sometimes, when a servant was away or busy, I went to the shop to deliver the preserves. I usually overheard her going on about her Robbie. Robbie this and Robbie that. "Wouldn't he look so dashing in a Hussar's uniform? Just like his grandfather, God rest his soul. He died fighting the heathens in India, you know ..." She just went on and on.

Sometimes Jemima came to the cabin, during her breaks from chores in the kitchen, and always gave me a hand. She busied about lifting the pot off the fire, or anything she thought too heavy for me. While she put the filled jars in boxes and carried them away to the storage room, she kept up a constant barrage of criticism.

"No good for you, missy, to work alone. Aah say to Mistress to git someone to help you. But she say, with her hands on her hips, ain't nobody around, Jemima. We not so rich folks to hire more servants. Besides, I git that girl oll the way from New Jersey and cost me a pretty bundle to pay fo her tickets. But aah say, mistress, she's yo kin. You gotta help the poor child. Her pa and ma less rich than yo. But, she say, when she little girl in Ir'land, she work just as hard."

I usually put my arm around her shoulder to comfort her and told her, "It's all right, Jemima. I can manage on my own. Really. Please don't upset yourself."

She often left the cabin dabbing her eyes.

The truth was I found all the hard work helpful in keeping Robert out of my mind. Weeks went by, and just when I thought he had forgotten all about me, I heard someone enter the cabin. My back was to the door, for I was stirring a mixture of fruit pulp in the pot hanging in the fireplace.

"Hallo, Puppet." It was his pleasant voice, and despite myself, I felt a rush of joy. He walked over and embraced me from behind.

While his hug made my blood race in excitement, I didn't wish to encourage him. "Please, Robert, let me go. I'm busy, can't you see? Or do you want this hot mixture over both of us?"

"Can you spare a moment, Puppet? I must talk to you."

"All right, what is it?" I said, trying to take the hot and heavy pot off the fireplace, using both hands.

"Here, let me help you." He took the pot in one hand and easily carried it over to the workbench and put it on top of the bricks.

"Please be quick, I can't let the mixture cool in the pot."

He held me by my shoulders and gazed into my eyes. His blue eyes looked pale, like the sky. "All right, I'll be brief. What I came to say—rather, to ask you, is: will you come away with me?"

"Come away? Whatever do you mean?"

"We could go somewhere, America maybe? Perhaps to Charleston to Aunt Nora's plantation, or anywhere in the world you wish, my darling Puppet. Let's run away together. What say you?"

I cannot recall what it was that, on hearing the suggestion, made me tense. Perhaps it was the voice of our Lord in my head, warning me to be wary of this temptation. I put the spoon I was holding on the bench and looked at Robert.

I said in a loud voice, "Really! Go away. As simple as that? Are you out of your mind?"

"No. I'm perfectly in my senses. I've thought long and hard. I feel it's the right decision for us."

"Pray, how did you come to this conclusion?" I asked sarcastically. Then, it suddenly dawned on me. "Good God, you have spoken to your mother about us, haven't you?"

"I told you I would speak to her, and I have."

"And what did she say?"

He did not reply and simply looked down at the floor. That gave me his answer.

"Right. Just as I thought. No wonder she's been looking at me strangely and treating me brusquely. She wants you to marry Nancy, doesn't she?" I said, again raising my voice.

He nodded sheepishly.

"So, you'd rather elope with me. Is that it?"

"Yes. You know, Puppet, I love you so much and want to spend the rest of my life with you."

"But how are we going to manage? Your parents will surely disinherit you. You've barely finished school. What kind of a life will it be for the two of us, working like the other slaves on your Aunt Nora's plantation? Have you thought about that?"

"I can work to earn our keep. I'm willing to do anything for you."

He had tears in his eyes when he said those words. It really melted my heart. I reached over and hugged him. Tears started to flow down my cheeks. Yet somehow, I managed to compose myself. I stepped back and dabbed my eyes with a kerchief.

"Robbie, look at me. Let me tell you something. I know you well enough to be aware of what you're really like. You wouldn't be happy working like a farm hand. You want to ride horses, be a cavalry officer, travel the world, live in a manor home, have valets and servants at your beck and call. And you *should* lead the good life. You deserve it. You are used to it. Just think about losing it all. You will come to resent me for it."

"So you won't come with me?"

"Robbie! As much as I want to, I'm thinking about *your* future life."

"No! I don't want such a life. What good are those comforts without you? You are the only one I love, Puppet." Saying this, he rushed out of the cabin. I imagine he didn't wish me to see him crying.

I started to run after him, but stopped at the door. It was as if my legs were in chains and I could go no further. I tried to shout after him, yes, yes, Robbie, let's saddle up right now and gallop off towards Charleston. However, the words would not come out.

Robert mounted Babur and galloped away. I watched him until he disappeared into the woods.

I went back inside the cabin and sat down on the bench. With my elbows on the table and my head between my hands, I cried my heart out. Did I make the right decision, I wondered? Dear God, have I lost him forever?

I slept badly that night. As a result, I woke up a bit late the next day. Remembering that Betty, the upstairs maid, was feeling poorly and would not be at work, I decided to tidy up before leaving the room. As my room was next door to my aunt and uncle's bedroom, we shared an adjoining washroom. After washing up, I cleaned in there, emptied the washbasin, and brought up fresh water in the jug. I was making the bed when I heard the customary knock on the washroom door on the side of the master bedroom. My side of the washroom door was closed and as I wasn't in there, I did not answer.

"Anyone in there? Guess not." It was Uncle Will.

Through the door, I heard water splashing in the washbasin and, later, the slapping sound of a razor sharpening on the leather strap, as he prepared to shave.

"Are you decent, Will? I want to talk to you." It was Aunt Fiona.

"Aye, come in. What is it, Fi?"

"Sorry to bother you at your toilet, but I have to rush to the post office. Has Robert spoken to you?"

"About what?"

"It appears our lad is coming of age."

"Ha! Really. Has he gotten anyone in trouble?" he said with a laugh.

"No, not yet, but he might soon."

"He's giving you fair warning, is he? To get the nursery ready?" Uncle was laughing heartily by then.

"No, no. Would you be serious for a minute, Will?"

"Aye. Is anything the matter?"

"Robbie wants to get married."

"Really! Nancy can't wait, is that it?"

"No, no. Not to Nancy. To your charming niece."

Uncle Will was silent for a long while. I sat down on my bed and crossed my arms about my chest to stop myself from trembling.

Finally, he said, "Has he told Nancy yet?"

"Apparently so. The Mitchells are furious."

"Don't blame them. This is going to be the talk of the town."

"The tongues are already wagging, I'd say. Let me tell you, Will, if he marries that preacher's daughter, he can kiss his commission goodbye."

"Now, now, Fi. They aren't such a bad lot."

"Not a bad lot! Did you see how she behaved at our bonfire? Picked a quarrel with sweet Nancy. Told her fibs that she'd been shopping at the most fashionable stores in Manhattan and implied that Nancy's a country bumpkin for never having been to New York. And did you notice all the lads gawking at Margaret, with their tongues hanging out? It was so embarrassing. I almost felt like asking her to leave the party and go to her room."

"That was Heather's dress, wasn't it? Didn't she lend it to Margaret?"

"She did, and I'd suggested it. I thought I was doing the poor girl a favour. Her mother literally begged me, in all her letters, to find a suitable beau for her. And how does she repay me? By showing not the least bit of interest in any of the young, eligible, well-off bachelors I presented to her."

"Whom did you introduce her to?" Uncle Will asked.

"Wilfred Campbell—only a little balding. Magnus Lanchester—not very portly and two farms to his name. George Rhinegold—so moral, and his sisters would be a great help around the house, since they're likely to never marry … Oh yes, and that rich water-miller's boy, Albert, but she seemed to know him already, heaven knows where from. Instead, she throws herself at our Robbie. I am simply disgusted."

"I suppose you told Robbie he cannot marry her."

"Aye. We had a long talk. I told him of the consequences in no uncertain terms. I didn't wish to bother you with this news until I got all the facts."

"And what did he say?"

"Can you imagine what he said? He said if we objected, he was going to elope with her to your good for nothing sister's plantation. That's what he said!"

"Good heavens. Not to that slave farm!"

"Aye. He's going live in a slave shanty with his harlot."

"What are we to do, Fi? Have you thought of anything?"

"I most certainly have—"

I was beginning to feel sick. I couldn't bear to listen anymore. I got up from the bed, tiptoed to my bedroom door and quietly slipped out. I didn't care for breakfast. Instead, I went for a walk in the woods, to clear my head of all the vile things Aunt Fiona had said about my family and me. How dare she judge me so harshly, I fumed?

It is said that eventually, we all have to face our Judgment Day, where our life thereafter shall be proclaimed. Nevertheless, I also believe that we have to face numerous judgment days here on Earth, where our subsequent life in this world is to be determined. That day was one such judgment day for me.

I went to the cabin and, just as usual, started preparations for the day's work making preserves. I gathered up an armload of jars and was taking them to the washbasin when Aunt Fiona entered the cabin.

"Good morning, Aunt," I said, keeping a steady voice.

"Good morning. Leave those. Come with me, I wish to talk to you." She spoke curtly, through pressed lips.

I followed her out of the cabin and she led the way to her favourite spot. The rose garden. The roses were in bloom and their enchanting scent was in the air. She stopped before a bench, sat down, and motioned at me to sit beside her. I did.

Dressed in a blue cape over a red velvety dress, her red hair brushed back and with a solemn look on her long slim face, she looked like a noblewoman. She sat straight and quiet for a long while, just looking around, admiring the roses and breathing deeply the fragrant air. Finally she spoke.

"Isn't it lovely here?"

"Indeed it is, Aunt."

"Then why are you bent upon destroying everything that Will and I have built?"

"*Destroy?* Whatever do you mean, Aunt?"

"You know perfectly well what I mean. Leading Robert on like that."

"I've done no such thing, Aunt. It is Robert who's been—"

"No, it is *you* who's been encouraging him. Wanting him to break off the relationship with Nancy he's been developing for so long, and marry you."

Her presumption that I was trying to get Robert to marry me was a shock. I was speechless. I looked at her, amazed.

"Don't look at me like that. You knew full well that he is fond of Nancy."

"Yes, but—"

"Then why did you lead him on? Running to the stables after him in the middle of the night! Really, child, have you no shame or modesty?"

"Honestly, Aunt. It wasn't at all like you think."

"Not like what? Lizzie told me she saw you from her bedroom window, following Robert into the stables and then, much later, scurrying back with your hair all tousled."

"No, Aunt. It was Robert who wanted me to go there and—"

"Yes, yes. I've spoken to Robert. He told me all about Babur being fidgety and Robbie asking for your help. He said nothing happened between the two of you, and that's good enough for me."

"I'm relieved to hear you understand, Aunt."

"But what I then don't understand is him wanting to run off with you."

"Because he's in love with me. We love each other."

"Nonsense. I don't believe it for a second. You're both so young; hardly know the meaning of the word. Besides, he's got his future to think of."

"What do you mean, Aunt?"

"He's got to get his commission. How can he do that if he runs away with you? I've spoken with Will, and we are both adamant about it. The moment he leaves this house with you, he is completely on his own. He will not get a penny from us. Do you understand?"

I nodded.

"We have made up our minds. We feel it would be best if you were to leave immediately, and go back home."

Go back home. Those words stunned me. The thought of going home in disgrace, facing the wrath of Mamma and Papa and being chastised for not earning my keep, was too much for me. Tears swelled in my eyes and rolled down my cheeks. I put my palm on my aunt's arm, but she moved her hand away.

Between sniffles and tears, I implored her, "Aunt Fiona, I beg you, please don't send me home. I promise not to listen to Robert's wild ideas. You know I need to earn money for my education. Mamma told me Papa will never be able to afford to send me to college."

"Then you'll have to find another job, won't you?" she said tersely. If she felt even the least bit sorry for me, she certainly didn't let it show.

"You know there aren't any jobs for women. Except in the cotton mills in the slums of Boston or Lowell."

"Well, you should have thought about it before, shouldn't you?" Her voice was harsh and unyielding.

I tried once again. "Aunt, I'll do anything you say. I won't be a bother to you at all. If you like, I'll move into the cabin with the Jenkins family. I'll work twice as hard for you. Just please, please, do not send me away." I tried to put my arm around her and wanted to place my head on her shoulder. She pushed me away, firmly.

She spoke again, in a sterner voice this time. "On top of it, you're now carrying on with that Miller boy. Is it to make Robert jealous?"

It felt as if someone had slapped me hard. Although stunned, I gathered enough courage to reply, "Not at all. I'm not seeing Albert. He only took me out riding once, to show me Ball's Falls."

"And we heard some gossip about that outing too."

"What has Albert been saying? It's all lies. I told him I never wanted to see him again. If you would ask him to come over, I can clear it up before you."

"It won't serve any purpose, Margaret. You have disgraced the good name of our family. The whole town is talking about you. It's best for you to go home. I telegraphed your mother and here's her reply."

She took a folded piece of paper out of her pocket and handed it to me. The telegram read:

Please send Margaret home at once STOP Advise arrival time of train in Jersey City STOP James will pick her up STOP With many apologies for her inexcusable behaviour STOP Much love to you all STOP Joan END OF MESSAGE

Mamma's phrase, *her inexcusable behaviour*, was like a dagger through my heart. I began to cry with my head between my hands.

"Now, now, child. Pray, control yourself." Aunt Fiona stood up abruptly and gave me her final instructions. "I want you to go up to your room, pack up your trunk and be ready within the hour. I've asked Frank to bring the carriage around. He will take you down to Niagara Falls, buy your ticket, and put you on the train for Jersey City. Your papa will meet you there. I have already wired the money for all your past wages to Joan. Here's some spending money for the journey." She dropped a couple of silver dollar coins into my lap and strode out of the garden.

I sat on the bench for a while. The rose bushes suddenly looked full of thorns with wilted flowers. It also seemed the sun had disappeared behind dull clouds. I felt engulfed in a dark shroud. I was not surprised Mamma was upset at the turn of events. However, I felt Papa would be more understanding. I had sat through many of his sermons when he had preached for courage in times of despair and advised praying to our Lord to be shown the path to salvation. I put my palms together and said a silent prayer to Him. I asked for forgiveness, if I had sinned, for I knew I had not. I asked for guidance and assistance in my future endeavours. It was then a strange calmness came over me. I felt serene and I knew my plea would be answered. I dried my tears, got up, and walked calmly towards the house.

In anticipation of the long journey in the grimy train, I wore a dark blue, high-collar dress with long sleeves and a matching bonnet. I felt utterly empty inside.

There was a knock on the door. It was Frank. "Your carriage is waiting, miss. Is your trunk ready? May I take it down?"

"Yes, it is ready. Thank you, Frank." I pointed to it.

I took one last look around the pretty room where I'd spent a comfortable month. I glanced out of the window at the lily pond, the picturesque garden and the lovely fruit trees in the orchard, the shining blue lake and the Forty Mile Creek yonder. The gulls were still circling there. Would I ever return to see this heavenly place again? I did not think so, as I closed the door behind me.

I came down the staircase, carrying my travelling bag, which was made from leftover material. In the foyer, Aunt Clara and Thomas were waiting.

"Goodbye, child. Have a safe journey. Be sure to give my love to your mamma," Aunt Clara said, hugging me. Her sympathetic voice lifted me slightly. I looked about for Elizabeth, but she was nowhere to be found.

Thomas handed me a box. "Some lunch for your journey, mistress."

"Thank you, Thomas." I managed a smile at him, for he knew I liked him to call me "mistress".

He simply bowed his head in respectful silence.

I walked out of the massive oak doors of Wallace Hall with a heavy heart, as I believed it was the last time I would pass through that grand entrance. Frank had the carriage door open for me. I walked down the steps towards it. Just before entering the carriage, I looked back and saw Aunt Fiona and Uncle Will come out of the house and stand on the stone landing above the front steps. I ran back to them. With tears in my eyes, I hugged Aunt Fiona and tried one last time to plead with her. "Dearest Aunt, is there any way or anything I can do for you to forgive me? Can you not let me stay?" I sobbed on her shoulder.

She pushed me back firmly. "Pray, control yourself. Behave like a lady," was all she could manage.

Uncle Will took me by my arm and led me back to the carriage.

"Goodbye, Margaret. God be with you, child," he said in a kind voice, and kissed me on the cheek.

Frank slapped the reins on the horses' flanks, startling them from their slumber. The carriage lurched forward. I was crying uncontrollably by then. As the coach rounded the driveway, I looked out of the window, to take one last look at the manor house. It was then I saw Robert standing by one of the windows on the second floor, his arms folded, his body rigid and his face expressionless. He just stared out from between the drapes, watching me drive away. He did not wave, and neither did I.

Chapter Twelve

Meeting at the Lake House Tavern

1967, July: Toronto, Ontario, Canada

ALEXANDRA JOINED ME ON THE SOFA in the living room of her parents' home. It was shortly after I had come downstairs earlier that night, in search of Doctor Margaret's apparition. I poured Alexandra a glass of wine and refilled mine. We sat together, entranced, reading Doctor Margaret's journal for much of the night. Eventually, the first rays of sunlight peeked through the windows; birds flew about in the garden, from the trees onto the lawn, looking for their morning meal.

Alexandra reached for a tissue from the box on the side table and dabbed the tears from her eyes. "Goodness, what a hard-hearted aunt. Imagine, sending her poor niece back home, knowing full well she needed the money for her college education—"

"Money for whose college education?" Alexandra's mother asked, as she came down the stairs in her pink dressing gown.

I closed the journal and put it down on the centre table. While Alexandra blew her nose into the tissue, I said, "Money for Margaret's college education, which her aunt wouldn't even let her work for."

"Good heavens. Both of you haven't been up all night reading that journal, have you?"

"Yes, pretty well, Mamma. We just couldn't sleep. It's such a poignant story," Alexandra replied, with tears still in her eyes. She then proceeded to tell her mother all the events we had learned so far in Margaret's life.

Peter came down, freshly shaved and showered, dressed in a white shirt and dark trousers. It being a Sunday, he was likely going to church later. He sat in a wing chair, coffee cup in hand, listening intently to Alexandra narrate the fascinating chronicle. I must admit I had teary eyes as well and I excused myself to go upstairs to wash up and get ready. Alexandra followed me up shortly and showered while I shaved.

I wanted to get an early start to return to Baltimore at least by Monday afternoon. But I was still curious about what had transpired the day before, back at Wallace Hall in Grimsby, and whether or not Bill Wallace had managed to get the crown back from his stepbrother, Gregorze. I felt I should at least give them a telephone call before we left Toronto and possibly stop by for a short visit on the way home.

After a hearty breakfast of delicious omelettes and strong cups of coffee, Alexandra and I were fresh as ever for the return journey. I suggested we give the Wallaces a call, to which she and her parents agreed, saying it was a good idea. I dialled the number. Bill answered.

"Walli, how good of you to call. We've been calling your home in Baltimore and there wasn't any answer."

"We're still here in Toronto, at Alexandra's parents."

"Oh yes, now I remember you mentioned you might be visiting them. Tell me, when are you returning home?"

"We're leaving right now. Just called to ask if everything is all right?"

"Everything is fine. Why don't you stop by here on your way home?" Bill suggested.

"We could, just let me check with my wife." I put my hand on the receiver's mouthpiece and asked Alexandra, "Shall we meet with them for a while?"

She nodded.

Peter interjected, "Don't go to their house, just in case the KGB is watching. Meet them someplace else."

I nodded. I was thankful for that suggestion; no doubt Peter was well versed in the ways of the KGB. I spoke again into the telephone receiver. "Bill, yes, let's meet. But how about someplace close to the highway? We're in a hurry to get home."

"The Lake House Tavern," Alexandra whispered.

"How about the Lake House Tavern, Bill?"

"Sure, that sounds good. Let's meet there at noon?"

"Lunch is on us," I said.

"We'll discuss that."

We said goodbye to Alexandra's parents and, promising to return soon, were on our way towards Grimsby.

"There it is." Alexandra pointed to a stone building with *Lake House Tavern* written on a signboard beside a picture of the century-old house, hanging on a post close to the Lakeshore Road.

I made the turn into their driveway and drove towards the parking lot adjacent to the building. There weren't many cars in the lot and I found a parking spot in the first row by the low brick wall at the edge of a ridge overlooking the lake. A glorious view presented itself. The bright sunrays reflecting off the water created a shimmering effect. Since we had arrived early, we sat in the car, admiring the vista. To the right, the land gently sloped to a small, wooded canyon where a stream flowed through it, out into the lake.

"That looks like the Forty Mile Creek," I said, pointing towards the ravine.

"That could be it. Look at those gulls. Don't they look lovely, sweeping up and down into the water?"

"Yes, how interesting." A group flew over our car, squawking with delight. Just then, I remembered what Margaret had written about seeing them when she'd been here with her cousin Robert. "Looks like they are welcoming us," I repeated Robert's sentence.

Alexandra smiled at me. "Hmm. Aren't you getting a bit romantic, dear?"

"No. You're the romantic one," I replied, as I reached over and put my arms around her. Our eyes met. Hers were turning moist again; no doubt, Margaret was still on her mind. I bent my head and kissed her on her soft lips. Our kiss lasted a while. I finally released her from my embrace, and sighed, "Woo, we'd better go in before they throw us off these premises for indecent behaviour."

She touched my cheek with her palm. "I love you, Walli."

"I love you too, Ola," I said, running my fingers through her blonde hair.

We got out of the car and walked towards the tavern's entrance. A dark blue Cadillac turned in from the road onto the driveway. Bill was driving and he waved at us. We waved back. I saw Jane sitting in the front passenger seat, and in the back seat there was another couple I couldn't see too well, except for their golden hair. I thought they were their children. Bill parked the car and the four of them got out and walked towards us.

It was then I recognised the heavyset man with a crew cut, striding next to Bill. I held Alexandra's hand and whispered, "Good God. Is that who I think it is?"

"Yes, that's him," she replied while I felt her hand shake a bit.

Bill came forward and shook our hands. "Alexandra and Walli, this is Karolina and her husband, Gregorze Barinowsky, whom I believe you have met," he said with a smile.

"Indeed, we have. Mr. Barinowsky, how are you feeling? " I asked, forcing myself to use my calm doctor's voice, as we shook hands with them.

"Very well. Thank you. Please call me Greg."

"Tell me, Greg, why did you bump our car?" Alexandra asked in a stern voice, as if she were interrogating a witness in a courtroom.

While Greg looked sheepishly at us, Bill interjected, "Alexandra, it's a bit of a story. Let's go in and we'll tell you all about it over drinks." He spread his arms out to usher us into the tavern.

It being a warm, sunny day, we opted for a table out on the patio. Greg asked that we take one in the corner, under a shady umbrella. The hostess led us to it. The marvellous view of the lake was before us and the sound of the gentle surf on the sandy beach tried its best to soothe our minds. The tavern staff busied about, serving the customers. A waiter took our orders. I asked about the specialty of the house and was informed it was steak and kidney pie. I ordered that and so did Alexandra, although she usually had fish when we ate out. She looked at me and we smiled, acknowledging it was what Margaret and Robert had partaken over a century ago at that very spot.

"Bill, do they still do the re-enactment of the Battle of the Forty Mile Creek?" I asked to start the conversation in a gentler tone.

"No. They stopped doing that a while back. Although they still re-enact the nearby Stony Creek one. Why don't you come over next June, and we'll go see it?"

"Yes. We'd very much like to." I turned towards Alexandra and asked, "Would your parents like to see it, in case they haven't already?"

"Oh, I'm sure Papa has. He's a history buff."

"So, Alexandra, which part of Russia is your family from?" Jane asked.

"My father's side. They're from St. Petersburg."

"Oh, we coming from there too." Karolina said in her Russian accent and nodding her head, which shook her shoulder-length, blonde hair.

Greg finally apologized. "Sorry for bumping your car. However, I was careful not to cause too much damage, was I not? I looked your Buick over in the parking lot. You can hardly see any dents. I'm glad I still remember some of my training. I'm a retired police officer, you know." He smiled and then, reaching into his pocket, took out a small, red velvet cloth pouch, tied with a drawstring; the kind they used in the past to carry money. "As a token of our begging your forgiveness, I would like to present you this." He offered the pouch to me, on both his palms put together.

I accepted the pouch and opened it. It contained a metal pendant on a gold chain. I pulled it out. A faded, old silver coin hung from the chain. There were inscriptions written in Greek around the edge and in the centre the head of an emperor whom I recognised as Alexander the Great.

"Good God, where did you get this?" I asked with raised eyebrows and my heart pounding.

"It belonged to my grandfather, Count Nicholai. It is recorded in our family register that it was given to him by an Indian sepoy named *Bhadur* Sharif. By any chance, could he be a relation of yours, Walli Sharif?"

"He was my grandfather."

There was silence around the table as they absorbed this information. Finally, Greg cleared his throat and admitted, "I'd suspected as much from the name, but when Bill told me your grandfather was employed by the Rani of Jhansi, it confirmed my hunch. I feel this heirloom should be returned to the family that originally owned it."

I stared at the pendant for a long time, unable to speak, overcome by a strange mixture of both delight and grief. At last, I shook Greg's hand, thanking him for this invaluable family treasure. I wanted to elaborate that I knew how Grandfather had found this coin, on the shores of the Arabian Ocean, in 1856. He was travelling on the very route that Alexander had journeyed in 327 B.C., on his return from the Macedonian expedition in India. More importantly, Grandfather was going to Persia to meet Count Nicholai and guide him safely into

India.

Before I could speak, the waitress interrupted us bringing our mugs of ale and placing them on the table.

"Here's to the Sharifs' health." Bill raised his mug in a toast. In return, we toasted the Barinowsky and the Wallace families.

After a few sips of ale, Alexandra asked again, "But, Greg, please do tell us, why *did* you bump our car? Even though ever so gently."

"Actually, I was trying to get you to stop. To warn you about the Soviet agents."

"You were trying to warn us about the KGB. And here we thought you were one of them!" I said with a laugh, and Alexandra chuckled a bit as well.

"Please, let me explain," Bill interjected. "Walli, ever since you returned from India, you have been trying to locate us?"

"Right," I replied.

"Now, we don't normally get the Toronto newspapers, and even when we do, we don't read the advertisements, anyway. Therefore, we didn't know you wanted to meet us. Actually, it was someone from the Russian Embassy who called, asking us to get in touch with you, because you had brought our grandmother's sea chest from India. While that was exciting news for us and we very much wanted to acquire that trunk, there was a catch." Bill took a sip of his ale after giving us this lengthy bit of information.

"Oh, there was a condition?" I asked with raised eyebrows.

"Yes. Before they would give us your name or telephone number, they wanted us to agree to hand over the Rani of Jhansi's crown and Grandmother's journals."

"But how did they know those items were in the sea chest?" I was puzzled at how much the Soviets knew.

"Oh, most likely Margaret mentioned it to someone, who told another, who spoke to somebody, and finally the word got to the KGB. You know how such gossip and rumours get around," Jane interjected.

"So you agreed with that arrangement?" Alexandra asked.

"No. I discussed it with Jane and Greg. We believed that while the crown would be most valuable in terms of the gemstones in it, it would be next to impossible that we could sell it. Because it belonged to the Rani and the state of Jhansi, the Government of India would demand its return. On the other hand, we would never let our dear grandmother's journals fall into the Soviets' hands. I told them they could have the crown, but not the journals. They wouldn't agree. So, there was no deal." Bill took another sip from his glass.

"But then, how did you manage to call us the other day?" Alexandra asked.

It was Greg who answered this question. "Ah, you know my grandfather, Count Nicholai, was a Russian agent too. I know a few things about counter-espionage."

"So what did you do?" I asked.

"I knew they wanted the crown very badly. Therefore, I went to the Russian Embassy, pretending I needed a visa to visit St. Petersburg. I then asked to see the KGB Colonel Yermolov, who had contacted Bill earlier. I told him I wished to make a deal. I would bring the crown and the journals to them if they would give me a visa plus a hundred thousand dollars. They ah'd, hummed, and finally agreed, but I would only get the visa after I delivered the goods and the money in St. Petersburg—in roubles, of course. We shook hands on that." Greg finished his ale and raised it to the waiter, asking for another one.

"Oh, that's why you came with a revolver and snatched the crown from Jane's hands." Alexandra exclaimed. However, on seeing Jane and Bill smiling, she frowned. "Why, you're putting me on, aren't you? It was all a set-up, wasn't it?"

"Yes, dear." Jane put her hand on Alexandra's wrist and explained, "Greg spoke to me and Bill about this deal he'd made with the Russians, to get Margaret's trunk. You know he was just as eager to have it returned to us."

"But why did you have to pull out the revolver?" Alexandra was in her cross-examination mode.

"It was to convince the KGB. An agent was waiting outside in a car. It looked very real for me to rush out of the house with the crown in one hand and a gun in the other. He drove me to my house, where Colonel Yermolov awaited my arrival with the goods."

The waitress brought our main course dishes. I was pretty hungry by then. I cut into the steak and kidney pie and put a hot forkful, dripping with gravy, into my mouth. It tasted delicious. I looked at the others and they seemed to be enjoying their dishes. I asked Alexandra and she nodded with a mouthful of the pie.

"Greg, what did the colonel say when you arrived home without the journals?" I asked.

"Walli, I know that if you have to tell a lie, keep it as

uncomplicated as possible. Hence, I simply told him the journals were not in that trunk. He really flew off his handle—called me an incompetent peasant. I reminded him that my grandfather was a count. He ignored that and decided to go to Wallace Hall to confirm I was telling the truth."

"But, Jane, what about the telephone call from Karolina? Didn't you say Greg was coming to get the journals?"

Karolina answered, "Oh, I am sorry. My English not good. I mean to say Greg come to warn you that Yermolov coming to take the diaries. I am sorry."

"I think I understood what Karolina said," Jane elaborated, "but I wanted you to leave quickly with the diaries. Explaining all about Yermolov would have delayed you."

"But, Greg, how did you arrive so soon at Wallace Hall, even ahead of Colonel Yermolov?" Alexandra asked, still looking confused.

That's a good question, I thought.

"I know a shortcut. There is a farm road through the fields between the two houses. I jumped into my pick-up truck and reached Wallace Hall in about half the time Yermolov took," Greg replied, looking rather proud.

"You must have been surprised that we got away even before you arrived?" I asked.

"Yes, I was. But I tried to follow you, to warn you about Yermolov."

"Yes, I got the message from your gentle bumping of our behind."

Greg laughed. "I wanted you to stop, to explain the situation. But my God, you zoomed away, leaving me behind in your dust. That's a big engine you got there. Is it a 440?"

"I'm not certain of the size. But I believe it's one of the GM's biggies."

While Greg and I were busy discussing GM cars and engines, Alexandra could not leave the story behind and interjected.

"But I don't understand one thing, Greg."

What's up now, I thought?

"Yes, what is it, Olenka?" Greg asked.

"Why do the Russians want the Rani's crown so badly, as you put it?"

Greg moved forward in his chair and put his elbows on the table. In typical secret agent style, he looked sideways to make sure no one was listening and spoke in a whisper. "Let me tell you something that's top secret. The Soviets are going to invade Afghanistan very soon. They know Pakistan has strong ties with Afghanistan and will never be on their side. So, they want India's support badly. The crown is proof that they helped the Rani in India's First War of Independence. By returning the crown, they hope they will get some backing from India for their campaign in Afghanistan."

It appeared the Russians' aim on Afghanistan was an open secret. Peter had mentioned the same plans to me as well. What an interesting strategy, to get India's support, I thought. However, I was curious about the journals and asked, "Bill, so what happened when Yermolov arrived at your place?"

"Nothing much, really. He came in, looked around, and asked about the diaries. We told him that they weren't in the trunk. Simple as that."

Everyone guffawed.

"Did he believe you?" I asked.

"It would seem so. Yermolov put the same question to some of our relatives. They also replied that they didn't know what he was talking about. He left satisfied enough. I believe they've gone back to Ottawa. I think we're okay for a while, but I'm sure sooner or later, they're going to find out that the journals do exist," Bill said.

"So what do you suggest we do, Bill? We can't hide them forever in the States," I said.

"I have the perfect solution," Bill replied.

"Really! And what's that?" I asked in amazement.

Bill was about to answer, but kept silent as the waitress came back to pick up the empty plates and asked if we would like any dessert. We refused dessert but ordered coffee, except for Greg, who wanted a cheesecake as well.

Bill continued, "You know, Walli, the main reason I do not wish the Soviets to have the journals is that Margaret was originally American, and with the Cold War going on, the Soviets would likely do their utmost to disgrace her and Count Nicholai's family. We know them; they'll likely add all kinds of untruths in there—"

"But why? Wasn't the count sent to India by the Russians to help in the Revolution?" I interrupted.

"Yes, but due to the fact the fact that the Russian plan failed, for whatever reason, they will try to pin the blame on our grandparents,"

Bill said.

"Ah! Is it the matter of those Russian invasion maps and how they mysteriously fell into British hands?" I finally began to understand the Barinowskys and Wallaces' concern.

Greg leaned forward. "Yes, Walli. That's it. You might not have heard, but there's an intense controversy about them. Grandmother's journal is just the medium they might use to disgrace my family, especially since we are White Russians."

"Oh, really! So how can I help?" I asked.

"Well, I know you doctors write rather quickly," Bill said with a smile and asked, "Can we request you to write Margaret's biography? A good friend of ours is a book publisher and we could have it out on the market in no time."

"Oh, I get it. Once the biography, based on the journals, is published, they would become just archive material and of no use to the Soviets. Bill, you're a genius." I pressed his shoulder.

"So, will you help us, Walli?"

"But why me, Bill? Why not yourself or someone else?"

"Walli, I'm humbled by your suggestion. I'm not a very literary person. You're from that area and know the history well. In addition, with your grandfather's connection to the count and Margaret, you'll be able to put together her story most effectively. You are the best person to pen the biography. I'm certain of it."

I then remembered all those dreams and nightmares I had been having, where Margaret visited me off and on, and thought, goodness, she wants me to write her story for the whole world to read. Not being able to refuse, I replied, "Bill, I don't have much free time. But for Margaret's sake, I'll make time, even if I have to miss my beauty sleep."

"Thank you, Walli. I knew we could count on you."

"I'll do my best. By the way, do you have a title for the book in mind?"

"We'll leave it completely up to you and Alexandra."

I looked inquiringly at Alexandra.

"I can propose a promising title," Alexandra said.

"What do you suggest, dear?" Jane asked.

"How about we call it *Doctor Margaret's Sea Chest?*"

Just then, a flock of gulls flew over, screaming their heads off. We looked up.

Bill remarked, "Looks like the gulls agree. It is the perfect title for the book."

"Can you do one thing, Bill?" Greg asked, suddenly.

"Yes, Greg, what is it?"

"Can you hold the publication until I have returned from Russia?"

"Of course, we wouldn't risk having you missing out on your bounty, Greg," Bill replied with a smile.

It was getting late and I wanted to be on our way. I motioned to the waitress for the bill, which she brought over in a silver dish and placed it on the table. I reached for it, but Bill held my hand. I protested, but he would not let go.

"Consider this a promotional lunch for your book," Bill said, picking up the paper.

"You are most kind and generous." I thanked them again for the hospitality, and especially Karolina and Greg for the return of the precious pendant.

As we got up and prepared to leave, Alexandra had a mystified look. She stood by her chair, holding onto the backrest, looking very much like a lawyer making her final summation in court. She said, "Greg, I'm still not clear on one point."

What could it be now, I mused.

"Yes, Olenka?" Greg asked with a bewildered look.

"I understand you're going ahead with your plan to visit the USSR?" When Greg nodded, she continued, "Do you really believe the Soviets are going to hand over a bag of roubles as soon as you land in Moscow?"

Greg concurred. "I guess you're right. They may not even want to see me."

Alexandra, the lawyer, was persistent. "So why are you taking such a big risk? Have you considered the possibility that you might be imprisoned? Unless there is a greater compelling reason—is there?"

Greg looked down at the floor for a while. He finally answered in a whisper, "Yes, there is. I have to get my daughter, Katya, out of there."

That revelation stunned me and, from the look on her face, Alexandra as well. The others, including Karolina, simply stood by calmly, looking at Greg.

It was Jane who broke the silence by saying, "But that's another story. Let's not hold up Alexandra and Walli. I'm sure Greg will tell us all about it some other time."

I nodded, and we started to walk towards the exit.

Instead of going out the front door of the tavern, we walked out the back gate from the patio towards the beach. A path led from there to the parking lot. I spied a lovely bed of rosebushes along the wall, with an abundance of flowers in a multitude of red, yellow, and pink.

"What a delightful collection of roses." Alexandra remarked. She stood there in deep thought, as if she remembered something. I went over to the rose bushes and plucked a red rose for her. When I returned, she was talking to Bill and Jane and I heard her ask, "Bill, whatever happened to Robert Wallace? We haven't heard you talk about him at all."

Bill stood in silence, very erect in his six-foot-two frame, and simply stared out towards the lake, apparently unable to speak.

Jane came to his rescue. "Alexandra, dear, why don't you read about Robert in Margaret's diaries? I'm sure she'll tell you all. It's very painful for Bill to speak about him."

"Oh, I'm sorry, Bill. I didn't mean to upset you." Alexandra said, putting her palm on his forearm.

"It's all right. Have a safe trip home," he said in a barely audible whisper.

Chapter Thirteen

A Medical College for Women!

1847, September: Elizabethtown, New Jersey
EVER SINCE MY "DISGRACEFUL RETURN FROM GRIMSBY",
as Mamma liked to put it, I was relegated to the charwoman's position
at the Wallace School for Children. Mamma, in an effort to supplement
Papa's meagre income, used to run a school.

The Common School System had not yet come into being in our
state, and children were still educated in small, single-room schools
such as Mamma's. The schoolhouse was located in a small, single-
storey frame building on the church grounds adjacent to our house. My
cleaning tasks consisted of sweeping and tidying up the schoolroom,
the office, a small library, the kitchen, and—lest I forget—mopping up
the outhouse. I did those chores happily, as I liked earning the pocket
money, although Mamma made me save most of the coins in a jar to
be spent only on church collections, birthdays and Christmas presents.

With the start of the school year, in addition to concentrating on
my studies, I busied myself with all the menial work. One afternoon
after school, while I swept the classroom floor, I overheard a pupil, the
daughter of a Doctor Levy who operated a clinic close by, talking to
Mamma in the office. Apparently, one of their maids had left and they
were looking for some help.

"Mother says the job would be just the cleaning downstairs, in the
clinic, and the vestibule. She wants to know if you can recommend
someone," the girl said.

Just as I thought, Mamma jumped at this chance to bring in some additional money. I heard her say, "Margaret is quite busy, although I think Elizabeth should be able to take it on. She's in the playground, I think. Let's go find her."

I continued sweeping and spotted, through the window, Mamma and the girl talking to Elizabeth. I snickered when I heard Elizabeth say in a loud voice, "No. I won't do it. I've seen that clinic. I will not clean up all the blood in the surgery rooms and then the toilets as well." I saw her walk away as Mamma stared after her.

Mamma came to the classroom door with the girl in tow, and called out sweetly to me, "Puppet. Can you come here for a moment, dear?"

I put the broom aside and walked over to them. "Yes, what is it?"

"Doctor Levy needs someone to help out in his clinic. It's in the evenings, mind, and requires cleaning the operating rooms and the privy. I know you did such a good job at your Aunt Fiona's preserves workshop. This should be no problem for you. I'll get Lizzie to take over here," Mamma said, putting her hand on my shoulder. "Would you be interested?" she asked with a squeeze.

I must admit the thought of working in a medical clinic enthralled me. Although I felt a surge of delight rush through my body, I hid my enthusiasm and said, "All right, Mamma. If you want me to take this job, I'll take it."

"Good. Thank you, Puppet. I'll let Mrs. and Doctor Levy know. I'm sure they will be happy to take you on." Mamma left with her final instruction, "And when you see them, do try to make a good impression, will you?"

I nodded, wondering what she meant by her last remark, unless it was a veiled reference to Aunt Fiona's comments. I stood leaning on the broom handle for a while, feeling elated. This was the opportunity I had been waiting for. It was the opening for me to embark on the road to a medical education. The Lord had answered my prayer.

The next evening, I got ready and walked over to Doctor Levy's house. He ran his clinic from the ground floor of an old, rambling, colonial-style mansion. Several rooms were used as offices and for surgery, and some had beds for convalescing patients. I had put on a dark blue, high-collar, long-sleeves with white cuffs gown. I had borrowed the dress from a girlfriend's mother, who worked as a servant. I also made sure to look the part by wearing her tight-fitting, white cotton maid's bonnet with the ribbons tied securely below my chin.

Doctor Levy sat writing at his desk in his office, which was littered with medical curios. The item I could not take my eyes away from was a full-length human skeleton hanging in one corner. Doctor Levy looked up, asked me to come in and motioned towards a chair. He was an older gentleman, tall and slim, with a bald crown and greying hair that fell over his ears. As I sat down, he straightened up and looked at me with steady brown eyes and a grim face. He appeared surprised, but after a moment, he relaxed and, leaning back in the chair, stretched his long legs and clasped his strong-looking hands about his chest.

Finally he said, "Tell me, Miss Wallace. What makes a fine young lady such as yourself wish to take on this tedious job?"

My heart skipped a beat; I thought my disguise had not had its effect. "I don't mind char work, sir. Oi like working with me 'ands," I tried hard to lie.

"Is that so? And have you done this kind of work before?" he asked, looking at my clean fingers.

"Yes, sir. Oi worked up in Canada this summer, for me aunt. And now, I'm working for me mom in the school, cleaning the floors and the toilets, like."

"Hmm …" He appeared to contemplate. "Too bad Mrs. Levy had to go to a meeting. She would have shown you around and explained to you the details of the difficult work. Anyhow, when she was told that *you* were coming, she didn't look too pleased. I don't think she would have considered you suitable. Perhaps you should reconsider."

I heard the rejection, but I wasn't going to be vanquished. I perked up my courage and said in a pleading voice, "No, sir. I'm interested in this job. Please, give me a chance, sir. I'm not afraid of doing 'ard work. I 'ave done it before."

"But, Miss Wallace, a summer job with your cousins and sweeping out your mother's schoolroom is hardly the experience needed for working in a hospital-like environment. There will be many sick people about here, you know. You will see bleedings, amputations and all kinds of surgery waste to clean up after. I dare say you might even see a dead body now and then. I don't think you will be able to stand up to these horrific sights. Would you?"

"No, sir. I'm not scared of seein' blood. I've seen dead bodies."

"Really, dead bodies! Like where?"

"I've seen me grandpa, at his funeral."

He laughed. "Miss Wallace, seeing a dead person in a funeral home is not what I meant. I'm really curious why you are so interested in this job."

"Yes, sir. I'm very much interested. Also, I do need this job, for I need the money, sir."

"Come now, Miss Wallace. I know Pastor James. Your mother runs the school. I don't think you're in the poor house. Besides, what do you need the money for? Pretty soon, some young man is going to come around and sweep you off your feet. Am I not right?"

I was certain that my masquerade as a maid was not working. Hence, I thought, why not tell him the truth, and in the proper accent. "No, sir," I replied firmly. "I am not ready for marriage yet. And I need to save money to go to medical college."

I saw his jaw drop. "Really? Medical college! Are you quite sure?"

"Yes, sir. That is *the* profession I am interested in."

"And how long have you had this idea?"

"For as long as I can remember."

He smiled and said, "Ah. Now it is getting clearer to me."

"How do you mean, sir?" I asked, feeling bewildered, and I must have displayed it on my face.

"Miss Wallace, let me tell you, I was born and bred in London. Your accent did not match any that I have heard in my fifty-five years."

I laughed and covered my face with my hands.

"And that attire. Is it yours?"

"No, sir."

"I didn't think so. I see that you are willing to look the part of a maid. But let me ask you again. Are you really certain you will be able to carry on the strenuous duties here? I must warn you, Mrs. Levy is very demanding."

"Why, yes, sir. I will do my best."

"Normally I would not have employed a young lady of your position. We asked your mother if she could *recommend* someone suitable. A more … mature woman, shall we say. Not a clergyman's daughter. I'm sure when your mother learns what her child has to endure, she may keep you away. Would she not?"

"You don't have to worry about Mamma, sir. I will not utter one word of complaint to her."

"Miss Wallace, I am impressed by your determination, especially your desire to become a physician. I'm not sure if you will get there, but this is a good place to start. All right, here's what I propose. You can begin working here for a trial period of one month. After that, Mrs. Levy and I shall evaluate your performance. You may, if you wish, leave before the month is over. Is this acceptable?"

I felt like running up to him and hugging him. However, I restrained myself by holding on to my chair's armrests. "Thank you, sir. You'll see I will stay for the month and much longer."

Doctor Levy told me how much he would pay me. In my excitement, I nodded, accepting it immediately. It was not much, but I would have worked there even for naught. He got up and we shook hands. I felt the warmth of his strong surgeon's fingers.

As I walked back home, in the darkness of the late summer evening, I said a silent prayer to thank the Lord for opening this door for me. I wondered if it was providence that had arranged for Mrs. Levy to be away that evening. Would she have been so understanding?

*****

I began my evening job at Doctor Levy's in earnest. The first few days were quite exhausting. After a whole day of school and helping Mamma with the house chores and then working in the clinic from six till ten o'clock in the evenings, I had barely enough energy left to crawl into bed. However, gradually I become accustomed to the routine and arranged my tasks such that, to Mrs. Levy's amazement, I used to sweep the floors, dust and tidy up the rooms, clean up the surgical tables, and rinse and wash out the privies well before my quitting time. Actually, there was another reason for my hurrying up and finishing the chores. It gave me some time to linger in Doctor Levy's office and examine his medical books and bric-a-brac.

After nearly a month, one day, while I stood staring at the human skeleton, Doctor Levy came into the office, looking for a book or something. At first, he ignored me and scanned the bookshelf on the other side of the room. Having found the item, he turned around and said, "Ah, there you are, Margaret. I have been meaning to speak with you. I wish to acknowledge your good work here. Mrs. Levy tells me you are a very efficient worker. Both of us are very pleased with your performance. Why, the place looks so spick and span, it's a pleasure to come to work in the mornings. So, would you like to continue on here?"

"Why, yes, sir. I would love to. Thank you, sir," I stammered.

"That's good. Oh, I see you are already interested in pursuing your medical curiosity."

"Yes, sir. I want to learn all I can."

"All right, if you wish to know more about Mr. Bones there, let me find you something," he said and, turning around, picked out a slim volume from the bookshelf. "Here, read this. But peruse it only in this office. You are not to take it out. Do you understand?"

"Yes, sir. Thank you."

He handed me the book and left the office, saying, "I don't expect you to understand everything in it. But you may ask me if there is something you wish to know more about."

I eagerly took the book to the desk and, putting the oil lamp a bit higher, opened the first page. It was a text titled *Introduction to Human Anatomy.* That was the first of countless other medical books I was to read.

*****

1850, March: Elizabethtown, New Jersey
Even though I had reached my teens, my parents were still very much against me entering the medical profession. There was a social taboo, at that time in the mid nineteenth century, against women becoming doctors. This was possibly because we in the old colonial States, even after having fought a war and obtained our freedom from the British, still cherished the Victorian traditions. Other than one notable exception, it was unheard of for young ladies to enrol in medical colleges and administer medicines or perform surgery. For, heaven forbid, they would then have to look at and touch the naked bodies of men. Perhaps performing such acts was thought to be similar to the job of females who practiced the world's oldest profession.

Like my siblings and the other children of the neighbourhood, we attended Mamma's school and, upon completing the curriculum, went on to jobs or sat for entrance examinations of institutions or academies of higher education. Although I had passed my examinations and received my certificate with high honours, due to lack of higher education and job opportunities for women, I continued to work for Doctor Levy. However, by that time, I was doing much more than simple cleaning jobs. On occasions when some male orderly or nurse was off sick, Doctor Levy asked me to help out in the surgery room. I said not a word about these special duties to my parents, and made up some excuse for why I was needed at the clinic in the daytime.

Mamma saw that I, having finished school, had lots of free time and asked me to assist in instructing some of the science classes. Even though I was not keen on teaching, I enjoyed doing this, for it gave me a chance to read some of the newer science books, which I used to borrow from the town library.

I learned as much as I could at Doctor Levy's clinic, for I longed to go to a medical college. I dreamt of studying in classrooms with floors and walls of polished mahogany hardwood and performing experiments in the laboratories, wearing those white coats.

Nevertheless, every time I approached my parents on this subject, Papa's stern answer was always the same. "Margaret, there are no medical schools for women. Don't you know, even Geneva Medical College will no longer admit females? You had better start thinking of doing something more useful with your life."

This always made me cry and I used to run to my room and lie in bed with my head buried in the pillow. Mamma did come over, after a while—when Papa had likely calmed down—to comfort me. Indeed Papa was right, for the medical institutions were steadfastly refusing to admit females. Although a few years ago, one exceptional school, the Geneva Medical College, had bravely enrolled and graduated a lone woman—to national headlines—it had also closed its doors to any more female students. On top of that, our very first woman doctor, Elizabeth Blackwell, having suffered much castigation, had left for Europe to work in hospitals there.

One day, my guardian angel smiled on me. That early spring day in 1850 is another of my unforgettable days. I was nearly twenty then, and in addition to my job at the clinic, was labouring in my mother's school not only as a teacher but again as a charwoman, for Elizabeth had discovered boys and was out so much, I was forced to do her work. That morning, I had gone to the schoolhouse to start the cleaning, which needed to be done early, before the start of the school day.

A priest, a friend of Papa, was visiting from Philadelphia for the weekend. He had delivered a guest sermon on Sunday and spent the night in the school's office, where we had placed a sleeping cot for him. As I walked up the path to the school, carrying a mop and pail, I spotted him waving at me while he rode away. I waved back his goodbye and entered the school to start the tasks. I folded up the cot, put it outside and proceeded to tidy up the office. While dusting the desk, I noticed a copy of a newspaper lying on top of other pamphlets, which the visiting priest must have left behind. It was the *Philadelphia Daily News*. As we rarely got any of those big-city newspapers, I enjoyed reading them whenever I found one.

I immediately decided to take a break and, sitting on the chair at the desk, started to flip through the newspaper. As always, I first read the commercial sections. There were the usual advertisements for women's apparel, and other items. Not that I could buy any of those expensive dresses, shoes and such things, but I liked to know what was available and especially their prices. I would later inform my girlfriends. I used to smile when I saw the look on their faces, not only at the prices, but also in admiration for my knowledge of the latest fashions.

I spied a small ad in the newspaper's column with the heading *Educational Institutions*. There, in between the large posters for all the military academies and other well-known universities, like Yale and Harvard, there was a smaller notice that I nearly missed. It was in small print and only about three inches long, titled *Female Medical College*. At first, I thought it was for some British school and was about to skip it, when I noticed the address at the bottom said *Philadelphia, Pennsylvania*.

While I mentally searched my mind how far it would be from Elizabethtown, three small words in the notice, each hardly wider than a fly, seemed to jump out and shine before my eyes, like bright stars. They read: *only ladies admitted*. With my heart beating wildly, I hurriedly re-read the advertisement. It stated, in part:

New Female Medical College incorporated by Act of Assembly in Pennsylvania ... Liberal teaching facilities, modern college buildings, fully equipped laboratories... Only ladies admitted... Send for catalogue... Signed:
William J. Mullen for the Religious Society of Friends.

I must have screamed with joy and, clutching the newspaper in my hand, I ran to our house. Mamma and Papa were still at the dining table, finishing breakfast, and looked up, startled by my scampering in and slamming of the front door.

I rushed to the table, holding the page of the newspaper. I thrust it in front of my father and said, out of breath, "Papa, look at this."

My father read the ad I pointed out to him, while my mother asked, "What is it, Margaret?"

Still panting from the exertion, I said in an excited voice, "There is a medical college in Philly that admits women."

My mother exclaimed, "Good Lord, why on earth would they do such a thing?" She looked at my father and asked, "Is that so, James, will they accept young lasses?"

My father, putting the paper down, replied, "Apparently so, Joan. I must admit I'd heard someone mention this institution to me a while back. Seems that even after Geneva, having had a dreadful experience of admitting that one lady, this one is now opening its doors. "

I gasped, and said, "Papa, you knew about it and did not tell me? How could you do such a thing?"

"Now, Margaret, it only came up by chance in a conversation I had with a parishioner, and he was not too sure about the facts, either."

I argued, "But you could at least have told me about it."

"It slipped my mind, but in any event, I do not believe this type of education is for you. We have advised you likewise earlier. On many occasions."

"And, pray, what is wrong with this education?"

"Most people regard these professions, such as medicine, military and clergy, as masculine duties."

"And why can't a woman perform these duties?"

"Now, Margaret, you should know that these occupations demand responsibilities which are more compatible with the physical and mental capacities of the male species."

"So Papa, what is a woman supposed to do?"

My mother then joined in, after having read the notice. She answered my question in a sweet tone, obviously to pacify me. "Well, Margaret, a woman is by nature designed to discharge her duties in other walks of life—no less important, mind, but more delicate and refined."

"Like having babies, you mean?" I retorted.

My mother kept her composure and said, "No, Margaret, not just children; a woman is like the flower of the human race, to be cherished and adored."

I asked, "And for what use? Except as an ornament, and to be tossed away when it wilts?" I continued to implore, "But what would be wrong in taking the medical path? Lady Magdalen used to help Jesus attend to the sick."

My father joined in and said, "We don't know all the facts about Mary Magdalen. There is a lot of hearsay about her. A woman entering this field would be like going astray and following the forbidden path towards perversion, against the laws of our Maker."

I knew exactly what he was referring to. Although I was considered naive, I had heard of the madams of Paris, New York and other large cities, who were believed to be engaging in those acts of perversion.

My mother also added, "Margaret, would you not agree that a woman works much better with a needle or a pencil than, say, with a rifle or a sword? And what about teaching children—have you not given any further thought towards that vocation?"

I replied, "No. I hate teaching. Many women fire rifles. A lot of them helped in the Revolution. As for taking the forbidden path, one can take it just as easily. Is there a need to go to a medical school to learn those things?" I again implored, "Please, Mamma, I am not trying to become a woman of the street, rather a doctor to heal people. I want to go overseas and serve as a medical missionary. Why can't I go to that college? See, it's only for women. There won't be any men to make fun of me, as they did to Miss Blackwell in Geneva."

While my father glared at me, my mother replied, a bit sternly now, as she was obviously beginning to lose her patience, "Now look, Margaret, your papa and I have endured many hardships to achieve a respectable status in life. We have brought you all up to be pious and virtuous children. What do you think the parishioners and your other family members would say if they learned the pastor's daughter was examining the nude bodies of male strangers? I would simply die with shame. Why are you so intent on bringing this humiliation on us once again?"

I believe, in the heat of the argument, I missed her last question and instead—turning her question around—I asked, in a sterner tone as well, "So is it quite all right, then, for male doctors to examine women's bodies?"

My mother did not reply, she simply put her hands to her forehead and bent her head. Tears flowed down her cheeks.

My father said in an angry voice, "Margaret, only for women or not, we absolutely forbid you to go to this college. We shall not take you there."

I was unmoved by all the forbidding commands from my parents. Still pretty inflamed by their attitude, I told them in a resolute voice, "All right! I will go to this college on my own. Even if I have to walk all the way there."

I believe my father understood my determination and said with a sigh, "Well, Margaret, you will be on your own, then. Pray do not count on any support from us."

"That will be just fine with me, Papa. I'll wash dishes to get by."

While my mother wept loudly now, I snatched the newspaper from the table and stomped upstairs to my room.

I sat at my writing table, pulled out a clean sheet of paper and composed a letter, in my best handwriting, to the registrar of that college, requesting their brochure. At that moment, I had no idea how I was going to support myself and pay for my studies. I contemplated, to take one day at a time, pray to God for His divine help and things would surely work out.

But just then, I remembered my mother's words about bringing "… shame on the family, once again …" and I realised what she was referring to, which she had not wished to mention in front of my father. In the heat of the argument, I had forgotten all about Robert and Aunt Fiona. Mamma must have been inferring to the most despicable way in which Aunt Fiona had dismissed me from the preserves canning job at her farm in Grimsby, and sent me back home in disgrace. All that was in an attempt to get me away from Robert, as she had mistakenly assumed that I was inciting her beloved son to run away with me and not marry the daughter of an influential regimental colonel she had chosen for him. Little did she know that it was in fact Robert who had confessed his love to me, and wanted to marry me, rather than the one *she* had chosen for him. Nevertheless, Mamma had strictly forbidden me to make any contact or write to Robert ever again. I imagined Aunt Fiona would have given Robert the same instructions. Hence, I had very little news of Robert ever since my return from Grimsby, except on one occasion, last year.

Uncle Tom had just returned from another trip to Canada and stopped over on his way back to his farm in Delaware. He'd no doubt escorted another group of runaway slaves on the Underground Railroad to freedom there. I was coming down the stairs to meet him, when I heard him talking to Mamma and Papa in the parlour. Papa had asked him how things were at Wallace Hall in Grimsby. Uncle Tom replied that they were all doing very well and how dashing Robert looked in his cavalry officer's uniform. My heart skipped a beat at the mention of Robert's name. When I rushed in to hear more of the news, everyone became curiously silent, and Uncle Tom changed the subject by asking me how I was, what I was doing and so on. So, Robert had indeed obtained the commission he longed for so very much. I was happy for him.

The sound of the front door opening and closing brought my mind back from those thoughts of past years.

"Hallo, Aunty Joan. I looked for Margaret in the school, but didn't find her. Is she home?" I recognised the voice of my cousin, Agnes, who lived not too far from us. Her father ran a furniture-making business.

"She's in her room, dear. You can go right up," Mamma replied, most likely wiping her tears and giving Agnes a kiss.

"What's going on? Everyone looks so glum." Agnes exclaimed, coming into my room.

"Don't ask, Agnes. I've had one of those discussions again with Mamma and Papa," I replied, dabbing my eyes with a kerchief.

"About going to medical college?"

"Yes, and even after I showed them this advertisement." I handed her the newspaper.

She read it and, throwing the paper in the air, ran up to me and embraced me. "Goodness, Margaret. How wonderful. There it is, finally, another medical college that will now accept women. So, when are you going?"

"How can I? Papa won't pay and Mamma isn't thrilled with the proposition, either. But, you know what, I will still apply," I said, lying down on the bed, while Agnes sat on the chair.

"Good for you. But how will you support yourself?"

"I don't know. I can barely scrape together the application fee they will want. Let alone the hundreds of dollars in tuition fees, and there would be room and board expenses on top of that. On the other hand, I don't know if they will even accept me. I understand that these institutions, in addition to good school grades, require years of practical experience and a number of references."

"I think you have all that. As for money, have you thought about borrowing it from someone?"

"Agnes. Be serious. Who do you think will lend me that much money? Uncle Tom's so busy with the Underground Railroad that he has neglected farming and is making very little. Unless your father, Uncle John, will be kind enough?"

Agnes thought for a while and replied, "No. I don't believe so. Mother and Father think pretty much like your parents. They strongly believe a woman's job is in her home. They don't want me to go to college even to study Arts or Literature, let alone Medicine. I feel so useless most of the time."

"I'm sorry to hear that, Agnes. However, you're going to be married soon and things will be much different. By the way, have you heard from Patrick lately?"

"Yes. I got a letter from Pat a couple of days ago. Says that he misses me terribly. He's all alone in Boston and can't wait till we're married. The poor boy." she said with a giggle. However, she grew silent, as if another thought had crossed her mind, and she asked in a hushed voice, "Heard any news about Robert?"

"No. Just what I told you I'd overheard Uncle Tom saying. He's got his commission and is a cavalry officer now."

"Is he married?"

"Most likely. You know, his mother's beloved Nancy was part of the deal for the commission."

"I don't believe he's married."

"Agnes, be serious. Why would he not marry her?"

"Well, for one thing, didn't he tell you he loved you and even wanted to elope with you?"

"Yes, but that was the eighteen-year-old lad in him talking. You don't know half of what he tried to do to me that night in the stables, until I made him stop."

"Yes, but if he was just after a roll in the hay, what I'm still puzzled about is why did he then go and talk to his mother about wanting to marry you?"

"All right, I'll grant you that he wanted to marry me, but when his dear mamma said no, that was that. He picked up his cricket bat and went home."

Agnes giggled and blushed a bit at my metaphor. "No, no. Dearest, you are forgetting one very important event. Didn't you tell me that he came to your workshop and asked you to run away with him?"

"Yes, Agnes. He did. But what was I to do? You know running away would have been disastrous for both of us."

"Fine. I'm glad too that you didn't elope with him. But my point is, don't you see, he did love you so very much."

I must admit I was taken aback by Agnes's assertion that Robert wasn't married yet and possibly still loved me. "Agnes, all that happened years ago. There's been too much water under the bridge. There's nothing I can do now."

"Oh, yes, you can."

"Like what? Take the next train to Grimsby and ask Robert to saddle up and ride away to his aunt's plantation in Charleston?"

"No, no. I know you still love him. Why don't you write to the poor boy?"

"If I did, his mother wouldn't let him see even a shadow of the letter."

"Isn't there someone you could use as an intermediary?"

"Like in a Jane Austen novel, you mean?"

We both giggled at that thought. Just then, there was a light tap at the door and Mamma came in.

"Now then, glad to see you both are hav'n a good time," Mamma said and, upon observing the newspaper on the floor, added, "Agnes, I hope you've talked some sense into Margaret about her harebrained idea of going to that institution. Can you imagine women cutting apart male dead bodies. Good heavens, just thinking about it sends shivers down my spine."

"Yes, Aunt. I *have* been taking some sense into Margaret. But I must run along now. You should see the long shopping list Mother gave me," Agnes said, getting up from the chair.

"And I have to go and finish cleaning up the schoolhouse," I said, getting up from the bed. We both scampered down the stairs like little kids. I am sure Mamma was wondering what we were up to.

Outside the house, Agnes said, "Oh, I just remembered one more thing. As you say, Uncle Tom might be dirt poor, but I'm sure Aunt Mary can help you get admission to that college."

"How can she?"

"Didn't the ad say the Philadelphia college is being started by the Friends' Society?"

"How right you are." I said, hugging her. "It escaped my mind completely. Aunt Mary's Quaker family could help with a good recommendation. I'm sure she knows someone in a high position in the Society."

"Yes, considering your efforts that time, in assisting Harriet and her parents' escape to Canada."

"Of course. I will be most disappointed if she doesn't mention in her letter to the college that I can look a Southerner slave-catcher in the eye and say boo to him."

We both bust out giggling. We hugged again and kissed goodbye.

"Don't forget to write to you know who," she whispered.

"Thank you, Agnes. You're a sweetheart."

*****

Agnes's words, *don't you see, he did love you so very much…,* rang in my head for days.

The prospectus from the Philadelphia Female Medical College arrived, along with the request to fill in the numerous application forms. They wanted school records and details of practical experience under a qualified physician to be attached. There was also the requirement to have letters of reference sent directly to the college.

I was confident I would meet all the admission requirements, but even if I was admitted, the thought of how to pay the tuition fees and other expenses was very much on my mind. Taking on a part-time job did not appear to be an option as, for one, there weren't too many jobs open to young women, and besides, I would have needed to concentrate all my time and energy towards the arduous studies.

Finally, as a last resort, I decided that I should write and ask Robert for a loan; indirectly, of course. For even if he did not love me and was likely married, it was the one thing he could do for me, his cousin. Nevertheless, how was I to get the letter over to him? Surely his mother would intercept it and send one of her nasty telegrams to Mamma. Agnes's suggestion of using an intermediary sounded like a good idea. Who could that be? Also, could that person be trusted? I racked my brain for a confidant in Grimsby. It suddenly dawned on me: the one person I could trust to hold my secret was indeed Mr. Jenkins.

On a late Saturday night, when all were asleep and the house quiet,

I sat down at my desk and wrote a letter to Robert. It read in part:

May 1850

Dearest Robert,
I trust that all of you at Wallace Hall are keeping well, as are we
all here in Elizabethtown. It was a thrill to learn from Uncle Tom, the
other day, that you had finally received your commission. I know you
must be very pleased, as your heart was set resolutely on it. I am sure
Aunt Fiona and Uncle Will are proud of you. I am so very happy for
you and can almost picture you in your dashing uniform.
How is Nancy? I am sure she will be a perfect wife for you. Have
you a family yet?
Unfortunately, unlike yours, my dreams of becoming a doctor
haven't materialised until now. There did not seem to be any medical
colleges that would accept a woman. But you will not believe your
eyes when I write you of what I saw recently in the Philadelphia
Bulletin ...

I added a covering note to Mr. Jenkins, asking about Jemima, Harriet's and his health. Also, I asked him if he could be so kind as to deliver my letter, personally, to Robert.

I inserted the letter to Robert in an envelope addressed to *Mr. Jenkins, Wallace Hall, Grimsby, Canada West.* I also completed the application to the Philadelphia Female Medical College, as well as one to Aunt Mary, enclosing a cutting of the college ad and explaining the situation to her. I posted the three letters the very first thing on Monday morning, as soon as the post office opened.

That evening, after work, I mentioned the news to Doctor Levy, taking care not to state my parents' opposition, and requested a letter of recommendation. He looked pleased that I had finally decided to apply and said he would be more than happy to send in a letter with all the details of the work I had done under his guidance.

*****

It was not long before I heard back from Aunt Mary. Her letter was full of encouragement. She wrote that her father knew an influential person in the Society of Friends, and she would be happy to request him to write to the college, recommending my admission. I was overjoyed to hear that. I replied to Aunt Mary with a thank-you note, that same day.

However, the days following my posting the letter to Robert were possibly the longest of my life. Each day after work, I would run into the parlour and look on the corner table where Mamma usually put the mail waiting to be read by Papa. Every time I was disappointed, as there was not a single letter for me. Nevertheless, just to be sure, I used to ask, "Mamma, are there any messages for me?"

"No, child. None for you."

Then, invariably with a sad face, I used to go upstairs to my bedroom and lie down, wondering what would become of me. Almost a month went by and alas, there was no news, either from the college or from Robert. How could he not even reply ... I sobbed.

Then one day, after finishing cleaning the school in the early hours and then teaching both in the morning and in the afternoon, I trudged into the house, wanting to rest my feet before the evening duties at the clinic. My mother was at the wood-burning oven, stirring the cooking pots on the top, preparing dinner. Just behind her, on the kitchen table, lay an envelope. It was addressed to me and had in the corner, the unmistakable red stamp of Canada with the Queen's smiling face and the crown on her head.

"Letter from Robert!" I shouted, with magically renewed energy, and ran up to the table to grab it. My heart sank when I saw that it had been opened. "Mamma, did you open it?"

"Yes, I did," she replied in the sweet voice she used whenever she wanted to assert her authority gently.

"How could you?"

"Why not, Margaret? We are so worried about you and wondering what on earth you are up to," she replied, as she continued to wash and peel some potatoes.

"What I am up to is slaving for you in that school of yours."

"Hush now, child. Pray read that letter first." She turned around and smiled at me, while drying her hands on her apron.

I sat down on a chair and, with shaking hands, opened Robert's letter, which began:

2nd Lieutenant Robert Wallace
Fort George, Niagara Falls, Canada West
July 1850

Dearest Margaret,

Thank you for your lovely letter. Sorry for the late reply, on account of my now being stationed here in Fort George, and poor Jenkins couldn't get away from Grimsby for a week, due to heavy work on the farm. It was so kind of him to have spent his day off riding up here to deliver your letter personally to me. You have already heard the greatest news. Through the kind efforts of my Upper Canada College riding instructors, who have high regard for my riding abilities and having given me an outstanding recommendation, I received an appointment in the Regiment stationed here at Fort George, close to Niagara Falls. I want to let you know that the appointment was purely through my own efforts. Father didn't have to pay a penny to buy me the commission. He is happy to see his son in a cavalry officer's uniform. Mother is not too elated, though, as, for one, Fort George is a half-day's ride away, and more so, she'd wanted me to join Colonel Mitchell's Regiment there in Grimsby, even though I heard he was demanding a hefty sum for my commission.

Dearest Margaret, your information is not all correct. I am not married. Nancy had many suitors and is already married to Albert Miller. I believe you may remember him. I still believe he married her for the commission in her father's regiment. I never cared much for her, anyway. Thank goodness, I didn't marry her. It would never have worked out.

But enough of old news about me. What interesting information. You finally found a medical college that would admit you! Isn't that wonderful? Your dream of becoming a doctor will surely come true soon. Too bad Uncle and Aunt Wallace are not supporting you. Now, what's this I read that you will be going there anyway? But how will you maintaint yourself? You know medical studies are so dear. And you say you will take on a part-time job? I don't believe you will be able to hold onto an evening job and still complete your studies.

Dearest Margaret, I know I might sound foolish and headstrong, much like the last time you were here. But that's the way I am. Will you ever forgive me for my most deplorable behaviour? I know I am forever asking for your pardon, but I promise not to make a habit of it.

Dearest, I am still very much in love with you, and if you still feel the same about me, the way you did before my shameful conduct, will you marry me?

Why don't we get married before you go to the medical college?

Although my pay will not be much, I am sure I will be able to look after you through your studies and forever. I know you didn't say "yes" to my proposal earlier, but I am asking you again. I realise the time was possibly not right then. However, it looks like the right time has arrived. Darling, shall I talk to Uncle Wallace? ...

I could not read the letter any further, as tears of joy filled my eyes. I looked at my mother and saw she had tears in her eyes as well.

"Mamma, Robert wants to marry me!" I said between sobs.

"Yes, I know, dear. I am so happy for you." She came to me and embraced me. I hugged her and sobbed while she ran her fingers over my hair.

Between sobs, I asked, "But what about Papa? How will he take this news?"

"Your papa and I have already discussed this—"

"I am happy for you, Margaret," my father said, entering the kitchen, clearing his throat. He had all this time been sitting in the parlour, still dressed in his church dark frock coat and white collar, waiting for me to come home.

"Thank you, Papa." I ran to him and hugged him. He put his strong arms around me and held me in a tight embrace. By then I was crying uncontrollably, with tears running down my cheeks.

"Now, now, hush, sweet child. We were never against you getting married. If that's what you want."

"But what about medical college?"

"You have only just applied, child. Let's see what their decision is. If they admit you, we will talk about it then," he said in a calm voice.

I knew that was his way of agreeing to something he wasn't too happy about.

"Oh ... thank you, Papa, thank you ... thank you so much." I put my arms around him and put my head on his broad chest. I wouldn't let go, until he had to gently pry my arms apart to free himself.

*****

About a week later, an official-looking envelope arrived. It was addressed to me, from the Philadelphia Female Medical College. Taking it straight up to my bedroom, I opened it with trembling fingers. Apart from the number of lengthy forms in it and information brochures, it included a nice covering letter signed by the college's registrar. The letter said the College Admissions Board had reviewed my application and were impressed with my record of education, practical experience and letters of reference. It continued to say that it was a pleasure for him to inform me that I had been accepted for admission for the fall semester, commencing on the first Monday in October 1850.

I threw up my arms in air and jumped for joy. While I felt elated that the Lord was answering my prayers, I did feel that some of the credit for my acceptance to the Quaker's Institution must be due to Papa's good name. For although we were not Friends, he must have been highly regarded in their Society for his anti-slavery stand and for all our family's efforts in the abolition activities. I wrote another letter of appreciation to Aunt Mary, thanking her for all her and her father's efforts in securing me the admission.

The very next day, I went to the post office and sent out the following telegram to Robert:

July 1850
To : 2ⁿᵈ Lieutenant Robert Wallace
Fort George, Niagara-on-the-Lake, Canada West
Dearest Robert. STOP. Yes. STOP. Forever Yours. STOP.
Margaret. END OF MESSAGE

Chapter Fourteen

Robert's Visit

1850, August: Elizabethtown, New Jersey
I OPENED MY BEDROOM WINDOW and took a deep breath of fresh air. The refreshing late summer breeze blew in, gently swaying the curtains. It was a bright Sunday afternoon. Flowers were in bloom in the gardens and birds flew in the park, chirruping as they hopped from tree to tree, no doubt looking for tasty morsels. In the street below, people strolled about. Ladies, parasol in hand, dressed in billowing crinoline skirts, ambled along, holding onto the arm of their men, who wore dark suits with white cravats and top hats. I spotted Elizabeth and David playing hopscotch at one end of the street with their friends. I spied the steeple of the church, which we had attended that morning and where we had listened to Papa's far-too-long sermon. Later, at home, we enjoyed a delicious meal, of corn soup and tender roast duck, prepared by Mamma with her special blend of seasonings.

I sat at my desk, trying to prepare the science lesson for delivery to the class the next day. A recent issue of *The American Medical Journal* lay open before me. I had borrowed it from Doctor Levy's office, with his permission, of course. I was intrigued by a detailed article, a monograph, which a British naturalist, Charles Darwin, had written recently upon his return from a voyage around the world. It was a forerunner, likely a rough sketch, of the famous theory he was to expound upon a few years later. He had conjectured on something that caused quite a stir among the medical community, not to mention the theologians. For Charles Darwin had touched on the very heart of our beliefs on the origins of the human race. He said he was beginning to form an opinion that we had all evolved from sea creatures, reptiles and, good heavens, apes! I was indeed curious to learn what the fuss was all about regarding what Mr. Darwin had written. Of course, I had not told Mamma or Papa about this article in the *Journal*, and kept the magazine hidden in my book-bag, for I knew they would never have let me bring it into the house. I flipped through the pages, looked at the illustrations of dinosaurs, birds, monkeys and other creatures, and wondered what, if anything, I could or should use from it for the lesson. Surely, just as lovers would dare steal a kiss in the park, I felt, if I were bold enough to talk about Charles Darwin's thoughts, I would hear no end of it from Mamma, and might have some of my students' parents calling on me. It might also be the last straw that could result in my parents changing their minds and breaking my dream of going to medical college. Nevertheless, I thought otherwise and decided to follow what my conscience advised me.

Although I had shown my admission letter from the Philadelphia Medical College to Mamma and Papa, they had taken it very nonchalantly and had virtually ignored it. The fees were due in October, just prior to the start of the term, and here I was practically penniless. What was I to do, I anguished?

I could not concentrate on the preparation of the lesson and my thoughts turned towards Robert. It was nearly three weeks since I sent him the telegram and there had not been a word from him. What could be the matter? Had he changed his mind? Good God, I hoped Aunt Fiona had not intervened, once again, to scuttle his plans.

My daydreaming was interrupted when I heard the sound of hurried footsteps coming up the stairs and towards my bedroom door. After a gentle knock, the door opened. It was Elizabeth.

"A pirate is waiting outside; wants to see you," she said, panting a bit from the exertion of darting up the stairs.

"A pirate?"

"Yes, with an eye patch, a beard, and a parrot sitting on his shoulder." Although she was nearly seventeen, she still had a bit of a squeaky voice, which became more pronounced whenever she was excited.

"You are putting me on. Oh, I know who it is. Is it not Sam, from school? He's always clowning around." I believed Sam had a crush on me and was calling often, of late.

Elizabeth shook her head, trying hard to keep a straight face.

Just then a conversation flashed through my mind of some years ago with a young man, at the Lake House Tavern in Grimsby, when he promised me, "Even if I have to, I'll hop over to you on one leg …"

"Does he have a wooden leg?" I asked.

Elizabeth nodded, this time with a broad smile, and replied, "Sort of a wooden leg."

"Is it Robert?" I asked in a whisper.

She nodded again and, reaching over, embraced me. "I'm so happy for you, Sister," she said with tears in her eyes.

I thanked her and, holding up my skirt in both hands, ran down the stairs, shouting, "Mamma, Robert is here!"

I stormed out of the front door and saw my beloved standing on the driveway, by the steps leading up to the porch. He did look convincing as a pirate and with that disguise could easily have qualified for a part in a theatrical play. He wore his jacket inside out and had a dummy parrot pinned onto one shoulder. The eye patch and the painted beard, together with a torn three-pointed hat with the skull and bones emblem on the front, made him look very much like a seafaring buccaneer. The *pièce de résistance* was the dummy wooden crutch strapped to his right knee. He stood on it with the lower portion of the support buckled to his thigh, in a poor imitation of a one-legged sailor. By this time, a group of inquisitive persons, mostly our neighbours, had gathered by the fence and were looking curiously at us.

I ran down the steps to embrace him, and doing so, nearly knocked him over. He stumbled, but regained his balance. There were murmurs of laughter from the crowd.

"Woo, easy now, gal, this sailor ain't got his landlubber legs yet," he said, trying to mock a drunken sailor's accent.

"I know it's you, Robert. You don't fool me one bit," I said, trying to appear stern and keeping a straight face. I heard the door open and close and, looking back, saw Mamma and Papa come out and stand on the porch. Elizabeth and David stood to one side with their hands over their mouths, trying to suppress their laughter.

Robert took off his hat and the eye patch and unbuckled the straps that held the wooden prop. He moved his leg up and down a few times to get the circulation going. Some more of our neighbours had gathered by the fence and looked on curiously at Robert's antics. "Hallo, Margaret. Was I that bad a pirate?"

"The worst one I've ever seen." I replied, still trying my best not to burst out into laughter.

He then spied Mamma and Papa standing on the porch, looking on in bewilderment.

"Good day, Aunt Joan, Uncle James," he said with a slight bow to them.

"Good day, Robert. What brings you here?" Mamma said, while Papa nodded.

"Oh, I just happened to be in the neighbourhood," he replied with a smile. Turning to me and saying, "Excuse me a minute, Margaret," he turned around and went over to his horse, which was tethered to the gatepost. Something large, wrapped in red paper, stuck out from the saddlebags. He pulled it out and brought it over to me.

He handed the wrap up to me, with those words I still remember to this day: "With all my love, Margaret, darling."

It was a lovely bouquet of flowers, roses, irises, lilies, daisies, magnolias and other exquisite kinds, all done in an eye-catching arrangement. I was speechless. Holding onto the flowers in one hand, I put the other around his shoulder. He held me in a tight embrace and through my moist eyes, I saw him looking at me with his deep blue eyes that sparked, as if to confess his love for me. My eyes blurred with tears of joy and the next thing I felt were his lips on mine.

We must have kissed for a while. I felt as if I were in another world, a soft and gentle land where one's dreams and wishes come true just for the asking. The sound of clapping from the on-looking neighbours brought us back down to earth. Still in an embrace, with our cheeks together, we looked up at my parents, who stood on the porch, and appeared rather amused. They likely suppressed their displeasure at our public display of affection.

"Well, sailor boy, don't just stand there waiting for the tide to come in." Mamma said.

"Come in, Robert. Do come in," Papa said, extending his arm.

Robert went up the stairs, shook Papa's hand, and kissed Mamma on the cheeks.

"You haven't joined the Union Army Cadets, have you, Robert?" Papa asked, looking at Robert's grey uniform jacket and trousers.

"Oh, no, sir. I am here at West Point, on a training course." Then, turning to me, he said, "Sorry, Margaret, I didn't get a chance to write to you. It all happened so suddenly. Another senior officer of our

Regiment, who was to attend this training, took ill. I was sent in his place."

"Come now, Robert. I know you wanted to surprise me, did you not?" I asked and he nodded slyly with a smile. David held the door open for us to go into the house.

"These are for you." He gave the dummy parrot, made of a nice green material, to Elizabeth, and the pirate hat to David. They thanked him, their eyes shining with excitement.

Papa waved back at the neighbours. "Thank you all, most kindly, for your attention. We'll let you know when the next show will be." There was a roar of laughter and clapping again from all those standing by the fence.

"Bravo, sailor boy." and "Good luck, Robert." some of the onlookers shouted. I am sure they all knew who Robert was, and the reason for his visit. Elizabeth must have seen to that. I hurried into the house before there were any more smart remarks.

Mamma brought in the tea tray and Elizabeth and I followed her, with plates of cakes and cookies, into the parlour, where Papa and Robert sat talking earnestly. Robert broke off the conversation and stood up.

"Oh, pray be seated, Robert. We are not at all so formal here, you know," Mamma said.

"Thank you, Aunt. May I help with something?"

"No, no. Just have a seat and tell us all about your parents and what's been happening at Wallace Hall. David will bring in the rest of the tea."

I smiled when he replied, "Nothing much, really. Just the usual."

"Oh, come now. It has been a while since we visited you. How are Fiona and Will?" Mamma persisted.

"Well, thank you. Mamma's preserves business is flourishing. Father is busy as ever, running the vineyards and orchards, although he hasn't been feeling too good lately."

"Oh, what is the matter with him?" Papa asked in a concerned voice.

"He feels a bit tired sometimes. It could be some after-effects of the bouts of cholera he had while serving in India."

"Could it be his heart?" I asked, for I'd read in some medical book that cholera can affect one's heart.

"It's possible. Our town physician, Doctor Nelles, wants to bleed him. But Papa will have none of that."

"You be sure to tell Fiona to take good care of him. Try some herbal medication. Goodness, he is so young."

"Yes, we are all trying to tell him to take it easy. It has been difficult with me being away. But he's hired more staff—that should help."

"So, what are your plans, young man?" Papa asked, sipping tea.

Robert had a mouth full of cookie and kept munching on it, while we all looked at him, waiting for his reply. Finally, he swallowed but still did not say anything and instead looked at me with questioning eyes. I knew what he asked. I simply nodded.

Robert gulped down the last of the cookie with a sip of tea and, clearing his throat, asked Papa, "Uncle James, may I have a word with you in private?"

"By all means, son. Why don't we go into the library?" Papa got up from his chair and walked towards the library. It wasn't much of a library—rather, a small room on one side of the house, between the parlour and the dining room, where Papa had a small desk. There was hardly space enough for two chairs, a desk and rows of bookshelves on the sides.

Robert gave me another loving look and followed Papa. He had straightened out his West Point jacket; the brass buttons and yellow piping on it matched his wavy golden hair. I sat on one side of the sofa and although I folded my arms around my bosom, shivers of excitement passed through my body. Was it really happening? Was Robert really here, talking to Papa?

Mamma, who sat next to me on the sofa, must have noted my trembling, for she reached out and put her arm around my shoulder. I leaned over to her and she held me in a warm embrace. Tears ran down my cheeks.

"Now, now, child. No need to cry. This is a happy moment of your life," she said, comforting me, as she ran her fingers through my hair.

However, almost a half hour passed and still Papa and Robert had not finished talking. I did hear some of their murmured voices, but from the distance and being in my excited state, I could not discern what they were discussing that was taking so long.

Finally, after what seemed like an eternity, Papa appeared at the door of the parlour. "Joan, could you please join us?" he asked.

Mamma got up from the sofa and I started to get up as well. She put a hand on my shoulder and gently made me sit down. "Wait here, child. Let me see what this is all about." She followed Papa into the library.

I strained to hear what they could be talking about. My heart skipped a beat when I heard the library door close. I couldn't restrain myself any longer. I got up, tiptoed gently to the dining room, and stared at the closed library door ahead, my heart beating like a steam engine. Although I heard some raised voices, especially Mamma's, I couldn't make out clearly what she said. When I listened to her say loudly something about a "disinheritance", I realised it must be Aunt Fiona up to her vile schemes again. I sank to the floor with my back against the wall and head in my hands, and sobbed bitterly. Elizabeth and David stood in the doorway, looking puzzled.

The library door opened and Mamma stepped out. "Ah, there you are, child. What are you doing there on the floor? Come, talk to your papa." She came over and, taking me by the arm, made me get up and led me into the library. I dried my eyes on my kerchief and straightened out my dress.

Papa stood by the window, gazing out, and Robert sat in a chair, looking glum. On hearing me enter, Papa turned around.

"Margaret, Robert here tells us that he wants to marry you and you have said 'yes' to him."

"Yes, Papa. I love him very much." I moved closer to Robert's chair and put my arm around his shoulder. Mamma closed the library door; perhaps she didn't wish Elizabeth and Robert to hear the rest of the conversation.

"But has he told you that his parents do not agree to this marriage?"

"No. But I don't mind, if Robert doesn't. Do you, Robert?"

"I love Margaret with all my heart. I don't care if my parents do not agree. I have my own life to live," Robert replied, looking at me with his charming eyes. I felt like kissing him at that remark.

"Indeed, son, you have your own life, but you have to live within a family circumstance. You are asking us to give you our blessing for this union. However, how can we, knowing full well that it would tear your family apart? It would be like ripping a strong limb off a healthy tree. If I agreed, the good Lord would never forgive me for this transgression." Papa spoke in his preacher's voice.

"But, sir, as I have implored you, pray do not look upon this as my dismemberment from my family. I will always be there for them. I know Father is not well. I may even leave the Regiment to go back and work on the farm."

"That's provided they will have you back. Robert, please do tell Margaret exactly what Fiona has told you," Mamma asked him in a stern voice.

"Aunt, I had written to Margaret. Mother was most upset at my having broken off with Nancy. Yes, and she's not too happy either with me asking her permission, again, to marry Margaret."

"But you are leaving out the most important part. What else did she tell you?" Mamma asked again.

"Dearest Aunt, you know she has a temper. She sometimes says things she doesn't mean. Yes, she did say something about disinheriting me. But that time is not here yet. It is way down the road. She will change her mind when the time comes, you will see."

"Change her mind! Not likely. That was precisely what she told Margaret three years ago, when she sent her back home, and it is what she is still telling you now," Mamma retorted.

Robert looked straight ahead, not knowing what to say.

"Mamma, is Robert's inheritance so important to you? We don't care. Do we, Robert?" I tried to calm Mamma. I saw Robert shake his head, agreeing with me.

"Nay, child. It's not the question of the inheritance, it's the whole way in which Fiona's treating the matter. Sending you out of her home, just on a whim. Now she implies again that you are not good enough for her son. It is as if we are some poorhouse folks. Who does she think she is, the Duchess of Grimsby?" Mamma took out her kerchief from her dress sleeve and dabbed her eyes.

Papa came hurriedly to her and embraced her. "Now, now, Joan, no need to get so upset. We'll work things out."

"Why should I not get distressed? My lovely child has to marry under these conditions," she said between sobs. Tears started to flow down her cheeks and she hurried out of the room.

"Robert, we're sorry it's coming to this. Let me apologise for that last remark by your aunt. She has the Scottish temperament too, you know," Papa said, putting a hand on Robert's shoulder.

"It's all right, sir. I know Aunt is disturbed."

"Look, son. I want to be able to look Cousin Will in the eye again. Now, is there any way you can get Fiona and him to change their minds? Perhaps tell them how we feel about it? Do you believe that might sway them?"

"Well, I can try again, sir."

"Good. Please send my compliments to Cousin Will and have him write to me. Can you do that?"

Robert nodded.

It was getting dark when Robert rode out at a gallop down the road from our house. Even though he had promised to come and see me next Sunday, that same eerie feeling came over me once more, as it did whenever we parted. I always wondered if I would see him again. When he had mounted his horse, I ran out to him and, holding onto his hand, asked, "Robert, what are we going to do if your father won't give his consent in the letter to Papa?"

"Not to worry, dearest. I have a plan." After a kiss and a squeeze of my hand, he rode off.

I sat on the swing in the porch, contemplating what the future held for me and what Robert had in mind. Mamma called to say that dinner was ready. I did not feel hungry and declined to eat. I made a fresh cup of tea and, cup in hand, trudged upstairs to my bedroom. I sat down once again at the desk, wanting to complete the science lesson I had to deliver the next day to my high school class.

Lighting the oil lamp, I opened the *American Medical Journal* and read meticulously the article on Charles Darwin's monograph on a theory—evolution by natural selection—he was developing that concerned the origin and evolution of the species. On the face of it, the hypothesis seemed simple enough, for it was based on the principle of transmutation of chemicals. For instance, lead could be changed to gold, but it was its application to the human species that intrigued and disturbed many people. The conclusion was most fascinating, as it suggested that humans and animals were from a common source, much like branches on a tree. Perhaps the discovery by Mr. Darwin I found most captivating was his observation that the birds on the Galapagos Islands were not a mixture of wrens, finches and other beaked ones. But they all were ground finches, which had uniquely adapted to those three different islands, where each had a representative finch of its own. It was interesting to note that they had diverged from their mainland colonies. How was it possible? Transmutation was the obvious answer. Darwin also attributed this to the process of natural selection, a progression that results in the organism adapting to its environment by selectively generating changes in its constitution and body. The life form's chances of survival are thereby enhanced, leading to its development from generation to generation. This thought nevertheless led to the inevitable conclusion that only the adaptable, or the fittest, were able to survive, and raised the question of God's role as the creator of the universe. However, the article did state that Mr. Darwin did believe in the existence of God, which I found curious, and I wondered what Papa would say to that.

The idea that creatures adapted and protected themselves from the environment sounded plausible to me. It dawned on me, then, why Negroes looked so different from us. It surely was because of how they had adapted themselves and learned to live in the harsh surroundings of their original homes in Africa.

I decided to go ahead with the lecture and worked late into the night, preparing notes. I realised I would need to make it interesting and understandable to high school students, hence I kept the information at the simplest level, and confined the talk to mostly birds and common sea creatures. I titled the lesson *Where We Came From: A Theory by Charles Darwin*.

From the many questions at the end of the class, I was happy to note that my lecture on Charles Darwin's philosophy was well received by the students. However, just as I had expected, Mamma was not thrilled, to say the least. I noted her sitting stone-faced at the back of the class, along with some of the other teachers. I was thankful she had not interrupted my talk, which I had made sure I ended by emphasising that the material I had presented was the philosophical conjecture of mostly one person, Charles Darwin, based on his extensive research and travel around the world. Nevertheless, at the end of the class, after the students had departed and I was collecting my books and papers, Mamma came up to me and said in a cold voice, "Margaret, what do you mean by presenting this nonsense to our group of impressionable young children?"

"It wasn't nonsense, Mamma. I researched this information from this reputable medical journal. Besides, they are high school students, not children." I showed her the publication.

"Rubbish! Utter rubbish. We should not believe all that we read in some tuppence magazine."

"Indeed, Mamma. I made it very clear that all this was theory and conjecture. It is for them to evaluate these thoughts, do further study, and make up their own minds."

"Child, you are so naive. We make so much effort to bring them up as good Christians. Have them believe in God and the universe He created. But here you are going about putting agnostic thoughts in their vulnerable minds."

"Good heavens, Mamma! I was definitely not trying to turn them into atheists."

"Then what else was your motive in presenting this gibberish that we have descended from the apes?"

"It is just a theory of the evolutionary process. It does not mean that God doesn't exist. Besides, is it not our duty as teachers to tutor all the latest thoughts there are for the students to know?"

"Indeed, but need to know, the truthful things. Not the harebrained ideas of someone who spent years sailing around the world."

"I disagree—"

"Well, child, looks like you have once again brought shame on us. Some of the teachers who sat in the class were disgusted as well. In fact, they wanted me, as the principal, to stop your lecture. However, I didn't wish to disgrace you in front of the students. It is very likely we will hear about it from their parents. Goodness, look at the time. Your papa will be home soon. I have to cook dinner. Please lock up the school after you."

"Yes, Mamma," I blurted, dabbing at the tears in my eyes with a kerchief.

Everyone was very quiet at dinner. Mamma did not say much to me, other than the usual instructions as I helped set the table and brought food out from the kitchen. Elizabeth and David took sly glances at me for although, being in junior class, they had not attended my lecture, they would have heard of it from the other students. I am sure Mamma must have briefed Papa fully on the events of the afternoon, for he sat glumly eating his food and hardly said a word to me.

After dinner, I cleared the table and was helping Mamma wash the dishes when I heard Papa come into the kitchen. "Margaret, when you have finished, may I have a word with you?"

"Yes, Papa."

I took off my apron, wiped my hands on it, and went to the library, where Papa sat at his desk, smoking a cigar.

"Ah, come in, child. Pray close the door." He motioned towards the empty chair.

I sat down. Although I knew what he wanted to talk to me about and that he perhaps expected me to break down in sobs and beg his forgiveness, I did nothing of the sort. I just sat with my eyes down, looking at my hands on my lap, and waited for him to begin.

"Margaret, what is this I hear? You delivered a lecture today on that agnostic Charles Darwin's speculations on the beginning of our wonderful universe?"

"Yes, Papa. It was merely from what I had read in the *Medical Journal*."

"Oh, I've heard many discussions on Darwin's ideas. From what I gather, they are a piece of hogwash. Not even worth the paper they're written on, if you ask me."

"No, Papa. I do not believe his theory is hogwash, as you say. He has produced it after painstaking research and detailed observation of life forms around the world, especially on the Galapagos Islands."

"The Galapagos! Those windswept pieces of rock out in the Pacific Ocean? How can he be so dim-witted as to think those animals there represent changes in evolution, which God in his wisdom has brought about on this Earth?"

"But don't you see, Papa. Those creatures are telling us—rather, showing us—the way in which we have evolved."

"Nonsense! That means God is irrelevant and the whole universe was created as if by chance, a message, which theologians will never accept. Evolution is in the hands of our Creator, an Act of God. We should not be putting such disbelieving ideas in young minds. Our first message should be to instil a love of God in their hearts."

Before I could respond, the library door opened and Mamma entered, wiping her hands on her apron, which she still wore around her waist.

I pleaded, "But Papa, that is your job, as a pastor. I am a science teacher. If I am not to teach them the latest scientific discoveries, wouldn't I be failing to fulfil my responsibilities?"

"No. I will not allow a daughter of mine to teach such blasphemous theories," Papa said, looking at me with angry eyes, and said, "I want you to go before that same class tomorrow and apologise for your conduct. You are then to retract all the statements you made today and instead deliver a lecture explaining the beginnings of our wonderful universe as told to us in the Bible. I believe you know the passages. I can help you with some interpretations, if you like. Will you do that?"

"Papa! You are not serious, are you?"

"Yes, I am most adamant that you should do this."

"Why, that would be asking me to confess to a crime I have not committed. Can you imagine how foolish I would look in the eyes of the high school-level children?"

"There is nothing foolish about repenting for one's sins."

"Oh, Papa, you are carrying this too far. Now you are making me out to be a sinner," I responded with tears forming in my eyes, and held my forehead in my hands.

"I am asking again. Will you do what I am asking you to do?"

I replied, now with tears running down my cheeks, "No. I would rather die before I did that. Apologise in front of the whole class and deliver a sermon to revoke all I had told them earlier? Never!"

Mamma looked at Papa and he nodded at her, which seemed to be a prearranged signal between them. Mamma then addressed me in her stern schoolmistress's voice. "Very well, then, Margaret. Just as I told you this afternoon, some of the teachers and I are most unhappy with your lecture. What's more, your Papa agrees with me. Hence, I have no choice but to remove you from your teaching position. You will deliver no more lessons in my school. I might have considered keeping you on, if you had undertaken the reparation your papa asked you to do. You may continue with the cleaning chores, if you like."

I started to sob loudly on hearing this harsh pronouncement on something that seemed so trivial to me. After all the hard work I had put into helping Mamma build that school, to be treated as such distressed me.

I dried my eyes and blew my nose and, composing myself, replied, "Very well, Mamma. I shall do as you wish, just the cleaning from now on." Tears once again started to stream from my eyes.

"There is one more thing. Where did you get hold of that medical journal?" Papa asked in an angry voice.

"Why, at Doctor Levy's, of course," I replied between sobs.

"Just as I thought. These persons who call themselves 'doctor' wish to poison the minds of our children. Margaret, you are to stop working in that clinic. I will have a word with him."

I could not bear it any longer and ran out of the library, through the front door, into the street and all the way to the park.

*****

Waiting for next Sunday, when Robert had promised to visit, was most excruciating. Now that I was relieved of my teaching duties and my job at the clinic, time seemed to stand still. It looked as if the minute hand on our grandfather clock in the hallway took nearly an hour to move from one mark to the next.

Just as I thought, Mamma and Papa had, as usual, overreacted to my scientific lecture, for there was hardly the avalanche of complaint from the students' parents that Mamma feared. In fact, Sam, one of the older students in my class, who called on me a few days after the infamous lecture, confided that a few parents had actually remarked favourably to Mamma on the fresh topic I had chosen to teach the students. Nevertheless, Mamma was not convinced of the merit of the subject. The reason there weren't any complaints, she believed, was due to *herself* delivering, the next day, the apologetic speech and a long, boring, sermon-like talk on the biblical version of the "Beginning". Sam said it had put half the class to sleep.

We sat out on the swing chair on the porch and poor Sam, knowing I was depressed, tried to keep a lively conversation going by telling me of all sorts of innuendos and happenings in the school and town. He also told me something that I did not quite listen to. He said he had overheard Mamma telling one of the teachers that she was planning to send me to Boston, to live with my married cousin, Agnes, and work in a cotton mill that was run by a friend of theirs. However, I had difficulty concentrating on what he said, for my mind wandered in thoughts of Robert, especially his last remark to me, "Dearest, I have a plan." What could he have meant by that? What kind of a plan was he scheming for us?

Sunday finally arrived. We all got washed and dressed, as was our norm, in our good clothes to go to church and later, enjoy a day of rest, just like God had done—which Papa reminded us often. I sat in my room, engrossed in Currer Bell's *Jane Eyre*, which had recently been published and, due to its rave reviews, was in big demand at the library. I could relate well to her Jane, but must admit that at first I did not think much of Mr. Rochester, due to his devious behaviour.

"Robert's here." David said, entering my bedroom without even a knock.

"How many times have I told you to knock first?"

"Sorry, Sister. But he is downstairs waiting for you."

"I heard you. Please tell him I'll be down shortly."

I took a few moments, looked into the mirror, pinched my cheeks, made sure my ringlets were in order and straightened out the lace around the bosom. After smoothing out the folds of my dress, I made my way gently down the stairs, very ladylike. Robert greeted me at the bottom of the staircase, and handed me another exquisite bouquet of flowers. After a kiss, he held me in an embrace for a moment. I looked into his eyes. However, they did not have their usual shine. Good God, something was the matter.

"Come into the parlour, Robert. I'll go and make tea," Mamma said and hurried off into the kitchen.

We went into the parlour with me holding Robert's hand. Papa was already there and motioned Robert towards a chair.

"So, tell us, are they keeping you busy at West Point? Is it a six-week training course you mentioned?"

"Yes, sir. They are instructing us in use of the latest rifles and other armaments, which we don't have in Canada as yet," Robert replied with a chuckle.

"Ah, but you will get them soon enough. Is there any new war on the horizon?"

"Don't know, sir. The Mexican-American war finished a couple of years ago. Apart from some small skirmishes here and there, things seem to be fairly quiet in Europe and America, at least."

"Good. That's what I always pray for, peace and quiet on earth."

Mamma entered with the tea tray and set it down on the centre table. I moved the vase into which I had put Robert's flowers to a side table.

"How are Fiona and Will, Robert? Have you heard from them?" Mamma asked, pouring tea into the cups.

"Very well, Aunt. Yes, I've just received a telegram from Father," Robert said, reaching into his pocket and producing a folded paper. My hands shook as I handed him his cup of tea. I tried to look into his eyes, but he looked away.

"Oh, is it in reply to that question I asked?" Papa inquired.

"Yes, it is, sir," Robert said, handing Papa the telegram.

It was a very short one, for Papa read it in a glance. He passed the telegram to Mamma and sank back in the chair, sipping his tea. I looked at him and he stared at me, although with some sadness in his eyes. He shook his head and whispered, "Most unfortunate."

"What is so unfortunate? May I have a look at the telegram, Mamma?"

She handed me the slip of paper. The paper shook with the trembling of my hands. The cable read:

Dearest Son STOP Please inform Cousin James that our answer is still no STOP Sorry STOP With love STOP Mother and Father END OF MESSAGE

I sat down on the chair with my head between my hands. However, strangely enough, it was as if I had anticipated this moment, for nary a tear escaped my eyes. I looked at Robert with inquiring eyes, as if to ask *what shall we do now, dearest?*

However, I must give Robert his dues. He was one of those soldiers who never gives up, irrespective of facing the most insurmountable foe, or even when defeat stares him in the face. He gathered up enough courage to have one more try at winning the acceptance of my hand from Papa.

"Uncle James, may I ask what is your opinion, sir?"

"My opinion? Well, it is immaterial now, isn't it? Cousin Will has given us a definitive 'no', and no it shall be. What else can it be, son?"

"But, sir, couldn't you reconsider? I know Father has said no for now, but I am sure, with time, and when he sees how much Margaret and I love each other, things will change."

"No, son, I will not be able to give my blessing to this union, knowing full well that your parents are against it."

Mamma interjected, "Robert, how can we agree when we know they will disown you?"

"Aunt, if it is the matter of the inheritance, I am sure I could take some legal action against them and get it ba—"

"Good heavens, child. What do you take us for? We know your parents are rich, but we are not gold diggers, either." Mamma nearly screamed at him.

Robert jumped from his chair, held Mamma's hand in both his and kissed it. "Please, please, forgive me, Aunt. I did not mean it that way. What you said … the gold, I mean … was far from my mind. I was merely thinking of Margaret and our future family."

Mamma was silent for some time while Robert held her hand. Finally, she looked into his eyes and, holding his flushed cheek in the palm of one hand, said, "It's all right, Robert. I was not offended and I am sorry for what I said. But you know what? I think you should leave now, while we are all still on speaking terms."

"But what will become of Margaret? How will she manage in medical school?" Robert asked.

"She is not going to medical college—rather, we are sending her to Boston. She will work in a cotton mill run by some friends of ours," Papa retorted.

Although Sam had warned me of their intention, this news hit me like a cannon ball. "No. I will not go to Boston!" I screamed. I got up and, crumpling the telegram, which was still in my hand, threw it into the fireplace. I then stormed out of the house.

I ran over to Robert's horse, which was tethered to the fence post. I held onto the saddle, as if not wanting him to leave, and sobbed bitterly with my head on the horse's warm flank. Finally, Robert came over and embraced me. We kissed passionately. Our lips did not part for a long time.

"Goodbye, my darling," he said softly and whispered in my ear, "Write to me when you get to Boston. I have a plan."

I held onto his arm and cried, "Robert, dearest, take me with you. I cannot live here anymore."

"I will," he said, as he galloped away.

Chapter Fifteen

A Visitor from Langley

1967, June: Baltimore, Maryland

IT WAS LATE AFTERNOON when, after an enjoyable lunch with the Wallaces and Barinowskys, we left the Lake House Tavern in Grimsby. We took the ramp onto the QEW Highway and headed for the US-Canada border at Niagara Falls. The single-span Rainbow Bridge there, when compared to the treacherous ferry services in the 1800s, made the crossing over the Niagara Gorge as convenient as driving onto Manhattan Island. We drove over the white line at the centre of the bridge that designates the boundary line between the two countries. National flags flew on either side of the line, as well as the United Nations' in between them, indicative of the strong bonds between the two countries. I glanced over to peek at the horseshoe-shaped falls. Mist rose from the force of water pounding on the rocks at the foot of the cataract. A small cruise boat named *Maid of the Mist*, brimming with tourists, plied the river.

There was a long queue of cars and trucks at the US checkpoint. The inspection of trucks was taking its time and we came to a dead stop. I moved the gear stick to "park" and stretching my arms, yawned.

"Are you tired, dear? Shall I take over the driving?" Alexandra asked.

It had been a long day and I was indeed tired. Agreeing to her offer and jumping out of the car, I jogged over to the passenger side, while she slid over into the driver's seat. It looked like it was going to be a long wait; hence, I folded my arms and put my head on the headrest.

*****

I found myself standing at the edge of the Niagara Falls. The noise of the thunderous streams had grown louder than I could remember. It seemed that much more water than I had ever observed before was flowing over the Falls, which were barely visible through the heavy mist. In addition, for some reason, the surrounding trees had become denser, almost like a heavily wooded forest growing up to the edge of the gorge. That's funny, I thought. Never seen trees that close to the water before, and where did all the buildings go?

I heard drumbeats. A small band of Indians emerged from the thicket. They were mostly men, warriors with war-paint, except for a lovely young maiden who walked between them. She wore a white doeskin robe and a wreath of red, yellow and white wildflowers in her dark, braided hair, which fell almost to her hips. Another group walked behind them, carrying a canoe over their heads.

"Hinum, Hinum. Where are you?" cried an older man, apparently their chief, for he wore a headdress adorned with an eagle's head and two bands of feathers that flowed down his back. "Can you hear me? I am Chief Eagle Eye," he shouted, raising both his hands towards the Falls. "I am here to make the ultimate sacrifice of my beloved daughter, Lelawala. Will you help us? Cure our sick from dying?"

Tears running down her cheeks, the beautiful maiden got into the canoe, which four braves were holding in the water. They moved aside as the chief came up, his lips moving, and with both hands on the stern, pushed the canoe into the river. The fast-flowing current caught the canoe and propelled it towards the Falls. The boat went out of sight for a moment, as the mist engulfed it. It reappeared shortly, just as it reached the edge and plunged over the cataract. The sight of Lelawala sitting cross-legged, calmly, in the centre of the canoe, holding onto the sides, was one to behold. I leaned over the edge of the escarpment to spot the canoe, but it was enveloped once again in the fog.

A voice thundered from the vicinity of the gorge, as if from a cave below. "Chief Eagle Eye, your daughter is safe. My two sons have caught her. Since she has promised to marry the younger one, he will now tell you how to protect your people."

A younger voice said, "Kill the snake that visits your village every year and poisons your water. Lelawala and I will henceforth live in the cave behind the Fall."

I leaned further over the edge, attempting to glimpse the cave. I lost my footing and plunged headlong towards the pulsating waters. Suddenly, someone caught me by the arm.

*****

"Wake up, dear, we're approaching the checkpoint." It was Alexandra, shaking me by the arm.

We cleared the immigration/customs inspection and were on our way. Alexandra looked curiously at me. "Did you have another nightmare? You shook in your nap. I was afraid you might be sick, and wanted to wake you."

"Yes, it was scary."

"Did that Lady Godiva appear again?" she asked, smiling.

"No, not her. This time it was Lelawala."

"Oh, you mean the Maid of the Mist? Did you see her go over the Falls in her canoe?"

"Yes, quite vividly. I'm amazed at the sacrifice she made for her people, even in those days."

Alexandra brushed her blonde hair back from her forehead and gave me a melting look. "Women have been making sacrifices for mankind for centuries, my love," she said, patting my arm.

"Hmm ... sounds like something Doctor Margaret might have done," I remarked.

"Do you think she gave up her life for a cause?"

"It seems that way. But for what purpose?" I wondered.

"I'm curious as well. It should be in her diaries."

I then remembered what Greg Barinowsky had told us over lunch. "I'm intrigued by what Greg said about wanting to get *his* daughter, Katya, out from Russia. Karolina didn't say much. Do you think he meant Katya is from a former marriage?"

"Possibly. But it almost sounded as if she is his illegitimate child."

"How interesting." I wondered why he wanted to get Katya out from Russia so badly that he was even willing to go back there. Had she been part of their sacrifice to escape from the USSR?

Having rested, I took over the driving again. By the time we reached Rochester, the orange glow of the setting sun reflected from the windshields of the passing vehicles and heralded the approaching darkness. As we drove through the city, Alexandra remarked, "Rochester. Hmm ... Dear, isn't this where little Margaret and her family stopped for lunch on their way to Grimsby?"

"Yes, and they ran into those slave-catchers here, didn't they?"

"Yes. I remember she wrote it was in one of the Dutch taverns. What was its name?" She flipped through the diary and, having located the sentence, said, "Here it is—the New Holland Tavern. Wonder if it still exists."

"Darling, it was way back in the 1840s—I doubt the place is still around," I said, gazing around to find a suitable hotel or a motel. The downtown's bright streetlights and those of the tall, concrete buildings and shops had come on, which, together with the neon signs and the headlights of the passing automobiles, made the place glitter.

My thoughts turned to what this area would have looked like when the Wallaces had driven down, likely on this very road, in their horse-drawn carriages over a hundred years ago. Images of wooden buildings, stores, feedlots, saloons with porches and railings with tethered horses came to my mind.

"Walli, look. There it is." Alexandra's remark brought me back to reality. She pointed to a pleasant-looking, red-tiled building with a sign that read *New Holland Inn.*

"Good God! So it is. It seems they've upgraded it to an inn." I made the turn into their driveway and parked in the lot behind the building. An old barn with a red hipped roof stood on one side of the parking area, and the main building was on the other end. It looked like a comfortable place. We picked up our suitcases and walked up to the lobby.

After checking in, as the clerk handed me the room keys, I asked, "How old is this inn?"

"I don't know exactly, sir. I believe it's been around since the Revolutionary days."

"That old, eh! The building's been renovated, of course?"

"Yes, sir. This main building is new. I understand there used to be a tavern here, which is now the dining room, through there." He pointed towards the hallway. "This wing with the guest rooms was added later. But the barn from the old days is still there." He pointed towards the back of the building.

"What's in the barn?" Alexandra asked.

"It was like a stable. A local company has rented it now. They run an antique shop in there. They sell beautiful quilts. Look, there's an original one, made by some Quaker settlers, hanging on the wall there." He pointed to the wall behind us. "You may buy one in the store, if you're interested."

We turned around and saw the quilt hanging like a tapestry on the wall. It was a typical quilt made of colourful square pieces with triangular patterns showing flying birds. Due to its age, the colours had begun to fade. I had a chilling feeling of déjà vu.

I turned towards Alexandra and said, "Doesn't that remind you of the one we just read about?"

The clerk looked quizzically at us.

Alexandra nodded and remarked, "Yes, I'd like very much to get one of those quilts."

We took the elevator up to our room and, after freshening up, came back down to the dining room for dinner. The hostess seated us at a table beside a window that looked out onto a small garden on one side of the Inn. The waiter, after clearing the plate setting for the other unoccupied seats, took our orders.

While we waited, Alexandra excused herself to visit the powder room. I looked around at the decorations from the Colonial period that adorned the room. It was then I saw, in a dark corner at the far end of the dining room, a lady seated alone at a small table. I thought she was either a performer or a saleswoman from the antique shop, for she wore a Victorian period gown in blue velvety material, with a low-cut front that displayed her ample bosom. Her blonde hair was done up in an eye-catching style and flowed in ringlets around her long neck. She looked very intriguing and I stared at her for a while, but when she turned her eyes towards me, I quickly looked the other way, out of the window. The view out of the window, strangely, looked much brighter than earlier. In the garden, a clothesline was set up and on it hung a solitary quilt. I felt astounded when I noticed it had the same square patterns of flying birds, possibly like on the one that had warned the Wallaces of the slave-catchers.

I turned towards the lady sitting alone at the corner table. She looked up at me. It was then our eyes met and she smiled. I recognised her. I was stunned. It was the lady of my nightmares, the one who asked me to gallop after her on that hot plain in India, asking me to save the Rani, and had recently emerged to ask me to write her biography. However, this time she seemed more like a real person than someone in a dream.

She got up and walked over to me. "Hallo, Walli."

"Hiii ..." I stammered back, standing up and looking into her sparkling blue eyes.

"I am glad you now have your grandfather's pendant."

"Yes. But why did he give it to you?"

"It was to bring us good luck during our escape from India."

"And when was that?"

Before she could answer, I felt a hand on my shoulder. I turned and saw Alexandra beside me.

"Why are you standing up, dear?" Alexandra asked, looking perplexed.

I motioned with my eyes for Alexandra to look in the lady's direction. Alexandra turned around.

"What is it, dear? I don't see anyone. Was there someone you recognised?" she asked in a puzzled voice, looking around.

I looked towards where Margaret had stood. But no one was there. That lady had simply melted away. "Yes. It's ... I mean, there was ... Never mind, it was just my imagination," I stuttered and sat down. Also, when I looked out of the window, it was now dark and the clothesline with the quilt was nowhere to be seen.

"Oh, dear. You must be tired from the long drive."

"And hungry too," I said. Just then, the waitress brought our drinks. I look a long sip of my scotch and soda. But Margaret's words still rang in my head: *it was during our escape from India...*

Alexandra had read Margaret's journal aloud during our drive that afternoon, and she couldn't wait to get back to it. After dinner, we went into the lounge and sat, snuggled together, on a cosy sofa by the fireplace. We ordered another bottle of red wine and, sipping on the soothing elixir, read the diary well into the night.

Margaret's account of her teenage years and her struggle to overcome the many obstacles in her life enthralled us. The words in the journal, written in a clear, tiny script, flowed before our eyes till we could barely read. We finally trudged upstairs to our room and, slumping onto the soft bed, rested our weary heads on the feather pillows. As sleep closed my eyelids, my thoughts were still for that determined little girl who, much like Lelawala, had sacrificed so much to become a doctor and serve mankind.

The next morning, after a quick breakfast, we resumed our journey.

It was almost noon when we passed though picturesque Harrisburg and I took the cut-off for Interstate 83 South, towards Baltimore. Alexandra resumed her recitation of the journal and reached the point where Robert left Margaret's home, disappointed at her parents' response to his request for her hand. Nevertheless, he had promised to meet her in Boston with an alternate plan. I was anxious to hear what that plan was, when Alexandra suddenly became silent. I glanced over and saw her flipping through the pages, as if she had lost her place in the book and was searching for the next continuing sentence.

"Is anything the matter?" I asked.

"Yes. That's funny. I can't find the next page. I reached the end of Volume I and thought the narrative would continue into Volume II, but it doesn't."

"What's in Volume II?"

"Volume II is titled *My Married Life* and starts some three years later, in 1853."

"Are you sure the continuation isn't on any other pages of Volume I? You know how people sometimes write at the bottom or on the side of some pages in their diary." I was tempted to look, but kept my eyes on the road.

"That's what I thought. But I've searched through and cannot find anything that would continue her story from when Robert left her."

"So, where does Volume II start?"

"It's three years later and she writes about her new life in Canada, in the town of Niagara-on-the-Lake, near Fort George, where Robert is stationed ... Goodness!" Alexandra stopped in mid-sentence and giggled a bit.

"What's that?" I asked, trying to concentrate on driving down the winding highway.

"She has two children already. A boy and a girl."

"Oh! How nice. It seems they couldn't wait."

"Apparently not. But you know, in those days, they started a family right away."

"What was the plan that Robert had thought up? Where did they get married? Doesn't she write anything about that?"

"Not a word. Let me check again in Volume I. Some pages might have come loose." Alexandra picked up that volume and flipped through it again. "Oh my God ... this is really strange!"

"What's that?"

"I thought some pages were missing, but that's not the case. The journal is still pretty tightly bound. Look, it seems someone has neatly cut out the last few pages, possibly with a razor blade. Here." She held the end of the journal open towards me.

I glanced over, for just a moment, and indeed there was a sharp cut where the last few pages had been. "Goodness, why would anybody do that?"

"It appears as if someone doesn't want us to read that part of her life. Since no one else seems to have read this, it's possible she herself cut those pages out," Alexandra conjectured.

"But why would she wish to hide that part of her story?" I asked, glancing at Alexandra.

"Well … the one reason that comes to mind is probably something happened after she wrote those pages that made that period too emotional for her. She didn't wish to recount it again. But how can we confirm this?"

Then I remembered how Bill Wallace had become rather emotional, outside the Grimsby Tavern, when Alexandra had asked him about Robert. "Do you think Jane Wallace might know?"

"Yes, of course she'd know. Tell you what, when we get home, I'll call her."

*****

The next day, I arrived early at my office at the hospital. After my week off, I was anxious to catch up. Debbie, the Head Nurse, had neatly placed on my desk a stack of files for the patients I was to see that day. My schedule of appointments, surgery and other commitments for the week lay on one side of the table. I was relieved to note that my calendar was not overly busy, it being summer time.

There was a slight tap at the door and Debbie entered. "Welcome back, Doctor Walli. How was your trip to Canada?" Her lovely smile and attractive features could put even the most stressed-out person at ease.

"The family visit went well. Thank you, Debbie. How was it here?" I replied, relaxing back in my chair.

"Not bad. We managed to survive without you," she said with a slight laugh. "A couple of your patients did call in, but one of the other doctors took care of them. I have their files at the bottom of that pile."

"Good. Thank you. Were there any emergencies … anything new?"

"No … there weren't any crises, except this gentleman called," she said, handing me a slip. "He wanted to see only you, and said he would wait till you returned. He asked that you please call him."

The name on the note read Richard Redford, followed by a telephone number. "Hmm ... Did he say what was wrong with him?"

"Not specifically. He said he had just returned from India and might have picked up a virus or something there. The hospital had referred him to you. Would you like me to call him to make an appointment?"

"Where was he was calling from? Oh … isn't this a Washington number?" I asked, looking at the area code.

"Yes, I looked it up. It's Langley," she replied simply, as if it wasn't anything extraordinary, and again smiled in her disarming way.

"Langley!" I exclaimed, raising my eyebrows.

Debbie just nodded.

"Okay, I'd better call him. It might be important. I'll let you know if he wishes to come in."

"Okay, Doctor, and welcome back again," she said in her charming voice.

"Thank you, Debbie. Glad to be back in the salt mine." I said with a laugh.

Debbie laughed in return and left the office, closing the door gently behind her.

There weren't any appointments that morning, and I spent the time working through the patients' files, looking up records and case histories, making notes, and calling colleagues to discuss current medical issues. I later dropped by my chief's office for our usual morning get-together. It was close to noon by the time I had caught up with most of the outstanding work. Debbie's note to call Richard Redford lay in front of me. I decided to call him before he likely left for lunch.

"Central Intelligence Agency, how may I direct your call?" A pleasant enough sounding female operator answered.

"Richard Redford, please."

"One moment, please."

I heard the clicking sounds of my call being forwarded.

"Redford."

"Hello, Mr. Redford? This is Doctor Sharif calling. I believe you wished to speak with me?"

"Ah, yes. Doctor Sharif. Thank you for returning my call. Yes, I called the hospital and they suggested I speak with you. I understand you are a specialist in Eastern diseases?"

"Among other things," I replied with a slight laugh. "How may I help you?"

"I was in India and some other Eastern countries not too long ago, and seem to have picked up a cold or something. I'm just not able to shake it off," he said with a sniffle.

"How are you feeling?"

"Not bad. But I've been coughing and sneezing. The usual." He coughed a bit when he finished the sentence.

"Any fever, pain, nausea or sweating?"

"Yeah, I do feel feverish and sweat a bit sometimes."

"Is it mostly at night?"

"Yes. I wake up occasionally in a sweat."

"Hmm … Well, why don't you come in? Let's have a look at you. Would this Friday morning be convenient?" I asked, looking at my calendar.

"Sure, Doctor. Would ten a.m. be okay? It will give me an excuse to take the morning off," he said with a slight chuckle.

"That will be fine. See you on Friday, Richard."

"Call me Dick, please."

I got home just after six p.m. and changed from my suit into casual clothes, sports shirt and jeans. Alexandra had called the office earlier, saying she was going to be at court that day and would be late, but would pick up some Chinese food on the way home. Since we were away, she had not been able to precook and freeze our dinners for the whole week.

While I sat in our family room, sipping a beer and trying to catch the news on TV, the events of that morning came back to my mind. In particular, my conversation with Dick Redford played in my head. It replaced what streamed on the TV. The fact that he worked for the CIA did not bother me much, for I did have some patients in the Police and other government agencies, but the timing of it was what intrigued me. Our social visit to Grimsby, to the Wallaces, to simply return their grandmother's trunk, had nearly turned into a nightmare. If it had not been for our fast getaway from Wallace Hall, we could have come face to face with the KGB Colonel Yermolov. Goodness, did Redford have a hidden agenda and wish to know about my visit to Canada, or was he really sick with an Asian flu virus, I wondered?

Alexandra arrived home with our favourite Chinese takeout food, especially the hot and sour soup and stir-fried shrimps and vegetables. While we ate, I told her about the call from Langley and the new patient I had acquired.

"Now, you be very careful about what you tell him, if he asks any personal questions," Alexandra cautioned me, while she picked up the last of the noodles with her chopsticks.

"Yes, miss," I teased and asked, "Why? Do you think he's fishing?"

"I should think so. Unless it's a bizarre coincidence that you ran into a KGB and a CIA agent in the same week."

"Well, didn't you know, darling, your husband is a VIP?"

"Yeah, but I don't want him to end up on the six o'clock news."

"Okay, so, what or how much would you suggest I tell him?"

"If he asks, I'd answer his questions truthfully, but avoid conjecturing or expressing any opinions."

"Should I tell him about the Rani of Jhansi's crown and Greg snatching it away from the Wallaces for the KGB?"

"Sure, I don't see why not. It's got nothing to do with us, after all."

"Thank you, dear. I'm so glad I can count on you for expert legal advice."

"Sweetheart, I believe you have run well over your free half-hour consultation."

"Oh, by the way, did you manage to call Jane?" I asked, knowing she had been busy that day.

"Yes, I found a moment during lunch. I wanted to make the thank-you call anyway, but I was just as curious as you to find out about Robert's 'plan'."

"And what did she tell you?"

"Just as I thought. Margaret was sent to Boston to work in that cotton mill. She boarded in the home of the mill owners who were known to her family. But as Jane mentioned, she was treated no better than a servant and made to do a lot of housework in addition to her ten-hour shifts at the mill. No wonder that as soon as Robert finished his training at West Point, they eloped. And guess where they went? He took her to his Aunt Nora's plantation, near Charleston, where else? Their aunt was happy to receive them for, as you know, Robert's family hadn't spoken to her ever since she ran away with the Southerner, the plantation owner's son. Jane said they had a grand wedding out in the gardens. All the neighbours and the elite of Charleston were there."

"Were Margaret's and Robert's parents present at the ceremony?"

"No. Jane said the parents did not attend, for sure. But she believed that one of the uncles and some of the children did. She thought Robert's sister, Heather, went there with the Jenkins, who posed as her slaves, in disguise. Margaret's brother, David, went with his Uncle Tom's family, despite the parents' objections."

"Good God, how heartless could the parents have been?"

"People had strong convictions in those days, you know, dear."

"No wonder Margaret decided to cut out the pages of her wedding's narrative from her diary."

"It would seem she wanted to erase the memory of those events," Alexandra surmised.

That thought captivated me. I moved closer to her and held her in an embrace. "How sad, having to cut the pages out," I remarked.

"I'd have done the same thing, if my parents hadn't attended our wedding."

I was moved almost to tears by her remark, for I recalled that my parents had categorically refused to attend our wedding. We kissed for a long while.

*****

Friday came with a promise of the weekend to follow. I arrived at the office at my usual time of about eight o'clock. There were patients' cases to be reviewed, reports to be prepared and filed away. I got busy making the summaries and had almost forgotten about the appointment with my new patient, when Debbie entered with a light tap on the door.

"Robert … I mean *Richard* Redford is here." she said, placing a file on my desk.

"Robert! Does he look like him at all?"

"Oh, very much so. Could be his brother," she replied with a grin.

"Have you asked if he's related?"

"No, not yet, but I might. I asked him to fill out the patient medical history form. It's in the file."

I picked up the file and glanced at the form. "Thank you, Debbie.

I'll go and get him," I said, getting up.

Debbie left the office and I walked over to the patients' waiting room. There weren't many there and I spotted him right away, sitting in a corner chair, reading a *National Geographic*. He looked to be in his thirties, with blond hair and similar features to Robert Redford, which no doubt had people likening him to the movie star. He looked up.

"Dick?" I asked, looking at him.

"Yes." He said and, putting the magazine away, came to the door.

We shook hands and I led him towards my office.

"Please sit down, Dick. Can we get you a coffee or something?"

"No thanks, Doctor Sharif. I had one on my way up."

"Oh, please call me Walli. How was the drive?" I asked, taking a fleeting look at the address on the form, and added, "I see you aren't too far from us."

"Yes. We're in Rockville. Traffic wasn't too bad for a Friday."

I went over his medical history. There were no major diseases or operations listed and everything seemed to be in order.

"Good. So, how are you feeling now?"

"Not too badly. Still have a bit of a cough, though."

I thought I heard a slight Bostonian-Irish accent. Overall, he seemed a typical Ivy League type.

I made him take his shirt off and proceeded with the examination by taking his blood pressure, listening to his chest and so on. While the blood pressure was normal, some erratic breathing was discernible in the stethoscope. But it could have been due to his smoking, which he had indicated on the form.

"Are you still experiencing fever and sweating at night?" I asked.

"Yes, sometimes. Although, haven't had one for a few days. What do you think I have? Could it be cholera, Doctor?"

"Good heavens, no. You'd be a lot sicker if you had cholera. I don't blame you for assuming that. Having read so much about it in books, most of us returning from India think we've caught it."

"Oh, I'm relieved to hear that."

"But, Dick, your fever and sweating at night bothers me. It might be indicative of something serious. I'd like to send you for some tests. An X-ray, blood work and an ECG? Would you mind?"

"Not at all. Better to be safe than sorry. That's why I came to see you," he said, putting his shirt back on.

I went to the sink, washed my hands and sat down at the desk. "Tell me, how long were you in India?"

"Nearly three months. It was a tour—visited several Eastern countries."

"You must be with the Near-East Division, then?"

"Yes. You seem to know a lot about the Agency," he said smiling.

"No, not much. Just what I've read in those thriller novels," I said with a laugh.

"When I called here, they told me you'd been on a sabbatical to India?"

"It was nearly two years ago. I spent about a year there. The Delhi hospital is again in need of help and wants me to return for another term."

"Are you going to go?"

"Haven't decided yet. Have to ask my wife first." I replied, with a chuckle.

"Yes, don't we all have to check with the real boss?"

I filled in a test requisition form and checked out the examinations. I handed him the form, saying, "Here are the tests I'd like you to take. Is there anything else I can do for you?"

Redford took the form and looked at it for a moment. "Yes, Doctor Walli, there is one more thing."

I leaned back in my chair, waiting to hear what he was going to say.

"When my division chief heard I was going to see you, he called me in and asked if I could talk to you about a matter of some importance. Do you mind if I discuss it with you?"

"No, not at all. I'd be happy to help in any way I can."

"However, as this matter is highly classified, I'd like your assurance that you will treat this in the strictest confidence?"

"You have my assurance, Dick. But am I under any investigation?"

"Oh, no, Doctor Walli, definitely not. For if you were, they would have handled it differently."

"I understand. So, what's it all about?"

"We had a report from our Canadian Bureau, in Ottawa, that the Soviet KGB office chief recently visited a farm in the town of Grimsby, where a car with license plates belonging to you was also seen. So, we would like to know if you met with Colonel Yermolov, and if you did, was there any special reason for the meeting?"

Just then, our hasty departure from Wallace Hall came to my mind and I recalled seeing a blue sedan parked on the side of the road with its hood up. So, they were the CIA surveillance agents. How right / Alexandra's father was.

I saw Richard gazing at me, waiting for my answer. I replied hastily, "No, no. I didn't meet the colonel. But I learned later from Mr. Wallace, the farmer, that he arrived there after we left."

"Did Mr. Wallace say what the colonel wanted to see *him* about?"

At that point, I figured I had better tell him the whole story: The finding of Doctor Margaret's sea chest at that hospital in India, my bringing it back to the Wallaces and its almost ceremonial opening in their home. He listened intently and did not look too concerned. But when I mentioned that the KGB had offered Bill Wallace's stepbrother, Gregorze, money and a family visit visa to the USSR if he would snatch away Margaret's diaries and the Rani of Jhansi's crown, he looked at me, amazed. I further revealed that the Barinowskys and the Wallaces, having had a change of heart, decided not to part with their grandmother's diaries. They gave only the Rani's crown away to the Soviets.

Redford remarked, "Goodness, another set of crown jewels from India. How does it compare with Queen Elizabeth's crown?"

"I just had a glimpse of it. It looks somewhat similar, but the centre piece diamond did not appear to be as large as the Koh-i-Noor."

"I happened to see the Crown Jewels a few years ago while on a trip to London, on display in the Tower," Redford said and added, "I cannot imagine any diamond being prettier than the Koh-i-Noor. But don't the Indians want this Rani's crown back, just like they wish the Koh-i-Noor's return?"

"I believe they would like to have it back as well, except they don't know who has it. Wait till word gets out that it's in possession of the Soviets; the clamouring in Delhi will be heard all the way to Moscow."

"Tell me, what did Doctor Margaret do in India?"

"It seems she was hired by the Rani to work in her palace as a physician. Apparently, there were some Russian military advisors there as well. Sadly, it looks like they all perished during the 1857 Rebellion."

"Hmm … But why don't the Wallaces wish to sell the diaries to the Soviets? And what do they want to do with them?"

"Oh, I think they don't want their grandmother's work in India distorted, which they are certain the Soviets would likely do. Would you believe, the Wallaces have asked me to write her biography."

"But of course. With so much knowledge of that area, you are the most appropriate person. How far along are you?"

"I haven't started writing it yet. My wife and I are reading Margaret's diaries at the moment." I did not mention the Russian invasion maps. It was not because I wanted to hide them from him, but somehow at that moment, I had an uneasy feeling. I was not comfortable about bringing them up. In addition, I did not reveal that the real reason Greg wanted so badly to visit Russia was to get Katya out. Besides, I thought I could always tell him about these items some other time.

"Didn't someone else write about the Tsarist agents in India? Kipling, was it?" Redford jarred me from my thoughts.

"Ah! I believe you're referring to his *Kim*. But the time period of that novel was much later than 1857, when Margaret was there."

"I see. So, at the moment, you're in the researching stage?"

I nodded.

"I can understand the Wallaces not wanting to hand over the private diaries of their grandmother, but tell me, why did the KGB want the Rani's crown? Surely they wouldn't want to sell it. Do they wish to display it in Moscow?"

"I'm not sure. Those kinds of things are for you folks to find out," I said with a laugh, and added, "and when you have the answer, could you please let me know, so I can write the ending of my book?"

He laughed as well and asked, "Tell me, did Mr. Barinowsky finally collect his bounty?"

"Not yet. According to the deal, he'll get the visitor's visa and will be paid once he gets to Moscow. But I imagine the prize money might be much reduced when he shows up there without Margaret's diaries."

"So, is he going to go there?"

"I'm not sure. I know they still have family there and wish to visit them. But now that he's got involved in this caper, he might be thinking twice."

"Hmm … how very interesting, the Soviets wanting those diaries," Redford mused and remarked, "Division Chief will be most intrigued on hearing this chain of events. I'm certain he'll want to get to the bottom of it."

"Looks like you have another assignment coming up, Dick."

"As if I don't have enough to do. Well, thanks, Doctor Walli. You have been most helpful."

"Any time," I replied.

"I'll get on with these tests, and what happens next?" he asked, folding the test requisition slip and putting it in his pocket.

"As soon as the results come in, I'll have a look and, if necessary, we'll call you in to discuss."

"I'll do that. And good speed with the biography. I'd very much like to read it. Please, invite me to the book signing."

"I'll do that, and I hope you'll buy a copy."

He laughed. We shook hands. He left with his head bent down, still barely missing hitting the top of the doorframe.

I made some brief notes on the meeting and, walking over to the nurses' station, handed Debbie the file.

"Did you ask him about Robert?" I teased.

"No. I couldn't gather enough courage."

"Next time, then. He'll be back."

"But you know what, Doctor Walli? I called my boyfriend and we're going to see Redford in *Barefoot in the Park* tonight."

"Hey, that's a great movie. My favourite actress, Jane, is in it as well." I said, walking towards my chief's office for our luncheon appointment. Boy, he wouldn't believe his ears when I tell him about my new patient, I figured.

Chapter Sixteen

The Colonel Gets His Wish

1856, June: Jhansi, India

AS I SIT WRITING THIS JOURNAL on the balcony adjoining my room on the third floor of the palace of the Rani of Jhansi, the vista of the fortress gardens and the citadels stretching out to the Betwa River reminds me of a similar scene from Fort George, overlooking the Niagara River. That memory brings tears to my eyes, for it was at Niagara that I spent the most unforgettable three years with my beloved husband, Robert.

*****

1854, January: Niagara, Canada West

Junior officers' married quarters were hard to come by in the Fort George barracks. Hence, we rented a log cabin from a farmer just outside the town. Although it was a mere one-room ramshackle of a hut, likely used by farm hands, it was our very first home. It was also all we could afford, as Robert was forced to get by on his meagre pay —what was left of it after all the deductions. Our "bedchamber" was at one end of the cabin, where we had also placed the babies' cribs. Our eldest, Bruce, was over a year old and needed a larger cot already, while our daughter, Vika, at only six months, was quite content to sleep soundly in her cradle. The other end of the room served as the kitchen. It had an old, beaten-down wood-burning oven and stove, whose smoke pipe ran across the ceiling and served to heat the cabin as well. A wooden table with a much-scratched top and four chairs took up the centre of the room. We had managed to find these and two worn-out wing chairs at an open-air market. The vendor had kindly let us have them at an additional discount when he noted that both Robert and I, having emptied our wallets and change pouches, still did not possess enough money to pay for the marked-down items. After much fixing, re-cushioning and reupholstering, the wing chairs looked somewhat presentable. They were placed in front of the wood stove, where we spent the long winter evenings talking or reading with the children on our laps.

While the living expenses of our family of four were manageable, as we had learned to live frugally, we barely scraped by. This was due to the regular remittances sent to Robert's Aunt Nora. Those payments went towards repaying the money she had so kindly lent us to cover all our expenses of the wedding in Charleston, my hefty medical college fees, cost of books, instruments, and the living expenses in Philadelphia. Although in her letters Aunt Nora did mention that there was no need to hurry to repay her, we were adamant about keeping our end of the promise, and a money order was sent to her as soon as Robert received his monthly remuneration. I am certain Aunt Nora's husband, Uncle Jacques, was supportive of her desire to help us. I have often wondered what Robert and I would have done if it had not been for their Southern generosity. Little did we know that in only a few years, all the goodwill between the Northerners and Southerners would soon be forgotten.

It was a bitterly cold morning. Snow had fallen overnight and the wind howled through the cracks in the plaster fillings between the cabin's logs. I had made hot porridge for Robert and he left at six o'clock, his usual time, for the Fort. After feeding Bruce and nursing the baby, I cleared up the breakfast platters. As I washed dishes in the basin, using water from a pail Robert had brought in earlier from the well, there was a knock on the back door.

"Are you up, Margaret?" It was Beatrice, our farmer-landlord's wife.

"Aye, Bea. Come in. I've been awake for hours."

Beatrice entered, along with a gust of cold wind and blowing snow, which she tried to keep out by quickly closing the door behind her. She held a milk pail in one hand and in the other, two pigeons with their throats slit and feet tied by a string. "I brought these for you, dear, just as you asked."

"Thank you, Bea. Robert has been craving pigeon pie for some time."

"I'm sure he'll like it. The pigeons are fresh. John killed them just this mornin'." She put the pigeons and the milk pail on the table.

"I'm glad he did that. I could never have enough courage to slay the poor creatures. Let me pay you for them." I reached over to a shelf of the cupboard for the tin moneybox.

She must have noticed that I did not have many coins in there and said quickly, "Aww … Not to worry, dear. Pay me at the end o' the month with the milk money."

"Thank you, Bea. You're too kind. Would you like some tea? The kettle's on the stove."

"Don't mind if I do. Give me a chance to put me feet up. I've been on the go since before sunrise." She took her coat and scarf off and, flinging them onto the back of a wing chair, sat down. She rubbed her hands and extended her palms towards the woodstove. "How are the childa? Sleepin' still, I see."

"They were up and about with their father, but went back for a nap after breakfast." I poured the tea and, handing her a cup, sat down with my cup in hand in the other wing chair. "It's a cold one, isn't it? Looks like I'll have to caulk the gaps between the logs."

"Aye, you can hear the wind screamin' in 'ere like hungry cats. I know Robert got no time, but you can't do it alone, love. Canna I get John and the boys to help ya?"

"Oh, no, Bea. That won't be necessary. I'll manage. There aren't that many cracks. It sounds much worse than it is," I replied quickly, for I knew we could never afford to hire workmen. Even if they would have worked for free, neither Robert nor I liked accepting favours.

"But you should be doin' somethin' more useful with your time, Margaret. You're a doctor, ain't ya?" she asked, looking at my diploma hanging on the wall.

"Well, not quite yet. The Upper Canada Medical Board wants me to take some courses at the medical college in Toronto and write exams before they'll grant me a license."

"What a lot of hogwash. If you ask me, it's that women's thing. They dinna want no lady doctors in this country."

"No, Bea. Those are the rules, the same for women as well as for men."

"So, when you gonna go to Toronto?"

"Well, if I could get someone to look after the children, I can go now, stay there for a couple of months, and take the exams this spring. Otherwise, as I've had to do so far, wait until next year. Unless ..." I trailed off, too shy to complete the sentence.

"Unless? Unless yo get another one comin', is that it?"

I merely nodded. I am sure my face had turned crimson.

"Oh, I'd be happy to look after yer childa. Shall I talk to John?"

"No. Not yet, Bea. Robert wants the children to stay with family. He's working on his mother. He said he'll talk to her again this Sunday, when he goes visiting. He's planning to borrow a sledge and take the children along as well. Thinks the presence of grandchildren might soften her heart."

"I hope she'll agree to look after your babes. But John tells me her husband isn't feelin' too well, either. When did you see her, last?"

"Not too long ago, actually. I ran into her at the Jams & Jellies in Niagara."

"Oh! What's she doin' in there? Dinna she 'ave her own shop in Grimsby?"

"Checking out the prices of her competitors, I guess."

"Did she speak to ya?"

"No. She took one look at me and left the store by the back door."

"Good Lord. How uncivilised can one get." Her owlish eyebrows shot up.

"Pray tell me, what's wrong with Uncle Will?" My voice betrayed my concern.

"John works for the colonel now and then. He don't rightly know. Says the gov's been feeling rather poorly lately. How're your parents, Margaret? They in India now, aren't they?"

"Doing well, I believe. Had a letter from Mamma not too long ago. She wrote that Papa is really enjoying preaching to the natives. Mamma is happy teaching at a small school, also run by the American Mission. Elizabeth and David are studying at that same school."

"That's good. They'll be making good money, then. I hear the pay's generous for goin' abroad."

"If I know my Papa, the extra money would hardly have been a factor in applying for an appointment at that Mission. Perhaps Mamma might have had other ideas."

"Aye, a bit o' extra money sure come in 'andy at times o' need. So, 'ow long they plannin' to stay out there?"

"A few more years, I understand. They want Elizabeth and David to go to college in the States."

"They'll be able to do for them what they weren't able to do for you."

I merely nodded, overcome with emotion, thinking about that time when I had begged Mamma and Papa to send me to medical college. My thoughts were interrupted by Vika's cries from her crib.

"Oh, look, your daughter's up. She be needin' changin'. I'd better go. John be wondering if a bear got me or what." Bea got up and started to put on her jacket and scarf.

"Thank you, Bea, for the visit. You are such a comfort to me. I don't know if I could survive here without you."

"Hush, child. What are neighbours for, if we canna help each other in our time o' need? Be sure to let me know if you be needin' an 'and with that caulking. Make sure you be keepin' the childa and yo'self warm." She kept speaking even when she was out of the door. I waved a goodbye to her.

*****

I watched Robert scrape the platter for the last of the pigeon pie. The morsel was followed with a long gulp from his tankard of ale. He beamed at me with a look that said he had truly enjoyed the meal. Little Bruce, seated next to Robert, was also doing his best to finish his small piece of pie. I had already nursed Vika and she lay peacefully in her crib, likely dreaming of wandering and picking flowers in an enchanted forest.

"That was an excellent pigeon pie, dearest. Your best one yet."

"I'm glad you enjoyed it. Are you sure the crust wasn't overdone a bit?" I asked, as I walked over to pick up his plate.

"No. It was baked to perfection," he said, most likely ignoring the bitter taste of the burned edges. He put his arms around my waist and gently pulled me to him. I bent down and he kissed me on the lips. A small, thank-you one at first, but he continued into a longer, more eager one. His passion surprised me, and we continued kissing until we heard Bruce.

"Papa! Me," Bruce said, extending his hands, wanting a kiss as well.

"Okay, but only a small one," Robert said, releasing me and picking him up.

I collected the platters and proceeded to wash them in the basin.

"Tell me, what else did Bea have to say?" Robert asked.

My mind was still on the ardent kiss Robert had given me and my lingering suspicion that it heralded bad news. I replied, "Nothing much. Oh, yes. She's offered to take care of the *childa*, if I choose to go to Toronto to sit for the medical exams."

"And what did you tell her?"

"I told her we'll think about her offer, for you'd prefer if the children stayed with your parents. Have you spoken to Aunt Fiona yet?"

Not hearing Robert's answer, I stopped washing the dishes and turned around. I saw him staring at my medical college diploma on the wall as he took another gulp of ale.

"Robert. Didn't you hear my question? Is anything the matter?"

"Oh. Sorry, darling. No, I haven't spoken to Mother yet," he replied finally, as if breaking from a trance. "I was going to ask her this Sunday. But it looks like there'll be a change of plans." He took another swig of ale.

Robert's words, *change of plans*, pounded in my head like drumbeats. My hands shook and I very nearly dropped the plates. I quickly finished the dishwashing, wiped my hands on the apron, and went over to sit in the chair beside him. Bruce was still in Robert's lap, twiddling with the brass buttons of his uniform. I ran my fingers through Robert's thick golden hair. "What is it, dearest? Please tell me. What happened today?"

"It looks like there will be a war in Europe, after all."

"So, what's that got to do with us? We're in North America ..." But, noting the expression on Robert's face, I realised I had been too hasty in dismissing the impact of the war in Europe on Canada. I had that all-too-familiar sinking feeling inside my heart. Robert's behaviour said it all. Nevertheless, I still asked, "Do you mean they want you to go out there?"

He nodded, staring at the snow-laden trees outside the window.

I put my elbows on the table and rested my head on the tips of my fingers. All the pleasant feelings and gaiety I had felt just a few moments ago vanished like they had been put in a gas-filled balloon and flown into the dark sky. The thought of Robert going away to war, and our separation, was too much for me. Tears welled in my eyes. Robert still held Bruce in his lap with one hand and put his free hand over my shoulder. He gently massaged my neck and ran his fingers through my hair.

In between sniffles, I asked, "But why you, Robert? Why do you have to go?"

"Darling, Britain has asked for help from her colonies, and loyal Canada has responded. A contingent of foot soldiers and cavalry officers will be sent."

"But how do you know *you* have to go?" I asked, tears rolling down my cheeks.

"A selection has been made, my love. My name is on the list. Don't cry, dearest—this is the way things happen. It's the life of a soldier. You'll see, the war will be over before you know it. I'll be back soon. You'll see."

"Mamma, no cry, no cry," Bruce also chimed in, attempting to stroke my hair with his tiny hand.

Eventually my tears dried, but it was his words, *a selection has been made,* that really sobered me.

"Robert, who made the selection?"

"I don't exactly know. It works on a chain of command. The final selection is made by the people at the top."

"But surely only experienced soldiers are selected, are they not?" I asked, blowing my nose in a kerchief.

"Yes, mostly, unless there is need for inexperienced staff for other duties. Why do you ask, darling?"

"Then how is it that your name got on the list, when you happen to be among the junior officers?"

"Well, I cannot say why exactly. Yes, there are other, more senior officers who weren't selected—"

I interrupted, "Could it be that someone deliberately added your name to the list?"

"Don't be silly, dearest. How could anyone add a name *deliberately?*"

"Why not? If a commanding officer wanted to select someone, he would be chosen, would he not?"

"Yes, it's possible. What are you driving at?"

"Let me ask you this. Did Colonel Mitchell have a hand in this selection?"

"Yes. He's the chairman of the nominating committee. But—" Robert stopped in mid sentence, as if a thought had flashed into his head. "I see what you're thinking. He acted to get even with me for not marrying his daughter. Is that what you're implying?"

"Yes. I believe he did it out of spite towards you. I understand he's been fuming ever since you broke off with Nancy."

"Nonsense. I can't believe anyone could be that malicious."

I got up and put my arms around Robert. With our son between us, I looked into his eyes and said, "Dearest, believe me, there are people in this world who are that despicable. In addition, I feel responsible for this. If it weren't for me, things would be different for you."

"Darling, let's not start those old reminiscences again. What happened in the past is past. It is done. It's time to move on. I love only you, and that's that. I'll not have us walk over old smouldering fires again."

"Okay, sweetheart. Let's not discuss it. However, can you promise me one thing?"

"Yes, what is it?"

"Will you talk to Aunt Fiona about the possibility of getting Colonel Mitchell to rescind your selection? I understand your parents are still very close to the Mitchells. A few words in the right ears can work miracles, you know?"

"Well, all right, darling. I'll talk to Mother. If it makes you happy."

"I shall be the happiest woman on earth. I don't know what I'd do if anything happened to you," I said, kissing him.

"Nothing's going to happen to me. You'll see." Robert held me tightly and kissed me passionately again, just as he had done earlier. The fever within us began to rise once more. I noted that Bruce had fallen asleep in Robert's lap. I tore my lips from his. "Let's put Bruce to bed first," I whispered into his ear.

It started to snow again that night. Wind gusted around our cabin and buffeted streams of snow at the walls, shaking them like an angry ocean smashes its waves against the wooden hull of a galleon. Outside, the pine trees swayed with the wind howling through their branches.

However, all the snow and the wind did not bother us. For during those hours of darkness, we were intimate as we had never loved before, not even on our wedding night. Robert was by nature a passionate man, but that night, possibly the thought of our impending separation must have given him new vigour. The logs in the wood stove had burned out. Cold wind blew in through the cracks in the walls and the cabin became chilly. But, as we cuddled under the blankets, his naked body felt as if he was on fire from another furnace burning inside him. I clung to him, wanting to hold him forever.

He covered my body with hot kisses. He took his time exploring, touching, pressing, kissing and licking deep down into the folds. My squeals of delight and pleadings for him to stop were of no avail. Wave after wave of shivers of pleasure ran up and down my spine. My back convulsed involuntarily. Ultimately, I could not take it anymore, for my body felt like it was exploding from within. I gently pulled his face up to mine. We kissed fervently and I felt his hard manhood on my belly. It seemed to have engorged to an exceptional hardness that night. I reached down to touch it, wanting to reassure myself that it wasn't a dream. Robert moaned with delight as I stroked and squeezed it.

"Take me, Robbie, dearest. Take me now. I cannot stand the wait any longer," I whispered into his ear, tugging at his member.

"Are you sure, darling?" he asked.

"Yes, yes, my love," I replied and bit gently at his earlobes.

Robert, being over six feet tall, with a strapping body and solid muscles hardened from years of horseback riding and military training, looked like a little giant. But, he was a master of the art of gentleness. Each time he made love, he would pause, withdraw and start again, always asking if I was comfortable, until he was fully inside me, up to its very hilt. I held him tightly, my arms around his shoulders and legs wrapped around his buttocks. The tension left me and I became his, truly his. It was a most exquisite feeling that I wished could last forever.

Robert lay motionless on top of me, for a long time, as if he also wanted to savour the moment. While we kissed madly, our tongues darting into each other's mouth, he began his slow rocking movement. As he increased his tempo, torrents of pleasure darted throughout my body. I thought of the times we had been intimate. The memory of the very first time he had tried to seduce me in the stables came to my mind. At that time, the vision of his mother had come between us, to taunt me. However, she was no longer there. She was gone from my mind—I hoped forever. I felt released like a bird. I floated freely on a cloud, in another world.

Between my moans of pleasure, I heard Robert groaning. His body sweated, as he now thrust like a runner sprinting close to the end of a race. He moved his head down to suck my nipples. He loved to do that as he finished. I hugged him tightly. I felt I was being carried to the heights of ecstasy. Finally, I descended gently back to earth.

I opened my eyes to look at Robert, but the window on the wall opposite our bed came into sight. It was then I saw, among the falling snow, a face outside the window, staring into our cabin. I gasped and raised my head to get a clearer view. It was Uncle Will, Robert's father, dressed in a black fur coat and a matching fur cap. His face looked sombre, more benevolent, like someone who cared. His voice rang in my ears, "Do not worry, I will protect you." But when I saw his eyes, they had turned all white, like marbles. I let out a scream and the apparition swiftly disappeared.

"What is it, darling? Did I hurt you?" Robert asked, withdrawing and running his hands over my hair.

I couldn't answer, except to say, "No, dearest. It was nothing." I covered my face with my trembling hands.

"There, there, darling, my love, my love." Robert whispered soothing words into my ear as he hugged me.

We lay there in each other's embrace. I heard Robert snoring gently. The ghostly image of Uncle Will was before my eyes for a long time, until I must have dozed off as well, from sheer exhaustion.

I woke to the sounds of boots shuffling on the floorboards. Robert stood before the mirror, buttoning his jacket, all shaved, washed and ready to head out to work. I looked at the clock on the mantel. It was nearly six o' clock. I threw the covers off and jumped out of bed.

"Darling, why didn't you wake me?" I went over to him.

He kissed and embraced me. "You looked so pretty, sleeping soundly. I couldn't bear to wake you."

"Sorry, I overslept. Let me whip up a quick breakfast for you."

"Thanks, but it's getting late. I'd better be going. I'll pick up something at the canteen."

"Are you sure?"

"Yes, darling," he said, kissing me, and added in a murmur, "Hmm … we were a bit fresh last night, weren't we?"

"Speak for yourself," I replied, smacking him playfully on the buttocks. He laughed and, giving me another kiss, left the cabin.

I felt happy. I yawned, stretched out my arms and watched myself in the mirror. I saw a girl with a glow, her blonde locks all ruffled and displaying the broadest smile on her face. The sounds of Robert's departure must have awakened the bairns. Bruce was standing up in his cot. I went over to pick him up and he smiled, no doubt imitating me. "What have you got to be smiling about, young man?" I twitched his nose gently and he giggled out loud. Vika woke up just then and cried gently, obviously wanting to be changed and nursed. Thus began another, what I thought would be a normal day. However, the events later that day proved me wrong.

The grey clouds that had brought all the snow the night before had moved on. The sun shone brightly, and the view from the cabin window, of the snow-covered fields and the pine trees with their branches weighed down, could have adorned a postcard.

It was just past noon and the children, having finished their meal, were cooing and giggling as they lay on the rug in front of the stove. Bruce was trying to teach his sister how to clap. I sat in a chair, mending woollen socks. There was a knock on the front door. I wondered who it could be as I went over and opened it.

"Hallo, Missy Margaret."

"Jenkins! Do come in."

He entered and removed his cap, but just stood there, gazing at the floor. His solemn face, sad eyes and hunched shoulders said it all. Although in my heart I knew why he had come, I did ask, "So, what brings you here, Jenkins? Is everyone all right at Wallace Hall?"

Tears started rolling down his cheeks. He stammered, "It's Mister Wallace, missy. He died last night."

"Oh, my God!" I exclaimed. My hand flew to my mouth, as the image I had seen last night outside our window came before my eyes. His spirit had indeed come to say goodbye.

"Have you seen Robert, yet?"

He nodded. "I've just come from the Fort."

"Come, please sit down, Jenkins." I led him to a chair. "So, what did Robert say?"

"He asked me to tell you to get the children ready. He's gone to borrow a sleigh and wants y'all to leave right away for Wallace Hall."

I offered Jenkins some tea and biscuits. He helped to pack my trunk, while I scurried about getting the children dresses. Soon we heard the jingle of bells on the horse-drawn sleigh outside and Robert entered the cabin. His eyes had never looked so sad. I ran to him and he held me in a tight embrace.

"Oh, my love. I am so sorry," I said, resting my head on his chest with tears in my eyes.

"There, there, dearest. We knew it was coming. His heart just gave out." Robert comforted me by running his hand over my back.

"He was always good to me, you know. I shall miss him."

"Yes, darling. We all will."

"Papa, Papa." Bruce came running over and hugged Robert's leg.

"How are we today, my little Brucie?" Robert tickled his belly and he giggled loudly.

"Go see Grandma?" Bruce asked.

"Yes, we will see your grandma."

"Grandpa?"

"No. Grandpa has gone."

"Gone?" Bruce asked with a puzzled look.

"Yes, gone to Heaven," Robert replied, pointing his index finger skywards.

Jenkins took my sea chest out and secured it on the back of the sledge.

Dressed in leather jackets, thick gloves, heavy boots and woollen caps, we settled comfortably in the leather seat. The children sat between Robert and me and we threw warm fur blankets around us for protection from the bitter wind. Robert snapped the reins on the horses' flanks and we were away with a jolt. Jenkins followed behind on his horse.

The sun was setting behind the trees as our sleigh skated in through the gates of the stone wall surrounding the estate. The imposing Wallace Hall loomed before us. I was reminded of the last time I had passed through those gates, some seven years ago. The lily pond was still there, to one side of the driveway, although frozen and no doubt being used as a skating rink. Wind blew through the front garden, shaking the dormant rose bushes so loved by Aunt Fiona. Grooms led horses into the stables and the log cabin still stood to one side, where I had toiled hard, making the jam preserves with nary a word of appreciation from my aunt.

Robert reined in the sledge horses in front of the entrance to the manor. Frank, the footman who had driven me out to the train station after Aunt Fiona had unceremoniously dismissed me, came hurrying out of the door. He expressed his condolences to Robert and, bowing to me, held the horses by their bridles. I took our sleeping Vika in my arms and, with her head on my shoulder, walked up the patio steps. Robert led our wide-eyed son; he seemed to have enjoyed the sleigh ride but looked confused, likely because we had not conversed much.

We entered the mansion. Heather, Kirsten and Thomas the butler met us in the foyer. I hugged and kissed my dearest friend, Heather. Her swollen eyes betrayed a sleepless night, likely spent crying. She greeted me and took Vika from me, into her arms.

Robert and I looked around for Aunt Fiona. We found her in the parlour, sitting on a wing chair by the fireplace, arrayed in her best black-laced mourning dress, like a grieving Madonna. She looked just the same as the last time I had seen her, the same slim face, prominent chin, long thin nose, and piercing blue eyes. Her red hair looked as exquisite as ever, betraying her Emerald Isle ancestry.

"Mother!" Robert went to her, kissed and hugged her for a long time.

"My dear son. How are you?" she asked.

"I'm well. Here are Margaret and the children."

I touched her shoulder. "Dearest Aunt," I said, bowing down in an attempt to kiss her. But she abruptly moved her head sideways, avoiding my lips, and bent down to look at Bruce, who stood in the middle of the room, gazing curiously at her.

"Ah! There's my grandchild. Come here, you little bunny." She beaconed him by extending her arms. He went running to her. She proceeded to make baby talk with him.

I stood there for a while and felt the edges of a long-forgotten headache start to throb in my temples. It took all my will to swallow back the anger, the hurt, and keep a pleasant smile on my face. How could she be so cold? Would she never let it go? Tears welled in my eyes.

Robert looked puzzled and turned around to talk to his sisters.

Drying my tears, I walked over to sit on a sofa by the window.

Finally, Aunt Fiona addressed me, stiff and formal. "Thank you for coming so promptly, Margaret."

In vain, I searched her face for any trace of softening. There was none. Keeping my voice even and lighter than I felt, I replied, "We came as soon as we could, Aunt."

"Is Father upstairs, Mother?" Robert asked.

Fresh tears welled in the matron's eyes. "Yes, he's lying in his room. The caretakers have just left. You may go up."

I accompanied Robert to pay our last respects to Uncle Will. He was laid out on his bed, neatly dressed in his dark suit, white silken waistcoat, and a blue cravat. However, when I looked at his face, a shiver ran down my spine. Although his eyes were closed, he wore the same expression as when he had looked into our cabin window last night. I turned to Robert and hugged him. I wondered what Uncle Will had meant when he said, "*Do not worry, I will protect you.*"

Uncle Will's funeral was held the next day. By the grace of God, it was bright and sunny, with little of the chilling wind that had blown for the better part of the week. Robert and five faithful servants of Wallace Hall carried the coffin to the private cemetery, situated a short way down the farm road. The family members followed the coffin in a procession that went into the graveyard, through a gate in the wrought-iron fence around the cemetery. Graves of generations of Wallaces were laid out in rows, each with a granite headstone and some with memorial pillars.

Grimsby residents had turned up en masse to attend the interment. They stood in silent bleakness. The local militia unit had offered to take care of the burial of their honorary colonel. They stood at attention with rifles at the sides, in two straight lines by the freshly dug grave. All looked splendid in their dress uniform red kilts, their bare legs in knee-length, grey woollen socks, defiant of the cold weather. The pastor from the Grimsby Presbyterian Church read the last rites and delivered a moving eulogy. They lowered the coffin into the grave while a lone bagpiper played Uncle Will's favourite, "Scotland the Brave", but in a slow tone and time. It brought more tears to our eyes. Finally, the militiamen fired a volley from their rifles, as a last farewell to their former commander.

Aunt Fiona invited the attendees to the house for the wake. I helped Heather, Kirsten and the maids serve tea and refreshments. The busy task helped to keep me away from Aunt Fiona and her silent disapproval. Amid the gathering, I spied Mrs. Mitchell, Nancy and her husband—my tormenter, Albert. I did not see Colonel Mitchell, although I wanted to talk to him about Robert's overseas posting. Nancy and her mother took a fleeting glance at me and quickly turned away to walk towards another room. I could not have cared less for their cold-shoulder treatment and, carrying my tray of hors d'oeuvres, spun around to walk in the opposite direction. I felt a tap on my shoulder. I glanced sideways and saw Albert, dressed in an ill-fitting captain's uniform, smiling with a drink in hand. I turned and held the tray out to him.

He was the perfect caricature of a spoiled rich brat given to the excesses of the affluent life. Although I believe he was just a year older than Robert's twenty-five, he looked much beyond his age. In the last few years since I had seen him, he seemed to have developed a much pronounced portly figure, puffed cheeks and a double chin; no doubt from overindulgence in food, wine and whatever else.

Picking up a sandwich, he said, "Margaret. My condolences. How are you and the children?"

Surprised at his civility, I replied, "Thank you, Albert. We are fine. How are you and the family?"

"We are well. They aren't too happy about my leaving for Europe, though."

"Oh, are you going as well?"

"Yes. Didn't Robert tell you? I've just been made captain, and will lead the contingent."

It did not surprise me to hear that, for I suspected his appointment could not have been on merit alone. "Congratulations. No, he didn't tell me. I'm sure he's happy to have a friend for a commander."

"I am sure he is. How about you, Margaret? Are *you* happy that he's going away?"

"No. Not at all." I cannot say what prompted me to ask, "Albert, is there any way … I mean, could Robert's selection be changed? Perhaps someone else might take his place?"

"Hmm … I see. You mean, could he be replaced?"

"Yes. After all, his father just passed away, and him being the eldest …" I saw him smile. Hence, encouraged, I added, "Albert, would you know of someone who might be wanting to go to Europe?"

He thought for a moment. I noted his grin change into a devious look that made me squirm.

"I suppose I could make some inquiries. I'm sure there's bound to be an adventurous type willing to take Robert's place."

Despite his stare, I felt elated and asked in an excited voice, "Could you, Albert? Robert's a good mate of yours."

"How about you, Margaret? Are *you* my friend?" he asked in a whisper, bending down and picking up another sandwich.

"Why, yes, Albert … I mean, we are not … enemies, are we?" I stammered, feeling embarrassed. In an attempt to make amends, I added, "I'm sorry for slapping you that time at Ball's Falls."

I saw an evil twinkle in his eye that made me feel sorry for having brought the subject up. He moved closer to me and whispered, "Don't mention it. It was probably what I deserved for finding you so desirable. Tell you what, why don't I drop by your cabin some afternoon. Would the children be asleep? We could … ah … discuss Robert's substitution some more?"

A feeling of intense rage, as if my blood boiled, rushed through my body. I felt like shoving the plate of food in his face. It took a lot of will power to restrain myself. I said to him in a low snarl, making sure others nearby did not overhear, "Never. Never will I stoop so low. Who do you take me for? You imbecile … you moron."

Albert was stunned at the ferocity of my remarks. He stepped back and shrugged his shoulders, as it to say, if I were not going to play, there was nothing he would do.

Thankfully, Robert, managing to break away from the visitors, came to me. He looked impressive in his attire of dark frock coat and silk cravat.

"How are you bearing up, darling? I see Albert's been keeping you company."

"Pretty well," I said, keeping my composure, and noted Albert walking away without a word to Robert.

"So … I suppose we should leave this afternoon?" Robert asked, taking a sandwich from my tray.

"We could, but didn't you say you had three days of bereavement leave allotted?"

"Yes. But I thought you would rather depart right after the funeral."

"Why don't we stay another day? I think Aunt Fiona will like that," I said, hoping to make one last attempt at breaking the ice, to improve relations with Aunt Fiona.

"Are you sure now? And of course there is the reading of Father's will tomorrow as well."

"Yes. We should stay for that, shouldn't we?"

"Good, let's stay till tomorrow, then. Besides, I think Mother's coming around to you," he said with a smile and squeezed my arm. He left to talk to some other guests who waited to pay their respects.

The following day, after the recital of the will and the departure of the lawyers, we sat in the parlour with heavy hearts, each trying to overcome our grief by reading, writing or some such activity. The sun shone through the windows, adding to the warmth from the roaring fireplace, but it looked bitterly cold outside. The wind had picked up again and, gusting frequently, swirled snow about like in a Siberian terrain.

I was glad that Uncle Will had not completely forgotten Robert, as he had threatened. Although the farm estate was left in the hands of Aunt Fiona, upon her death it would transfer to Robert. Monetary sums were also bequeathed to Robert and others. I was relieved that we would be able to repay all the money to Aunt Nora. With the leftover funds, if Aunt Fiona would not look after our children, I could even have taken them with me to Toronto and hired a governess there.

My thoughts were interrupted by the sound of the parlour door opening. "Colonel Mitchell to see you, ma'am," the butler announced.

"Show him into the drawing room, Thomas." Aunt Fiona stood up and started to walk to the foyer. Robert did likewise but looked at me, as if wanting to know if I wished to accompany them.

As Aunt Fiona walked by me, I asked, "May I join you?" From her look, I soon realised it was a mistake.

She turned around and, looking at me with her cold blue eyes, said, "That will not be necessary."

I was shocked. While Kirsten followed them, Heather sat in silence, her eyes on the rug.

I heard the colonel say in his booming voice, "Mrs. Wallace, Robert. What a tragedy. My heartfelt condolences. Sorry I could not attend the funeral. I was called away to Toronto, on account of this talk of war with the Russians ..." His words trailed off as they went into the drawing room on the other side of the foyer. I sat in one of the window ledge seats with the sun radiating on me and, clasping my hands, I whispered a little prayer.

"What is it?" It was Heather, squeezing onto the seat and putting her arms around me.

"Oh, I do hope your mother can dissuade Colonel Mitchell and have Robert's selection cancelled."

"I do wish it too. I'd hate to lose my only brother. Shall I go and listen?"

"Yes, please. Can you find out what he's saying?"

Heather was gone for a while. I tried to occupy myself by reading a magazine but just kept turning the pages, unable to concentrate. The horrible sexual proposition that Albert had made to "help" Robert came to my thoughts. I felt like rushing into the drawing room and informing the colonel about the degenerate mind of the officer—his son-in-law—he had selected to lead the contingent. I controlled myself, preferring to suffer in silence.

Heather returned. From the look on her face, I guessed what the colonel's answer was. She stood by my side, put her arm around my shoulder and whispered in my ear, "I'm sorry, Margaret. He won't listen. But he says the British permit their officers' wives to accompany them and you may go with Robert, if you wish."

"What nonsense!" My temper flared up. I jumped up and walked hurriedly towards the drawing room. When I got to the foyer, Colonel Mitchell was already coming out of the drawing room. He looked at me and I saw the contempt boiling in his hard eyes, which made me take a step back. He didn't even nod or say anything to me. Instead, he turned back and spoke to Aunt Fiona.

"As I said, Mrs. Wallace, if Margaret is concerned about Robert, she can accompany him to Europe. I will arrange that. That is the most I can do, and frankly, it is more than enough."

I had to steady myself by placing one hand on the round centre table. I gathered enough courage to stammer, "Please, sir. Could you not reconsider? Robert's the head of the family now."

"Sorry, Margaret," he said, not sounding sorry at all. "The decision has been made." He marched to the vestibule. Robert helped the colonel with his uniform greatcoat. He put on his fur hat, which had the regimental insignia pinned to it, picked up his cane and, with a curt "Good day to you all", strode out of the door.

Aunt Fiona, with teary eyes, started to climb the stairs, holding the railing with one hand. Her legs wobbled. Feeling sorry for her, I rushed up to her, wanting to steady her by holding her elbow. She jerked my arm away.

"Don't touch me," she shrieked. "Don't you dare come near me. Do you hear? Ever again."

"Mother!" Robert exclaimed.

I stood at the foot of the stairs in stunned silence. She ascended, with some effort. Halfway up the curved staircase, she stopped to catch her breath. She turned around to glare down at me. Wagging a finger, she said, "This is all your doing. Do you know that? All your doing."

Chapter Seventeen

Across the Atlantic and up the Thames Estuary to London

1856, July: Jhansi, India

BRITAIN AND FRANCE declared war on Russia in March of 1854. However, preparations had begun much earlier, following battles between the Turks and Russians along the Romanian and Bulgarian borders and naval engagements in the Black Sea. I am still confused on the main cause of that war. There seemed to be as many theories as people could conjure. Only this morning, the Rani came to my chambers, followed by her entourage, carrying trays of our *choti-hazri*. Although she was a rather short lady, she made up for it by her beauty that mesmerized those in her presence. While normally she wore sets of heavy jewellery and numerous strings of pearls, it being early, she did not even have her customary diamond and pearls studded large nose ring. I must admit it gave her lovely oval, lighter shade of brown, face a rather charming look. She was clad in a minimum of silken red and yellow robes, which accentuated her athletic figure and prominent breasts.

After settling comfortably on a divan, while sipping a cup of *chai*, she looked at me with her large dark eyes and asked how much of my memoirs I had written. When I mentioned I was up to the war in Crimea, she inquired about the origin of that conflict.

"I'm not sure, Raniji. But you know, someone told me the discord started in Bethlehem."

"In the Holy Land! How so?"

"Apparently, an argument developed between the Orthodox and Catholic monks over decorations for the manger. A fight ensued and some of the Orthodox monks were stabbed and, unfortunately, died." I paused to accept a plate of fresh fruit salad from a maid.

"But Margie, why did the Russians and the British get involved?" Rani asked, looking confused.

In between bites of sweet, aromatic pieces of mango and bananas, I replied, "Raniji, you know how one small event leads to bigger and bigger incidents? The Russians took the side of the Orthodox monks and the French the Catholics. Russia blamed Turkey for the mismanagement of the Holy Lands and went to war against them. The French and the British came to Turkey's aid. That's how it all started, I'm told."

"You mean the British went all the way to Crimea to help the Musselman Turks!"

"It may sound strange, but that's what happened," I said, setting my cup of tea aside.

The Rani seemed lost in thought, and we ate in silence. After our breakfast, she motioned to the servants to take the trays away and asked those lingering to leave us alone. She then moved onto the side of the divan nearer to my chair.

"Margie, I have just heard from Delhi. The Mughal Emperor informs me of a Russian offer to help train our troops, free of any charge or encumbrances. What do you think about this proposal?"

"Well, I don't know, Raniji. I'm no military expert. But from what I saw of the Russians in the Crimea, they seem to be good soldiers."

"Yes, so I have heard. Margie, as you can see, we do not have much wealth now. The British have taken over so many of our lands. The East India Company grabs all our production for a pittance. We can hardly maintain a small force to defend ourselves. Should one of our neighbouring kings choose to attack us, only *Bhagwan* can protect us." She clasped her palms and looked skywards.

"Have you asked the British for help?"

"Yes, so many times. But there are always excuses and promises to 'look into the matter', and when their aid does come, it is with so many strings attached."

"I do see the predicament your kingdom is in, Raniji. In that case, if the British will not assist, why not take what help you can get?"

The Rani moved closer to me. Putting one hand on my shoulder, she said, "Doctor Margie, I'm glad you agree. Let me tell you more news. A Russian military officer is due to arrive here shortly. I'd like you to meet him. But, for the moment, can you please keep this news to yourself?" she asked, squeezing my shoulder.

I nodded.

*****

1854, March: Toronto, Canada West to London, England
Our small Canadian frigate, the *HMCS Mississauga*, pitched and yawed, battling the waves of the angry Atlantic on her way towards the British shores. While Robert had been to England and Scotland earlier with his parents, this was my very first trip to that famous isle. My excitement was like that of a schoolgirl going to her first dance. On board, along with a contingent of foot soldiers we had picked up from Toronto and Montreal, were some cavalry officers of the Niagara Regiment. Among them was Captain Albert Miller. I could not imagine what Nancy saw in him. Unless it was all the riches his family possessed, which they had acquired from operating the many non-unionised mills with starving, poorly paid and brutalised labourers, whose ranks I had almost been forced to join.

From his appalling behaviour at Uncle Will's wake, I knew Albert bore a grudge against me; I believe likely not from the break-up between Robert and Nancy, but from the other incident, when he had called on me while I worked at Wallace Estates, and I had reluctantly agreed to go out riding with him. I had been cautious ever since and especially when one of the farm girls, Rebecca, a pretty sixteen-year-old, had warned me about him. She had whispered that he was the type of brute who never took "no" for an answer. When I asked if she had told her parents about it, she tearfully replied, "Yes, but they didn't believe me and said I was making it up. Anyhow, it would have been my word against his, and my family are afraid of losing their jobs."

One morning a few days into sail, after breakfast, Robert and I stood on deck, admiring the vast expanse of ocean around us. It being early spring, there was a nip in the air. I draped my homemade woollen wrap tightly around me and snuggled close to Robert, trying to get some of his warmth to flow to me. The crew went about their business, doing the things needed to make sure the ship stayed in shape and on course. Some wiped the deck and polished the brass-plated equipment, while others kept a lookout from atop one of the three masts for any stray icebergs.

"Ah, there you are." It was Albert, with Nancy on his arm, strolling lazily towards us. They looked warm and comfortable, dressed in their long, burgundy-coloured fur coats and matching hats.

"Good morning, Nancy, Albert," Robert said, nodding stiffly.

"How are you, Margaret? Trust the sailing is agreeing with you?" Albert asked.

I ignored the sneer in his voice, putting as much amicability into my own as I could muster, and replied, "Very well, thank you. I'd heard a lot about the seasickness, but it hasn't caught up with me yet." Trying to be friendly, I asked, "How about you, Nancy—how are you feeling?"

"Fine. I'm quite used to sailing, actually. We go across every year for our holidays, you know. Have you been to England at all?" Nancy asked, her face expressionless and her nose lifted a bit.

"This will be my first visit. Although my cousins in Scotland have been writing, I've been too busy, what with my studies and then the children—"

"Yes, how are the children? Are they with those *farmers*?" she interrupted.

Before I could answer, Robert replied, "No. They are with Mother."

"Oh! She changed her mind, then, did she?" Nancy exclaimed.

"No, there wasn't any change of mind. She never said she wouldn't look after them. I am amazed that some persons will carry on the gossip," Robert replied, his face getting a bit flushed.

"Isn't it such a lovely day?" I said, trying to change the subject.

But from the silence and the look on Nancy's and Albert's faces, Robert's last remark had not gone over too well.

"How are our horses, lieutenant?" Albert asked in an authoritative voice.

"Fine, I think, sir. I'm sure our grooms are caring for them."

"Have you looked in on them today?"

"No. Not yet, sir."

"Well, as you are the officer in charge of the livestock, I suggest you had better go down and have a look."

"Yes, I will do that, sir." Robert snapped to attention, turned, and marched off towards the gangway leading down to the hold.

Some of the nearby sailors stopped working and looked at us curiously. I noticed that while Albert's face sported a smile, Nancy broke off into a giggle and tried to hide her face behind Albert's back.

I was quite mortified. The two of them were behaving worse than school children. "Excuse me, I'd better go and see how Betsy, my mare, is faring," I said, and followed Robert.

I found him in the hold, massaging the flanks of his charger, Harold. The poor horse, being constrained in a cramped stall, likely felt relieved and looked back at him with big, adoring eyes. Robert's face was still flushed with anger.

"The gall of that man. To dress me down like that in front of the men, not to mention you and Nancy."

I hugged him. "Now, now, dearest. Don't go upsetting yourself like that," I said, running my fingers through his hair. "Albert is simply flaunting his new appointment. We all know how he got promoted, don't we? We'll be in England soon, and hopefully you'll have another commanding officer."

*****

That incident on the deck was not the end of Albert's shenanigans. He continued to pick on Robert for the pettiest things and made him do all kinds of unnecessary chores, while his favourite officers lazed around, drinking ale. For instance, he made Robert, in addition to his numerous other duties, the officer in charge of the early morning drill. Robert therefore had to get up well before sunrise every day, get dressed and go out on deck and stand around watching the drill sergeant exercise the soldiers.

On most evenings after dinner, there was the usual smoking and drinking session and some of our pipers and drummers played military tunes. While I liked to listen to the music, I did not care much for the limerick recitals, which got racier and racier as the evening progressed. The verse usually started with a line that went something like "there was a young lady from somewhere or the other, who wore such and such unmentionables", and who usually ended up having the time of her life, or some such embarrassment. The men loved it. The other ladies and I normally excused ourselves and strolled to our cabins on the lower deck.

One night, I was returning alone, as the other women had left earlier and Robert stayed behind to smoke and talk to some of the other officers. On the second deck, I spotted Albert. He walked in my direction from the end of the long corridor. When he got closer, he just stood in the narrow passage. I tried to go past him, but he remained there, blocking my way.

"Ah, Margaret. At long last, we get a chance to be alone. Shall we go up on deck for a breath of fresh air? I'll bring a bottle of brandy from my cabin." From his slurred speech and heavily alcohol-laden breath, which likely could have caught fire if he had stood closer to an oil lamp, it was clear he was on one of his usual binges.

"No. Sorry, Albert, I have to retire. I'm tired."

"Oh, in that case, let me put you to bed. Shall I rub your temples, my dear?"

"No, no, thank you. I'll find my own way." Just then, the ship lurched and I stumbled towards him. Catching me, he pulled me to him in a tight embrace.

"Oh, come on, Margaret. I know you want to. I've been smitten with you ever since I set eyes on you."

"I'm flattered, Albert. But please let me go. What would Nancy say?"

"Don't worry about her. She's asleep. Why don't we go up on deck and have some fun? It's such a lovely night. I'll make it worthwhile for you and Robert. I'll recommend him for a pay increase."

"No, no. I don't want to. Please let me go." I tried to wriggle out of his grasp, but he held me firmly and pressed me against the door of a cabin. I felt his chest crushing my breasts and his whole body pressing against mine, including his protruding belly and the risen member between the legs. I was afraid to cry out, or make too much of a fuss over his drunken actions, for I feared he would make Robert's life more miserable. I searched desperately for a way to escape.

As there was no one in sight, I banged on the cabin door, hoping there might be someone inside who would come out to rescue me from this monster. There was no response. It only encouraged him. He opened the door and, lifting me by my waist, carried me inside and slammed the door shut with one foot. Before I knew what was happening, he had thrown me onto the lower bunk. My head received a glancing blow from the bedpost, knocking me out.

Fortunately, I recovered shortly, when I felt him jump on top of me and smelled his foul body odour and sour brandy breath on my face.

"H—" I tried to shout.

He pressed his large, beefy right hand over my mouth, almost choking me, and whispered, "Go ahead, scream all you want, wench. I'm going to give you what I've been wanting for a long time."

He slid his left hand down my leg and started to pull up my dress and underclothes. I glanced at the door and, to my horror, saw that while I had lain unconscious, he had bolted it. His red jacket lay on the floor. I felt ensnared, like a trapped animal. I tried to scream, but only a low moan emerged. Attempting to free myself by beating my fists on his back and moving my head from side to side was not much help, either. It only made the fiend press his hand harder over my mouth, covering part of my nose as well. I had difficulty breathing and felt myself slowly sinking, as if down into an ocean.

"Stay quiet, bitch," he whispered hoarsely in my ear, "otherwise I'll have my men feed your children and the high and mighty Wallaces to the wolves."

At the mention of my children from his vile lips, a new fury awoke inside me. Just at that moment, the image of Uncle Wallace—the same face I had seen outside our log cabin window the other night—passed before my eyes. I looked into his eyes and pleaded for help. I heard the image repeat what it had said earlier: *"I'll look after you ..."*, and it faded. That sight seemed to spring new life in me. I sensed a supernatural being had injected fresh blood into my veins. A strange feeling, like I had gained the strength of a whale, came over me.

I was wearing a low-cut dress and Albert, with his head on my bosom, kissed the exposed area of my breasts. I reached up and grabbed his hair on either side of his temples. Pulling his head up, I rolled like a whale and bashed his head on the bunk post. He tried to bring his free hand out from under my dress, but it caught in the folds of the petticoat. I managed to strike his head, hard, a few more times on the post. He went limp and his hand fell away from my mouth. I released his hair and he rolled off the bunk onto the floor with a light thud. Breathing heavily, I wanted to scream for help but restrained myself, fearing it would bring some of his cronies, who might put me through an ordeal much worse than he had been trying to.

I jumped out of the bed. He lay sprawled on the floor in semi-consciousness, swaying from the motion of the ship. To my amazement, I noticed the brute had already undone the buttons of his breeches and underwear, and his now-limp member lay drooping to one side. I had heard a good kick there does wonders to tame even the fiercest bull in heat. I steadied myself, holding on to the bunk post, and directed a swift kick with my boot at that spot.

He groaned and reached over to cover his groin with both hands.

I leaned down and said, in the same heavy, whispering tone he had used on me a little while earlier, "You bastard. Don't you dare try to harm my children, Robert, or anyone in our family, or else I'll have you court-martialled. You know what the penalty for rape is, don't you? There is a line-up of Wallace farm girls willing to testify against you. You son of a bitch."

He merely moaned painfully.

I smoothed down my dress and, looking into a mirror on the wall, straightened out my hair and rubbed my cheeks to make sure I looked respectable. Unbolting the door, I walked out into the corridor. The sounds of the pipers and drummers still playing upstairs floated down. Thankfully, no one was around to see me leave. I walked towards my cabin, feeling like a boxing champion who had just knocked out an opponent.

The ship had started to roll and sway much more heavily then, and I had to press my hands on the walls to steady myself. A group of sailors came along the corridor. Each stood aside, almost at attention, to give me a clear passage. However, as I stumbled from the rolling, a dozen hands came up to assist me.

"Steady as you go, ma'am," one of the sailors cautioned.

"Why has it got so rough all of a sudden?" I asked.

"Oh, that's because we're approachin' the English Channel, ma'am."

"Really, are we there finally?" I asked, intense relief spreading through me at the thought of ending the dreadful voyage.

"Aye. I reckon we be in Port of London pretty near noon tomorrow," a crusty old hand replied, without bothering to take the wooden pipe out of his mouth.

I thanked the sailors and each bid me a good night.

I was relieved to see that Robert was not yet in our cabin, for I had feared he would have raised an alarm on not finding me there. I cared too much for his career to give him even a hint of what had just transpired, for if he knew, God knows what he would have done to Albert. But that would only have brought the wrath of the Army on him, because, as the farm girl had mentioned, in such instances the blame was mostly placed on the woman. She was usually labelled either "unchaste" or "loose". Some would have even uttered "she had likely wanted it". Hence, I was determined to wipe out the humiliating experience I had been through. I summed up all my courage and resoluteness. From my past life-experiences and the training at the Medical College, I managed to control myself and not turn into a hysterical wreck, as some other woman might have.

Although in the end, I did feel somewhat pleased at having taken some revenge for Albert's actions, I was not foolish enough to believe that it was the end of my conflict with him. I had merely won a battle and there would be other encounters. I would have to be ready to deal with them, as and when they occurred.

Having decided to behave as normally as possible, I undressed quickly, washed and slid into bed. Picking up Dickens's latest novel, *David Copperfield*, which Heather had given me as a going-away present, I read propped up on a pillow. Soon enough, there was a light tap on the door and Robert entered.

"Puppet, I have great news." He sounded excited.

I guessed right away what it was, for he had also been feeling miserable at having to endure the long voyage. "Yes, I know. We're going to dock in London tomorrow," I said.

His jaw dropped at my having stolen his line. "Is there anything you don't know?"

"Well, is there anything left for you to teach me?" I asked with a broad smile, and playfully threw a pillow at him.

"You just wait right there. I have a couple more tricks in *my* medical bag I haven't shown you, Doctor." He proceeded to undress hurriedly.

*****

Early the next day, we entered the historic Thames River estuary. It was one of those exhilarating spring days. Everyone hurried through breakfast, to get a good spot on the deck and watch the banks of the Thames slip by, as our tiny frigate, flying the Canadian flag, gently sailed up the river. Robert, not having been this way, was glad we were going to sail right into the London Pool. He was relieved that we would avoid the long, cramped coach ride from Southampton that he had endured with his parents on the previous visit.

"Look, there's the Nore lightship," Robert said, pointing to a small boat anchored close to the shore. "This is the lighthouse which has guided the mariners' entry into the Thames for centuries."

I recalled reading about it and must admit I was disappointed at its size, for I had expected it to be a much bigger ship. We passed by pleasant-looking towns with rows of brick houses, dotted with church steeples and towers here and there, all set back from low-lying marshlands. Someone mentioned that those towns and villages dated from the first Viking settlements. I imagined Viking boats coming up this very way into London. But the flashes of burly, hairy Scandinavian men mutated into Albert's image. I had to suck in a deep breath to steady myself and clear my head.

We stopped at Tilbury to take on a pilot. Several naval vessels were anchored at the docks. On noticing our Canadian flag, some of the steamers blew their horns in welcoming blasts. An old fort loomed over the cliffs.

"Robert, that looks like a really old fort. When do you think it was built?" I asked.

Robert hesitated a bit, searching for an answer.

From behind us, a voice I despised and would never be able to forget, replied, "That is Tilbury Fort, built by Henry VIII in the 1500s."

We turned and saw Nancy and Albert standing behind us. My hand tightened convulsively on Robert's arm. Nancy looked fresh as ever, all dressed up in a feathery bonnet and a pink dress, as if she were going to be presented to Queen Victoria herself. The weasel at her side looked his usual groggy self, from lack of sleep and too much boozing. However, he seemed none the worse from last night's head bashing and foot treatment.

Determined not to show the slightest bit of weakness, I said cheerily, "Why, thank you, Albert."

He simply tipped his hat and looked away, avoiding my eyes.

Robert said, "Excuse me, sir, I'd forgotten to mention it. But just before we left, I received a letter from one of my Upper Canada College old boys, a Lieutenant Alexander Dunn. He wrote that he will try and meet us at the London Docks."

"Is that so. Which regiment is he with?" Albert asked.

"The 11th Hussars, sir. The very one we are to join."

"Well, you should be in good company. I read in the dispatch that another Canadian, Captain Nolan, just returned from India, might be joining us."

"Nolan! I've heard a lot about him. It will be a pleasure to meet him."

Albert took Nancy's elbow. "Come, my dear, let me show you Greenhithe and the Ingress estate." He led her to the other side of the ship, walking with a slight limp, the reason for which I did not have to guess.

Robert and I also crossed the deck to look at the Ingress mansion, which was just coming into sight. It indeed had a lovely architecture. Its central dome reminded me of some of the Italian mansions I had seen in paintings. The thing I liked best about that estate was the picturesque gardens and lawns, which extended from the manor right down to the edge of the river.

From that point onwards, the banks of the Thames looked rather grim. Endless rows of docks, warehouses, waterside steps and other landing places came into view. All teemed with every imaginable kind of craft, either loading or unloading their cargo or passengers. Closer to the Isle of Dogs, our frigate's sails were all wrapped up and tugboats took over, pulling the ship round the numerous bends and twists of the river. The Thames narrowed and the other vessels passed by in close proximity. We heard welcoming yells from the sailors of those ships and the responses from ours. Metropolitan London's skyline finally came into view. The dominating dome of St. Paul's Cathedral and the massive lantern that adorns its top were visible. At the same time, another sense of London, other than sight and sound, welcomed us.

"Ah! Thaar be London," said another old hand, sniffing the air.

As the crusty sailor had predicted, it was just past noon when our frigate entered the locks of St. Katharine's port. Shortly, we pulled alongside the dock and gangplanks were attached. A welcoming military band played as our contingent of soldiers stepped down, led by Albert. I noted he had sobered enough to resemble a commanding officer. Canadian soldiers lined up on the dock for an inspection. Officials from the Horse Guards, taken around by Albert, welcomed and inspected the troops.

With the formalities over, the ladies disembarked next, picking their way daintily down the walkway and holding up their dresses and petticoats. The pandemonium around the docks was the same I had experienced at the wharves in New York and Boston. Crowds milled around, looking for one thing or another. Children darted about, trying to sell flowers and all kinds of ornaments and trinkets. Supplies were being loaded on and off the ship. Porters scurried around, carrying baggage.

I made sure that our porter brought down the two sea chests and portmanteaux. As I stood beside our luggage, waiting for Robert, I saw grooms bringing the horses down another gangplank from the back of the ship. Robert finally rushed over, accompanied by two British officers.

"Margaret, I would like you to meet Captain Edward Nolan and Lieutenant Alexander Dunn, both originally from Toronto."

I shook hands with the two smart officers. Nolan was older, although the shorter of the two, but looked to be a well-seasoned officer. Dunn was a rather tall fellow, about Robert's age, but even Robert, at his six feet, had to look up to talk to him. We chatted with them for a while, bringing them up to date on the happenings in Upper Canada. In return, they told us about the war brewing in Europe.

Albert strode over, with Nancy in tow. Robert introduced them to Nolan and Dunn. Albert spoke very briefly to them and seemed to be in a hurry. "Robert, I'm afraid it's time to leave. We will stay in London awhile and join up with our new regiment in a few days. You are booked at the ... let me see," he consulted a list in his hand, "ah, yes, at the Portobello Inn in Kensington."

"Thank you, sir. Are you staying there as well?" Robert asked.

"Er, no. We always stay at the Grosvenor House in Piccadilly. It's central. Nancy finds it convenient."

"Oh, I love that place. It's so close to all the best shops, Piccadilly Square, Regent Street and St. James's Park, too, you know," Nancy chimed in.

"Ah, well, yes. Better get some rest. We have a meeting with our new commander, Lord Cardigan, at the Horse Guards, early tomorrow," Albert advised. He looked tired and ready for bed.

I held Robert's arm and proposed, "Oh well, Robert, while you are gone tomorrow, I'll see what there is to see around Kensington."

Albert retorted, "No, Margaret. Your sightseeing will have to wait a bit. His Lordship wishes to meet his new officers *and* their wives." He took Nancy by the elbow. "Come, my dear. We mustn't keep the carriage waiting." They turned and walked away.

Nolan and Dunn tried to keep a straight face. "The Grosvenor

House! Robert, your captain has connections," Nolan exclaimed.

"It's his Mrs. with the connections," Robert said.

"Good God. Is she actually going to Turkey?" Dunn asked.

We nodded.

"But how's she going to manage? There aren't any shops at the battle lines," Nolan remarked.

We couldn't hold it any longer and burst out in laughter.

Nolan waved his arm and an East Indian soldier, wearing the British army red coat and white breeches but a red turban, brought his horse over. I looked curiously at him, for it was the first time I had seen an East Indian person. Nolan introduced him as "Najeeb, the best groom you will ever find". He added, "I wouldn't part with him for even a dozen *naatch* girls in exchange."

Najeeb put the palms of his hands together and bent his head in the customary Indian greeting to us.

We bid farewell to Nolan, who informed us he was leaving shortly on a mission to purchase horses in Europe and we wouldn't see him until we were in Turkey. Dunn departed after inviting us for Sunday dinner, at his home in the City, where he lived with his parents. We accepted.

Robert extended his arm towards me. "Come, milady. Your carriage awaits."

We walked to the carriages, the porter following behind with our trunks and the other items on a wheelbarrow. Robert helped me onto the carriage and asked me to wait while he went and made sure Betsy and Harold had got off the vessel all right. I sat in the carriage and gazed out the window at the families walking by, their children at their sides and babies in their or governesses' arms.

My thoughts turned to our own Bruce and Vika. I wondered how Aunt Fiona was looking after them. Tears formed in my eyes as I recalled the most heart-wrenching separation with them at the docks in Niagara. I had hugged my adorable Bruce for a long time, and repeated to him that he was to be a good boy while he stayed with Grandma. His mamma and papa would be returning very soon. I just couldn't let Vika out of my arms to go to Heather, who stood waiting patiently. I kept kissing Vika and looking at her sweet face, while she reached up and played with my hair with her tiny hands. I cried profoundly. Finally, with the ship's bells and whistles going off for all to board, and at the imploring of Robert, I had handed Vika to Heather.

She had whispered, "Don't worry, Margaret. I shall look after them as if they are my own."

Now, sitting in the carriage, as I dried my eyes, I wondered if I would ever see my darling children again.

Robert interrupted my thoughts when he climbed into the carriage and said, "Harold and Betsy are fine. Appears they made the journey well. Their grooms are taking them to the Cavalry Barracks." He must have noted my sad face and teary eyes, for he asked, "What is it, my love? Have you been crying?"

I hugged him and whispered, "It's nothing, darling. I'm so glad to have you next to me."

It was beginning to turn grey and dismal as our carriage left the St. Katharine's dock and cantered along the Tower Hill Street. We passed under the shadows of the famous Tower of London. Robert pointed up at its stark, terrifying walls and informed me that "It was there that Anne Boleyn was beheaded."

I enjoyed observing the various landmarks of London that Robert kept pointing out. But the carriage seemed to take forever to reach our inn. We stopped frequently because of the chaos in the streets, caused by too many people and coaches. There were row upon row of black, soot-covered brick buildings with shops below and what seemed to be residences above, their windows covered with drapes. The one arresting image, which drew my attention, was that of the destitute children who simply stood or sat on the front steps of their homes in shabby clothes. So these were the children Charles Dickens wrote about, I thought.

The carriage finally stopped in front of a rundown building. A weathered sign on the wall announced that it indeed was the Portobello Inn. An old couple greeted us and showed us to our appointed room, up three flights of stairs. The room was probably nowhere like the one in the Grosvenor House, but functional. A lovely view of the rooftops of London could be seen from the round skylight window. We had to make do with what we were given, for we had neither money nor connections to upgrade the accommodation. Robert did not have the heart to ask the old gentleman to help him with our luggage. While I assisted with the lighter portmanteaux, he carried our heavy sea chests on his back, one at a time, all the way up.

I was up early the next morning. I wished to dress appropriately for presentation to the Earl of Cardigan. I selected my best dress, a

morning gown of pink taffeta with a white lace collar and sleeves
puffed at the shoulders. I was glad I had purchased an expensive
bonnet, in light rouge silk, which went well with that dress and let my
ringletted hair fall elegantly down the sides. Robert said I looked most
charming. He was his handsome self in a new, clean uniform, which
was still that of his Canadian regiment. Albert had said that later on he
was to visit the tailors to be fitted in the 11th Hussars' uniform, the blue
pelisses and the pink pantaloons that were nicknamed "cherry
pickers".

After a quick breakfast of kippers and eggs in the inn's dining
room, we hurried to our appointment. The carriage let us out at the
Whitehall Road, close to the Thames Embankment. We crossed a large
parade ground leading to the imposing Horse Guards building,
constructed in the Venetian Palladian style of the 1650s, which served
as the headquarters of the Household Cavalry.

We were shown into a large room, which could have functioned as
a banquet hall or a ballroom. Large paintings of famous British
military officers, Wellington, Cornwallis and others, along with a
number of well-known battle scenes, adorned the walls. Heavy red
velvet drapes hung down beside sizeable windows and doors. We were
the first to arrive. The other officers, some with their wives, came in
shortly. We sat in chairs at the back of the room for a while, drinking
tea served by solemn-looking butlers, and chatted about our first night
in London.

It was with great effort that I threw myself into the pointless, light-
hearted conversation. At length I was congratulating myself on almost
having forgotten the swirling cesspool lurking in the back of my mind,
when Albert strode up with Nancy trailing him, like a frolicking
lapdog. In her elaborate attire, she resembled at best an actress trying
to look like a duchess, and with so much rouge, she would have made
a woman of a bawdy house envious. They did not greet or look at me,
and I was glad.

Albert was in a hurry, as usual, and—although *they* were late—
complained that while we sat there drinking tea, the earl could arrive
any moment. He quickly ordered us to stand in a row at the front of the
room, according to the officers' rank and seniority. Obviously, Robert
being most junior, we were at the far left of the line. This suited me
well enough; I couldn't get too far from the villain.

The front double doors finally opened, and Lord Cardigan

strode in, followed by his entourage of aides and assistants. Albert marched up and managed a decent enough salute. Cardigan looked splendid in his form-fitting uniform and walked, very erect, to the front of our line. Although his greying long sideburns and moustache betrayed his age—which, I had been told, was about fifty—he looked much younger and, I dare say, very charming.

"Ladies and gentlemen, on behalf of Her Majesty, I have the honour of welcoming you and thanking you for your courage in joining this endeavour at our time of need ..." So began his speech.

My mind wandered to other things, the smell of the paint and polish in the room, the paintings on the walls, the grounds and the view of the river through the windows. I heard patches of the speech, when he informed us we were to set sail very shortly for the Bulgarian frontier, where fierce fighting raged on between the Russians and Turks. I listened attentively when he mentioned, "I'm sorry to say there have been heavy casualties, and a large number of injured and wounded. Not only that, there are reports of widespread sickness with diseases such as cholera and dysentery ..." He finally finished by emphasizing that "... such is the state of affairs; however, I expect every man to give his very best ..."

I had feared this news of illnesses at the front, and meant to have Robert make inquiries if there would be any opportunity for me to offer my medical services, either as a doctor—if they would have me —or in any other capacity. This sounded like a perfect time and I made a mental note to have Robert—rather than speaking to Albert, who would certainly have vetoed the idea—approach either Lord Cardigan himself or one of his ADCs.

The presentation portion of the meeting got underway with Albert escorting Cardigan along the line. Of course, the first one to be introduced, standing at our rightmost end, was Nancy.

When Albert presented her, she bobbed a perfect slow curtsey, as if she had been practicing, and squealed, "So pleased to meet you, milord. My father, Colonel Mitchell, has spoken so much about you. You know him, don't you?"

"Er, can't say that I do," Cardigan replied, looking confused. "What was the name again?"

"Mitchell, Colonel Mitchell." She repeated the name twice.

I pinched myself to suppress a giggle.

Cardigan looked around to his ADCs with a puzzled expression, as if seeking some help, but none was offered. Finally, Albert came to the rescue and said, "My lord, Colonel Mitchell is our Niagara Regiment's commanding officer and made the arrangements for our assignment to you."

"Oh, then he would have dealt with the Horse Guards. Sorry, ma'am, I am not acquainted with your father. However, I trust you will have a pleasant stay with us. Good day." He then moved on to the next officer.

Finally, it was Robert and my turn. "Lieutenant and Mrs. Wallace," Albert announced.

Robert bowed and I managed an awkward curtsey, my very first one.

"Wallace ... Wallace ... Hmm ... Wasn't your father, Major William Wallace, in our service for a while?"

"Yes, sir. He served in India with your regiment, milord," Robert answered proudly while the others in the line turned their heads to look towards us.

"Yes. Bill Wallace. I thought I recognised the name. I believe he had to return to Canada on account of his father's ill health. Was it not?"

"Yes, sir. Grandfather suffered a serious heart attack and Father had to return to look after our family farm."

"A fine soldier, your father." Cardigan then turned to me and shook my hand. Looking at me with piercing eyes, he said, "Well, Mrs. Wallace. It appears that farming life agrees with you."

I must have blushed at his veiled compliment. "No, no, milord. I do not work on the farm."

"Oh! So tell me, how *do* you spend your time, ma'am?"

"I'm a doctor, sir. I mean ... I am training to be one," I stammered.

Albert interjected. "Mrs. Wallace is an American, milord. She went to medical college in the United States."

Cardigan gave him a quick glance, as if to say *be quiet and let the lady speak for herself.* Then, turning to me, he asked, "Oh, yes. I have heard the American medical colleges have started admitting women. Tell me, when did you graduate?"

"About three years ago, sir. Unfortunately, I haven't been able to work the required period in a hospital as yet to get my license."

"Hmm ... have you spoken to Florence yet?"

"No. If you mean Miss Nightingale, sir?"

"Yes. I believe she's approached the government for help in setting up a hospital in Turkey. God knows there are enough sick out there needing medical attention, just as she predicted."

"I'll be more than happy to help her, sir. That is, if she'll have me."

"Tell you what. I'll make arrangements for you to go and see her. She's at her home in Embley Park. Lieutenant Wallace will be busy; my personal carriage and footman will be at your service."

Albert quickly interjected again, "Oh, that won't be necessary, milord. I am sure Mrs. Wallace can find her way to Embley Park."

I could have slapped him for interfering in my affairs.

"Nonsense, Captain. This is the least I can do for the daughter-in-law of one of my former officers." He then turned to one of his aides and asked, "David, could you please make arrangements for Mrs. Wallace to visit Miss Nightingale? Thank you."

"Yes, sir," the ADC replied, hurriedly scribbling down the order on a small notepad.

That concluded the formalities and Lord Cardigan departed, bidding us all a good day. No sooner had he left than the other officers came to Robert and shook his hand, congratulating him on having made such a good impression on Lord Cardigan, for it was well known that the Major-General did not hold officers who had served in India in high esteem, let alone those from the Dominions. I saw Albert and Nancy leaving the room, as if in a huff, without saying a word to Robert.

*****

I sat in Lord Cardigan's luxurious carriage, looking out of the widow, while the four horses pulled it with speed towards Embley Park. It was a landau with padded leather seats and polished dark wood and brass exterior. I realised why he had insisted that I take his cab, for Embley Park was quite a distance from London and travelling in a public coach would have taken me the better part of the day. We finally rolled in through the iron gates of the impressive mansion and up the curving driveway, which reminded me very much of Wallace Hall. The footman jumped out from his rear seat and opened the carriage door, which had the earl's family crest on it.

Seeing Florence Nightingale come out of the door towards me felt like an angel was floating over to welcome me. Her slim build and the attractive, almost round face gave her the angelic look.

"Welcome, Doctor Margaret, welcome," she said, extending her arms to me, and we embraced as if we had known each other for a long time. She led me into her drawing room, which was decorated in a charming Victorian style. "I've been most anxious to meet you, ever since I heard from Lord Cardigan that another American lady doctor was in town," she said, motioning me to sit in a wing chair by the fireplace.

"Miss Nightingale, how do you mean *another* American lady doctor?"

"Please call me Florence, my dear. Sit down, sit down. Yes, that's right, you may not know, but I did meet Doctor Elizabeth Blackwell in London a few years ago."

"Oh, is that so. She graduated some years earlier than me. Actually, she's been a great inspiration. It seems I've been living in her shadow for a long time."

"Yes, she's just as good-natured as you are. May I call you Margaret?"

"Yes, please, by all means," I replied, a little overawed.

Florence continued, "I asked Elizabeth to join me in a hospital venture in London. But, alas, she told me her heart was in America. I was really sorry to see her leave."

"I believe she's practising in New York at the moment."

"I wish her all the best. But I do hope, Margaret, you will not disappoint me?"

"What do you have in mind, Florence?"

"Well, would you believe it? Finally, the British government has agreed to my proposal to set up a hospital, with proper nurses, in Turkey. What with this ghastly war brewing up, they have taken heed of my warning."

"Florence, that is marvellous. Oh, to be able to treat the wounded in a hospital, as they deserve, instead of in those terrible battlefield tents they used in the Napoleonic Wars."

"Right you are. So, would you be able to help us there?"

"It will be my pleasure, Florence. My husband and I are going there anyway. When will the hospital be operational?"

"Like all good things, it is taking its time. Most infuriating. It will be situated near Constantinople, in a small town called Scutari. We have an excellent military doctor, Menzies, out there now. So far, we have chosen the buildings and are making arrangements for their purchase. The medical equipment was due to be shipped, but there is another delay. However, Doctor Menzies is prepared to work out of tents, if need be."

"It sounds very interesting. I am already excited and feel like starting immediately."

"Good. I'm very thrilled as well." She was silent for a while, as if thinking of something. "There is just one more thing, Margaret."

"Yes, Florence?"

"I was in the City yesterday, and spoke with the British Medical Board officers about engaging you. They are agreeable, but so hidebound. Since you do not have a British medical license, we will not be able to call you a doctor. Would you be willing to work as Doctor Menzies's assistant?"

"Yes, of course. I would not object to those terms. I am anxious to get started in my profession. It is the wounded and the sick I care about, not titles."

"Good. I am glad to hear that. I'll write to Doctor Menzies to expect you and, before you leave today, I'll give you a letter of introduction."

"Will you be going there as well, Florence?"

"Yes, I definitely will be there. However, it will be in a few months. I'm waiting for my nurses to finish their training first. Good heavens, look at the time," she said, nodding towards the clock on the mantelpiece. "It is well past noon. Would you like to join me for lunch?"

"Thank you. I would love to. But after that, could you please show me around the exquisite garden I admired on the way in?"

"It will be my pleasure, Margaret." She got up and pulled on a cord to summon her butler.

Chapter Eighteen

Fun in Vauxhall Gardens, to War in Crimea and a Medical Position at Last!

1856, August: Jhansi, India
IT WAS A SPECIAL DAY at Jhansi. Not that they did not have a celebration for a festival of one kind or another almost every month, but that day, a nobleman from the neighbouring principality of Bithur was coming for a visit. While his name was Nana Dhondu Panth, he was lovingly called "Nana Sahib" and sometimes even addressed as the "Raja of Bithur", for although he did not have a kingdom to speak of, he had inherited the lands, estates and what was left of the vast fortune of the last Peshwa of the Maratha Confederacy. Even though he had been appointed the Peshwa's heir in his Last Will and Testament, the British did not transfer the pension that had been awarded to the Peshwa as part of the terms for handing over his kingdom, the pathetic reason being that Nana Sahib was an adopted son. No doubt, losing a large pension would rile up even the best of men, and I am led to believe that such was the circumstance in the case of Nana Sahib. The Rani had told me he was one of her childhood friends.

I had just finished my rounds, examining the patients in the *hakim-khana*, when the Rani came excitedly into my chamber, followed by her handmaidens. "Margie, come quickly. Nana Sahib is arriving at the palace gates," she squealed. "I would like you to be part of the welcoming group."

"Me! Why do you want me to welcome him?"

"He is bringing his *vakil*, Azimullah Khan, to meet you. Azimullah has just returned from London after pleading Nana's pension case before Queen Victoria."

Azimullah? That name rang a bell. I wondered if he was the same gentleman I had met in the Crimea at the Russian camp. The Rani was in a hurry and I did not bother her with questions.

"Oh, all right," I said, and followed her.

A lady-in-waiting handed me a basket of rose petals.

Rani turned to me and asked, "Margie, did you ever meet Queen Victoria when you were in London?"

"No, Raniji, I can't say that I actually met her. But I had the opportunity of seeing her once, though."

"Really! When was that?"

My thoughts turned to the morning I had seen the Queen and her family, dressed regally, standing on the balcony of Buckingham Palace.

*****

1854, April: London, England

There was a strange excitement in London. After nearly forty years, Great Britain was once again sending her armies to fight battles on foreign soil. The war fever had reached almost hysterical proportions. Bands played popular military tunes in squares, parks and on street corners. Crowds cheered as troops marched towards their embarkation points. Sparkles of light from the soldiers' bayonets glimmered, as if the fog were generating a bizarre kind of lightning. While the company of soldiers marched in their colourful uniforms, motley groups of bedraggled women, the regimental wives, stumbled behind them. Wrapped in shawls, with hungry, haggard looks, each woman carried her worldly possessions in a bundle slung over the shoulder. The Army of the East was on the move.

One early morning, as was our custom, Robert and I collected our horses from the stables and took Betsy and Harold out for their daily exercise. We trotted around St. James's Park, which was, as usual, shrouded in the morning fog. We took one last round and in the final gallop down The Mall had to slow down as we approached Buckingham Palace, due to a large crowd having gathered before the gates. Although it was still early, the sun had just begun to cast its rays over the buildings and the haze was beginning to lift.

We halted alongside some other riders, who informed us the Queen was to appear when one of her favourite regiments marched past the Palace. Sure enough, as soon as the band started to play and marching feet could be heard, Her Majesty, along with an entourage, emerged onto the palace balcony. Robert pulled out his field glasses from the saddlebag and trained them in their direction.

"Who can you see, Robert?" I asked with excitement.

Robert replied, rotating the lenses, "Well, I can see the Queen and Prince Albert. There are a few princesses and, ah, that must be Bertie. Here, take a look." He handed me the glasses.

As I rotated the telescope, the blurred circular view cleared and the group on the terrace came into focus. It thrilled me to see Queen Victoria for the first time. While prone to plumpness, she appeared very pleasant. She wore a regal blue gown under a flowing cape. Her distinctive centrally parted hairstyle, tied in a chignon behind her ears, was clearly visible underneath an elegant bonnet. Along with the prince and princesses, she waved to the crowds amid loud cheers. This was my glimpse of the lady who directed the future of millions of people in her Empire, upon which the sun never set.

While Robert was busy with one training session after another, I spent the days in London, walking around Kensington Gardens, Hyde Park and some of the nearby street markets. In the shopping districts, I could only window-shop, for we had hardly any money to spare. I am sure Nancy must have needed to buy extra trunks to store all the latest gowns and dresses she likely acquired. During the long afternoons, I usually sat on a bench in one of the parks and read. Such tranquil moments were often interrupted whenever children ran by, or stopped and, leaning on the bench, asked, "What are you reading?" I chatted with them until their mothers or governesses ushered them along. Their smiling faces and inquisitive eyes reminded me of our Bruce and Vika. I had to restrain myself from bursting into tears, until they were gone some distance. However, our most memorable evenings were when Robert and I strolled together, enjoying the highlights and amusements of London. Thanks to the gaslights, which prolonged the evenings, we were able to spend more time outdoors.

Alexander Dunn, the old school chum of Robert's, was kind to us, knowing we were alone in London. We met him often. He invited us a number of times to dine at his house. His father had been the Receiver

General of Upper Canada, but upon his wife's death had moved to England. As they still owned property in Canada, Alexander had mentioned his desire to marry and return to settle in Toronto, one day.

One evening, wishing to reciprocate Alexander's kindness, we invited him and his lady friend for an outing at the famous Vauxhall Gardens. Since Alexander introduced her only by her first name, her name escapes me. She looked a bit older than him, but was an attractive and charming woman nonetheless. Besides, the way they looked into each other's eyes made it evident they were very much in love. Was she the one Alexander had wanted to marry and relocate with to Canada? I have often wondered.

The four of us had a marvellous time at the Vauxhall, which really was a huge amusement park. The whole place was so lit up that it made night appear like day. We listened to the fiddlers and the singers and watched many acrobatic and comic performers. I had not laughed and had so much fun in a long time. For dinner, we went to a restaurant inside a gazebo and were seated at an elegant table set with white linen, fine china, silver and crystal glasses. Robert ordered champagne to mark the occasion and we clinked glasses to "happier times ahead".

We had nearly finished dinner when Robert whispered in my ear, "If I were you, I wouldn't look back."

I have never been able to comply with such instructions, and that night, fortified with champagne, I couldn't help turning around. To my astonishment, saw the very persons I did not wish to set eyes on. It was Nancy and Albert, standing outside our gazebo. Nancy looked just as miserable as she had back home, some years ago, during the bonfire when Robert had broken off with her. Robert, ever the gentleman, jumped up.

"Good evening, Captain, Nancy. Would you care to join us?"

Albert looked inquiringly at Nancy. She simply nodded.

"Thank you. Don't mind if we do," Albert said, and with Nancy on his arm, climbed up the steps into the pavilion. The waiters scurried around to place two more chairs at our table.

"Fancy meeting you here, sir," Alexander said and introduced his lady friend, again by her first name only, as Miss Amelia or some name like that.

We had almost finished our dinner. Nancy and Albert declined to order food, saying they had eaten already. Instead, they joined us in drinking wine.

"So, tell us, Margaret. What have you been doing with yourself?" Nancy asked.

"Oh, not much. Just riding and sightseeing," I replied.

"Why did you not visit me at the Groov'nor House? We could have gone out shopping."

I thought, the gall of the woman, wanting me to call on her. However, I checked my temper and replied in a cheery voice, "Oh, is that what your hotel is called? My goodness, all this time I've been trying to find the Governor's Home. Most of the hansom drivers told me they'd never heard of that institution."

While Nancy looked as she was still trying to figure out my farfetched tale, there was much laughter all round. Just then, the waiter came over and asked if we would like to try their specialty drink, the rack punch. Alexander insisted we should try some, saying, "One hasn't lived till one has tried the Vauxhall's rack punch."

The special concoction was brought over and poured into wine glasses with much fanfare. We clinked glasses again, this time, "to Canada". I took one sip and its harsh, bitter taste made me conclude that it was not for me. I believe Nancy and the other lady did the same. Nevertheless, the gentlemen seemed to enjoy it. Even Robert, who did not drink much, had a second glass. It was with some apprehension I noticed, from the corner of my eye, that Albert was gulping down one glass after another.

Shortly, the garden's famous fireworks started. We stood up and walked to the railing to watch the dazzling display. Albert did not join us and kept sitting, I am sure, to indulge in a few more glasses of the punch. When we got back to our seats, he looked like one of those typical drunks one sees dropping off their stools in a tavern.

"Sho, tell me, ma'am, haven't we met before?" he asked Alexander's lady friend, looking at her with beady eyes.

"I do not believe so, sir," she replied in a low voice.

"Nanshy, don't you think we know this pretty lady?"

Nancy didn't say a word and just looked at something in the distance.

"Why, I coush have sworn we met you at Cardigan's soiree," Albert persisted.

"I do not recall meeting you, sir," the lady replied calmly once again, although I noticed she took a quick, agitated glance at

Alexander.

"Oh, by jove, I have it. You are Mrs.—"

"The lady said she doesn't know you, sir," Alexander interrupted in a voice so loud that those seated at nearby tables and some of the passers-by turned their heads to see what was going on.

"Lieutenant. How dare you butt in? I am talking to the lady," Albert said in an equally raised voice, which drew more attention from the crowd that had begun to gather.

"The lady doesn't wish to speak with you, sir," Alexander replied, again in a loud voice.

"Nonshenshe. What business is it of yours? I am trying to ascertain if I know the lady."

"Albert!" Nancy said, putting her hand on Albert's arm.

"You stay out of this, Nanshy," he said, slapping her hand away. "I am trying to find out which street Alex picked her up from?"

"It's none of your business, sir," the lady said. She got up, picked up her half-full glass of the rack punch and threw the liquid across the table, onto Albert's waistcoat. While we looked on in stunned silence, she coolly put on her cape and asked, "Alex, dear, can you take me home, please?"

While Alexander left with the lady on his arm, the others around us clapped and cheered. I heard a voice in the crowd say, "'Ere, want another glass o' bubbly, miss?"

It seemed some of the punch had gotten into Albert's eyes, as he patted them with a kerchief and Nancy tried to wipe it off his waistcoat. Robert and I just sat there, wondering what to do next. I was glad the three officers were dressed in mufti, for if the news of this fracas had reached Cardigan's ears, he very likely would have flown into such a rage that his profanities could have been heard outside the officers' mess.

All the uproar and commotion brought the maître d' over, looking very morose. "Seems the gov'ner 'ad a bit much o' the punch. Shall we put 'im in a cab, ma'am?" he asked Nancy.

Nancy nodded, dabbing her teary eyes. I will have to admit I felt sorry for her at that instant, but cannot say the same for Albert. The maître d' waved his arm and two burly men, who looked as if they dug graves for a pastime, came over and, taking Albert by each arm, dragged him out towards the gates. Nancy followed, still wiping tears from her eyes. Robert and I stayed on a bit longer to savour the sights and sounds of Vauxhall Gardens.

Albert, having made such a fool of himself and got what he deserved, did not help to quell my anger at him. I was still determined to repay him for his disgusting behaviour during the voyage from Canada towards Robert and me, and especially for what he had tried to do to me in that frigate cabin.

*****

1854, May: Sailing for Turkey

The peaceful sojourn in London soon ended. In late May, the day of our departure arrived and we set sail from Plymouth aboard a troop ship named, I believe, *Glendalough*, headed towards the Mediterranean. However, this sailing was much worse than the one I had experienced crossing the Atlantic. The tiny ship rolled and pitched constantly, as we encountered one storm after another. I was sick to my stomach and spent quite a bit of time in either the cabin or leaning precariously over the railings. Robert held me for my dear life, as the cold surf drenched me from head to toe. I had thought my nausea was due to a bout of seasickness, but little did I know there was another reason for it.

I was also distressed to see our poor horses suffering much more than we did. I cannot imagine how they coped in the deplorable conditions down in the hold. The poor creatures were tethered together in cramped rows. Someone had the bright idea to put them in slings. However, it did little to support them from the rolling and pitching, and merely produced sores on their bellies. In addition to Robert's and our groom's attention and, despite the awful stench, I used to go down often to check on Harold and Betsy. Fortunately, they appeared to fare better than the others. Some of the horses kicked and screamed constantly. The grooms were forever sponging their nostrils with vinegar, or dousing them with buckets of water. My heart skipped a beat whenever I noted an empty stall. Upon inquiry, the groom's predictable answer was, "Sorry, ma'am, 'e went mad. 'Ad to be put down."

*****

1854, June: Scutari, Turkey

Everyone except me flocked to the railings to catch their first glimpse of the Greek islands, as our ship approached the Dardanelles region. After brief stops in Malta and Gallipoli, we entered the narrow straights of the Bosporus, the great divide between the West and the East, to sail towards the gigantic, pond-like Black Sea. At Robert's coaxing, I managed to drag myself out onto the deck and, holding onto his arm, gazed at the picturesque sight of the approaching fabled city of Constantinople. Amidst the palm and cypress trees, blue and white domes and slim minarets of the numerous mosques gleamed in the sunlight. The main city, Constantinople—or Stamboul, as the Turks preferred to call it—was situated on the west bank of the channel, and a smaller town, Scutari, was located on the eastern edge. The *Glendalough* sailed into the Asian side of Turkey and docked at what looked to be the remnant of a wharf.

The horses and equipment were unloaded with great difficulty. Turkish porters, in their distinctive red fez caps, scurried about on the rickety pier, clamouring to be hired. Robert engaged a sturdy-looking fellow, who brought our luggage in his donkey wagon to the military campground. The campsite was situated in front of an impressive palatial-looking building, the Selimiye Barracks, which, we were informed, were built by a sultan in the seventeenth century. The Army Headquarters and the hospital were located in that building.

Other regiments, having arrived earlier, were already camped. The sappers got busy and erected our tents in no time. However, upon inspection from the division commander, Lord Lucan, they had to be moved back, for he considered the rows too close together. After moving the rows apart, we had hardly settled in when our brigade commander, Lord Cardigan, came trotting by on his fine charger— named Ronald, I believe—and guess what? He ordered us to move the tents forward, for he felt they were too far apart. The tents were relocated to where they were pitched originally. Anyhow, it felt good to be back on land. Robert and I spent a restful night in our tent.

The next morning, I was woken early by a most melodious strain, which sounded like a religious chant, from the direction of a nearby mosque. Later, I was to learn it was the Mohammedan priest's call to prayer, much like our church bells. I did not mind it, really, for I had to get up early anyway to prepare for my meeting with the doctor in charge of the Barracks hospital. I peeked out of the tent towards the latrines and was glad to see the inviting steam rising from the bathing enclosures.

I hurried to the women's baths area before a crowd could gather. The orderlies had the hot water ready, and they poured it into a bath barrel and discreetly stepped away from the tent. I closed the tent flaps and, undressing quickly, jumped into the barrel. After the long sea voyage, the hot water felt heavenly. I lingered in the heat, letting it soothe away the aches and pains from my body.

I was on the way back to our tent, carrying my unmentionables wrapped in a towel, when I spotted Nancy in the long queue that had built up by then. I tried to ignore her and pass by the other way.

"Margaret!" she called and waved to me.

I walked up to her, reluctantly, and we exchanged greetings.

"When are you joining the hospital?" she asked.

"Today. I'll be going over there right after breakfast."

"Already! But you've only just arrived."

"Some of us have to work for a living, you know," I tried to humour her. When I saw a look of annoyance in her eyes, I added quickly, "So, how about you, Nancy? What are you planning to do today?"

"Oh, Albert managed to get the day off and we might go into Constantinople to see the sights and do a bit of shopping. We might also call on the British Ambassador. Father knows him."

"Well, have fun. I'd better be going," I said and hurried towards our tent.

For the first meeting with the hospital superintendent, I took care not to dress too elaborately. I selected a simple, high-collared, dark blue day gown, with a matching bonnet. Robert was getting ready to report for a drill or something. As I was leaving the tent, with my letter of introduction from Florence Nightingale in hand, he hugged and kissed me.

"Shall I ask for a day off?" he asked.

"No, dearest. Save your leave for later."

"Are you sure you are going to be all right, going alone?" he persisted, looking serious.

"Of course, darling. The hospital is right there." I pointed towards the building.

"Now, don't spend your first pay advance all at once."

"No? And here I was planning to buy a harem dancer's costume."

"Well! In that case, go right ahead, and take some belly dancing lessons as well. I feel like some entertainment tonight."

"We'll see about the *entertainment*, my love. I have to get paid first." I laughed and headed for the imposing Barracks building.

On reaching the edifice, I asked some soldiers who were walking by for directions to the hospital entrance. They pointed to the wing where the medical facility was set up. The ground floor of the structure was slightly elevated, above what looked like a basement floor consisting of a row of cellars, each with a rusting iron-barred window, almost like that of a prison.

I climbed up the steps to the entrance and approached the sentry. He asked me to wait and called for the sergeant on duty.

"Yes. Can I help you, ma'am?" asked the burly sergeant, sporting a handlebar moustache.

"I'd like to see Doctor Menzies, the superintendent."

"You cannot stay here. There is no more room downstairs. Not even on the floor," he said, motioning towards the cellars.

"What's down there?" I asked. My inquisitiveness got the better of me.

"That's where the women and children are livin'. Got nowheres else to go. Now you look like a real lady. Donna 'e have someone to look after 'e?" he asked, looking me up and down.

"Look, sergeant, you don't understand. I'm not here looking for accommodation. I have a job in this hospital. I have an appointment letter right here from Miss Florence Nightingale," I said, waving the letter in his face.

"Aw, you mean yo're a nurse, like?" he asked with a lecherous smile on his face.

"Yes, something like that. Now then, would you be so kind as to let me pass and tell me where I can find Doctor Menzies?"

"Aw, all right. Follow me, please."

I could not blame the poor fellow for being so cautious, for I had overheard someone say that women of ill repute were wandering around the town like stray cats.

On entering the building, the first thing that hit me was the curdled milk-like stench of the place. Filthy dust bunnies lay about on the floors and in corners. Dirty utensils, clothing and personal items littered the tables. I had experienced dreadful hospitals in Philadelphia, New York and Boston, but this was the worst I had ever seen. The sergeant led me through several wards filled with moaning and groaning patients lying on rows of cots, bundled in sheets that must have at one time been white. The conditions there were simply appalling.

We went up another flight of stairs to the third floor. On reaching Doctor Menzies's office, the ever-careful soldier asked me to wait. He knocked on the door and opened it ajar.

"A lady's here to see you, sir. Says she's go' a letter from Miss Florence."

There was silence for a moment. Finally a voice said, "Ah, yes. Do send her in, Scott."

I thanked the sergeant and strode into the room. Two gentlemen were seated at a desk on one side of the room and, upon seeing me, got up. One was dressed in a British Army uniform and the other in a dark frock coat and trousers with a matching cravat. The one in the dark coat came forward and shook my hand. He was a middle-aged gentleman with a white goatee beard and long whiskers that grew wider as he smiled. He reminded me of a picture of Charles Darwin I had once seen in a medical journal.

"Good morning, Mrs. Wallace. We have been expecting you. I'm Doctor Duncan Menzies, and this is Major Sillery. He looks after the military side of our hospital's organisation."

The major bowed to me.

"Good morning, gentlemen. I am pleased to be here and trust I can be of some assistance," I replied, handing Doctor Menzies the letter from Florence. I did my best to suppress my nervousness and excitement at finally being welcomed at a hospital.

Doctor Menzies pulled another chair up to his desk and bade me to sit down. He proceeded to explain the general workings of the hospital and stressed how short of staff and funds they were. Major Sillery interjected from time to time to fill in any military detail.

"The shortage of staff and supplies were pretty evident from what little I have seen of the hospital floors, Doctor," I remarked.

"We are in a little better shape than when we first arrived here. You should have seen the filth we found accumulated in the building. Looked like the place hadn't seen a broom for centuries." Doctor Menzies pointed to the floor.

"How about that dead horse we saw lying on the ground floor, Duncan? Wasn't that a pretty sight, eh?" Major Sillery said with a laugh.

While I felt a dead horse was no laughing matter, I joined them in their mirth.

"So, when are you expecting more equipment and supplies?" I asked.

There was silence for a moment as both men looked at each other, likely at a loss for an answer. Finally, Major Sillery replied, "We are expecting some soon. As you know, Florence will be bringing help and, we trust, funds as well. But in the meanwhile, we have to do the best we can." Having said that, he got up and added, "Well, Duncan, I'll leave you to acquaint Mrs. Wallace with the hospital and her quarters."

On hearing that, I said, hastily, "Oh, no, sir. I will not be needing any *quarters*. I am staying with my husband in the camp."

"Sorry to advise you, ma'am. I believe the Light Brigade will be moving north to Varna in a few days. I'm afraid you will have to stay here." The Major thought for a moment and added, "Hmm ... I dare say you will need some money for living expenses. I'll have the quartermaster advance you this month's half pay. Would that be sufficient?"

"Yes. Thank you, sir. You are most kind," I replied, trying to look calm. The thought of Robert moving away had my heart beating fast.

"Very well. I am pleased to meet you, Mrs. Wallace, and trust you will have a pleasant stay here." The Major bowed and left the room.

Doctor Menzies rose and asked if I would like a cup of tea. I accepted, saying that would be nice. He went to a side table, where a tea tray was placed. Lifting the tea cosy from the pot, he poured two cups and brought one over to me.

"There is one more thing, Mrs. Wallace," Doctor Menzies said, sitting down. "As Florence explained to you, you will be working as my assistant, not as a doctor. Hence, you will go into the wards only if accompanied by me, or one of the other doctors. We have the same rules for the other female staff here. I hope you know our reasons?"

I nodded and replied, taking a sip of the tea, "Yes, I understand, doctor."

"Good. You will share this office with me, and that desk over there shall be yours." He pointed to a desk on the other side of the room. I noted it already had two stacks of files on it.

After finishing our tea, Doctor Menzies took me to show me my accommodations. It was in one of the four towers of the Barracks, which, he explained, was reserved for Florence and the nurses she was bringing over. The tower had five rooms and a kitchen. Only five rooms for about fifty women, I wondered, and asked Dr. Menzies about it. He simply replied that there was shortage of space in the Barracks, and it was all they could allocate.

"Look, there is a nice view of the Bosporus and Constantinople from here," he said, opening the window in one of the rooms. "Why don't you take a bed in this room? Two other women are also staying here. They are hospital help, engaged in washing and cleaning." He pointed to their cots. "They are pleasant ladies. You will have good company. Do you mind sharing?"

"No. I don't mind at all. This room is fine," I replied, noting that at least it looked cleaner than the wards. I was also relieved that I did not have to live down in the cellars, in the dungeon-like conditions the sergeant had pointed out to me. "I'll bring my belongings over tomorrow."

We went back to his office and he assigned me my first job, which was to sort through the two stacks of patients' files. I was to bring them up to date with the particulars of the patient's illness and enter the treatment details from the scribbled notes made by the doctors on pieces of paper that lay in another stack. It appeared the files had not been updated for weeks. There was another list of persons who had died, and their files needed to be closed with a notation "Deceased", and the date. With such a backlog of records, the hospital was evidently indeed short of staff.

I took off my bonnet, rolled up my sleeves, picked up a quill pen and, dipping it in the ink bottle, got to work. Dr. Menzies came over a few times to see if I was doing the entries and making the notes properly. He smiled when he observed that I wrote in a neat, clear hand and got the spelling of the medical terms correct, despite the doctors' quick, scribbled notes, some of which were pretty near illegible.

An orderly brought over lunch trays, of soup and sandwiches. I drank the soup down quickly and nibbled at the sandwich while continuing to work. I noted that while some of the patients had injuries incurred either at the battlefront or from accidents, the majority were suffering from cholera and dysentery. I wondered why.

I was enjoying my work—for writing the medical conditions took me back to my college days—when there was a knock on the door.

"Mrs. Wallace?" A young soldier peeked into the room.

I nodded. He came over to my desk. "I'm from the paymaster's unit. I have a packet for you, ma'am. Could you sign here, please?" The soldier handed me the packet and I signed in the ledger he presented.

It was my very first pay packet. While it contained only a few notes and some coins, I held it in both my hands and pressed it to my bosom. Tears of joy formed in my eyes. I looked up towards Heaven and thanked God for all His mercies and happiness He had bestowed upon me. Dr. Menzies, sitting at his desk, smiled when he saw my joy.

Through the rest of the afternoon, I worked diligently, in my usual quick way. I believe I am blessed with an excellent memory. I need to look at a name or a number just once and I will remember it—at least for a good while, anyway. By the time the evening shadows arrived and the rays of the setting sun shimmered off the Bosporus waters, I was nearly finished. Doctor Menzies got up from his desk and came over.

"Goodness, Mrs. Wallace. You have completed almost all of them. This is remarkable." He picked up a couple of files and flipped through them. "No one will have trouble reading these. You should have seen how some of the other nurses wrote in here. One would have needed a magnifying glass to decipher their scrawls." Placing the files back, he took out a watch from his waistcoat pocket and looked at the time. "It's nearly five o'clock. Normally we work here until six. This being your first day, why don't you leave the rest till tomorrow?"

I protested a bit, saying I would like to finish all the files, but he insisted and I thanked him for his kindness. I was glad to be leaving early, as I wanted to buy something special to celebrate my first day at work as a doctor; well, a sort of a doctor, anyway.

Leaving the building, I saw Sergeant Scott was still on duty. I asked him if there was a market nearby where I could shop for food and wine. He told me of a bazaar just a furlong or so down the road. He pointed to it and cautioned me at the same time to be wary of the natives. The marketplace being not too far, I ventured out there. I did get a few curious stares from the throngs of Turkish men, dressed in colourful garb, and women in scarves with veils across their faces. I did my best to ignore them. Strolling down the bazaar, I found a wine shop that looked decent enough. The Greek owner spoke only a smattering of English, but was fluent in French. As I had picked up quite a bit of French in Canada, we were able to converse sensibly. He brought out several bottles of different types of wines and champagnes from Bulgaria, Germany, France and elsewhere. I selected a bottle of French champagne—Robert's favourite—and some cheese and bread.

It was nearly dinnertime when I reached our tent and was thrilled to see that Robert had anticipated my desire to celebrate. He had had the soldier-servants set up, in front of the tent, chairs and a camp table decorated with a white tablecloth, plates and cutlery. My heart melted on seeing in the centre of the table a vase with some pleasant-looking flowers.

"How was your first day at work, Puppet?" Robert asked, coming out of the tent and buttoning up a fresh shirt.

I ran up to him, hugged and kissed him. Thanking him for the flowers, I handed him the shopping bag. He was ecstatic when he pulled out the bottle of French champagne. For dinner, we had my favourite, roast duck. Robert had silvered, no doubt, the cook's palm.

Most of our friends came by and offered their congratulations on my appointment. However, there was no sign of Nancy and Albert, and I was glad of that. I guessed they were still in some Stamboul harem or the other, with Albert likely drunk and rolling on the divans.

We sat, sipping champagne and enjoying the pleasant Mediterranean spring evening. Robert was silent for a while and I felt there was something on his mind.

He finally said, "I have some bad news, Puppet. The Regiment will be moving up north to Varna, in a couple of days. Cardigan has already left."

"Yes. I know. Major Sillery told me at the hospital."

"I'm sorry, my love, you'll be left alone here. Unless you want to leave your job and come with me?" He reached over and held my hand.

"No, darling. How can I? I've just started. You go ahead. I'll be all right here. They have a room for me at the hospital. Besides, I'll only be in your way, with you fighting in those battles."

"Yes, there will be some of them. We've heard the Russians have crossed the Danube and the Turks want our help to drive them back. But I'll be back soon. You'll see."

Later, lying together in the narrow cot, he asked about my sickness and when I told him that I felt much better, but we might have an addition to our family, he was overjoyed. He said this called for a double celebration. He kissed me all over for what seemed like an eternity. When I begged him to stop, he loved me in his familiar, gentle way. In the end, he held me tenderly as I fell into a soothing sleep.

I dreamt I was a seagull and flew over the palaces and mosques of Constantinople and north to Varna. I saw the fighting at the Danube and the red-jacketed riders driving the grey-coated men across the river. My flight then took me across the Black Sea, over to the Crimean Peninsula. I circled the town of Sebastopol, and when I saw to the east the town of Balaclava with a picturesque harbour, I decided to rest there. I flew over some lush hills and alighted on a tree branch overlooking a scenic valley. I had barely landed when I felt a human hand grab me.

I awakened with a start, but relaxed when I realised it was only Robert caressing my breasts. He roused me up for the second celebration.

*****

1854, July: Scutari, Turkey

The parting from Robert was most tearful, to say the least. I stood at the dock and waved at his ship as it departed. I then ran up to the top of the hospital's tower and watched it sail away, until it was reduced to a white dot.

I busied myself in my work during the day, and spent the long evenings reading or staring out of the window towards the Black Sea, in the direction I believed Varna was. Soon enough, there was some jubilation in Scutari. We heard the Turkish army had managed to hold off the Russians all by themselves. The Russians were in retreat. The British forces had not seen much action and might not be needed after all. The mission seemed to have been accomplished—we would soon go home. I worked industriously at the hospital to make the days pass quicker while waiting patiently for our return orders. I performed all the tasks assigned by Doctor Menzies, as meticulously as I could, and was happy to note that he looked pleased with my performance.

"Margaret, I see you are coming along very well. Much, much better than I had ever expected." he once remarked.

He gradually started to take me along on his rounds of the wards. It was sporadic at first, but when he noticed I was of considerable help to him—in taking notes and prompting him of a patient's history from memory—I soon became his constant companion. On the other hand, conditions at the hospital had not improved and, in fact, even deteriorated considerably, due to shortages of every necessity. The expected help from Britain in the form of additional supplies and funds, and Florence Nightingale with her group of nurses, had not yet arrived.

We started to receive from Varna shiploads of sick soldiers suffering from cholera, which had broken out in epidemic proportions there. As there were no more beds in the hospital wards, the unwell had to be laid on the floors and in the corridors on straw mattresses. Daily, corpses of the dead were carried out and buried in the yard in hastily dug graves. At that time, the only medicine known to alleviate the suffering of cholera victims, laudanum, was in very short supply. Opium helped as well, but that was virtually unavailable. Doctors prescribed it for only the worst cases.

I had read in an old wives' medical book that red pepper in water worked wonders. When I suggested this to Doctor Menzies, he said he had never heard of it. But after some thought, he agreed, saying, "It can't hurt. Why not give it a try." So, we did. It was not just my imagination; other doctors noticed it as well. There was a marked improvement in the conditions of some patients; at least those who were not in the advanced stages of cholera.

I had also read in some of the newer medical journals that patients' hygiene and good sanitary conditions were important in controlling the outbreak of diseases. However, my suggestions that the patients' bedding and clothing be changed regularly, and the sick be taken out daily for fresh air, were voted down by the other doctors—although Doctor Menzies seemed to be in favour of it. In those days, doctors did not believe in the benefits of cleanliness, fresh air and exercise to treat diseases. Confinement and a warm bed was the usual therapy administered. After much prompting by me, the doctors agreed to send patients out for walks, which indeed helped them to recover much quicker.

I prayed every night for Robert's safety, for there was no news from him. I used to ask every ailing soldier arriving from Varna about him. My heart sank when I heard that instead of returning home, the British, assisted by the French and Turks, had decided to launch a campaign on the Russian territory itself. The Crimean Peninsula. The objective was to capture the Russian naval base at Sebastopol, thereby blocking the Russians from launching ships from there, to attack Turkey and, for that matter, any other parts of the world.

Finally, in September, a long-awaited letter, from Robert, arrived. He was part of the invasion force that had landed on the western shore of Crimea and was proceeding towards Sebastopol. Nevertheless, I was relieved to learn that he was all right and had not participated in the terrible battle at the Alma River. He wrote that Lord Lucan was so far keeping the cavalry division in reserve. He preferred to have them sit on their horses, watching, while the infantry exchanged fire and bayoneted the enemy. I laughed out loud when I read, "The troopers are getting anxious and have started calling the general 'Lord Look-on'."

Doctor Menzies heard me and came over to my desk. "Is that a letter from Robert? How is he?"

"Yes. He's fine. They are camped somewhere in the hills of Balaclava," I replied, and read the joke.

He guffawed aloud. When he stopped laughing, he composed himself and said, "This reminds me. We have a request for help, from the hospital just set up at Balaclava. They are short of doctors and need experienced staff urgently. As a rule, I wouldn't send female personnel to the front. But seeing you have gained considerable knowledge here and observing that you are a diligent worker, I'm willing to make an exception. I would hate to see you go, but would you be interested in serving at Balaclava? You don't *have* to go, if you don't wish to, mind."

I could not believe my ears. *Not wish to go!* "Yes, Doctor Menzies. I would very much like to be where the battles are," I replied, as calmly as possible, and added, "I thank you, sir, for your consideration. I am willing to take the risk, if it means being closer to my husband."

"Yes. I understand. Good, then. I'll forward my recommendation. It's up to the Balaclava hospital's administrator. I understand the facility is set up in a ship docked at the harbour, but I trust you realise you may have to go up to the battlefields?"

I nodded, unable to speak, for I had a lump in my throat and tears in my eyes.

My prayers to the good Lord were being answered.

My acceptance at the Balaclava hospital-ship came in a few days and I was soon aboard a steamer, sailing across the Black Sea, bound for Crimea.

*****

1854, late September: Balaclava, Crimea
My first sight of Balaclava, in the early morning mist, was that of a tiny, crumbling fortress atop a row of bare hills. Compared to the massive Russian fortifications of Sebastopol we had sailed around, to evade their big cannons, it appeared to be something built during the Crusades. No wonder we had captured Balaclava "without firing a shot", as I was informed by a sailor standing beside me on the bobbing deck.

"Where are all the British ships, then?" I asked, not seeing any vessels.

"They be in the 'arbour, ma'am. It's inside the land, in a pond, like. We'll be towed in there," replied the sailor.

"Does anyone live in Balaclava? It looks like a piece of rock to me."

"It be a fishin' village, habited mostly by Greeks and Turks, ma'am. The Russians 'ave fled to Sebastopol."

As we approached land, a tiny inlet in between the gigantic rocks that plunged into the sea came into view. Tugboats arrived to tow our ship into the harbour. Sailing gently through the curved channel, we approached the port of Balaclava. Just as the sailor had said, the harbour resembled a lake surrounded by a ring of mountains. From a distance, one could hardly see any buildings, for every inch of shoreline was occupied by vessels huddled together like bees, their masts swaying. As we got closer, we could see rows of soiled, white-stuccoed buildings—with disintegrating green-tiled roof—on one side of the pool. Our ship was led to the docks along a small street in front of the village.

My portmanteaux and reticule in hands, I stood on deck beside my sea chest, which the kind sailor had gone down and brought up. While the vessel was being secured, I anxiously scanned the faces of the people lined on the pier. I spotted Robert first and waved frantically to him. As there were several other women, all dressed similarly in bonnets and colourful dresses, gesturing to their loved ones, he did not notice me straight away. He looked towards the other end of the ship. But when he turned my way, the broadest smile appeared on his handsome face.

The gangplank having lowered, I gathered up my skirt and prepared to disembark. I tipped the sailor a shilling, asking that he please take my trunk down. He looked most pleased to receive the money and, saluting me his thanks, hoisted the coffer on his strong shoulder. We were the first ones off the boat.

Robert came running to me and held me in a tight embrace. He kissed me gently on the lips and, taking a sly look at my belly, asked, "How are you, my darling."

"Very well," I replied, my eyes becoming moist. I put my gloved hand to his cheek and said, "I'm so glad you are safe and sound."

"No fear of any injury. We've hardly seen any action yet."

I noted a young man wearing a dirty white shirt, baggy trousers and a red fez take my sea chest from the sailor.

"This is Selim, our new servant."

Selim put his fingers to his forehead and bowed to me.

I looked inquiringly at Robert, as if to ask, where did you find him?

"Oh, he came with the house I've rented for us."

"Really, Robert! A house?" I raised my eyebrows. "I could have stayed with you in camp."

"The camp's up in the hills. It's no place for a woman. Mrs. Duberly has already moved out to that ship," Robert said, pointing at a vessel. "Besides, your hospital ship is also here. That one, I believe." He pointed at another vessel, docked nearby.

Having heard earlier that Mrs. Duberly, the paymaster's wife, was also there, I was looking forward to meeting her. "But Robert, will they let *you* stay out of camp? Didn't Albert object?"

"He did. But I went over his head to our brigade commander. When he heard of your arrival, Lord Cardigan readily approved my request. Said, 'under the circumstances, it is justifiable'." Robert mocked the earl's aristocratic accent.

"I'm so glad we'll be together," I said, hugging Robert and thinking once again of Uncle Will's spirit, likely looking after us.

"Look, it's nearly lunchtime," Robert said, peeking at his gold pocket watch. "Let's take you home so you can settle in. It's not too far."

Selim tried to hoist the sea chest onto his shoulder and had some difficulty. He was a slim lad, likely a member of the few remaining Crimean Tartar families. Robert helped and he managed to carry it on his back, stooping slightly and holding the side strap with one hand. We walked out of the docks and onto the street, lined with a row of houses and shops. We passed by a sleek yacht whose name, *Dryad*, was painted across the bow. Robert informed me it belonged to Lord Cardigan.

My first sight of our Balaclava home was not one of disappointment, as I had feared. It looked like a pleasant, two-storey country house with a courtyard and stables in the back, where I spotted our horses. I pressed Robert's arm and asked, "Robbie, it looks lovely. How on earth did you manage to find it?"

"It was good luck, I suppose. I just happened to ride by and the owners were locking up. They are Greeks, in the shipping business, and live on a farm inland. This is one of their houses; they'd rented it to a Russian family who absconded without paying their rent. Mr. Constantinopolis is happy to lease it to us. I had to submit the first three months' fee in advance, though."

"I suppose you had enough money left over from Uncle Will's gift?"

Robert nodded.

We went inside and found the house was fully furnished. The Russians had seemingly left in a hurry. There was everything one needed downstairs, in the parlour, in the kitchen, and in the bedroom upstairs. I noticed a metallic bathtub propped up to one side of the staircase. I did not care for the odour that prevailed in the house, though, and the gaudy linen and bed covers, as well. I made a mental note to air out the place and buy new sheets. I wondered if I would find any.

Having learned of the acute shortage of food at the front, just before leaving Scutari, I had managed to purchase some fresh beef. I took it out of my reticule and handed the package to Selim. "Do you know how to cook beef?"

"Yes, madam. I make shish-kebab."

I had seen the kebabs being sold by the street vendors. I said, "I haven't tasted them yet."

Robert said, "If it's beef, I don't care what they're called. We haven't dined on fresh meat since we captured a Russian supply wagon weeks ago."

We sat in the parlour and lunched on tea and biscuits, while Selim prepared our dinner. Robert asked whether I had had any news from home, for he had not received many letters from his mother. I opened my reticule and read the recent letter from Heather. Our children were well, although she had written, "Vika does turn her baby head around, as if expecting to see you ... while Bruce constantly asked for you in the weeks following your departure, he seems to have resigned himself to accepting your absence. We all pray for your safety and wish you will be back here with us soon ..." Reading that brought me to tears. I put my head on Robert's chest and sobbed. He had moist eyes as well and embraced me tightly, while he stared out of the window.

Selim turned out to be a cook sent from Heaven. He put together a splendid dinner. For starters, he served a delicious cabbage soup, which we spooned from the bowls to the last drop. The beef kebabs, cooked over an open flame, were spiced with some Eastern spices that I did not know. Although I found the meat was chilli-peppered a bit too much, Robert loved it. For dessert, Selim brought out delectable flaky pastry filled with nuts and honey, which, he informed us, was from a bakery in the village. I had also brought a bottle of Robert's favourite champagne, which went very well with the meal.

After dinner, we sat on the couch, huddled together, and talked late into the night. I told him all about my work in the Scutari hospital and he brought me up to date on the war. It would seem that the Crimean campaign would not be over in a matter of days, as the British commander-in-chief, Lord Raglan, had believed. Following the landing and initial Allied successes in the battles and skirmishes, the Russians had retreated into Sebastopol and were defending it stubbornly. Robert thought there had been a missed opportunity, likely due to reluctance on the part of our French allies, to storm Sebastopol immediately following the Alma battle. The French, fearing heavy losses, had persuaded the British to wait and lay a siege around the seaport. Apparently there were not enough Allied troops for an effective cordon and the Russians were able to send in troops and supplies from the north. Although the Allied naval and land forces carried out heavy bombardment of Sebastopol's defences, it was having little effect. All the ruptures in the fortifications were speedily repaired overnight and the ramparts looked as solid as ever.

As we climbed up to the bedroom, Robert mused, "I fear we are like mice in a cage. The whole Russian Army might come barrelling down, like a pack of hungry bears, into Crimea."

"So, what's stopping them?" I asked, bewildered.

"Possibly not having a railway line right into the peninsula from Moscow. They have a long march from the end of the line," he replied with a laugh.

Relieved, I slapped his arm. "You had me worried for a while."

Later, as we lay together in bed, cuddling and kissing, he ran his hand gently over my belly and whispered in my ear, "Would it be all right?"

"Yes, darling. The baby is not due for months."

Needless to say, the night was spent most blissfully.

*****

Despite the war that raged around us and the food shortages, we spent pleasant days in Balaclava. Fortunately for us, the Allies preferring to lay siege to Sebastopol and bombard the enemy, the cavalry was not being used much. Hence, Robert spent his time mostly in parades held every morning before dawn, and on scouting duties. I engrossed myself in my tasks at the hospital-ship. The chief surgeon was impressed with my medical knowledge and experience gained at Scutari, and relied on my opinions and reports on the patients. On my days off, Robert took leave as well, and we used to pack a basket and climb up the hill to the small citadel, named the Genoese Fortress, which, we were told, was built in the 1500s to ward off the invading Ottoman Turks. While lunching, we enjoyed the panoramic view from there. Robert taught me how to use the telescopic spyglasses he brought along.

One morning at the hospital, I had just returned from a round of examining the patients and was writing up reports when there was a knock on the door. An orderly entered and said the chief surgeon wished to see me in the examination room. I closed the files and hurried to that cabin. Upon entering the room, I was amazed to see, of all people, Lord Cardigan sitting in the examination chair, and the chief surgeon standing next to him.

"Ah, Mrs. Wallace. I believe you have met his lordship? He remembered you and asked for you," the chief said.

"Yes, sir," I said, curtseying to the earl.

"Mrs. Wallace," Lord Cardigan said in a casual voice.

"Is there anything I can do, sir?" I asked.

"Yes, there is. Lord Cardigan thinks he might have cholera. I understand you have seen many cases in Scutari. I should like your opinion, please."

I looked at the earl and, while he looked rather pale, he seemed well enough. Nevertheless, I asked him about the kind of food and water he had consumed recently.

"Damn horrible stuff at the camp. I don't see why Raglan wants me to live there. I have a perfectly good boat sitting here," he said in a growl.

I got the message. So, his lordship wishes to stay in his luxurious yacht, does he, I thought as I walked over to him. Motioning towards his eyes, I asked, "May I?"

"By all means."

I opened his eyes wider, one by one, using my thumb and forefinger. They looked clear enough. "How about your motions, milord. Are they regular?"

Cardigan looked embarrassedly at the surgeon, who nodded as if to say *answer the doctor*.

"Damn bad case of the runs," he barked, looking the other way.

"Does Lord Cardigan have any fever?" I asked, looking at the Chief.

"Yes. His lordship's temperature has been high, occasionally. Is that not so, milord?"

"Yes, yes. I have been sweating in this blasted heat," Cardigan said with a scowl.

"So, what do you think, Margaret?" the chief asked, looking at me with his steady brown eyes.

I was tempted to say there was nothing wrong with his lordship, but I suddenly remembered his kindnesses to me for introducing me to Florence Nightingale and recently allowing Robert to stay in town with me. It's payback time now, Margaret, a voice said in my brain. "Well, sir. While it seems his lordship has a mild case of dysentery, what with the fever and the unhealthy conditions at the camp, it could get worse. I would recommend Lord Cardigan take complete rest in sanitary surroundings."

"Good. Thank you, Margaret. Could you please put it down in your report and let me have it? I have to courier it up to Lord Raglan," the chief surgeon said.

Lord Cardigan said, "Thank you. Mrs. Er ... may I call you Margaret?" He looked rather relieved and the colour was back in his cheeks.

"Yes, please, milord," I said, curtseying, and walked out of the cabin.

That evening during dinner, Robert said, "Can you believe it? Cardigan has received Lord Raglan's permission to sleep in his cosy yacht and dine on gourmet meals cooked by his French chef. The other officers are most upset. Rumour has it the surgeon thinks he might be catching cholera. Ha!"

I just smiled. Later someone informed me that his lordship had been nicknamed "The Noble Yachtsman".

*****

I heard daily reports of the Allies and the Russians continuing to exchange fire from their entrenched positions. Ambulances constantly brought down the sick and injured from the front lines. At times, the roar of the cannonades made it difficult to speak to injured soldiers. From snippets of conversation, I gathered the siege of Sebastopol was not going quite as planned and it was feared we would have to endure the harsh Crimean winter. I was told that while the British force was itching for an assault on the fort, it was continually being postponed. The reason being given, again, was the lack of preparedness of the French. To be fair, their lines being closer to Sebastopol, they were receiving the full force of the Russian bombardment. Daily we heard loud explosions from their positions, which, we were informed, were their ammunition and gunpowder magazine carts. These undoubtedly led to great losses of lives and armaments. Several attempts by British and French ships to pour volleys of cannon fire at the Russian fort proved unsuccessful. A number of Allied vessels were sunk, or suffered heavy damage and losses of men from the Sebastopol guns.

Possibly because they did not have an enemy to battle, the British Light and the Heavy Brigade commanders—the brother-in-laws, Cardigan and Lucan—took to quarrelling among themselves. I heard that on several occasions Lord "Look-on", even with his cavalry division lined up, missed opportunities by not ordering attacks on Russian troops who happened to come by, and let them get away. Cardigan, although in his yacht at those times, was furious and berated his officers, advising them they should have charged regardless of Lucan's orders. This and other incidents led to constant arguments between the two relatives.

On the other hand, there were frequent false alarms. Reports of enemy troop movements towards the British camp kept coming in. These led to rapid arousing and deployment of the troops. However, when they got to the stated location, not a Russian was in sight. Needless to say, Robert was very frustrated at the way things were turning out. He constantly grumbled, and confessed, "I'm getting sick of it. The men are at their wits' end."

One late October evening, the weather had turned chilly and rain pelted the windows of our small house. Robert and I were getting ready for bed when there was a knock on the front door. Robert put on his smoking jacket and went downstairs. I heard him welcome Lieutenant Alexander Dunn. They spoke in whispers; I could not make out why he had come at that late hour. I donned my dressing gown and, after quickly brushing my hair and looking into the mirror, hurried downstairs. I saw them standing in the hallway, still talking softly.

Upon seeing me, Dunn said, "Good evening, Margaret. Hope I didn't wake you?"

"No, Alexander, you did not. Why don't you come in? Would you like some tea?" I asked.

Robert turned to go upstairs and said to Alexander, "Please sit down and tell Margaret what's happening. I'll get dressed."

Alexander hung his rain-soaked cloak on the wall coat rack, and sat down at the edge of a chair. He moved aside his long sabre, which rattled on the floor. "No, thank you. I shan't have any tea. It might be another cry of 'wolf', but it looks serious this time."

"What looks serious?"

"A Turkish fellow has brought news of a massive Russian force gathering in the hills to the north of us."

"Is he reliable?"

"The Turkish officers think so. Hence, Lord Lucan has called a meeting to discuss this matter."

"Will they attack?"

"They might. We're like sitting ducks here. But one never knows."

Possibly to ease my mind, Alexander asked about my family. I informed him of their welfare and inquired about his lady friend in London, taking care not to sound too inquisitive, for I now knew she was the wife of his troop commander. He said he had received several letters from her, saying she missed him and was looking forward to his return. He also confided that once she obtained her divorce, they would likely settle in Canada.

Robert came down the stairs, looking elegant in his uniform. "So, let's see what Lord Look-on wants, eh?"

I went up to him and he hugged and kissed me. "Do be careful," I said.

"Not to worry, dear. I'm sure it's another false alarm. Don't you think so, Alexander?"

Alexander nodded.

They put on their parkas and forage caps, and set out into the pouring rain.

Although it had been an exhausting day at the hospital—having assisted the surgeons perform several amputations—I could not sleep. I lay in bed, reading Ellis Bell's *Wuthering Heights*, which another officer's wife had kindly lent me. I found the Earnshaw and the Linton families' saga quite fascinating, but could not concentrate and kept turning the pages back, to pick up the complex plot. My mind kept drifting to what the meeting up at the cavalry camp was all about, and why Robert had been so hurriedly called. I feared they might decide to make an assault on the Russian army. Surely, they would not attack at night, and not in this miserable rain.

I must have dozed off and wakened when I felt someone gently remove the book from my hands, and turn the lamp down. It was Robert.

"Keep sleeping, Puppet. Don't let me disturb you."

"What happened? Was it a false alarm?" I sat up, wide-awake.

Robert replied, as he wiped his wet hair with a towel, "Yes, it looks that way."

"Who was that spy? Why didn't they believe him?"

Robert started to undress. "He looked genuine enough. Said he is a cousin of our Selim. That was why Lucan sent for me."

"And is he?"

Robert sat down on the bed and, taking off his boots, threw them in a corner. "Yes. He responded reasonably to my questions. Seemed to know Selim well. But they are all related here, you know," he said with a laugh.

"What did Lucan decide to do?"

"His lordship had already dispatched a message by his ADC to the C-in-C at Sapoune Heights."

"I am sure Lord Raglan would have been most happy to receive it, in the middle of his after-dinner brandy."

"Might have given him indigestion, I'd say. Would you believe his reply?"

"What was it?"

"He simply scribbled on the note 'very well'. When we asked the ADC if there were any verbal instructions, he said his lordship had asked to be kept informed of the situation."

I felt relieved to hear that. But just to be sure, I asked, "That was all? He didn't want any action taken?"

Robert said, getting underneath the sheets, "Yes. I don't blame the old goat, though. He is likely still recovering from the abuse the infantry gave him when he ordered a futile all-night march, just three days ago."

"I'm glad he didn't order another mobilisation," I said, running my fingers through his damp hair.

"Yes, so am I. But can't say that for Nolan. He was itching to go."

Wondering why Robert had not said a word about Albert, I asked, "Was Albert there? As your troop leader, why didn't he come to fetch you?"

"Ha! Are you serious? He was likely too inebriated to even realise there was a war on. I'm sure poor Nancy would have done her best to get him up, short of throwing water on him. Besides, we're not on speaking terms at the moment."

Surprised on hearing it, I asked, "Why? Did anything happen between the two of you?"

"No. Nothing," he said, looking at the ceiling.

While I felt there was something amiss, Robert appeared exhausted, and I did not press him for details. We kissed goodnight. I blew out the lamp and turned towards my side of the bed.

I tried to get sleep to come back to me, but it remained far away. The events of that evening kept churning in my head. I shivered, wondering if Robert's prediction had come true. Had the Russian bears come waddling down into the Crimean peninsula to attack us poor, defenceless lambs?

Chapter Nineteen

The Charge of the Light Brigade

1854, October: Balaclava, Crimea

THE NOISE OF THE SHUTTERS banging against the wall woke me. They must have come loose in the cold autumn morning wind that rushes from the Black Sea up the bleak, rocky hills of the Crimea, down the escarpments into the valleys and trenches like angry ocean waves. The draught howled about the house and the floors creaked as if in agony. It was the twenty-fifth of October—another day branded in my memory, for it is not only a date of importance to the British military, in remembrance of their gallant battles at Agincourt and Balaclava, but for me as well.

The day began with an ominous sign. I turned over in bed and put my hand out to Robert's side, only to find an empty space. Reaching over to the bedside table, I groped for my pocket watch and, flipping up its cover, observed it was past eight o'clock. Startled, I sat up in bed, realising I had overslept. An unexplainable fear gripped me when I became aware that Robert was not yet back from the daily much-detested, early morning inspection that pernickety Lord Lucan was putting the cavalry division through. Normally he would return by seven, wake me up, and we would have breakfast together, before I set off for the hospital. A shiver ran through me as I imagined the reason for his absence. In view of the previous night's report, by the Turkish spy, it could only have been a call to battle.

Getting out of bed, I peeked through the second-floor bedroom window. The sun was just rising above the distant hills and shone on the tiled rooftops of the village. The Black Sea looked a gloomy grey and the vessels docked in the harbour bobbed on the waves, their masts still shrouded in haze. There seemed to be an air of unusual excitement in the village streets. Although the shops and taverns had not yet opened, the locals and some Turkish soldiers seemed to be scurrying about, in contrast to their normal lazy stroll. Some carried bundles over their shoulders and appeared to be heading towards the docks.

Lord Cardigan's groom waited outside the yacht, brushing the chestnut charger, Ronald. My mitigating thoughts—that it could not be so bad since Cardigan was still in his yacht—were short-lived. There was the unmistakeable sound of clomping hooves. My fears returned when I saw Fanny Duberly, on her horse, trotting along the promenade. She turned northward and galloped up the road towards the hills. She resided aboard the nearby-docked *HMS Shooting Star,* and for her to be up this early and riding out towards the cavalry camp surely meant something had to be amiss.

I put on a wrap and went downstairs. I saw our servant in the kitchen, cooking breakfast. "Selim," I called out, "where is my husband?"

"Master not back yet, madam."

"But it's so late. What's happening? Have you heard anything?"

"Yes, my cousin say big Russian army coming," Selim said, pointing northwards. "Madam want coffee?"

"Yes, in a minute. Where did your cousin come from? What exactly did he say?"

"He come from the hill. He say Russians attack the Turkish soldiers. We fight bravely, but they kill many."

I knew the Turks were assigned to man the cannons in the protective line of redoubts up in the hills a few miles north of Balaclava. So I asked, "But what is he doing here in town?"

"Turkish soldiers must run. What can they do? No help come from the British or French."

It was no secret that except for the cavalry Light and Heavy Brigades and a small regiment of Sir Colin's Highlanders camped in the Balaclava hills, all the Allied infantry divisions were encamped much further west, in the ring around Sebastopol. Hence, Balaclava was virtually unprotected.

I asked, "What about the cavalry? Did they not help?"

"Russians fire cannonballs. Not possible for horses to charge."

That was a bit of a relief, knowing that the cavalry was not involved. However, being aware of enough military tactics, I realised that further counter-attacks were possible and Robert would surely be caught up in the battles to follow. Hence, comprehending why Fanny had ridden out in haste, I decided to follow suit.

Rushing back to the bedroom and throwing my clothes on, I reflected on Lord Raglan's unwise decision to ignore the Turkish spy's intelligence report. The British were using the Balaclava port for sending up supplies, cannons, armaments and troops. However, there were not nearly enough soldiers to defend the city. We were as vulnerable as a bank at night with its vaults left open. The Russians must have known this, and probably wanted to capture Balaclava to cut off the supply lines up the Crimean Peninsula. That would have been disastrous for the Allied campaign.

I put one of Robert's blue woollen military greatcoats over my dress, for I was cold and did not wish to get mud all over my beige outfit. I gulped down the steaming hot Turkish coffee and pastries that Selim brought up. The coffee tasted like it had a mountain of sugar, and the cookies were drowned in honey. Despite my numerous instructions to him not to sweeten my coffee and to forgo honey on the cakes, he rarely remembered. However, there was not enough time to admonish him.

I poked my head out of the room and shouted, "Selim. Which horse has Robert taken?"

"Master take Harold, madam," he replied and asked, "I saddle Betsy for you?"

"Yes." I was relieved to hear that Robert was riding Harold, the fine black charger he had brought with him from Upper Canada. Although Harold had not been in a real battle yet, I believed he was well trained for the likely gruelling task ahead of them that day. Before leaving, I took one last look around the room. I saw Robert's spyglass lying on the folding table and, picking it up, slipped it into my coat pocket.

Outside the back door, Selim had Betsy saddled and waiting for me.

"Did you pack my medical bag?"

"Yes. Madam go to hospitaaal?" Selim asked, as he handed me Betsy's reins and cupped his hands to make a foothold to help me up sideways onto the saddle.

"No, I am going to the hills. They will need me more up there. Can you go to hospital and tell the sergeant I will not be there today?"

"Yes, madam," Selim replied. He looked anxious, but kept up a brave composure and bowed. As I trotted away, he called after me in a grim voice, "God be with you, madam."

Leaning over to pat Betsy, I felt for the medical kit in the saddle bag and slid the spyglass in there as well. I wheeled Betsy onto the road and proceeded northward towards the hills. I wondered what the chief surgeon would say when I did not report at the hospital-ship. For a moment, I felt like turning back, but that day my heart was not for the port.

I cantered along and passed several Allied military officers, hurrying on their way up or down the road. "Big battle up ahead, ma'am," they shouted. "Please go back to town." I, of course, paid no heed. Approaching the crossroad that branched towards Sebastopol or to the hills, my heart pounded with fear when I heard the unmistakable thumps of cannon shots and crackles of musket fire. Good God. The battle was still raging.

"Ma'am, kindly stay on the south road. Do not go into the north valley," were the instructions shouted to me by other soldiers jogging by. Several hills run along the breadth of the Crimean peninsula, like fingers of a giant hand. Valleys with vineyards and rivers lie between the rocky knolls. General Raglan, the commander of the British force, had set up headquarters at the plateau of a western hill called the Sapoune Heights. I heeled Betsy into a gallop on the winding road towards the HQ.

As I approached the general's command centre, it was nearing mid-morning and the sounds of the cannons had eased. A Union Jack, the French Tri-colour and the red Turkish flag with the crescent moon fluttered from the tops of the three poles of a large tent. The sun was trying to filter its rays into the foggy valleys. A number of Raglan's staff officers were at the crest of Sapoune Heights, peering down through their field lenses, observing the troop movements below. Lord Raglan had indeed chosen the location of his HQ at a strategic point. It offered a clear view of the two valleys, the north and the south, separated by a hill, the Causeway Heights.

A collection of military wives and tourists dawdled along one side of the Raglan camp. Some of these curious visitors had paid a fair sum to come on pleasure ships all the way to the Crimea to witness Britain's first war since Waterloo. We called these motley people "the travelling gentlemen". This assortment also peered down into the two valleys to catch a glimpse of their near and dear ones, or just to enjoy the sight and sounds of a real-life battle. Littered amongst them were their wicker picnic baskets, plates of cold meat and chicken, other food and wine goblets. As I approached these picnickers, one of the gentlemen seemed to recognise me; he might have seen me on the hospital-ship. He came up to me, wine glass in one hand and, raising his hat with the other, said, "You are a bit tardy, Madam Doctor—you just missed a good show."

"A good show? Whatever do you mean, sir?" I asked in astonishment.

"You should have seen our Sir Colin's Highlanders' 'thin red line' and General Scarlett's Heavy Brigade cut the damn Rooshians into ribbons. Ah, but the most amusing sight was the flight of the Turkish bumblebees."

I was not sure I had followed all that, and asked anxiously, "Oh, but did the Light Brigade see any action?"

"No, not yet. But they should be up next," he replied, like someone at an opera waiting for the next act. I was amazed at the lengths some people would go to see blood and gore. However, I was relieved to learn that Robert might not have been in a battle. I thanked the gentleman for this piece of comforting news and moved Betsy along. The gentleman raised his wine glass to me in a toast.

I spied Nancy standing by the tent, talking to an officer. She looked lovely in a pink floral dress and matching bonnet. The Vauxhall Gardens incident was long forgotten, and we were on friendly terms again. I rode towards her. As soon as she saw me, she ran up and took my hand to help me dismount. We greeted each other like lost sisters, with hugs and kisses. Nancy was able to get to the headquarters before me, for she and Albert did not reside too far from there. Albert, in his usual manner, had likely pulled some strings and rank to have him allotted a room in a comfortable farmhouse nearby, which had been requisitioned for General Raglan and his staff officers.

"Oh, Margaret, I'm so glad to see you. But I thought you would be at the hospital," Nancy said.

"Nancy, so good to see you too. No, I didn't go to the hospital today. I feel I might be more useful here. I'm sorry I'm late. Robert did not return from the inspection to wake me. Pray, do tell, what's been going on here?" I asked in an excited voice, holding both her hands. Little did she or I know what was to befall us during the rest of that fateful afternoon.

"Oh, Margaret, you wouldn't believe it. Russians attacked our gun positions on the hill over there," she said, out of breath, pointing to the Causeway Heights. "The poor Turkish gunners there were hardly a match for them. They tried to make a stand, but eventually had to turn and run down the hill towards town. Someone said they should have stood their ground. Honestly, can you blame them? What's a defenceless creature to do? Especially when faced with such odds and, what's more, with no support from either the British or the French. Some of those poor souls were cut down by the pursuing Cossacks even before they were halfway down the hill."

"Really!" I said with revulsion. "And then what happened? Pray continue."

"Well, can you believe the gall of some of those 'travelling gentlemen', flinging all sorts of insults at the Turks, like *cowards*, *run to your mammas, you so-and-so's*, and other unmentionables," she said, nodding towards the sightseers.

I shook my head. "How mean-spirited of them, especially since we are here to protect the Turks from the Russians!"

"Yes, and what's more, they completely failed to notice that actually not all the Turks ran into town. Rather, most of them stayed at the bottom of the hill to join up with Sir Colin's small infantry force. They and the Heavy Brigade's charge managed to repulse a large Russian cavalry attack. Without their gallant action, the Russians would be in Balaclava by now."

"Oh! So that's who they've been calling the 'thin red line'," I said, finally understanding what the travelling gentleman had told me earlier.

"Indeed. But you know what?" she said in a whisper and with a worried look.

"Pray, Nancy, what is it?" I asked, baffled.

"The Russians are stealing our cannons on that hill. Because the infantry hasn't arrived yet, our cavalry is being sent to recover them. General Raglan dispatched an order to Lord Lucan hours ago, but there hasn't been any movement. Raglan is fuming and is planning to send another message." She pointed towards the north valley.

"Oh, Nancy, that couldn't be so bad. There are only Russian infantry and a few Cossacks there. They may not even resist the recapturing of our cannons. Cheer up."

"Margaret, I have an eerie feeling. I'm worried for Robert and Albert," she said, wringing her hands.

"Don't fret, Nancy. Come, let's go and see what's happening," I said, putting my arm around her slim waist and leading her towards the tent.

She turned to me and said, "By the way, Margaret. There's something I should tell you ..."

I felt surprised. "Yes, what is it? Are you unwell?" I asked, wondering what could be the matter.

She said, "No, no. I'm well. It's something ... but it can wait. Let's go and see what Lord Raglan is doing."

I then remembered what Robert had said last night, and wondered if it was related to another of those squabbles between him and Albert. However, I put it out of my mind.

In front of the tent, on canvas folding chairs, sat our one-armed commander-in-chief, General Raglan, the French General Bosquet, the Turkish Commander and other senior officers. Raglan looked splendid in his plumed cock hat and black uniform coat with gold piping. He was dictating a message to an officer. A line of mounted messengers stood to one side. General Raglan took the pencilled note in between the fingers of his good left hand and brought it close to his spectacled eyes. Apparently satisfied, he motioned towards the messengers. When the first one in the line moved his horse forward, Raglan waved him aside. A thrill ran through me when he pointed a finger and said, "I want Nolan." All eyes were on the one next in line, Captain Nolan. Darting his horse forward, he took the message from the general's hand. He looked superb, dressed in a blue uniform with a red and gold forage cap, astride his charger with the distinctive tiger-skin covering showing beneath the saddle. As was customary, I believe, he waited for any special instructions. These came in the form of a terse comment: "Tell Lord Lucan the cavalry is to attack *immediately*."

"Yes, milord," Nolan said. He saluted and trotted over to the ridge to take a steep goat path that would enable him to scramble down the hill.

"What a daredevil!" someone exclaimed.

I ran to Betsy, tethered to one side along with other horses, and took out Robert's spyglass from the saddle bag. Nancy and I raced to the edge of the hill to get a better view of the north valley, where the cavalry brigades were positioned. The whole valley, some five hundred feet below, was like a giant, couple-of-miles-long football field. On the hill on the right side, the enemy was hitching up the abandoned British cannons. I noted some Russian cannons being placed at the bottom of the hills, both on the right and left of the valley. But they looked to be few in number and possibly Raglan thought the cavalry should be able to dash by them.

Raglan had likely selected Captain Nolan because, he was known to be one of the best riders in the Army, and could get the message down to the battlefield the quickest. I spotted him riding tortuously down the hill, in a wild manner; riding low in the saddle, likely to ward off any sniper fire, almost to one side, holding onto his horse's mane and neck as the poor creature slipped and slid down the hill. He had probably picked up this riding style from the North American Native warriors. Nolan was born in Upper Canada to a British military family; his father was stationed there during the War of 1812.

I imagined Robert's joy upon spotting his old friend, Nolan, ride by his position. I tried to locate Robert, but the distance and the fog kept me from doing so. I could only make out what I thought to be his spot in the line. The Hussars' blue jackets and bright cherry-coloured coveralls were visible in the round lens of my spyglass. I followed Nolan and watched him hand the message to Lord Lucan.

The sun reflected off the officers' gold-braided pelisses as they conferred. There seemed to be some confusion. There was much arm-waving and head-nodding. Harsh words appeared to be exchanged, as if the message was not clear. Later, we were informed that both Lucan and Cardigan, from their vantage point, could not see the abandoned British cannons being pulled away, and wondered: "Attack!" "Attack what?" "Which guns?" Nolan's arm gestures may have made them believe the cannons were at the end of the valley, rather than up on the hill to their right. Hence, the order was likely misinterpreted to mean: Attack and capture the guns at the end of the valley. *Immediately*.

"Tell me what's happening, Margaret? Please let me have a look." Nancy tugged at my elbow.

With much reluctance, I handed the telescope to her. She eagerly adjusted and moved it around, as if attempting to seek out someone. In the distance, the faint sound of a trumpet played the order to mount, and then a sharper one to advance.

"Good God … they are … off," Nancy said in a shaky voice.

The thinning fog revealed to the naked eye the Light Brigade with their commander, Lord Cardigan and the aides, at the head of nearly six hundred and sixty riders, formed in three rows. They started to move, slowly at first, and then in a trot down the long north valley. Behind them, Lord Lucan and his staff led close to seven hundred members of the Heavy Brigade in another three-row formation. The Heavy, having taken part in a successful charge earlier that morning, obviously, followed in support of the Light. It sickened me to hear a loud cheer from the watchers on our ridge.

The riders had not ridden far when Nancy gasped, "I don't understand it. Would you look at that," she said.

"What is it now, Nancy?" I asked with apprehension at her remark.

"Look," she said, handing me the glasses. "They're going straight down the valley and not turning towards the abandoned cannons on the hill to their right!"

I hurriedly looked through the lens and, having confirmed her assertion, exclaimed, "Indeed they are!" I trained the glasses towards the end of the valley to determine what could be so important for the Brigade to move in that direction. By then, the haze had cleared and as I rotated the lens to adjust it, the end of the valley came into focus. The scene I saw in the spyglass was one of those horrifying visions that remain embedded in our mind forever and come back to haunt us in nightmares. The circular view in the spyglass slowly focused on a row of huge cannon barrel lines across the valley. Beyond the guns stood a mass of grey-greatcoated riders. Those were indeed the "jaws of hell," which Lord Tennyson later recited to the world in his immortal poem.

I lowered my spyglass and, covering my mouth, muffled a moan.

"What is it?" Nancy cried.

My mind froze, my breath came in gasps as I clutched the spyglass. "It looks like they're riding to their death," I said, covering my face.

Before my words could sink in, Nancy waved her hand excitedly in the direction of the Light Brigade's front line, where the riders moved in an unhurried trot. "Isn't that Nolan? Please let me take a look." She took the glasses from my hand and pointed them towards a lone rider who had broken his formation and was galloping ahead of the front line to the leader, the unmistakeable shape of Lord Cardigan wearing his dark fur busby with its golden strap around his chin.

"Indeed it is Captain Nolan. Looks like he's tying to tell Cardigan something," she said.

I recognised Nolan's tall silhouette, and thought that although he had—likely with permission from the CO—admirably joined in the charge, it was very daring of him to ride up to Cardigan like that. Nolan waved his sabre and pointed to the right, as if to make Cardigan aware of the correct position of the guns they were ordered to retake. Lord Cardigan appeared to be annoyed by Nolan's breach of protocol and, in his true fashion, seemed to ignore him. Cardigan continued to ride, maintaining a stiff posture, looking straight ahead.

There was silence in the valley, except for the muffled sound of the horses' hooves on the soft ground and a neigh now and then. The hush did not last long. A Russian cannon fired from the hill on the left. The shell, most likely intended for the leaders, burst above them in an orange glow, spewing metallic fragments like those in a firework display. The pieces miraculously missed Cardigan and others. However, Nolan, a few feet away, was not so lucky. A metal splinter pierced his chest. I suspect it penetrated his heart and killed him instantly. While the sword in his raised arm dropped, his body stiffened in a kind of rigor mortis and he continued to gallop on with his arm still raised. As the crowd on our ridge watched in silent horror, Nolan finally fell, and his rider-less, bewildered horse turned and ran back through the lines.

Russian cannons and rifles then opened up a near-constant barrage of shots, shells and bullets. Yet Cardigan galloped on, followed by the Light Brigade. As other riders began taking hits, I trembled in anticipation of what was likely to follow. I dared not think of my dear Robert's fate. I then noticed Lord Lucan leading the Heavy Brigade away to the right. At first I thought it might be an adroit flanking manoeuvre, but to my amazement, they swung around and rode back towards their starting position, out of range of enemy fire. This evasion left their Light Brigade comrades to charge on ahead alone, to face the cannonade. I could barely believe it. What a cowardly act. Later, I heard Lord Lucan was heavily criticized for his decision and, in fact, was blamed for the loss of nearly half of the Light Brigade. In contrast, I knew it was my duty to be down there on the battlefield, amongst the dying and the wounded, to administer what little medical help I could. I was determined to fulfil my obligation.

The French general was also following the battle through his spyglass. In a brilliant move, he had sent one of his cavalry regiments to attack the Russian cannons on the left hill. They did their job superbly, for we saw the Russians hitching up their guns and disappearing over the crest of the hill. This saved many lives of our Light Brigade riders, as they continued to charge forward.

General Bosquet collapsed his telescope and, turning towards the officers, exclaimed, "C'est magnifique, mais ce n'est pas la guerre!" There was a murmur of agreement and nodding of cock hats.

"What did he say?" Nancy asked, knowing I spoke French.

"I believe he said, 'This is magnificent, but it is not war'." I hurriedly took the spyglass from Nancy, telling her, "I have to go down there." We ran to Betsy. I kissed Nancy on the cheek, and she helped me get into the saddle.

She said with tears in her eyes, "Do be careful, Margaret. And look after our husbands."

I told her I would do my best.

I heeled Betsy and we trotted out of the camp. I received curious glances from some of Lord Raglan's officers, but they were naturally too busy watching the cannon fire and carnage below to pay much attention to me, let alone stop me from going down to the valley. Because I rode sidesaddle, I could not take the straight, precipitous route down the hill that Nolan had taken a short while ago. I had to go on the road that led to Sebastopol from the back of the hill and try to find a cut-off that would lead me to the north valley. As I galloped down the meandering road, holding onto the pommel, I saw a small pathway leading from the road to what I believed would be a shortcut to the valley. I reined in Betsy and made her turn into that path.

Betsy obediently trotted onto the pathway, which narrowed to a small trail along the side of the hill, through the brush of shrubs, graperies and wildflower bushes. We went quite a distance. Eventually, I realised it was not the right way to the north valley. However, having gone so far, I decided to continue and find another way, rather than turn back. My thoughts were for Robert's safety and I wished to get to him as soon as possible.

The trail led to a small grove of trees. I decided to go through it, thinking there ought to be a path out from there to the valley. As I approached the thicket, a group of riders suddenly sprang out from behind the trees. Two of them came on either side of me and, taking hold of Betsy's bridle, made us stop. They had grim-looking, bearded faces and were dressed in the Russian Cossacks' uniform, grey overcoat and bearskin caps. One of them pulled out his pistol and pointed it at me, as if to warn me not to fight or try to run. They shouted at me in Russian, which I supposed was a demand to know who I was and what I was doing there.

"I am a doctor. I am going to help the wounded," I replied.

They did not understand at first, but when I kept repeating, "Doctor ... doctor," they finally seemed to comprehend. The two Cossacks alongside me and the two more in front roared with laughter and said some thing like, "Da, da, doctoro ... haha." They obviously did not believe me that I was a doctor, let alone a woman doctor. One of them, who likely spoke a few words of English, pointing a finger at me said something that sounded like, "You, spee ... spee ..."

I kept repeating that I was a doctor and pointed in the direction of the north valley, indicating I wanted to go there. Finally, another horseman came out of the grove. He was dressed in a more stately uniform and seemed to be an officer. He said in perfect French, "Mademoiselle, we do not believe that you are a physician. Rather, we are of the opinion that you are a British spy."

While I was relieved to note that this officer, a young man of about twenty, was obviously an educated person, I was horrified to hear him refer to me as a spy. I knew the harsh penalty meted out to undercover agents in those days. I hastily replied, in a trembling voice, using my faulty Canadian French, "No, no, monsieur. I am not a spy. Nothing could be further from the truth. I am indeed a doctor and am on my way to care for those wounded in the battle."

"Ah, but shouldn't you be in a hospital? And why are you coming from the British headquarters? We have been watching you, you know," the officer said.

"Oh, I only went there to determine what was happening. I have no intention of spying on Russian positions. Please, sir, let me go. The wounded are lying there on the battlefield, dying and in need of my help," I pleaded with him.

Just then, one of the Cossacks, who was alongside Betsy, reached into the saddle bag and pulled out the spyglass, which he must have noted sticking out. He waved it at me playfully, smiled mockingly and handed it to the officer. The officer examined the glasses, looked through them and, likely after ascertaining they were genuine, asked me with a smile but in an ironic voice, "And how do you use these to examine your patients, mademoiselle?"

I was furious at that suggestive remark, but controlled my temper and replied calmly, "Nay, sir. You are well aware they are not for medical use. As I am unfamiliar with this country, I use them to find my way around," I replied, taking care not to mention they were Robert's. I begged again, "Please, sir, it is getting late. Keep the glasses, if you like, but do let me go."

The young officer ordered, in a stern voice, "Sorry, mademoiselle. You are wearing a British military uniform and carrying a spyglass. Based on this evidence, I cannot let you go. You will have to accompany us to our camp. You can plead your case to our captain. Kindly hand the reins of your horse to my man."

I was so stunned I could hardly speak. How stupid of me to wear Robert's jacket and take his spyglass. Thinking of Robert in the valley with all the cannon and musket fire and me not being able to assist him put me in a stupefied spell. One of the Cossacks wrenched Betsy's reins from my hands and trotted forward, pulled her along. We followed timidly behind them, in a single file along the narrow path.

I do not recall much of the ride to the Russian camp. When we reached it, I saw a signboard outside that read Mackenzie Farm. I had heard about this farm, which belonged to an old Scottish settler and had obviously been confiscated. We rode in and dismounted before a group of tents in front of an old farmhouse. The soldiers ushered me into one of the tents, furnished with only a folding table and some chairs. It seemed it served as an interrogation room. A Cossack brought in a tray holding a jug of water and glasses, which he placed on the table. He poured me a glass of water and made some hand gestures, which I took to mean I was to sit there and not try to escape. I sipped the cool liquid, to calm myself, and waited. Noticing a small opening between the tent flaps, I peeked through it with just the corners of my eyes. I saw people dressed in strange uniforms, coming and going in and out of the farmhouse. So, these were the Russian "bears" we were fighting.

After what seemed an eternity, but in reality must have been only about five or so minutes, there was some movement outside the tent. A sentry lifted the flap and another tall officer, dressed in a dazzling white uniform with gold braiding, a shiny brass helmet and black leather boots, entered the tent. The other young officer who had brought me in followed behind.

"Ah, so you are the young mademoiselle Lieutenant Lapinsky says is claiming to be a British doctor?" he asked, in perfect English, extending his hand.

I got up from the chair and, taking his hand, said, "Indeed, sir. I am."

He held my fingers and looked me in the eyes. With a gentle smile on his face, instead of shaking my hand, he bent down and kissed it! I found that comforting, given the mental state I was in, although I was not used to that European way of greeting a woman.

"And your name is … mademoiselle?"

"Doctor Margaret Wallace," I replied and asked in return, "Pray, who may I be speaking with?"

"Count Nicholai Barinowsky, Captain of the Tsar's Guards."

"Pleased to meet you," I replied offhandedly, so as not to sound too anxious or bewildered by his presence. Since he said he was a captain, he must have been a bit older than Robert, about thirty, I thought. I pleaded with him, "Please, sir, I have to go. There are wounded and dying soldiers on the battlefield. I must take care of them."

"Mademoiselle claims to be a doctor, yet we saw her coming out from the British HQ and not only is she wearing a uniform, but is also in possession of a spyglass." The young lieutenant recited the charge, as if he had been practicing it. It seemed he was aiming to get a promotion for what he thought was a great catch.

I ignored the lieutenant and, turning to the count, said, "Sir, I can explain all this."

He beamed at me with a charming smile and said, "All right, mademoiselle, please sit down and let us hear your story."

The count and I sat down at the table while the lieutenant stood and fidgeted, moving his weight from one leg to the other. The afternoon sun shone down on the tent, stifling the air inside. I mopped beads of perspiration that had formed underneath the bonnet on my forehead. The count refilled my glass of water and poured himself one. He then took off his helmet, freeing his curly golden-blonde hair. The cascading curls fell well below his ears. He looked like a perfect nobleman, about to relax by the fireside with a glass of brandy. The count's mesmerising persona and his gentle deep blue eyes upon me took me aback. When he gestured with his hand, as if to ask me to proceed, I hurriedly offered my explanations.

While he continued to sip water as if drinking wine, I told him I resided in Balaclava near the hospital-ship and, it being cold, had borrowed the coat from an officer. I had heard of the impending battle and decided to go to the field instead of the hospital, for I thought I would be more useful there. I had gone to the general's headquarters to determine where the battle was. Yes, I always carried a spyglass, but only to find my way around. However, indeed, despite the spyglass, I had got lost in the woods when the lieutenant found me. "And that's the whole story, sir."

While the count reflected on my statements, possibly wondering what to make of them, the lieutenant again interjected, "Sir, this is just a fabricated tale. It looks like the British are dreaming up new ways to disguise their secret agents. Have you ever heard of a woman doctor? I do not believe women are even allowed to attend medical schools," he said pompously, as if to appear knowledgeable of worldly affairs.

"Lieutenant, it may be so in Russia, but not in other countries. I do recall someone mentioning to me that they are now permitting women to become physicians in America. Is that not so, mademoiselle?" When I nodded, he asked, "So, have you any proof that you are really a medical doctor?"

I immediately thought of my medical bag. "Yes," I replied, "I do have a medical kit in my saddle bag. Please send someone to fetch it."

"Lieutenant, please bring the lady doctor's medical bag."

The young lieutenant marched stiffly out of the tent to get the bag. The count looked at me curiously and, with a grin, asked, "You are not really British, are you?"

"No, Canadian—rather, American, sir. I was born in New Jersey."

"Yes, you do look a lot more attractive than the British women I have met," he said with that enchanting smile of his.

Bewildered by his frankness and, unable to reply, I might even have blushed. I was stammering a word of thanks to him when the lieutenant returned with my medical bag and spyglass in hand. He placed the bag on the table, but held onto the telescope.

"All right, then, can you please show and describe each instrument to us?" the count asked.

I opened the bag and without any hesitation, proceeded to draw out and explain the functions and specific uses of each of the medical tools and instruments. I showed him the usual first aid items, such as large forceps for pulling out bullets, rolls of bandages, ointments, scissors, and so on. He smiled and nodded knowingly when I showed him a stomach and enema cylinder-pump. Next was a small canister-type bloodletting lancet, which he said he had seen used before. When I pulled out a long scissor tool with a tongue depressor and a cutter at its ends, he was curious and wished to know more about it. I informed him that it was a tonsillotome, used for removing infected tonsils. Likely to test my knowledge, he asked me to show how it was used. I requested him to open his mouth wide and, holding his chin by the thumb and forefinger of my left hand and with the tool in my right hand—although I did not insert it inside his mouth—I demonstrated how it was operated with the fingers of only one hand.

While the count observed my exposition with interest, the lieutenant was getting impatient. He held the spyglass and rolled it between his hands, all the while glaring at me. He then proceeded to extend and retract the telescopes, as if agitated. The captain seemed impressed with my apparent proficiency with the tonsillotome. While I was in the middle of showing him a binaural stethoscope, I heard a childish scream from the young lieutenant.

"Mon dieu, capitaine. Have a look at this," he shouted to the count, showing him the spyglass extended to its full telescopic length.

"What is it, lieutenant?" the count asked, standing up to look at the spyglass. I stood up as well to see what the fuss was about.

"This proves she is a liar, sir. She *is* a spy, just as I thought," he said and pointed his finger at something etched on the last shaft of the telescope. My heart sank when he said out loud, "The inscription here says 'Belongs to Lieutenant Wallace'. This confirms it, sir. This woman is a lieutenant in the British Army. Did she not tell us her name is 'Wallace', just a moment ago?"

Overcome with shame, I slumped down on the chair and, resting my elbows on the table and my face between my hands, looked away from them. Tears welled in my eyes.

There was silence in the tent as the count looked at me quizzically and the lieutenant glared.

The count asked finally, "Now, mademoiselle, how do you explain this?"

"Well, sir, for a start, you can address me as 'madame', for I am married," I replied, dabbing my eyes. "That spyglass actually belongs to my husband."

"But why did you not tell us this before?" the lieutenant asked in a raised voice, staring down at me. The count looked at him disapprovingly.

"It's simple, sir. He's a lieutenant in the 11th Hussars and presently in a battle in the north valley," I replied.

"Ah! So that's why you are anxious to get to the battlefield. Is that not so, madame?" the count asked.

"Yes sir," I replied, tears now running down my cheeks. In between sobs, I added, "I am so worried about him … he might be lying there, wounded … no one to look after him…. Please, Count Nicholai … I beg you … kindly let me go."

"Yes, madame, you shall leave immediately. Your husband may very likely be in need of your assistance," the count said, and proceeded to pack the medical instruments back into my bag. When he came to the spyglass, he paused a moment and, holding it up to me, said, "I'll have to confiscate this telescope. A doctor should have no need for it. Is that acceptable to you?"

Overcome with emotion, I could merely nod.

Nevertheless, the arrogant lieutenant shouted, "This is most improper, sir. I request permission to take the prisoner to General Menshikoff's headquarters for further interrogation."

"That will not be necessary, lieutenant. Please bring Doctor Margaret's horse and arrange an escort to guide her speedily to the north valley."

"Begging your pardon, sir. This woman is a liar and a spy. Her whole story is nothing but a fabrication. I strongly recommend that her statements must be verified by Prince Menshikoff's staff before she is released."

The count's face reddened. He walked close to the lieutenant. Standing over six feet tall, the count had to bend down to stare into the shorter man's eyes. His voice remained calm as he addressed his subordinate. With his hands on his hips, he said to him in a calm voice, "Lieutenant, I am aware that the British permit their soldiers' wives to accompany them onto the battlefield. Also, I am fully satisfied that this lady is a doctor. I am in charge here. There is no need to take her to the prince. Is that understood?"

"Yes, sir," replied the lieutenant in a curt voice. He saluted, about turned and marched out of the tent.

The count picked up my medical bag in his left hand and extended his right elbow towards me. I took his arm and he led me out of the tent.

Two Cossacks stood beside Betsy, waiting to ride as my escort. Upon seeing me, Betsy neighed and nodded her head in excitement. I patted her face and said a few loving words to her. One of the Cossacks cupped his hands to help me mount.

Just then, I heard the creaking and closing sounds of a door. I looked towards the farm building and saw an East Indian man coming out of the veranda towards us. At first I thought he was Captain Nolan's groom, since he looked a bit like him, and I stared at him. However, this man was dressed in a white turban, dark jacket and white, baggy trousers. When he got closer, he looked different. He was of fine, light-complexioned features and walked very erect, almost with an air of nobility.

"Ah, Count Nicholai, there you are. I was looking for you." But upon seeing me, he hesitated and stopped at some distance. "I am sorry. I did not realise you are busy."

"It's nothing, Mr. Azimullah. A British lady has lost her way."

"How unfortunate for you, ma'am. Perhaps you would stay for some tea?" Azimullah asked in a perfect Oxford accent.

"No, thank you, sir. I must be on my way."

"I trust you will find your way back safely," the Indian man said.

I thanked the count again and extended my hand. He kissed it in his usual courteous manner. While the lieutenant glared at us from a distance, the count waved and said, "*Au revoir*, madame," and also, "*dos vi'daniya,*" in Russian, which I later understood to mean "goodbye".

As I trotted away, I turned around to glance at him. Although I was most worried about Robert's safety, I could not help thinking what a handsome figure he made, in that splendid uniform. Both the count and Mr. Azimullah waved, and I gestured back. At that moment, we three likely thought it was goodbye. Little did we know it was indeed an *au revoir*, for we were to meet again some years later in another faraway land, in another conflict, with other emotions to overcome and other passions to satisfy.

Chapter Twenty

The Aftermath of the Charge

1854, October: Balaclava, Crimea

THE TWO COSSACK escorts led me at a gallop towards the north valley. Betsy, having had a good rest, water and feed from the Russians, had no trouble keeping up with the Dons. It was past noon by the time, travelling through the pine forests, we reached a small pass leading into the western end of the valley. A part of the basin was in sunlight, while shadows of the southern hill crept down the slopes onto the other portion. The Cossacks reined in their horses, as we had reached British-held ground and they likely feared for their safety. They pointed the direction to me then turned around and rode away, bidding me "*dos vi'daniya*". Although it had been a hectic morning and I was feeling tired, the thought of seeing Robert rejuvenated me. I heeled Betsy and galloped into the vale.

Except for an occasional crackle of gunfire, a sinister silence enveloped the glade. It seemed the battle was over, for the Russian cannons, which I had heard booming all morning, were silent. At first sight, it looked like any pleasant late summer day, but as I galloped onto the battlefield, the eerie sight of a devastated army came into view. Bodies—complete and in parts—of riders and horses lay strewn all over the muddy, trodden ground, like timbers from a shipwreck on a beach. The lifeless men indeed looked as if they had faced the "jaws of hell".

Those fortunate enough to have survived the combat and able to ride or walk were regrouping at the western end. I did not venture

towards them, instead headed down to the eastern side, preferring to
follow a stream of men and women walking out to look for their
missing family and friends. As I hurried past them, my heart pounded
in desperation to find Robert, and horrifying thoughts of him lying
wounded, needing help, passed through my mind.

Russian riflemen still occupied the hills and took occasional pot-
shots at stragglers. A matronly lady walking ahead of me was hit in the
arm by a bullet ricocheting from a rock. I jumped down and quickly
tied a bandage around the wound. I advised her to go back to camp and
seek medical attention; she paid no heed and continued to limp along
to find her man. Some Cossacks busied themselves scavenging the
bodies of dead soldiers for whatever they could carry away. I took out
the medical orderly's white scarf from the saddle bag and tied it
around my right arm, hoping it would save me from becoming a target.

As I rode further onto the battlefield, more fallen soldiers came
into view. The searchers staggered around as if in a drunken stupor,
turning over bodies and calling out names. An occasional heart-
wrenching yell and wail rose into the air, indicating a female had
found her loved one, if only in body and not in soul. At the edge of
freshly dug graves, military chaplains stood administering last rites to
the dead. Slowing Betsy into a gingerly walk between the bodies, I
bent down to scrutinise the faces. Trembling with fear, I could not
even call out Robert's name. While one part of me believed he had
survived and was either back safely at the camp or perhaps had been
taken, injured, to the hospital, the other part of my brain feared the
worst.

Unexpectedly, Betsy whinnied and sped towards a horse standing
in the middle of some motionless bodies. On seeing us approach, that
horse neighed back, bobbed his head and stomped his feet with
excitement. It was our faithful charger, Harold. He stood, as if
dutifully, next to a body on the ground. My heart beat wildly. Betsy
galloped uncontrollably towards Harold. Getting closer, I saw four
soldiers lying around Harold. I jumped down and, snatching the
medical bag and a water bottle, ran towards the blue-coated, rouge-
trousered figure. The other three wore grey uniforms, those of Russian
Cossacks. It looked like there had been a fierce skirmish. Two of the
three Russians lay dead with swords clutched in hands. They had deep
wounds to their heads and necks. The third's decapitated head lay
beside him with a fur hat on and eyes still wide open. The sight

horrified me, and I dashed past the bodies, looking away from their blank, staring eyes. The blue-coated soldier lay some distance from the others. A dark pool of blood had oozed out of a large wound on his chest and several deep cuts on his left hand and thigh. His sabre was sheathed and lay in his belt alongside his left leg.

I shouted, breathlessly, "Robert … Robert … my love … is that you?"

To my amazement, he turned his head in my direction. It was Robert. My God, he was alive! My heart thumped harder than it had ever done before. I sprinted with all the strength in my legs and, reaching him, knelt down by his side. Hurriedly opening the medical bag and taking out a handful of bandage rolls, I stuffed one into the large hole in the middle of his chest and put some pads on the other wounds. He did not need them, however, for the haemorrhaging had virtually ceased.

He managed a slight smile and whispered, "Margaret. Puppet. My love … I'm glad you've come."

I kissed him and, while running my fingers through his hair, noticed they were damp with blood from another cut to his scalp. "I'm very happy to see you, dearest. Sorry I got here so late."

"Don't be sorry. There's nothing you could have done for me. I'm the one who should be sorry for not returning safely to you," he whispered.

"My darling, you've lost a lot of blood. Can you move your legs?" I asked, hoping I might be able to put him on Harold and take him to a field hospital.

"No. I've no feeling anywhere, except in my right arm," he said, moving it slightly.

I took his right hand and squeezed it gently. He must have felt the squeeze, because he smiled, but did not squeeze back. Instinct told me to get someone to help, to pick him up and take him to hospital. However, I gasped when I saw the extent of his injuries. The worst one was the hole in the centre of his chest. It was a bullet wound. Using sharp scissors, I cut his jacket around the wound and, putting my finger inside, felt the bullet lodged there between the ribs. Getting out the large pair of bullet-pulling tweezers and asking Robert to stay still, I inserted them deep into the wound and felt the tweezers grasp the bullet. I got up on my feet and, using both my hands to hold the instrument's handles, pulled with all my strength. At first slowly and then with a jolt, the bloodied bullet popped out. However, I knew it would be of little help. The bullet might have missed his heart, but he had already lost a lot of blood. It was a miracle he was still alive, although just barely breathing.

"Sorry, Puppet, someone shot me. I tried, but couldn't get back on Harold. Is he all right?" Robert asked.

"Yes, Harold looks unharmed. He's right here beside you. Oh, my love, you're so brave. You reached the cannons. You did your duty," I said with awe and to give him some comfort in what I dreaded were his last moments.

"I just followed our leader. I'm glad Harold is all right. How is Albert? Did he reach camp safely?"

"I don't know about Albert. I haven't been to camp yet. Why do you ask? Was he here with you?"

In reply, he simply nodded, ever so slightly. His normally rosy cheeks had turned pale. He was fainting. My heart sank, realising he was dying and I could do little. I cradled his head in my lap and poured some water from the water bottle over his lips.

He recovered a bit and said, "Ah. Thank you, dearest. That feels good. Please kiss our children goodbye from me, little Bruce and pretty Vika. Tell them I'm sorry I left them so early, but their papa loved them very much. Please tell Mother I cherished her dearly …"

He was barely audible. I leaned my ear down to his lips to hear the words that were to be his last. I started to cry.

He said, in a barely perceptible whisper, "Puppet, don't cry for me. Sorry I will not be around to hold our new baby. I'll watch him from Heaven. Can you promise me one thing?"

With what must have been his last bit of energy, I felt a gentle squeeze of my hand. His remembering my pregnancy brought another flood of tears in my eyes. Somehow, I managed to compose myself and moved my ear closer, nearly touching his lips, "Yes, my love?" I asked, sobbing, as tears ran down my cheeks.

"Please marry again. I want you to. Will you do that for me?"

I looked into his eyes and saw him watching me, as he lay dying. Before I could reply, his face took on a serene look. It lost its rigidity and turned into the young boy's countenance I had fallen in love with on Grimsby beach, years ago. His eyes lost their brightness and looked up towards Heaven, as if seeking out his Creator. His hand, still clutching mine, went limp. I realised he had left me. He did not wait for my reply to his question, for very likely he did not wish to hear me say, "Never." I could not have replied, anyway, for I sobbed and shook uncontrollably. All I could do was gently run my hand over his face and close his eyes.

Kneeling next to him, I moaned and cried loudly. Holding my joined hands up to Heaven, I said a prayer for him. I prayed to God to grant him a place in Paradise, for he was truly a good man, and to forgive his sins, if he had any, although I knew of none. He was kind and caring for others and nary a harsh word for even his adversaries. He loved his parents, although at times they misunderstood him. Most of all, he truly loved his family, his children and especially me, which I know in my heart of hearts, for in his quest to provide a better life for us, he even sacrificed his life.

A group of soldiers were trudging by and must have heard me weep. They came over. One asked, "Has he gone, miss? Shall I get the chaplain?"

Unable to speak, I simply nodded.

I unrolled the blanket tied behind Betsy's saddle, and we covered my Robert with it. The kind soldiers helped dig a grave while we waited for the priest. He arrived, looking sombre and tired. His black robe was all dirty from the mud and splattering of blood. His eyes looked glazed, likely from having seen so much carnage. He stood by Robert and read the passage, Isaiah 26:3, from the Bible:

Thou wilt keep him in perfect <u>peace</u>,
whose mind is stayed on thee,
because he trusteth in thee…

Along with more kind words, he administered the last rites to Robert.

With many helping hands, we lowered Robert's body into the grave. While the soldiers were shovelling the earth back in, I felt like jumping into the last resting bed with my Robert. I wanted to embrace him and somehow perform a miracle to bring him back to life. I might have jumped in or collapsed had it not been for the same matronly lady whose wound I had bandaged earlier. Having buried her own husband, she came by, hugged and comforted me while I cried uncontrollably.

They had removed Robert's cap and belt with the sabre and revolver still in its holster. An old soldier picked it up. "Keep these for his childa, ma'am. They'll want to know what a brave fighter their da was," he said, handing them to me.

I thanked the kind soul and, remembering Robert usually carried a wallet, I asked, "Sir, did you see a wallet?"

"Nay, sorry, ma'am. I looked in all the pockets of the gov'nor. The pouches are the first thing them mongrel Cossys are stealin'. But it is strange, though."

"What is so strange?"

"The Cossy didn' bother takin' the lieutenant's revolver, nor 'is sabre! Suppose 'e was in an 'urry." He then held my hand and put the bullet I had extracted onto my palm. "I found this on the ground, though. Looks like it was what done 'im in."

In response, I only squeezed the bullet in my fist and, holding it to my chest, sobbed bitterly.

Having performed their kind deed, the group of caring souls moved on to help bury some other unfortunate warrior. I was left alone, with Betsy and Harold standing patiently beside me. I sat by my Robert's grave for a long time, looking at the mound of raw earth, imagining him lying peacefully below. All the happy times we had enjoyed passed before my eyes.

In due course, while most of the wives, after weeping their hearts out at the side of their loved ones' burial spots, left the valley, I did not wish to leave. However, the sun was setting over the hill and dusk, like a dark shroud, began to envelope the valley. I spied some wildflowers that looked like poppies swaying in the wind close by. Plucking a bunch, I laid several on the grave and carried a handful.

I tied Harold's reins to Betsy's saddle and mounted her with a heavy heart. She turned her head and looked at me with her large, doe-like eyes. I detected some tears there. I turned back and saw the same in Harold's eyes. My God, the horses know, I thought as we trotted along the road out of the valley, back towards the Balaclava village that Robert had died saving.

I noticed our cavalry still gathered in groups at the far end of the valley. I asked a passing officer why they were still assembled there. He said the stand-down order had not been given yet and suggested I get speedily to the safety of the village. He feared a Russian counter-attack was imminent. I wondered where Nancy was and, although I normally could not care less for Albert, how her husband had fared. I wondered why Robert had asked about him even in his dying moments. I was sorrowful at having seen Captain Nolan fall earlier that morning and I also wished to know how our other Canadian friend, Lieutenant Alexander Dunn, had coped. However, it was getting late and I decided to go back to the house.

Selim stood waiting at the gate of the courtyard. His face dropped when he saw my teary eyes and Harold's empty saddle.

"Master not coming?" he asked, helping me down and taking the reins.

"No."

"In hospital? Yes?" he said in a hopeful voice.

I shook my head. To avoid letting him see me crying, I bent my head and walked quickly into the house. I went into the kitchen to fetch a vase for the bouquet of flowers. On the counter lay a large bowl of Greek salad and a platter of lamb kebabs on skewers, ready for grilling. These were Robert's favourite. The sight of Robert's dinner made me cry again. I ran upstairs and threw myself onto the bed.

A short while later, there was a knock. It was Selim. I asked him to come in and he stood there with tears in his eyes.

"Sorry to hear Master dead. He like my brother."

"Thank you, Selim. He liked you very much too."

"Madam want dinner?"

"No, Selim, I can't eat anything right now. Please make me some tea. I'll be down shortly," I said, my eyes still full of tears.

Having recovered a bit from the dreadful events of the afternoon, and after a wash and change of clothes, I went downstairs into the sitting room. It was getting chilly and Selim had lit the fireplace. I sat down on the chair beside the hearth and he brought me tea and biscuits. They tasted most agreeable, for I realised I had not eaten the whole day. Having taken only a few sips of tea, I heard someone knock on the front door. Selim opened it and Nancy and Lieutenant Alexander Dunn walked in.

I stood up and Nancy rushed over and hugged me. "Oh, Margaret, I'm so sorry, most sorry, to hear that Robert ..." She couldn't speak anymore and started to sob loudly. I was overcome with grief again and we cried together.

Alexander came over and put his large arms around both Nancy and me. We stood in an embrace for a while. "Now, now, ladies. Don't fret so much. Take heart. Robert did his duty and is now in the hands of his Maker," Alexander said, stepping back.

I suddenly realised Albert was not there and asked, "Nancy, how is Albert?"

Nancy, still too distraught to speak, continued to sob, hugging me. Alexander answered, "Captain Albert's in hospital. We've just come from there. Although he's badly injured, the surgeon thinks he'll make it."

Finally Nancy said, between sobs, "Oh, Margaret ... you will not believe this ... who would have known...." She started to cry again.

"What is it, Nancy? What happened?" When Nancy did not reply, I turned towards Alexander and asked, "Pray tell me what happened?"

"Yes, Margaret, you should know. Let's sit down and I'll tell you as much as I have heard." He led us to the sofa, where Nancy and I sat down. Alexander took the chair. Nancy still kept her arms around me and put her head on my shoulder. I looked at the lieutenant, wondering what was so important he wanted to tell me.

But before Alexander could speak, Nancy sat up and exclaimed, "He saved Albert! He saved my Albert's life. Oh, I hope Albert will live to know this. I pray Robert's bravery wasn't for naught ..." She started to cry again, dabbing her eyes with a handkerchief.

Although too bewildered to understand what Nancy said, I realised she was distraught. I rubbed her shoulder. "It's all right, Nancy. The doctors will take care of Albert. Let Alexander tell us what happened." I looked expectantly towards him. "I'm confused. Pray do tell what took place, right from the beginning, if you don't mind." I also called out to Selim to bring us some tea and get dinner ready.

Nancy reclined on the sofa and closed her eyes, saying, "I couldn't eat anything."

Alexander leaned back in the chair, cleared his throat, lit a cheroot and, throwing the match into the fire, started to relate the astonishing events of that afternoon. He began with Nolan's arrival down in the valley with the confusing message from Lord Raglan, the arguments between the commanders and the decision, finally, to attack the cannons.

"We were shocked to see poor Nolan take the first hit. He was obviously trying to tell Lord Cardigan to change course. Cardigan ignored him and we galloped on towards the batteries. Robert, Albert and I were on the left flank of the charge. Despite the heavy cannonade, each gun firing almost a shot per minute, and many of us taking hits, we managed to reach the battery. Due to much smoke, we couldn't see the cannons. It seemed Lucan had misjudged their number. He had thought the row comprised fifteen cannons, but in reality, there were about ten. To our astonishment, the 11th rode by on their right flank and we found ourselves at the back of the gunners."

"Oh, so Robert and you all made it to behind the cannons! Then what happened?" I asked, shivering with excitement.

"Well, some of the Russians tried to hitch up their cannons and flee, but we attacked the gunners. They tried to put up a fight; some poor souls even used their swab rods like lances. We soon disabled them. One or two of our men jumped off their horses and tried to capture the cannons. The smoke was like a thick blanket, obscuring our vision both behind and in front of the guns. I heard officers call for Cardigan, but he was nowhere to be seen."

"Oh! Where was he then?"

"It seems he rode right through between the cannons and, wheeling Ronald around, simply galloped back to base."

"Really! Then how did you manage without the leader?"

"Colonel Douglas took command. However, we didn't turn around. Douglas must have seen the Russian cavalry brigade appear from behind the cannons and had the trumpeter call us to re-form. We lined up and prepared for another charge. I recall there were about eighty of us regrouped there."

I couldn't believe my ears. "Do you mean to tell me only eighty of you actually charged a brigade?"

"Yes. But we owe our courage in part to the smoke and the assumption of support, in the form of the Heavy Brigade and our infantry, coming behind us. We were wrong, of course. And you know what? It fooled the Russkies too."

"Amazing!"

"Yes, but not for long, though."

Selim brought in cups of tea on a tray and handed them to us. Alexander took a long sip and sighed. His stressed face seemed to relax a bit. He rubbed his handlebar moustache and continued with the narrative.

"Yes, we charged the Russians and, to our surprise, even though they were a much larger force, they turned around and fled. My only explanation for their behaviour is they must have believed—on seeing us charge—there were more of our cavalry coming behind us. We chased them almost to the end of the valley, where a river runs across.

They were trapped. The only way out was over a narrow bridge, and it would have taken a long time for them to get across."

"Oh, so you had the Russians snared there?" I asked, sipping my tea to calm myself.

"We thought we had. However, that narrow bridge proved to be both a boon and a bane for us. I saw some of the Russians trying to get across the bridge. However, the majority stopped and wheeled around at the river. I must have instinctively turned my head backwards to see how much support was there. As the smoke cleared, I could see none. Warning bells went off in my head. I knew our meagre force would be no match for a Russian cavalry brigade. Robert was riding next to me and must have realised this as well. He pointed his sabre at the Russians re-forming at the river bank."

"Good God. What did he do?" I asked, wondering if Robert hadn't acted foolhardily.

"He did the right thing. As I was the Troop Leader, he asked me to inform Colonel Douglas of the danger."

"Oh, and did you talk to him?" I asked with apprehension, for I knew Alexander and the CO were at odds over another matter.

Alexander replied with a knowing smile, "Yes, I did. While on most occasions, Colonel Douglas and I do not have much to say to each other, I rode up ahead, pointed with my sabre at the Russians. By then, they had about-turned and were advancing towards us, although very cautiously. I didn't need to say anything more. The colonel comprehended the precarious situation. He asked me for an estimate of the support he believed was behind us. When I advised him there was none, he stared at me as if in disbelief. Quite astutely, he immediately raised his arm and asked the trumpeter to sound a halt. We noted the Russian Hussars were closing in on us and their Cossack regiments were attempting to go around our flanks, to attack us from the rear. The order to wheel about and retire was given.

"No sooner had we turned around than we saw a line of lancers some distance ahead of us. At first, we thought they were the remnants of our 17th. It turned out to be wishful thinking. On closer look, their pennants revealed they were, in fact, the Russian Uhlans in a three-row-deep formation."

"So you were in danger of being surrounded?" I asked, with the battle formations now playing in my mind.

"Cut off would be more like it, and with the possibility of being annihilated. Fortunately, Lord Paget and some men of his 4th Light Dragoons, who were close by and in a similar predicament, joined ranks with us. We formed rows as tightly and orderly as possible, given the circumstance and time. We made the final dash for home in a somewhat circular formation. The best horses and soldiers were in the outer circle, with officers and men all mingled together. I was at the rear and kept a watchful eye, with my long sword at the ready to slash at any Russian cavalryman who dared challenge us. When the Russian Hussars saw us approaching their Uhlan lancers, they dropped back, perhaps giving the task of finishing us off first to the Uhlans."

"Oh, my God!" I exclaimed. I noted Nancy was now sitting up and listening intently.

"I looked ahead and saw the formation of Uhlans, their lances pointing, ready and waiting for us. We approached them at the fastest speed our horses could muster, each man bent in his saddle with his head low alongside his horse's, to give as small a target as possible to the enemy's lances. Then the Uhlans made a strange manoeuvre. Possibly in an attempt to outflank us, they wheeled some of the right-end squadrons, thereby opening a break in their formation. Colonel Douglas must have noticed it and led us straight for that gap. The Russians did attack our flanks. We parried their lances with sabres and most of us managed to get away. However, some were not so lucky. Fierce hand-to-hand combat ensued. We were getting the better of them and, upon seeing the British breaking away, the Russian batteries and riflemen on the southern hill started firing into the mêlée, hitting both their foe and friends."

"Good God. How could they shoot their own soldiers?" I asked, bewildered.

"I'd never seen or heard of it, till then."

"So was it then when Robert got hit with a bullet?" I asked, remembering the wound on his chest.

"No. Not just then. A majority of us managed to break through the Uhlans' three-deep ranks. Due to the cannonade, it was every man for himself. Hence, our rows were broken and spread out. I'd seen Robert and Albert getting through the Uhlan lines and riding up ahead with others. As I said, I was at the rear of our group and, on noticing two of our men being attacked by a group of lancers, I'd gone back to help them. I took care of the Russians and we managed to gallop away to our base.

"Upon reaching our lines, I looked around for Robert and Albert, and was surprised on not finding them in the line. I inquired and was informed that Albert's horse was hit and he'd fallen off. Robert went back to help him. That was the last anyone saw of them. Just then, there were shouts of 'bravo' from the men. We saw Albert ride in slowly on a small pony with a Cossack saddle. Blood poured down his neck from cuts to the side of his head. I ran to him and helped him dismount. I asked about Robert and whether we should go back and help him.

"Albert simply shook his head and mumbled something. 'Robert's shot through the heart,' I believe he said. I still wanted to go and see for myself. I mounted my horse but Colonel Douglas bid me down, saying there were strict orders to stay put. No one was to leave the ranks until the stand-down was issued. I implored him to make an exception. He refused, saying, 'Robert's shot through the heart. He is very likely dead. Nothing you or anyone can do for him.' Margaret, please believe me, it was a most frustrating moment of my life, not being able to go back and help my very good friend. Later I heard from the chaplain you were present at his burial. How did you find him? When you got there, I mean."

Hearing of my Robert's valiant act to save a fellow officer, even though he was not on good terms with him, brought another flood of tears. I mopped my eyes and replied, "By the time I got there, he was barely alive. Albert was probably right. Robert wouldn't have made it back to base, let alone the hospital. Even though I managed to extract the bullet from him, it was no use. He'd lost a lot of blood and passed away ..." I put my head between my hands and started to sob bitterly.

Both Nancy and Alexander said comforting words, and eventually I regained my composure. Remembering the bullet was still in the pocket of my coat, which hung on the rack by the door, I got up and fished it out from the coat pocket. I showed it to Alexander. He took it between his thumb and forefinger and rotating it, examined it.

"That's funny," he said with a quizzical look. "It looks like one of our standard issues. Look."

I bent down to observe it closely and, true enough, it had markings in English etched on it. He then unhooked his holster cover and pulled out his service revolver. Opening the clasp, he rolled out the chamber and let a cartridge fall into the palm of his hand. He placed the bullet I had given him alongside his cartridge. Although a bit mangled, it matched the one at the tip of the cartridge.

"Ah! I know what it is. It's those damn Cossacks, stealing weapons from the bodies of our men and using them on us."

Selim came into the room and announced dinner was ready. We got up and, with heavy hearts, sat down at the dining table. We ate the lamb kebabs, not with pleasure or enjoyment but rather from hunger, and drank the wine to curb our sorrow.

While we dined, someone knocked on the door. Selim opened it and announced it was Cornet David, one of Lord Cardigan's aides.

"Sorry to bother you, ma'am," he said apologetically, taking his cap off. "Lord Cardigan sends his condolences and regrets he is not able to come personally. But he asks if Mrs. Wallace would be so kind as to join him for lunch tomorrow, aboard the *Dryad*?"

"Thank you for the message, David. Please tell the lord I am very much touched by his consideration. I shall be there tomorrow."

The Cornet bid us goodnight, bowed and left.

After dinner, Alexander asked if he could escort Nancy back to her quarters, up on the Sapoune Heights, in Lord Raglan's farmhouse.

"No, thank you," she said. "I should stay here, if it's all right with Margaret? I wish to be closer to the hospital-ship, and see Albert the first thing in the morning."

"Of course you may, Nancy," I replied. "And besides, I will appreciate some company tonight."

Alexander left, thanking me for the dinner and again offering his heartfelt sympathies. I got some spare blankets and pillows and made a bed for Nancy on the couch. We sat for a while and recounted the good times we had had in Grimsby, till the last of the embers in the fireplace died out. Nancy looked very tired and started to doze off. I kissed her goodnight and, with a heavy heart, I trudged upstairs.

I undressed, washed and put on my nightdress, but sleep was far from my eyes. Putting on my woollen housecoat, I sat down at the writing table and wrote a letter to Robert's mother in Grimsby and to my parents, who were then in India. I enclosed a poppy in each of those letters. The letter to my parents began:

Dearest Mamma and Papa,
It is with the deepest sadness in my heart that I write to inform you of the heartbreaking but valiant death of our beloved Robert, who was killed today, the 25th of October, in the charge of the Light Brigade,

fighting for his Queen. He performed his duty with courage and dignity. In his memory, which shall live forever in my heart, I enclose a poppy which grew in the field where he now lies, and shall continue to grow in his remembrance till eternity ...

I woke up with a start. It was still dark outside. I had gone to bed and fallen into a deep slumber from sheer exhaustion due to the events of the day. The pocket watch on the bedside table showed it to be close to three o'clock. I then remembered what had awakened me from the bad dream. It was an image of Albert's face, all bloodied and battered, looking menacingly at me, and in the next vision was Robert's lovely visage, asking me in his dying whisper, "Is Albert all right?"

Although a cool breeze from the Crimean shores blew into the room, I broke into a sweat when a horrible thought crossed my mind. *No, it could not be! No, no! Never, never!* However, there was only one way to find out. To be certain. It had to be tonight, before it was too late.

I threw the bed sheets off, got out of bed and dressed hurriedly and as quietly as possible. Without lighting a candle and holding onto the railings for guidance, I tiptoed slowly downstairs. I heard Nancy snoring in the sitting room. In the hallway, I put on Robert's greatcoat and, gently opening the front door, slipped out of the house.

In the dimly lit street, a cold wind swept from the sea and whipped against my body. I tied the straps of my bonnet tightly around my chin and put my gloved hands into the coat pockets for extra warmth. I felt for the fatal bullet in the right-hand pocket and held it between the fingers. I wanted to take care it would not fall out as I walked hurriedly, with my head bent, towards the hospital-ship, docked a couple of furlongs away.

The sentry at the gangplank recognised me and snapped to attention. I bade him good morning and walked onto the dimly lit deck of the hospital-ship. I went past a number of patients lying bundled up on cots on the main deck. I knew the person I wanted to see would be in one of the officers' cabins. I went down to the second deck and entered the main office. The duty sergeant sat at his desk and the orderlies lay dozing on the benches. I hung my bonnet on the hook, but kept the greatcoat on.

Upon seeing me, the sergeant stood up, bowed and said, "Good morning. Most sorry to hear about your husband, ma'am. He was a brave soldier."

"Thank you, sergeant. He was one of the many who died today, doing their duty," I said, trying to keep a brave composure.

"Yes. We lost nearly half the Light Brigade. Such a tragedy. But aren't you a bit early this mornin', ma'am?"

"Aye, couldn't sleep. Also, I heard Captain Albert, from my home town, was brought here? I'm anxious to see him. Do you know his cabin number?"

The sergeant looked through a sheaf of papers on the desk. On one page, pointing at a name on a list, he replied, "Yes. Captain Albert's in cabin fourteen. But I dare say he would be sleepin' now."

"Thank you, sergeant. Oh, I'll just look in for a bit and see if he's all right. I shan't be a moment," I said and, picking up an oil lamp, headed towards that cabin.

Cabin fourteen's door had two names on the nameplate holder. One read Captain Albert Miller. I opened the door as gently as possible. The hinges squeaked and I feared the sound might awaken the men. I entered the room and had to cover my nose due to the terrible stench of blood and sweat from the unwashed bodies. I raised the oil lamp high to let the dim light shine on the two bodies lying on beds on either side of the cabin. They continued to snore and I was glad they had not roused from my entry. The person on the right had the unmistakable heavy shape of Albert. I approached him silently. The wound was just above his right ear. It looked bad, as the bandage was crimson from oozing blood. His jacket and sabre belt, with the service revolver holster, hung on a hook next to the bed. I made sure my back was to the officer on the opposite bed and, bending down to make it look as if I was examining Albert, I opened the cover of the holster. Slowly removing the revolver, I slid it into my coat pocket. I left the cabin just as silently as I had come in. I was glad there weren't any doctors about, for they certainly would have questioned my presence at that time of the night.

I walked over to the chief surgeon's office in the cabin situated further down the hallway, where, as his assistant, my desk was also located. I sat down and with trembling hands drew out the revolver from my pocket. It was the same kind as Robert's and Alexander's. While I fumbled with the catch, trying to open the chamber cover, I heard footsteps coming to the office. I hurriedly slipped the revolver underneath a stack of papers.

Someone turned the knob and the door slowly opened.

Trembling, I asked, "Who is it?"

"Ah, there you are, ma'am. Only me. I was wondering if you might be wantin' some tea?"

"No. Thank you, sergeant. I shall be going back shortly. I'm leaving some notes for the surgeon."

"How is the captain?"

"Looks like he has a fever. His wound is still bleeding and the bandage needs changing."

"I'll get someone to do it first thing in the morning." He then left, closing the cabin door behind him.

I pulled the revolver out from under the papers and attempted once again to open it, trying to remember the way Alexander had undone his. I recollected it, and gave the revolver the slight sideways jerk Alexander had used. The chamber rolled out. It was empty and, from the smell of gunpowder, it looked as if all the rounds had been fired recently. Holding the piece by the butt in my left hand, I drew out the bullet from my coat pocket with my right hand. I put it over one of the holes in the chamber. My heart leapt when I saw it fitted exactly. Was it the same weapon that had killed my Robert? While my anxious mind said it was, I still would not believe it. I could not fathom Albert would stoop so low as to shoot one of his fellow officers. And for what reason? What was his motive? Did he lust for me so much? Or was it because Nancy was still in love with Robert? With these thoughts and a heart just as confused as the one I had arrived with, I returned Albert's revolver to his cabin and left the ship.

As I stepped off the hospital-ship's gangplank, the dark night sky over the Black Sea was changing to a lighter shade, announcing the imminent arrival of the grey dawn. The wind had died down and it felt a bit warmer. The streetlamps were being turned off, leaving the narrow lanes of the town in eerie shadows from the moonlight. Although I trembled in the dim light, I was at least happy I had partly confirmed my fears. Those and other thoughts of Robert's death swirled in my mind. I pulled Robert's greatcoat about me and, putting my head down, hurried back to the house. However, I felt I would require more evidence to verify my conjecture. Fortunately, I did not have to wait too long for that.

*****

"Tell me, Margaret. Have you made any plans for the future?" Lord Cardigan asked, lighting a cigar.

We were aboard Lord Cardigan's sleek yacht and had just finished lunch, which was arranged for the widows of his officers. The other wives and I ate what we could, for none of us was particularly hungry. We sat subdued, most likely with the memories of our loved ones still fresh in our minds. However, Cardigan, dressed splendidly in his bright uniform, looked none the worse from the horrific events of the day of the charge. I still cannot believe how miraculously he escaped, with just a few scratches from the Russian lances. The widows and officers seated around the dining table turned their heads towards me, waiting to hear my reply.

I stammered, "I'm not sure ... milord. One part of me badly ... wants to go back and be with my children and parents. Yet another part ... wishes me to stay here ... help the sick and wounded."

"Widows will be returning to England. You can go there, or we could send you to Canada, if you wish. But did you not say your parents were presently in India?"

"Yes, milord."

"Well then, how would you like it if you were transferred to medical service in India?" he asked, taking a puff of the cigar and blowing the smoke towards the ceiling.

I have never liked the smell of a cigar, especially so in my maternal condition at that time, and it very nearly nauseated me. However, on hearing what he said, I took a quick breath through my mouth and managed to recover hastily. "Really, milord? Why, that would be wonderful. If I could be with my parents, I would send for my children and still work in my profession," I replied with my heart lifting almost to the ceiling. It was the first bit of good news I had heard in a while. The prospect of having my mother next to me at the birth of my third child further comforted me.

"I was there in thirty-seven. A fine country. We have regiments going there all the time. I have seen excellent reports about your medical abilities. I'm sure they could use your help. I'll talk to the chief surgeon about transferring you to India."

"Thank you, sir. I always try to do my best. When would it be possible?"

"Oh, I should think it would be fairly quick," he said and, turning towards his ADC, added, "David, could you please see how soon Doctor Margaret can be booked on a ship for Calcutta?"

"Yes, sir," Cornet David replied, scribbling the instruction in his notebook.

"Thank you so very much, sir. You have been most kind to me. I couldn't have asked for anything more."

"Not at all. It's the least I can do for the widow of an officer. After all, your father-in-law also served in my regiment."

As I left the yacht, I curtseyed and thanked the earl again for all his kindnesses. Although I had heard several uncomplimentary words about him and knew he was not well liked by his troops, I could not feel any bitterness towards him. True, he was accused of having abandoned his men during the charge and ridden back to safety, but had he remained at the cannons, the events would not likely have been any different. It would not have saved my Robert's life. While walking back to the hospital-ship, I said a silent prayer of thankfulness to my Saviour, for continuing to open the doors of opportunity for me in the face of adversities.

I arrived back at the hospital-ship, rather elated at the prospect of finally going to India, something I had dreamt of since childhood. The duty sergeant greeted me and advised that Captain Albert's Mrs. was with her husband and wished to see me. I hurried over to Albert's cabin. At my knock, Nancy opened the door.

"Oh, Margaret, I'm glad you've come. Can you have a look at Albert? He looks so sick."

I went over to his bed. He lay still, although breathing rather heavily. I touched his forehead and it was just as hot as earlier. I felt he needed more laudanum, but with the influx of all the injured soldiers, the supplies at our small hospital were running very low. Besides, there weren't enough doctors to look after near half the patients. "He has high fever. Not a good sign. We could try bleeding him. But Nancy, I think he should be moved immediately to the Barracks hospital, in Scutari."

"Oh, Margaret, yes. But how? The doctors here are too busy. Could you talk to someone?"

Albert must have heard me. He said, in a low moan, "No, Margaret, no. Don't let them take me away to Scutari. I want to stay here, under your care. Robert saved my life."

Nancy bent down and ran her hand over his head, saying, "It's all right, dear. It's all right. Margaret says it's best if you go to Scutari and receive proper medical attention."

At his mentioning Robert, I asked, "Albert, when did you last see Robert?"

"So sorry, Margaret. He fought off three Cossacks attacking me. One of them shot him through the heart," Albert said in a rasping voice.

Anxious to learn what had happened there, I asked, "How did you escape?"

"I killed that Cossack."

"But Albert, didn't the Cossack shoot at you too?"

"No, he didn't … he didn't … Margaret, I want to stay here with you …" Albert's voice trailed off and, closing his eyes, he slipped into unconsciousness.

Nancy stood there with one hand over her mouth, looking mesmerised. I patted her on the shoulder. "Nancy, he's not making much sense. I'll go and talk to the chief surgeon."

I found the chief at his desk and advised him of Albert's poor condition. He said he had seen my notes and was aware of Albert's and other similar critical cases. He was already planning to move them to the base hospital in Scutari. I must have looked somewhat shaken and pale myself. He advised me that, as it was already late afternoon, I should go home early and return fresh the next morning. I thanked the doctor and proceeded towards the gangway.

As I passed by the main office, the duty sergeant called after me, waving a brown paper envelope. "Ma'am. A package for you."

It wasn't a large package, more like an oversize envelope, and had *Doctor Margaret Wallace* written across it in strange-looking handwriting. I took it from him. "Thank you, sergeant. Who is it from?"

"Don't know, ma'am. It came a short while ago. A Turkish chap handed it to the sentry and disappeared."

"Oh," I said, "it might be something for my Turkish servant, from his family. They probably don't know exactly where I live." I put the package under my arm and strode towards the house.

Selim wasn't in the house, and I remembered he had taken the horses to the blacksmith for new shoes. I put the package on the table in the hallway and, after putting the tea kettle on the stove, went upstairs to wash and change.

The kettle started to whistle and, hurrying down, I made myself a strong cup of tea. Settling in the sitting room sofa and putting my feet up, I sipped the tea, hoping it would smooth my rattled nerves after seeing Albert and hearing his account of Robert's ill-fated assistance. It sounded logical enough. As Alexander had thought, the Cossack might have shot Robert with a stolen British revolver. However, something was odd in Albert's narrative, which my mind would not accept. Was it the way he had asked me to look after him?

Despite the soothing effect of the tea, I felt miserable and wished to be with my children and my mother. It had been so long I could hardly remember when I last saw them. I then spotted the strange-looking envelope lying on the hallway table and thought, if it were for Selim, why would they write my name on it? Perhaps it really was for me. I walked over, picked up the envelope and brought it back to the sofa. I sat with it on my lap for a while, staring at it. I pressed it between my fingers. A bulky object was in it. While the item felt familiar, I could not place it. Finally, I decided to open it. It was a rather strong envelope, like the type used in military dispatches. I could not tear the flap with my fingers and had to use one of the knitting needles from a baby sweater I had just started, lying on the side table.

As I tore open the cover, a large, black leather object fell onto the floor. When I saw it, my heart leapt into my throat.

It was my Robert's wallet.

Chapter Twenty-One

Vengeance Is Mine

1854, October: Balaclava, Crimea

WITH TREMBLING HANDS, I picked up Robert's wallet from the floor. It was a black leather, folding type, with several compartments. His identification card was still in the front pocket and in the back pouch, his money. There were only a couple of pound notes and some coins in there. I did not think any money was stolen, for I knew the poor soul usually did not carry much. Tears filled my eyes as I recalled the time when Robert and I, mere teens in Canada, were walking along Grimsby beach and I had wanted him to take me into the Lake House Tavern for an ice cream. He made several flimsy excuses and finally, when I insisted, he confessed to having no money. Then I remembered the fat drummer boy, Albert, had come running and, after punching Robert to the ground, pulled on my pigtails. While I cried in pain and before Robert could recover, Albert ran away. Robert had shouted he would teach him a lesson for hurting me, along with some unkind words. Was that incident the beginning of the hostility between them, which still brewed?

The wallet's side compartment contained several photographs. They were smaller size prints of the ones taken before our departure from Grimsby. We had dressed up in our best outfits and driven over to the photographer's studio on Main Street. The sitting had taken some time, not to mention the cost, but Robert said they were well worth the money, for he wished to keep the images of me and our children close to his heart.

My hands shook as I held up the pictures, which were already yellowing at the edges. My tears fell on the first photograph. It was of me sitting on a stool, very erect, with my hands on my lap and looking sideways at the camera. I had spent hours doing my hair; it was parted in the middle and rolled up at the back in a neat chignon, which the photographer wanted to capture. I suspected he also wished to display my prominent décolletage. The next one was our family group photograph. I sat on a chair with Vika in my arms. Robert stood beside us, looking most elegant in a dark frock coat over a waistcoat, a high-collar shirt and a cravat. Bruce stood in front of him in a smart navy uniform with a sailor's cap, his grandmother's birthday gifts. There were some more pictures of Robert's parents and his sisters.

While I was putting the photographs back in the wallet, I noticed another one in the next compartment. I took it out. My hands quivered so much I nearly dropped it. Seeing that picture was another shocking moment, to add to the countless ones I had already experienced in the last few days. It was a photograph of Nancy. She stood in the middle of an artificial floral arrangement, staring solemnly at the camera. In her arms, she held a bouquet of cheap-looking flowers. However, the worst part of the picture was her dress, the most vulgar, tight fitting and low cut I had ever seen, displaying her prominent bosom and bottom. And on top of that, the photograph had been painted over in bright colours! I was certain she would have paid a fair amount for it, most likely thinking it made her look pretty. It definitely did not.

I knew Nancy and Robert had been in school together and, as Robert had mentioned to me, he was fond of her. For some reason that was still not clear to me, they had broken off. However, seeing her picture in Robert's wallet raised new doubts in my mind. Why did he carry her picture? Did he still love her?

I heard the back door open and Selim entered. I hurriedly put the photographs into the wallet and slid it under a cushion.

"Would madam like dinner?"

"Yes, but just a Greek salad for me. I'm not very hungry. Madam Nancy might want something more. Please ask her when she comes in." He nodded, and as he started to go towards the kitchen, I thought of the envelope and asked, "Oh, Selim. Did someone, perhaps a Turkish man, come to the house to deliver a package?"

He turned and replied, "No, madam. No Turkish man. It was Frenchman. He say he has letter for you from the French g'neraal. I say him to go to hospital."

"Good. Thank you. I got the letter," I said, waving the envelope at him.

I then noticed there was indeed a letter in there and took it out. It read:

Madame Doctor,

I return your husband's wallet with my deepest sympathy. If you wish to know some important information concerning your husband's death, please come to the dell where you met Lieutenant L.

I will be there the next Sunday and the Sunday thereafter, at noon.
Yours very sincerely,
Captain N.B.

My mind went into a whirl. Who was this Captain N.B.? Surely not that Russian, Count Nicholai Barry ... or some such name? Well, it had to be, for I remembered the young lieutenant's name was Lapinsky. However, how they had gotten hold of poor Robert's wallet was beyond me.

To ease my mind, I stared out of the window. The sun was setting over the Black Sea and its last rays shone through the windows, casting an orange glow in the room. Outside, in the busy street, villagers hurried home with loaves of bread and food items in their arms. The harbour docks looked congested with numerous vessels, their masts swaying gently. I spotted Nancy walking up the street. Grabbing the wallet and the letter, I threw the envelope onto the burning logs in the fireplace, and hurried upstairs to the bedroom.

I hid Robert's wallet and the letter in my sea chest, under some dresses and petticoats, except for Nancy's picture. I put that in the thick volume of *Vanity Fair* that Lord Cardigan had loaned me from his library in the yacht. I heard Nancy come in and ask Selim if I was home. He replied affirmatively and inquired if she wanted some tea and what she would like for dinner. She asked what I was having and, when informed, said she would have the same. The back door opened and closed. She had probably gone out to the privy.

I was tired and lay on the bed, reading a bit of the interesting novel about the exploits of William Thackeray's heroine, Becky Sharp. I soon lost concentration, as that photograph of Nancy preyed upon my mind and I began to get a throbbing headache. Getting up, I undressed, walked to the washstand and poured some fresh water from the tumbler into the basin. I washed my hands and splashed cold water on my face. I felt much better and refreshed after a body wash and a good scrubbing with the hand towel. I dressed in a dark gown and, as it was getting chilly, put a blue pashmina cotton shawl I had purchased in a Turkish market over my shoulders. Picking up *Vanity Fair*, I went downstairs to the sitting room.

Nancy lay on the sofa bed, her eyes closed and one hand over her forehead.

"Hallo, Nancy. Aren't you feeling well?"

"I have a terrible headache," she replied, sitting up and propping herself on a cushion.

"I have one as well. It must be the weather. Shall we have a glass of wine?"

"That would be lovely."

"Selim," I said, "will you bring us some wine?"

He came over with two glasses of red wine on a tray and informed us that dinner was ready. We took the wine goblets and walked over to the dining table. Selim served us the tasty Greek salad that he made so well, especially with the delicious goat cheese. I was amazed that he was able to find cheese in the market kiosks, because they looked so bare. On my inquiry, he informed us it was sent over from his family farm, situated inland.

"Cheers, Nancy," I said, raising my glass to her.

"To Robert," she said and burst into sobs.

I had tears in my eyes as well and remained silent for a while. I finally said, "Yes, to Robert. Thank you, Nancy."

We took a sip of the wine and started on the salad and hot bread.

"How is Albert?" I asked, taking another sip of the wine.

"He's still the same, has high fever and is delirious. I believe they will be moving him to the main hospital in Scutari on the next available ship."

"I'm sure he'll get better treatment there, now that Miss Nightingale has arrived with her trained nurses."

"She's finally here? How marvellous! I'm dying to meet her. I know you saw her in London. What's she like?"

"A most remarkable lady. Very angelic," I replied, thinking of my meeting with Florence at Embley Park. We ate our dinner and talked a bit about those memorable days in London and our families in Canada.

All the time I wondered how to phrase the question that was on my mind. Afterwards, we retired to the parlour and, with wine glasses in hand, sat by the fireplace.

"Nancy, pray tell me, did Albert say anything more about the last time he saw Robert?" I asked, trying to sound as casual as possible.

"No. Nothing more than he said the other night, while you were there. He keeps mumbling about how much he is indebted to Robert for saving his life and sorry that he could not stop the Cossack from shooting poor Robert."

"Didn't Albert say that he himself had killed the Cossack and taken his horse?"

"Yes, I remember him saying that."

"How did Albert do that? Did he say that *he* shot the Cossack?"

"No. As far as I recall, he said something about slashing him with his sabre. Why do you ask?"

"Because it sounds strange to me, that Albert wouldn't have used his revolver earlier. That way he might have shot the Cossack before my Robert got shot."

"Oh, I don't know. All this fighting and killing is beyond me. I am very distressed about our Robert's death. Margaret, can you take me to his grave, please? I should like to pay my last respects to him."

"Yes, Nancy. I will, perhaps tomorrow, provided there aren't any Russians near there ..." I paused a bit. Her words, "our Robert", gave me the opening. I inquired, "I know you and Robert were once close, but tell me, were you two ever engaged, perhaps privately?" I asked delicately.

She looked at me and I saw tears in her blue eyes. She pushed back a flock of blonde hair from her forehead. "No, not formally. You know, we were together in school, and very fond of each other. Our parents wanted us to get married."

"Would you have married him?"

She was silent for a while and then answered, "Yes. I would have, if he'd asked me. But we drifted apart and stopped seeing each other."

"Why did it happen? Did Robert stop caring for you?"

"No, he didn't, he still ..." She stopped in mid-sentence.

"How about you? Did you still care for him?"

She was silent for a while and, after dabbing her eyes, said, "Yes, I did."

"You married Albert when you were quite young. Weren't you?"

She simply nodded.

Then it suddenly dawned on me and I had to ask, "Did you *have to* marry him?"

She covered her eyes and started to sob.

I put my arms around her and held her in an embrace. "It's all right, Nancy. It's all right."

Having cried a bit, she composed herself and said, "Thank you, Margaret. I'm glad you understand."

"So, how about recently? Did you see much of Robert? I mean, while I was working at the hospital in Scutari."

Her face turned crimson. She averted her eyes and replied, "No. Nothing more than the usual. Albert and I saw him often and Alexander was with us some of the times as well."

"Were the two of you ever alone?"

"Not often. We went riding a few times. Albert never takes me out. Why do you ask?" Her brow knitted and she looked at me through narrowed eyes.

"Then how do you explain this?" I took out her photograph from the book and placed it in her lap.

She looked shocked. She picked it up, slowly, with both hands. Tears once again welled in her eyes and flowed down her cheeks. In between sobs, she asked, "Where … did you … find this?"

"In Robert's things. It's a recent photo, isn't it? Not from your school days, I mean."

"Yes. Margaret, please believe me. It's not what you're thinking."

"So, how did Robert come to possess it? Why did you give it to him?"

"It was when he was leaving Canada. I hadn't decided if I was going to accompany all of you. Robert thought he may never see me again and wanted something to remember me by. That's all."

"Didn't Albert say anything? About Robert taking you out riding."

"He didn't like it. You know how he is. He gets furious over the most trivial matters."

"Did he speak to Robert about your riding out together?"

"Yes. They argued a few times. I'd been meaning to mention it to you."

I then remembered something and asked, "By the way, what was it you wanted to tell me? When we met at General Raglan's headquarters the other day."

"Yes, it was just this. Something that happened between Robert and Albert."

"Oh! What happened?"

She blew her nose in a handkerchief. "All right, let me tell you what occurred. A few days ago, Robert took me out riding. We galloped for a while in the woods and, it being a hot day, were resting under some shady trees, on the banks of a pleasant river. Suddenly Albert rode up. He'd likely followed us. They exchanged harsh words. I tried my best to separate them, but they came to blows. Robert knocked Albert down. He sat up and pulled his revolver out. I shrieked at him to stop. Fortunately, Robert acted quickly, kicked and knocked it out of Albert's hand. Albert grabbed Robert's foot and pulled him to the ground. I kept shouting at them to stop it, but they paid no heed. They continued to scuffle on the steep riverbank. I was afraid they might fall into the fast-flowing stream and could have drowned."

"Oh my God. And did they fall into the river?"

"No, they didn't. But they would have if my cries had not brought some passers-by, who separated the two."

"Well, at least they didn't draw swords. Tell me, Nancy, why was Albert so angry?"

"Albert is the way he is. He wants to control everything. Always wishes to get his way."

"But he drew his weapon. Surely something must have really infuriated him. Were you and Robert in a compromising situation, by any chance?"

On hearing that, she seemed to flare up and said, "Honestly, Margaret! How could you think such a thing? No. Nothing like that. Robert might have had his arm around me, but it was just that—" She stopped abruptly, as if she had said too much. Tears welled in her eyes once again.

I did not like what I was hearing. The suspicion and fears I had been trying to suppress rose again within me like angry ocean waves. I clutched my hands to my bosom and, bending my head, said a silent prayer. Dear God, let it not be true. Please let it not be true.

"Margaret, what is it? Is anything the matter? Is the baby troubling you?" Nancy asked, putting a hand on my shoulder.

"The child's fine. It's nothing. I'm just tired. It's been a long day. I think I'll turn in."

I picked up the book and, bidding Nancy goodnight, went upstairs to my bedroom. I left her photograph with her, for I would have no use for it and neither would my poor Robert. While I lay in bed, Albert's growl of a whisper to me that night in the frigate cabin, on the way up from Canada, came back to me: *"I'll feed you and your family to the wolves."* I shivered when the thought flew through my mind: Could Albert have murdered my husband? And what was he going to do next?

*****

I spurred Betsy into a gallop along the road towards the hills that ring Balaclava in the north. It was one of those exceptionally warm Crimean autumn Sundays. The sun flowed down its energy, which the wind carried over to me in streams of hot air and blew through my black, high-collar dress and bonnet. It was the day of my appointment with the writer of that mysterious letter, Captain N.B.

Earlier, although it was my day off, I had got up before sunrise and asked Selim to set up the metallic bathtub in the bedroom, and fill it with hot water. While taking a leisurely bath and slapping balmy water over my shoulders, I wondered what could be so important that Captain N.B. wanted to tell me. Nancy was still asleep downstairs and I also thought about excuses to make to her, for going away somewhere. However, I didn't have to worry about that. Someone knocked on the front door and a messenger told Selim that Mrs. Nancy Miller was wanted at the hospital. Although I was concerned that it might have something to do with Albert's condition, I was glad she would be away when I left for my appointment.

I reached the road I had come down from Lord Raglan's headquarters on that fateful day. No British soldiers were around, likely because the Allies were then concentrating their efforts on capturing Sebastopol. Most of the guns and men were moved to the siege lines around that town.

I saw several paths and each looked nearly the same as the one I had taken previously. I tried several of those lanes, only to reach dead ends that forced me to return to the road. I was getting exasperated, when suddenly a flicker of sunlight flashed over my face. I looked up and saw someone at the entrance to one of the pathways, signalling me with a mirror. I rode in that direction and, sure enough, it was the very trail I had taken before. It was like finding one's way through a labyrinth. The lane led to that same wooded dell where those Russians had captured me. I cantered along that path and soon entered the grove of pine trees where I had met the cranky Russian lieutenant.

Coming into the shade from the bright sunlight, I was blinded for a moment. As my eyes focused, two riders standing motionless ahead of me gradually came into view. I stopped a short distance from them. We stood still for a while. They looked around; it seemed to make sure I had not been followed or had sprung a trap on them. My eyes fell on the taller rider, who wore a white uniform with gold amulets and a shiny brass, plumed helmet. He rode forward and stopped at my right side. Our eyes met. He was the same Russian captain who had interrogated me.

"Good day, madame. Are you sure no one followed you?" he said with a slight bow.

"Yes. Quite sure, no one knows I'm here, Captain, er ... ?"

"Nicholai Barinowsky, madame, at your service," he replied curtly and added quickly, "My deepest sympathies on the loss of your husband."

"Thank you, sir. You are most kind. But pray tell me why you wish to see me? "

"There is something important you should know."

I felt angry and said in a raised voice, "I am intrigued, sir. First, your men kill my husband and steal his wallet, which obviously came into your possession, and now you have something to tell me?"

The captain raised his hand and said, "No, madame. My men did not kill your husband."

"Then who did?"

"Sergeant Boris here saw it all happen. I will let him tell you in his own words, which I shall translate." He waved his arm at the sergeant and said something in Russian, which sounded like, "Boris, come here."

Sergeant Boris trotted forward, stopped in front of me and bowed. He was a heavyset man, with a full, greying beard, and dressed in the Cossack uniform: a thick grey greatcoat, a bearskin cap and brown leather boots. The captain asked him to recite to me what he had seen on the battlefield that day. When he started the narration, Captain Nicholai translated the sergeant's gruff Russian words.

"Madame, that day I was asked by milord Count Nicholai," he said, pointing at the captain, "to go to the battlefield and collect the dead British officers' wallets, along with any papers in their pockets, and bring them to him. I was there on the ground doing my duty, going through a dead officer's pockets, when at some distance, I witnessed a terrible scene. I saw your husband, the young lieutenant, riding back from his retreating group to help a British officer. I believe he was a captain, a rather portly gentleman with a dark moustache. Do you know that captain, madame?"

I nodded.

The sergeant continued his narrative. "It seems the captain's horse was shot and he had fallen down. I saw three of our Cossacks galloping towards the captain. There was no one else around to help him, except your husband. Your husband was very courageous. He dashed towards the Cossacks and approached them from the rear, on their weaker left side. With a slash of his sabre, he nearly decapitated one Cossack and started to parry with another."

"Didn't the captain help?" I asked in a trembling voice.

"Yes, madame. But only with his revolver. He got up and shot at the third Cossack. He missed and the Cossack galloped up to him and cut him on the side of the head. I believe the captain's cap helped him by glancing off the blow. It likely saved his life, although he fell down again. By that time, your husband had thrust his sabre into the second Cossack's chest and finished him off. The third Cossack, after cutting the captain, turned around and came up from behind your husband and tried to slash him on the neck. Fortunately, the lieutenant's horse reared up and the sword only struck him a glancing blow on the shoulder. The lieutenant fell down. I was certain the Cossack would now kill him. But he rolled over and in one movement, got up and thrust his sabre up at the Cossack. It went through the Cossack's neck. He fell from his horse, shrieking and bleeding. Your husband held that Cossack's horse by the reins and walked the horse over to the captain, who was still lying on the ground."

"Really! But the captain told me that *he* killed the Cossack and took the horse," I said in disbelief.

"No, madame. If he said so, he is lying. It was your husband who took the horse to the captain and helped him to mount."

"Then what happened?" I had a premonition of what had taken place next. However, I still did not believe it and wanted to hear it from the Russian. I again clasped my hands together and pressed them tightly to my bosom. Dear God, no. No, dear God, please, no, don't let it be so, I prayed silently.

"Here's what happened," the sergeant said. "After helping the captain get on the Cossack's horse, your husband walked over to his faithful stallion, who stood obediently to one side. Suddenly I heard a gunshot, and saw the lieutenant fall to the ground. At first I thought one of our riflemen had shot him, and I scanned the hills. However, I could not see anyone there. It was then I observed the smoking revolver in the captain's hand. Your husband, the strong man he was, did manage to stand and, with blood pouring out of his chest wound, staggered over to his horse. I think the captain tried to shoot again, but the gun did not fire. It was either jammed or it was empty. Unfortunately, your husband could not climb onto his horse and slid down to the ground, while trying to hold onto the horse's neck."

"Did the captain do anything else?" I asked, wiping my tears.

The sergeant shook his fur cap. "No. The captain only looked down to assure himself that your husband was dead. He then turned the horse around and rode off towards the British camp. Madame, I was so grieved on seeing this treacherous act that I broke milord Count's orders. Although he had forbidden me from getting involved in the fighting, I got on my horse and tried to catch the captain. On seeing me coming after him, he spurred the horse viciously into a breakneck gallop. I fired at him, but missed due to the range. I had to turn back for I saw some British cavalrymen coming my way. The captain managed to get away. I'm sorry I was not able to put a bullet in his heart, just the way he did in your husband's."

Tears fell down my cheeks. In between sobs, I managed to thank Count Nicholai and the sergeant for their kindness. Not wishing to hear any more, nor wanting them to see my anguish, I wheeled Betsy around and slowly started on my ride back to Balaclava. I fully believed what they had narrated, as there was no reason for them to lie to me. It was all out of the goodness of their hearts. Furthermore, most likely the count had wished to make some amends for having detained me. Not that it would have mattered. It seemed that Albert had eventually managed to do to my dear Robert what he had wanted to do for some time. But why? Was it rage? Jealousy? Or was it something else?

As I rode back, my grief slowly turned into anger. My heart beat faster and faster and I began to sweat as blood raced through my body. I felt like a kettle heating up, which would eventually blow steam out with a loud scream. Breathing heavily and shaking with rage, I stopped under the shade of a tree to regain control of myself. A firm resolve to avenge the murder of my beloved husband took hold of me. But how was I to do it? I thought about reporting Albert and having him court-martialled. However, I knew it would lead to nothing. He would most likely be acquitted, for where was the evidence? That one bullet? A Cossack could have fired it from a stolen revolver. Surely, the Russians would never testify, and even if by a remote chance, they agreed to do it, who would believe them? In the end, it would boil down to Albert's word against mine. And I knew very well whom the jury would believe. A Queen's officer would never stoop so low as to shoot another fellow officer. Never. For where was his motive? Would Nancy testify against him? For one thing, she may not be permitted to do so and even if she was, I didn't believe she had the strength in her spine to do that. Yes, it would just be my word against Albert's. I could visualise the headlines in the *Times*, reported by Mr. William Howard Russell: *Army Wife Accuses Cavalry Officer of Husband's Murder*. Why, I would likely be the laughing stock of the whole British Army! I could just hear the jokes in the taverns, "'Eyah, 'ave ya 'eard the one about the 'mad woman of Balaclava'?"

In conclusion, I deduced there was just one option left open to me. It was about time I took action myself and avenged not only Robert's murder, but also my honour, which Albert had so blatantly tried to steal that night in the frigate's cabin on the way over from Canada. I knew I had to do it, and I had to act promptly. For as long as he was in the hospital, there was a chance. It would be more difficult once he was discharged. I could not let this murderer get away. But how was I to do it? Yes, I knew how men could be killed in their sleep. However, there was always the danger of being seen or caught. It had to be a natural way, one that no one would suspect. Something that would cause his heart to stop beating? Yes, that would be perfect. I knew just the herbal tonic which, in the right amount, would have the desired effect. Having made this decision, I spurred Betsy into a gallop towards the hospital-ship.

"Isn't this your day off, ma'am?" the duty sergeant asked in surprise when I entered the main ward's office.

"Oh, I just came in to see how Captain Albert is. Did you send for his wife earlier?" I said, hanging up my bonnet and greatcoat.

"Aye. We sent for the captain's Mrs. 'cause they left for Scutari about an hour ago. 'E was still very poorly and the surgeon 'ad him transferred on the first available boat."

I felt as if the deck had collapsed below my feet and I held onto a peg on the wall to steady myself. "Really! I knew he was to be transferred, but this was so sudden."

"Yes, ma'am. As you were gone ridin', Captain and Mrs. were most sorry for not bein' able to say goodbye to you. I believe they left a note for you. Lemme see, where is that letta." He rummaged around on the desk and handed a paper to me. Then, as if he had suddenly remembered something, he said, "Ah! Before I forget, the chief surgeon wants to see you, ma'am. 'E said it could be tomorrow, but 'e is in his office. You can see him now, if you wish."

I thanked the sergeant and walked down the companionway to the chief's office.

"Come in," the surgeon answered to my light knock on the cabin door.

Upon seeing me enter, he stood up from his desk. "Ah! Margaret. So good of you to come in, even on a Sunday. Pray be seated." He motioned to the chair in front of his desk. He was a slim, tall man with a bald pate and a prominent nose. Dressed in a dark suit, he looked more like a preacher than a physician. Throwing his coattails aside, he sat down and, leaning back in the chair, stretched his long legs to one side of the desk. "I say, have you had tea yet?"

"No, sir. But I'll pour it." I got up and poured two cups from the tea service that lay on a side table.

"Ah! Thank you," he said, taking a sip and looking at me with kind brown eyes. It seemed he had forgotten why he had called me in.

I took a sip of the tea as well and waited. Finally, I asked, "Did you wish to see me about something, sir?"

"Ah, yes. Now what was it? Right. Cardigan tells me you wish to go to India?"

"Yes, sir. As you know, my parents are there, and I haven't seen them for quite a while."

"Yes, but how are you feeling? You know, in the family way?" he asked, looking at my abdomen, which had just started to show a bit.

"I feel fine, sir."

"You are now, what … about three or four months?"

"Yes, about four months, sir."

"You know it could take over two months to get to India. How do you feel about such a voyage?"

I took a sip of the refreshing tea. "I believe I will be all right, sir. I'll manage."

"Well, Margaret, you might be in luck." He took a long sip and, opening a drawer, drew out a piece of paper. "I have just seen in the dispatches a request for female medical help at a new hospital in Delhi. They are calling it … " He searched for the name. "Yes, St. Stanley's. Hmm … an appropriate name. Apparently, Florence has turned the request down. Says her staff's too busy in Scutari. Now, mind, I'd rather you stay here. Nevertheless, if you are keen on going, I can send up a recommendation. Would you be interested?" he asked with another smile. Gulping the last of the tea, he put the cup and saucer down on the desk.

"Yes, sir! I'd be most interested," I said delighted.

"Good. Now where in India did you say your parents were?"

"They're in Futtehgurh, at the American Mission."

"Fatte … what? Where on earth is that?"

"It's close to Delhi, sir," I replied with a slight laugh.

"All right, let's have a *dekko*." He smiled again, obviously trying to impress me with his knowledge of Army Hindustani. Getting up, he walked over to the large globe that stood on a footstool in one corner of the office. I joined him there. He rotated the globe until the map of India was in front of us.

"So, here's Calcutta," he said, pointing to a dot, "and there is the Ganges River. Good God, can you see? It flows right across the continent, from Kashmir to the Bay of Bengal." He traced his finger along the black squiggly line. "Oh, there is Lucknow, the capital of Oudh, the kingdom we've just annexed. Here's Delhi. Ah, but it isn't on the Ganges, rather on one of its tributaries. What's it called?" He peered down to read the name of that river. "The Jamuna—here it is, can you see? But where the devil is your folks' town, Fathegan, did you say?"

"Futtehgurh, sir. It seems the town—village, rather—is too small to be on your globe. It would be somewhere here, about a hundred miles from Delhi." I pointed to a spot an inch or so away from Delhi on the Ganges River.

"Well, that would suit you fine. You could gallop up to work and be home before dinner every day, couldn't you?"

"Not in my condition, sir." I laughed, sharing his banter.

"No. I wouldn't ride too much, if I were you," he said with a smile, looking at my belly. "You would have to stay in Delhi. Our resident officer, Fraser, says the king there is most friendly. I understand he's readily agreed to Fraser's proposal for setting up the hospital. I am sure some arrangements will be made for your accommodation. Why, I believe the Frasers would love to have you stay with them."

"I'm sure Papa will know someone in the mission there who could put me up."

"Good. I'll start with the paperwork immediately. Oh yes. I understand Cardigan is arranging to get you there on one of our troop ships. Now, Margaret, I'm asking again. Are you positively certain you're up to making this long journey?"

"Absolutely, sir. I wouldn't miss it for all the gold in the world."

"Good. I dare say you're looking rather tired. Why don't you take the rest of the afternoon off and rest up?"

"Thank you, sir. I will," I replied and left his office. I was too polite to remind the chief surgeon that it was already my day off. I was glad he did not ask me to go back to work. It might have meant helping with some ghastly amputations of a soldier's arm or leg, which were taking place regularly.

I went home and, just as the doctor recommended, spent the rest of the afternoon in the parlour, curled up in the chair before the fireplace. I read a good bit of *Vanity Fair*, but my mind wandered. I thought about Albert's fortunate transfer before I could reach him and execute what I had planned. In some ways I was satisfied that God had answered my prayers. Through divine intervention, I was relieved of my duty. Perhaps God would provide retribution in some other way. I remembered a passage in the Bible that Papa used to read in his sermons. I opened the Bible, which I kept on the side table, and read:

Romans 12:19-21
Beloved, never avenge yourselves, but leave it to the wrath of God, for it is written, "Vengeance is mine, I will repay, says the Lord." To the contrary, "if your enemy is hungry, feed him; if he is thirsty, give him something to drink; for by so doing you will heap burning coals on his head." Do not be overcome by evil, but overcome evil with good.

Would I have to wait for the Lord's vengeance? Or perhaps He might present me with another opportunity? I shuddered at the thought of having to take someone else's life. Nevertheless, if that was the way Providence wanted me to act, I was willing to find courage deep within me to fulfil my duty.

"Dinner is ready, madam." Selim interrupted my thoughts.

The appetizing aroma of roasted duck wafted from the kitchen. I had continued our family tradition of having baked fowl on Sundays. Although I missed Nancy, for she had been good company during the last few days, I was not sorry to see her gone. Finding her picture in Robert's wallet had once again scrubbed the old wounds I had received, on account of her, from Robert's mother.

While munching on the duck's leg, holding it with my fingers, I read Nancy's farewell note. It said simply that she and Albert were sorry they could not say goodbye to me prior to sailing for Scutari. However, they hoped they would have an opportunity to see me there. She closed by adding it would really be a shame if they left for Canada and I for India without meeting each other. As I ate dinner, I wondered what fate had in store for us.

There was a knock on the door. Selim answered it, and in walked Cornet David.

"Sorry to bother you, ma'am, during your repast," he said, removing his bicorn hat and giving me his customary elegant bow. He looked his usual harried self.

"Not at all, David. Would you like to join me? There is a whole duck here."

"Er … no thank you, ma'am. Though it looks most appetizing. I have to be present at the *Dryad*. Lord Cardigan is having another soirée. I just wanted to give you this." He handed me a thick manila envelope, which seemed to contain several papers.

"What's in here?" I asked, taking the envelope from him.

"Your transfer papers and tickets. For your passage to India."

"My goodness. So soon?"

"Yes. There are ships leaving shortly, to transport the wounded to Scutari and Malta. We have managed to find you a connection from there to India."

"Thank you so much, David. I see you went through a lot of trouble," I said, flipping through the papers.

"Not at all. It was my pleasure. Incidentally, I'll be informing Calcutta of your arrival. Shall I also send a telegram to your parents?

They are at the Futtehgurh Mission, are they not?"

"Yes, they are. Could you please do that?"

"I'll take care of it. Have a safe journey, ma'am."

I thanked him again. He bowed and left.

*****

1854, November: Scutari, Turkey

The minarets and domes of the mosques on the Turkish shore gradually came into view, as our ship glided through the gentle Black Sea waves towards Asia Minor. Dawn was breaking while I sat on my sea chest, wrapped in a blanket and holding onto a guy rope on the swaying deck. I had had to spend the whole night there, for every inch of the boat was occupied by the injured and sick soldiers. The few cabins were filled with the critical cases, while others lay along the passages and on deck. I was promised a cabin when some of the patients were disembarked at Scutari, and I would continue on to Malta. I was to change there to a larger vessel bound for Alexandria and then, after a camel ride across the desert to Cairo, board another ship for the final cruise to Calcutta.

"Would you care for some tea, miss?" A sailor came by, holding a huge, steaming kettle. Another, carrying a basket of what looked to be large, round biscuits, followed him.

I fished out a tin cup from my reticule, lying at my feet, and held it out. The sailor filled it with the weakest-looking tea I had ever seen, and a hard, cardboard-like biscuit was handed to me. At least the liquid was warm. However, even after breaking the cookie in two and dunking a piece in the tea, it required considerable effort to chew and swallow the tasteless morsel. I had checked mine to make sure there weren't any worms in it, although I noticed others tapping the biscuits on their palms, attempting to get the critters out. Feeling those usual pangs of hunger that women in my condition normally get on having to eat for two, I fished out a can of pilchards from the store of food I had packed in my carrying bag. The tin can was easily opened, having a key attached to its side, which was hooked onto the seal-strip, and the lid slit off by rotating the key around the container. I placed the pieces of fish on the biscuit and poured the remaining oil over them. The sardines tasted heavenly, although the hard biscuit still needed a great deal of chewing.

I was watching approaching Scutari's Eastern-style dwellings and the four corner towers of the Barrack Hospital when the captain came by. "Good morning, ma'am. Did you say you wished to look in at the hospital?" he asked, towering over me.

I wondered why he asked. "Yes. Are we not going to stop here for the day?"

"No, ma'am. That will not be possible. We have some folks pretty close to death. The surgeon wishes to leave for Malta as soon as possible."

My heart sank. I was expecting to see Albert and execute the vengeance plan that had been brewing in my mind for a while. "So, how long are we going to be in Scutari?"

"We'll leave as soon as we've unloaded this lot," he said, waving his arm in the direction of the wounded lying on deck. "It may take a couple of hours. I'm not letting any passengers get down here."

"Oh, please, sir, can I pop over to the hospital? It's just across the docks. There's a family member I must see. I shan't be long." I lied about the family bit.

He thought for a while, frowned and said, "I'd rather you not. But all right, I'll make an exception, for your family. But, mind, if you're not back within two hours, we'll leave without you. I hope you understand?"

"Yes, sir. I'll be here well before your departure."

The captain stood there looking at me for a moment. He then stooped and, bringing his bearded face closer to me, whispered, "Do be careful, ma'am—walking in the streets, I mean. There are reports of attacks on Europeans."

"Yes, I've heard," I whispered back. Then, patting my reticule, I said, "I have something in here to protect me."

He glanced at it and smiled, for he must have seen the outline of Robert's revolver in there. "Good. If it comes to that, I wouldn't hesitate to use it, if I were you." He got up and left, saying, "We'll have your cabin ready, ma'am. Don't be too long"

Our ship was towed slowly alongside the dock and moored. As the gangplank was attached, I stood by the railing, reticule in hand, at the front of a queue of scrawny-faced men with bloodied bandages. Some were barely able to stand and others needed to be supported by their comrades. Sailors were readying stretchers to carry the debilitated. Walking along the boardwalk, I wondered if I still had enough time to carry out my scheme. Albert's wretched face came before my eyes and my heart raced. I was certain he would be watched over by the staff and there would be patients close by in the crowded infirmary. If it had been dark, I could have slipped something in his tea. Now I would have to get him out of the building. But how? Would it be possible in the short time? Surely Nancy would be around. I clasped the reticule to my chest, scooped up the hem of my dress with one hand and, ignoring the imploring, outstretched hands of the urchins and hawkers, hurried down the lane towards the Barracks.

As I entered the doorway, the familiar stench I had borne for weeks during my stay there greeted me. Sergeant Scott was at his usual post, the front desk. Recognising me, he immediately stood up, bowed and said, "So sorry to hear about your husband, ma'am. Are you now back with us?"

"Thank you, Scott. He did his duty, like the others," I replied, wiping a tear from my eye. "No, I'm not staying. I'm on my way to service in India. I wish to see Captain Miller. Is he here?"

"Aye. He's in the officers' ward. Let me take you to him."

I followed the sergeant along the hallways, which stank of filth and human bodies. We squeezed by patients, some fortunate to have a cot, while others lay upon torn mattresses on the floor.

"India, eh!" Sergeant Scott turned towards me. "Don't be surprised if you see me there, ma'am."

"Why, are you being transferred?"

"I've been meaning to volunteer for a while. It's a good country, not like this wretched place. An' the pay's good. Although I 'eard there be some trouble brewin' with the natives. You be very careful there, ma'am." We entered the officers' ward. "There's the captain," Scott said, pointing to a bed in the far corner.

"Thank you, Scott. Be sure to look me up when you're in India."

"Aye. I will." He bowed and left.

I approached Albert's bed. He lay with his head bandaged and eyes closed. It appeared he had just finished breakfast, for an empty mug and plate lay on the side table. Spiking his tea was out of the question, then. It would have to be accomplished outdoors. Where was Nancy? How to carry out my plan raced in my mind. Albert must have heard the rustle of my petticoat and opened his eyes.

"Ah, Margaret! So good to see you." He raised both his arms, as if expecting me to bend, hug and kiss him.

I stood straight. "How are you, Albert?" I asked in a cool voice.

He looked pale and seemed to have lost a considerable amount of weight.

He dropped his arms. "Not too good … I'm afraid. No one here … to care for me. Have you changed your mind about India?" he said in a slurred voice.

"No. I'm just visiting. Have to leave shortly. Where's Nancy?"

"You just missed her. She's gone to Constantinople … talk to the British Ambassador … an old friend of Colonel Mitchell … try to get me out of this hellhole."

I felt relieved on hearing Nancy was away. Seeing Albert and hearing him talk about the despicable colonel brought additional anger into my head. I had to do it. It was then or never. I silently prayed to the Lord for help. It seemed my plea was answered instantly.

Albert threw off his bed sheets and sat up with some difficulty, his feet dangling to the floor. "Good that you're here. It's time for my morning walk. Could you please hand me my coat and walking stick?"

His clothes hung on a peg beside the bed. I helped him into his blue pelisse, the greatcoat and boots. He buckled on his belt with the money pouch and holster attached. The butt of a revolver was visible through the side of the holster cover. He turned and, with his back to me, opened a drawer of the night table and slipped something inside his coat pocket.

While the other patients looked on, I held him by his left arm and he stumbled along, steadying himself on the walking stick.

"Where do you normally go?" I asked, as we went out of the hospital's back door.

"Usually not far. But now that you're with me, can we walk to that park?" He pointed with his cane towards a pleasant-looking waterfront commons. It had numerous shady trees and looked empty at that time of the morning.

Perfect. Thank you, Lord, I thought. "All right, if you wish. I've just enough time to take you there."

We staggered towards the playground and wild thoughts raced through my mind again. How was I to do it? Although using my revolver was the easiest, it would be risky. The noise would surely attract attention and I would be arrested well before reaching the ship. I saw it anchored some distance from the park. Strangulation? No. I ruled it out for, despite his illness, he was a much stronger person and would overpower me easily. Yes, it would have to be with the sharp surgical scalpel I carried in the reticule. One jab and it would cut to his heart instantly. I would have to make it look like a robbery. Take his money and throw his wallet to the ground. Yes, that should work. No one would suspect me of the crime. I would be long gone before he was discovered, slumped on the bench. Let the bastard feel and suffer how my Robert had bled to death.

We wobbled to the park and, observing a secluded spot with some benches, I asked, "Shall we sit there for a while?"

Albert had been breathing heavily and seemed to appreciate the suggestion. "Yes. Let's, please. I have to catch my breath. Ah, it feels so good to have you beside me, Margaret."

Yes, just like that night in the frigate's cabin, I thought.

We sat down on a bench, me with my reticule on my lap, Albert leaning back. We stared out towards the Black Sea. The waves beat gently on the shore. Ships sailed by and there was a faint clattering of hooves from the town. Although it was late fall, the weather was mild, as is normal in the Mediterranean. The sun had come up and it felt comfortable despite the cool ocean breeze on our faces. I looked at my pocket watch.

"Do you have to leave so soon, Margaret?"

"No. There is still time."

"Good. You know, I'm really enjoying your company. Thank you so much for coming to see me."

"It's all right. I was on my way, anyway."

"Won't you change your mind about going to India? Why don't you work in this hospital? I wish you would."

"No. I have to go away from here."

He then reached out and held my hand. "Margaret, *my dear*, you know I care about you."

I moved my hand away. "Please don't."

He persisted and attempted to put his arm around me. I slid sideways. "My darling Margaret. Tell you what. Why don't *I* transfer as well to a regiment, going out there. Then we can *both* go to India, together. Would you like that?"

"No, thank you. I'm perfectly capable of going there myself."

"Dearest. Why do you treat me so? Do I not deserve some attention?"

"You will get what *you* deserve."

"Whatever do you mean?"

I was beginning to lose my temper and asked in a raised voice, "The way you treated Robert. Tell me. Did he say anything before dying?"

He turned and looked at me, bewildered. His eyes twitched. "No. Nothing. As I said, we were too busy fighting off those damn Cossacks. There wasn't any time to talk."

"Yet you found time to shoot him."

"Good heavens. Whatever gave you that idea?"

"Did you say Robert was fighting a Cossack, who shot him?" I wanted to confirm his earlier statement.

"Yes. He was on his horse, fencing the Cossack, who drew out a revolver and shot him."

"Then how would you explain the fact that we found Robert with his sabre in the scabbard?"

His jaw dropped. Yet, he recovered his composure and said, "Oh, I don't know. Someone might have sheathed it. There were Russians all around us."

I said in a slightly raised voice, "That someone, in fact, saw you shoot him. I also have the bullet I extracted from Robert's body. It matches your revolver's bullets." I took it out of my coat pocket. "Here." I held it between my thumb and forefinger.

He looked flabbergasted. "That bullet, fired from my revolver? Ridiculous. Who? ... Who saw me shoot? ... There was no one there."

My hands shook in anger. Putting the bullet back in my pocket, I shouted at him, "Yes there was. A Cossack soldier saw you. You son of a bitch. You shot my Robert. Tell me, why did you do it? Tell me!"

His face took on a grave look. It was like that of a soldier going into battle. "I did it because I had to. He deserved it."

"Why? Why did he deserve it?"

"There's lots you don't know, about Nancy and him."

"What? Nancy told me there was nothing going on between them."

"Oh, there was plenty going on." He looked angry and growled, "You should have seen the two them ... makin' out by the river. They said they were going riding. Ha! I caught them."

When I heard that, tears welled in my eyes. "No. No, Albert, it wasn't the way you think. My Robert would never act improperly. Nancy said they were just holding hands or something."

"Ha! Is that what she told you? I caught them in the act. He was lying on top of her … kissing her … Saw it with my own eyes."

I was stunned. Tears rolled down my cheeks. I took out a handkerchief from inside my sleeve and wiped them. "I don't believe it," I said, sobbing.

"Have you told anyone else? About Robert's shooting, I mean."

I shook my head.

"Who is this Russkie? Is he a prisoner?"

"No."

"Then, where did you meet him?"

"I'm at not liberty to say."

"Good. Let's keep it a secret between us. Shall we?" He again reached for my hand and I pushed his arm away.

I dried my tears and blew my nose. "No. There should be no secrets. I want to know what really happened. I'll report the incidence to the authorities. They'll question Nancy and, if possible, the Russian witness. They'll have to tell the truth."

"No, Margaret. Don't do that. I might be hanged. What's more, it'll bring shame on our families. Robert's name would be in the newspapers. Just think of that."

"I'll let the court-martial decide. If you're found guilty, you'll get what you deserve."

Thinking about Robert, I again started to cry. While I was wiping tears, I saw him unbutton his coat and, putting his hand into the inside pocket, draw out a large, folded-blade knife. As I sat, shocked, and bewildered, he snapped open the nearly six-inch-long blade. Good God, I thought. He had come prepared to attack me.

Before I could move, he grabbed my wrist. "Give me that bullet, and tell me who this Russian witness is. Or I'll slit your throat, you wench," he demanded in an enraged voice.

"No." I tried to free my wrist. He clenched it tighter, with his left hand.

To my horror, Albert swung his right arm at me, the knife in his fist. Perhaps instinctively, I snatched the reticule and raised it up to try and protect myself. The knife sliced into the canvas bag and jammed in a can of sardines or something in there. He had difficulty pulling it out. He let go of my wrist and, using his left hand to hold the reticule, pulled the knife out. Freed, I leapt up. He tried to stand but stumbled and fell back onto the bench. I put my boot to the edge of the park bench and pushed with all my strength. The bench rolled over, with

Albert in it. It fell with a loud thud. Albert tumbled on the grass. The knife flew out of his hand.

Thinking I had killed him, I peered across the overturned park bench. He lay motionless. I looked around to see if anyone had observed this incident. While some persons walked in the distant hospital grounds, they were too far away to have seen anything. No one seemed to be around in the park or on the beach, except for some fishermen in a small boat out in the sea. They were rowing towards shore. I walked around the bench towards the prone figure. He moved his arm. Although a bit relieved to see him alive, horror gripped me when I realised what he was trying to do. He had his hand inside his greatcoat, fumbling with the cover of his holster. In a moment, he pulled the revolver out.

"Stay where you are, you bitch," he shouted, trying to get up.

I wished I could get Robert's revolver out of the reticule and duel it out with Albert. Finish him there. However, I put the reticule under my arm and ran towards the beach as fast as I could. Glancing back, I saw Albert stand and, revolver in hand, move unsteadily in my direction. By that time, the Turkish fishermen had reached shore and were dragging their boat up the sandy beach. I shouted and waved to them. The group saw me and, leaving their boat, walked towards me. Albert must have seen them and it very likely made him hold his fire. If he had fired, he would surely have shot me.

On reaching the fishermen, I said excitedly the few words of Turkish greeting I had picked up from Selim. I am not sure if they understood. They made hand gestures, which I understood as asking if there was something wrong. I pointed towards Albert. His silhouette, with the gun in hand, told the fishermen the story. They moved boldly towards Albert. He waved his revolver at them and they stopped. Albert picked up his walking stick and plodded towards the hospital.

The fisherman said something to me in Turkish, with the word "police" in the sentence. I gestured that there was no need for that. I thanked them and took a path that led towards the docks.

While walking to the ship, I reflected on my action and believed I had made the correct decision. Reporting the matter to the police or the Army authorities would have delayed me and made me miss my connections on the passage to India. At that time, I wished for nothing except to get away from Albert as fast as I could.

The sun was setting over the Bosporus, by the time my ship finally sailed away from Scutari. I stood at the railing and watched the fading shoreline. I felt disappointed and regretted at having failed in my attempt to avenge my poor Robert's assassination. I did not believe a word of what Albert had uttered about having found Robert and Nancy in a compromising situation. It was his masquerade. Tears filled my eyes. I wondered if there would be another opportunity to set matters straight. I looked up towards the setting sun. In between the rays, a vision came to me. It was that of our Lord. He held his hand up towards me, as if telling me not to worry, and saying:

Vengeance is mine…

Epilogue

[Ham ne mana ke taqhuful na karo gay, lekin]
I concede you will not be heartless, yet
[Khak hojaying gay hum, tumko khabar hone tak]
I shall have turned to dust, before you hear of it
-- *Mirza Ghalib, Delhi, 1797 - 1869*

1967, July: Baltimore, Maryland
ALEXANDRA PUT DOWN MARGARET'S JOURNAL. She could not read any further. Tears ran down her cheeks as she reached for another tissue from the nearly empty box on the side table. She dabbed her eyes and, seeing I had tears in mine as well, handed me a hankie. It was late Sunday night and we had spent the better part of the day and the night on our living room sofa, reading the doctor's journal. The title on its hard cover, written in a flowery Victorian hand, read *Volume II, My Married Life*.

"My God. What a tragedy to have your husband shot by a fellow officer," Alexandra remarked as tears continued to well in her eyes.

"It seems it was the eternal love triangle situation," I said, putting my arms around her and squeezing her gently.

"Yes, but why did Albert have to kill Robert? Didn't he know he could never have Margaret?"

"It was by sheer coincidence she found out he was the murderer. I'm wondering if Albert wanted to make her think he tried to save Robert's life and hoped to get some sympathy and, possibly, love in return," I said.

"Love! That man deserves no love. Especially after he tried to rape Margaret in that ship's cabin, and even attempted to knife her on that park bench. These people are psychopaths. They have no feelings. If they get it in their twisted minds to do something, they'll keep on trying until they succeed. I've seen enough of them in courtrooms to know how they think."

I had obviously hit a nerve, as Alexandra looked agitated. I tried to calm her down. "Yes, I agree. Albert does sound like an evil man. It's a shame he managed to get away from Balaclava. Margaret had a better chance of confronting him there. It was a hopeless situation in Scutari."

"She tried but failed. I do hope she eventually manages to get even with him and avenges Robert's murder."

"She's leaving for India, and I don't know if she ever got an opportunity to meet him again," I said.

"Oh, I'm sure she would have hunted him down to the ends of this earth. You'll see. Shall we start with her *Volume III: My Life in India?*" Alexandra asked, stifling a yawn.

I looked at the clock on our mantelpiece; it was past midnight. "Better leave it till tomorrow. It's getting kinda late. I'm sure you have a busier day tomorrow than mine. Oh, yes. I forgot to mention—Dick, you know the CIA agent, is coming to see me at ten o'clock."

"Is he really sick, or it is just a front for something else?"

"No. It looks like he has a mild form of malaria. He must have gotten a bad mosquito bite when he was in India."

"Why was he in India?"

"He didn't say. But it could be something to do with what your father alluded to."

"You mean the Soviet plans to invade Afghanistan?" Alexandra asked, her thin eyebrows raised.

"It's possible. Don't you think the US would want Indian and Pakistani support to assist Afghanistan if the Russians do invade?"

"Yes, I would think so. But what can those poor countries do to help? They don't have any money to spare."

"Moral support goes a long way. It seems it's the very reason the Soviets want the Rani's crown and Margaret's journals."

"Oh, you mean by returning the crown, they might win over the Indians?"

"That would appear to be the Russians' motive."

"I guess you have a point," Alexandra said, yawning, "but it's getting too late for me to think clearly. Let's go to bed."

The next day, Dick Redford arrived for his scheduled appointment, promptly at ten a.m. I went to fetch him from the waiting room. He looked well enough, but had a slight redness around the nose, possibly due to the virus infection. He seemed pleased to see me. We shook hands and I brought him to my office. After hanging his trench coat and jacket on the rack, he walked to the patient's chair.

"So, how do you feel, Dick?" I asked when he sat down.

"Well enough, Doctor Walli, but still have this slight cough and sneezing. It's persistent. Can't seem to get rid of it."

I took his temperature and blood pressure, which were normal.

"Anything in the test results?" he asked.

"Yes, that's why I asked you to come in," I replied, putting my instruments away and washing my hands. I returned to my desk and opened his file. "Your blood test showed a mild trace of malaria." But when he raised his eyebrows at the mention of malaria, I tried to calm him down. "It's nothing to be alarmed about. This type is fairly common in India. I've seen it often enough. It can be cured easily, with antibiotics."

"Oh, it's a relief to hear that."

"It might have gone away on its own, but one can never be too sure. I'm glad you came in." I scribbled a prescription and handed him the note, saying, "Here's a treatment of thirty tablets. Take one a day with plenty of water. Why don't you come back in a month and let me see how you're doing?"

"Thank you, Doctor Walli. I'm glad I decided to seek medical attention." He put the prescription in his pocket and started to get up, then it seemed he remembered something. He sat down and asked, "So, how's the book coming along?"

"Good. I've started on the first few chapters. I thought it would be a simple biography. You know, the kind no one really reads." We laughed and I added, "But it's turning into a really complex tale."

"Oh, how so?"

"Doctor Margaret lived in the mid-to-late nineteenth century, which was a very interesting period. At first she had to struggle to become one of the first women doctors in North America, then she got involved in the wars in the Crimea and India. Not to mention the Tsarist agents out there." I told him the other details I had learned so far from her journals.

Dick listened intently and, when I had finished, asked, "So, when is Greg Barinowsky going to the USSR?"

I had had a feeling he would ask that question. "I don't know the exact date, but I believe it will be soon. The Wallaces and the Barinowskys will be visiting us next weekend. I'll know more details then."

"Er … Doctor Walli, I mentioned what you told me last time to my division chief and he's most fascinated by the turn of these events. You know, the finding of the Rani's crown, the doctor's journals, and the Soviets' interest in obtaining those items. He, of course, wants to learn more, but there's one thing that puzzled both of us."

I sat up a bit in my chair and, trying not to sound too alarmed, asked, "Yes, what's that?"

He coughed and blew his nose into a handkerchief. "We just couldn't figure out why Greg Barinowsky would go to all these lengths, setting up a mock robbery of the Rani's crown and handing it over to the Russians, just for a visa to visit Russia. Now, I know you mentioned they still have family out there, but why does he want to go there so badly he's willing to risk his neck? Is it something to do with his folks?"

At that point, I thought I might as well tell him about Katya, for he was bound to find out eventually. "Er … Dick, yes, you're right. It has to do with his relatives out there. In fact, a daughter from an earlier … marriage … possibly … I'm not certain. He wants to bring her out."

Dick mused for a while, then said, "Hmm … well, I'll speak to the chief. It's possible we could help him."

I cannot say why that offer from the CIA did not surprise me, but I knew there would be a catch. Hence, I asked, "In return for what, Dick?"

He smiled. "We'll have to discuss that with Mr. Barinowsky. Did you say they were coming over next weekend?"

I nodded.

"Would it be possible for me to drop by your house for a social chat?"

"I'll speak with my wife. I'm sure it would be all right. How about I call you?"

"Yes, that'll be fine." He looked at his wristwatch. "Goodness, I've overrun my appointment. Your staff will be most upset."

"Not if you tell them you have a brother named Robert. They've been dying to find out."

He laughed. "Oh, that. Yes, I get asked that question a lot. No, no such luck. I'll set the record straight on my way out." He put on his jacket and trench coat and left my office with a wave.

That evening over dinner, I narrated to Alexandra exactly what had transpired between Dick Redford and me. She listened attentively, sipped her wine and did not interrupt even once.

When I had finished, she said, "Well, it seems we're getting dug in deeper into Margaret's affairs. However, it cannot be undone. We offered to help and here we are, getting entangled with the CIA and the KGB. We'll have to do the best we can. I must admit I wanted to remain aloof at first, but after reading those journals, I've gotten obsessed with her story. I want to get to know all that happened to her. But be cautious, darling. Don't do anything we might regret later."

I nodded. "Yes, dear. Let's be very careful. So, is it okay for Dick to come over next Sunday to meet our Grimsby visitors?"

"Er … yes. But I don't think it would be proper for him to come to our house. Let's meet him at a more neutral place. How about at the golf club?"

"Hey, that sounds like a swell idea. Why didn't I think of it myself?"

"Because you're too busy writing prescriptions to think of your own welfare."

I laughed. "All right, I'll call the Wallaces tomorrow and, if it's okay with them, let Dick know."

*****

The following Sunday afternoon, from the living room window I spotted a blue Cadillac drive up the driveway. The Wallaces and the Barinowskys had arrived. They were on their way to Florida for a holiday and we had asked them to stop over to pick up the parts of Doctor Margaret's journals we had finished reading. Earlier in the week, I called them and Greg said he would be happy to meet with Dick Redford. I also spoke with Dick and he agreed to the meeting venue, at the nearby Twin Oakes Golf and Country Club.

It was a congenial reunion. There were warm hugs and handshakes all around. We ushered them into our living room and I asked if they would like a drink before dinner. It was white wine for the ladies, scotch on the rocks for Bill and vodka straight up for Greg. I poured myself a Scotch as well, as I had not had one for a while.

Jane Wallace remarked, "You have a lovely house here. I adore mahogany furniture." She looked around the room and took a peek at the garden from the bay window. "What do I see there? Roses in full bloom already! Ours have only just started to show."

The others also joined in with compliments as they tilted their heads to gaze out of the window.

"Oh, thank you. This is just a regular two-storey house, not as grand as your castle, we're sure," Alexandra said.

"Not at all. Wallace Hall isn't what it used to be in Grandma Margaret's days," Bill said.

"How is the fruit preserves business Margaret's aunt, Fiona, started?" Alexandra asked.

"It's still thriving, although not what it used to be. All the canning factories sprouting around us are flooding the market with mass-produced products," Jane replied.

Greg Barinowsky nodded and gulped his drink down. I took his glass and refilled it from the vodka bottle at the bar.

"It's a shame, isn't it? Fresh farm produce isn't in demand as it used to be," I said, handing Greg the drink.

Alexandra excused herself and left the room, saying she wanted to go and check on the dinner. Karolina followed her, offering to help.

"It's not only the farm produce—it's the same with other agricultural products. The water mills around us used to conduct a roaring business. They've closed down," Bill said, taking a sip of scotch.

The mention of the water mills reminded me of Albert Miller and I asked, "Margaret wrote about a Miller family. How are they?"

"Not very well, I'm afraid. After their mills closed down, they had one business failure after another. They still live in their big house in town, although it's really run-down now," Bill replied.

"What about Albert Miller? He must have lived a comfortable life?" I asked.

"No. Unfortunately not. The poor fellow died young, just like our grandfather, Robert," Bill said.

"Where did he die?" I asked.

"Wasn't it in the Crimea, love?" Bill asked, looking at Jane.

"Yes, I believe so, or that's what I've—"

"No, no, he survived Crimea," Greg interjected. He sipped his drink and continued, "One of his grandsons told me he died in India, fighting in the war there. What do they call it, Walli? Mutiny or something?"

"Yes, the Sepoy Mutiny. Some call it the Rebellion," I replied.

"Right. But you know, the funny thing is, when I asked which battle or town he was killed in, his grandson didn't know. In fact, he said none of the family knows. Sounds very mysterious to me," Greg said, finishing his drink. I poured him another shot of vodka.

"But how did he get to India from the Crimea?" I asked.

"Oh, we heard he was the adventurous type. Quite a ladies' man, they say," Jane answered and asked, "What did Margaret write about him, Walli?"

"Er …" I was at a loss for words. Fortunately, Alexandra came in and announced that dinner was ready. "It's somewhere in her journals, Jane," I said, as we got up and walked over to the dining room.

Our guests took their seats at the dining table, and while Alexandra got the dinner out, I poured them wine, either red or white in accordance with their wishes. The aroma of the grilled rack of lamb wafted down from the large serving platter and raised murmurs of delight around the table. As I carved the chops and handed the plates, the pendant with the Greek coin, which the Barinowskys had given me in Grimsby, rolled out from underneath the shirt and hung loosely over my chest. I had polished the silver coin and it shone.

"That necklace suits you, Walli," Greg remarked.

"Makes you look like a Greek warrior." Bill joined in.

"If you like, I can go and change into my suit of armour," I replied.

"Leave that for later, dear, your dinner will get cold," Alexandra said, amid laughter all around.

"Tell me, Greg. Where exactly did your grandfather obtain this coin?" I asked.

"I don't know where, exactly. But as I mentioned, the pendant was in our home in St. Petersburg for as long as I can remember. There used to be a slip of paper in the box, in Grandmother's hand, which said she'd received it as a gift from an Indian Sepoy named Sharif Khan *Bhadur*. Father brought it out to show only very special guests."

"Do you remember your grandmother, Greg?" Alexandra asked.

"No, I never met her. I was just a baby when they had to leave for the Urals, during the Revolution. Alas, we never heard from them again. It's possible they were executed by the Reds."

We ate in silence for a while, then Bill asked, "Walli, so what does Richard Redford wish to speak to us about?"

"It's Greg he wants to meet. I believe he said they can help Greg."

"Really! Help us get Katya out?" Karolina asked, wide-eyed.

I nodded.

"In return for what?" Greg said with raised eyebrows.

"I don't know, Greg. That's something you'll have to ask him. We'll see him tomorrow."

"I hope he can help, but I don't want him making things more difficult for me," Greg remarked.

"What does Katya do there?" Alexandra asked.

"She's a ballerina—or rather, was. I believe she's only an instructor now," Greg replied.

"Well, that should make it easier for her to get an exit visa," Alexandra conjectured.

"One would have thought so. But it's not that easy. We need to grease many palms. That's really the reason I wish to go there. See what I can do," Greg said.

"Well, the money from the deal of the Rani's crown should help a bit, shouldn't it?" I asked.

"Yes, that's what I'm hoping. I went to the Soviet Embassy in Ottawa not too long ago, and met Colonel Yermolov. He's still upset over not having obtained Margaret's journals. I again assured him they were not in her sea chest and reminded him I had risked my family's wrath in stealing the Rani's crown. I insisted he should keep his end of the bargain. He said he's discussing my visa and the *reduced* reward money with Moscow. I'm still waiting to hear from him."

"Well, Greg, with both the KGB and the CIA helping you, you shouldn't have any difficulties." I remarked.

"Very often that help is like a candy with a bitter pill at its centre," Greg said with a sarcastic laugh.

I poured them more wine and we toasted to Greg's success in having his daughter with him soon. I then remembered a name from my last visit to Delhi. I asked, "Greg, was Katya ever in the Soviet diplomatic service?"

"Yes, I believe so. After leaving the ballet, she joined them. But I don't think she's with them anymore. I'm not sure, having lost touch with her. Why do you ask?"

"I believe I met her in Delhi."

Everyone turned and stared at me in surprise.

"So, *that* was the Katya you mentioned, dear?" Alexandra asked, breaking the suspense.

I nodded.

"How did you meet her?" Greg asked, almost in disbelief.

"Oh, she'd come to the hospital, wishing to sell her book. A novel, I believe, about the Russian Revolution. Similar to Pasternak's *Doctor Zhivago*. I haven't found time to read it yet," I said, not wishing to divulge all the details—and particularly my encounter with the Soviet agents in that park in Delhi.

"Yes, now I remember. I heard she left the foreign service right after her term in India," Greg said, sipping the red wine.

Jane remarked, "Isn't that a lovely coincidence, Walli, you meeting both our Russian and Canadian families."

I nodded, yet wondered whether Katya's parting from the Soviet service had anything to do with her not managing to obtain the sea chest. Was she dismissed?

"Do you have any pictures of your India trip, Walli?" Jane asked.

"Hundreds! Let me set up the slide projector and show you," I said and led them to the family-room.

*****

The mid-morning sunlight reflected from the stonework of the Twin Oakes' clubhouse as I drove my Buick station wagon up the driveway, past the green, manicured golf grounds towards the parking lot. Our visitors looked relaxed and rested after their long journey from Grimsby the previous day, yet I wondered if they felt uneasy about meeting a CIA agent. I drove into the parking area and we waited in the car. We were a bit earlier than the ten a.m. meeting time I had arranged with Dick Redford.

Exactly at ten o'clock, a dark blue Oldsmobile drove into the parking lot. Dick was the driver, but another man sat on the passenger side. Dick parked the car some distance from us. He got out and walked towards us. He wore a blue suit, a matching tie and a hat. The other man, wearing a dark suit, remained seated. We alighted from our car. I shook hands with Dick and introduced him all around.

"Did you all have a good trip from Canada?" Dick asked.

The visitors mumbled yes, and nodded. We stood in silence,

looking at each other, waiting, as if for a movie director to tell us what to do.

Dick finally broke the silence. He sniffed into a handkerchief. "Walli, sorry I won't be able to join you for the round today."

"That's too bad, Dick. Are you feeling okay?"

"I'm fine. The division chief is with me and we have a meeting this afternoon. He wishes to see Greg alone. If that's okay with you, Greg?" He looked at Greg.

"Sure. I'll even see the president, if he wants to see me." Greg said. That broke the ice and we all had a good laugh.

I suggested, "All right, Greg. While you go chat with the chief, we'll wait in the coffee shop."

"Okay, I'll find you there," Greg said.

"Don't get lost, though," Bill said.

We had another laugh. I shook Dick's hand and he led Greg towards the blue Olds. We picked up our golf bags from the back of the station wagon and walked towards the clubhouse.

In the coffee shop, we ordered coffee and seated ourselves at a table by a large glass window overlooking the greens. It was not long before Greg arrived. He purchased a beer at the bar and, bottle in hand, joined us at the table. He took a chair with his back to the wall. We looked expectantly at him. He did not say anything and kept drinking his beer.

Bill finally asked, "So? Did you talk to him?"

Greg looked around and, satisfied no one else was within earshot, said in a whisper, "Good God. You won't believe this. They know all about my Katya. The chief said they have a file on her!"

"Really!" Karolina exclaimed.

Greg nodded. "But he said they would be willing to help me get her out."

"What did you say, dear?" Karolina asked.

"Of course I said yes. I can use all the help I can get."

"And what will you have to do for them?" Alexandra asked.

"They want me to contact an arms dealer. Buy some rifles, ammunition, those sorts of things. They believe it should be easy for me. I speak the language and know the country. Also, I'll be going there on approval of the KGB."

"The Americans are buying Soviet rifles! Have they stopped making guns in the States?" Bill said with a laugh.

"Where will the arms go?" I asked.

"They didn't say. Could be anywhere. South America, Cuba, Africa, who knows. There are rebels in every country."

"If it's to Afghanistan, I'll be surprised," Alexandra said.

"Why would you find that surprising?" I asked.

"I was at a business luncheon not too long ago. Some senators were there and I overheard some talk about the president not wishing to send any aid to the Afghanis."

"It seems the government is having a change of heart. They must have gotten wind of all the Soviet help going there," I said.

"But I still don't get it. Why give the rebels Soviet-built weapons?" Bill said with a chuckle.

"Well, you wouldn't want to give them American rifles, for everyone would then know where the aid was coming from. 'Specially if the president's denying any help to the Afghans," Alexandra said, using her sharp lawyer's logic.

"Ah!" Bill said.

Greg, having finished his beer, got up to get another one. He asked if anyone else wanted a drink. Bill asked for a coffee refill.

"How thrilling! All this talk of arms shipment and spy defection is making me want to get in the action," Jane said, rubbing her shoulders. "I wish I was a twenty-year-old again."

"Aren't you, my dear?" Bill said, putting his arm around her.

Greg returned to the table. "Walli, tell me. How was my Katya, when you met her? Did she look well?"

"Yes, very well."

"And she's writing novels now. What was that book you mentioned?"

"As I said, I haven't read it yet. The book's still in my flight bag." I chuckled. "If I remember correctly, its title is *Lara's Story*. I think she said it's based on a true story."

"But of course. She's likely telling our Grandmother Margaret's story. She was called Lara, because Margaret was too difficult to pronounce," Greg said. "Walli, may I borrow that book?"

"Yes, you may. Goodness, Margaret being Katya's great-grandmother never occurred to me," I said. "So how are you planning to get her out?"

"I was thinking Berlin, but Dick said travelling by boat from one of the small towns in the Crimea to Turkey is a better route."

"Crimea—that was where Margaret was, wasn't she?" Jane asked.

Alexandra must have remembered that Margaret was expecting when she left Balaclava for India. She asked, "Jane, do you know of Robert and Margaret's child who was born in India?"

Bill, had been listening somewhat quietly so far, suddenly exclaimed, "What? Did Margaret have a child in India?"

Alexandra said, "Bill, we haven't reached that far in her diaries yet. Margaret wrote that she was with child when she left the Crimea."

"Well, that certainly is a bit of news to us. Isn't it, Bill?" Jane said, holding Bill's hand.

Greg also put his arm around Karolina. Both looked surprised at the revelation.

I suggested, "Well, why don't we have a quick round of golf and then hurry home to read Margaret's journal about her life in India?"

Everyone nodded. Picking up our golf bags, we headed towards the first tee.

Glossary

Al-hamdo-lillah	praise be to God
Ameen	amen
Azadi	freedom
Baba	father
Bahen	sister
Bakra-Eid	Islamic celebration in remembrance of Abraham's sacrifice …
Bara Saa'b	big boss
Bechari	poor woman
Beta	son
Bhabi	sister-in-law (younger)
Bhabijaan	sister-in-law (elder)
Bhadur	brave warrior
Bhagwan	God (Hindu)
Chai	tea

Chakra	wheel
Chapatti	leavened bread
Charbagh	rectangular layout of a garden (Mughal style)
Charpoy	a cot comprising a wood frame and four legs, with netting of jute or cotton that serves as a bed
Chaukidar	gatekeeper (security guard)
Choti-hazri	light breakfast
Dada	grandfather
Dadi	grandmother
Dadi-Amma	elder grandmother
Daulat	wealth
Dekko	look
Der ayat durust yat	come late but come safely
Dil-e-Nadan	Troubled Heart
Dilli-wallahs	Delhi residents
Divan	a low, wide, four-poster platform for sitting in living rooms
Diwan-e-Khas	a hall for special visitors of the king
Dos vi'daniya	goodbye
Ghats	steps with landing (dock) to a river or sea

Ghazals	a form of Indian poetry
Gully	Side street
Hakim	physician
Hakim-khana	clinic
Harimzadi	a female manager of the harem (king's concubines)
Harmonium	an Indian musical instrument, something like an accordion
Haveli	mansion
Hookah	a tobacco smoking pipe where the smoke is drawn through a water base
Huzoor	sir
Inshallah	God willing
Jaldhysay	quickly
Jamadaran	sweeper-women
Janat	Paradise
Kamchor	lazy person
Karas	wide golden bracelets
Khooni-Darwaza	gate of blood
Ki madat say	with His help
Lassi	drink made from yoghurt and fruit

Lehnga	a loose, ankle-length skirt
Maalis	gardeners
Masala-dosa	a south Indian specialty composed of a delicious lentil pancake filled with spiced mashed potatoes
Mashallah	God be praised
Mian	honourable
Moazzen	the caller to prayer, usually in a mosque
Naatch	dance
Namaz-e-janaza	funeral prayer
Nameste	I bow to you (Indian/Hindu greeting)
Naushabhai	brother-in-law
Pakoras	battered and deep-fried vegetables
Purana	old
Rani	queen
Rasmalai	cottage cheese-balls fried and sweetened in honey
Russki-log	Russian people
Sarangi	an Indian musical instrument, like a violin
Sahiba	Mrs. or mistress
Salaam	peace be on you (Muslim greetings)

Samosas	Deep-fried patties of either vegetables or minced meat filling
Serai	rest house
Shaitan	Devil
Shalwar-kameez	a long shirt and baggy trousers
Sowar	cavalryman
Subedar	sergeant
Subhan-Allah	God is Merciful
Tabla	bongo drum
Taj	crown
Talwar	a curved sword, like a sabre
Tandoori	chicken barbecued in a tangy marinade
Topi	a cap shaped like a boat
Vakil	lawyer
Wah	wonderful, lovely
Walai-kum-Salaam	peace be on to you too
Wallah	person

ACKNOWLEDGMENTS

I am most grateful to all my lecturers at the McMaster University's Creative Writing Program, who taught me everything about writing fiction. I am thankful for their constant encouragement and suggestions in the evolution of this novel. I am indebted to my writing circles' partners: those in the McMaster class groups; the HisFicCritique Group (moderated by Anne Whitfield); Historical-Fiction-Writers-Critique Group (moderated by Mirella Patzer); and the CAA-Virtual Branch (moderated by Anne Osborne). Thank you all for your wonderful critiques that were of invaluable help to me in developing this novel.

I am much obliged to the Beta Readers of this novel, for their many insightful suggestions and brilliant comments, cited at the beginning of this book. I am truly appreciative of my skilful editors: Ranjan Chaudhuri, Victoria Grossack and Victoria Bell for not only their superb edits, but also for the many helpful suggestions.

I found the McMaster University Library's historical volumes collection stacks a most valuable source for reference material and am thankful to the Librarians for their prompt attention to my many inter-library loan requests. I am grateful to Mr. James Capodagli, Head, Health Information Center Library - SUNY Upstate Medical University, for information on the Geneva Medical College during its early period, 1853 – 1857. I am also indebted to Ms. Lisa Grimm, Assistant Archivist, Drexel University College of Medicine, for very useful information and help in directing me through their digital collection archives on the Female Medical College at the time of its inception in 1850.

Although this is a work of fiction, the following sources, among many others, were of particular value during research, in setting the historical backdrop of this novel.

Kaye, Sir John William. *A History of the Sepoy War in India, 1857-1858*. W. H. Allen, London, 1880.

Walsh, John Johnston. *A memorial of the Futtehgurh mission and her martyred missionaries: with some remarks on the mutiny in India.* J. Nesbit and Co., London, 1859

Sen, Surendra Nath. *Eighteen Fifty-Seven*. Ministry of Information and Broadcasting, Government of India, 1957.

Kinglake, A. W. *The Invasion of the Crimea*. William Blackwood & Sons, Edinburgh and London, 1877.

Duberly, Frances. *Journal Kept During the Russian War*. Longman, Brown, Green and Longmans, London, 1856.

The translations from Urdu to English of Mirza Ghalib's couplets (at the beginning of Prologue and Epilogue) and ghazal (on page 57) are my own efforts.

The quotation of the few opening lines of the song *Let My People Go*, (on page 155) is believed to be sung by Negro slaves since the late eighteenth century. It was located on the Internet, and is understood to be an open source.

I am most grateful for all the love, help and support of my wife, Alexandra, in enabling my thoughts to transform into this novel.

About the Author

Waheed Rabbani was born in India and was introduced to Victorian, Edwardian and other English novels, at a very young age, in his father's library. Most of the numerous books had been purchased by his father at 'garage sales' held, by departing British civil service officers, towards the end of their terms in India, during the Raj.

Waheed was educated at St. Patrick's School, Karachi, Pakistan, and graduated from Loughborough University, Leicestershire, England. He received a Master's degree from Concordia University, Montreal, Canada. While an engineer by profession, Waheed's other love is reading and writing English literature. Waheed also obtained a Certificate in Creative Writing from McMaster University, Hamilton, Canada.

Waheed and his wife, Alexandra, are now settled on the shores of Lake Ontario, in the historic town of Grimsby.

Printed in the United States
136752LV00006B/25/P

9 781849 231770